THE BRINK OF FREEDOM

THE BRINK OF FREEDOM

STELLA LEVENTOYANNIS HARVEY

Signature
EDITIONS

Cover design by Doowah Design.
Cover photo: Arrested refugees immigrants in Fylakio detention center Thrace Evros Greece (file 20101009), Creative Commons, by Ggia.

Photo of Stella Leventoyannis Harvey by Joern Rohde.

This book was printed on Ancient Forest Friendly paper.
Printed and bound in Canada by Hignell Book Printing Inc.

We acknowledge the support of the Canada Council for the Arts and the Manitoba Arts Council for our publishing program.

Library and Archives Canada Cataloguing in Publication

Leventoyannis Harvey, Stella, 1956-, author
     The brink of freedom / Stella Leventoyannis Harvey.

Issued in print and electronic formats.
ISBN 978-1-927426-76-0 (paperback).
--ISBN 978-1-927426-77-7 (epub)

     I. Title.

PS8623.E9446B75 2015   C813'.6   C2015-905904-6
                                     C2015-905999-2

Signature Editions
P.O. Box 206, RPO Corydon, Winnipeg, Manitoba, R3M 3S7
www.signature-editions.com

to
all asylum seekers

May you find safe passage
and a welcoming world
at journey's end

At his best, man is the noblest of all animals; separated from law and justice he is the worst.

— Aristotle, 5th century BC philosopher

The real destroyer of the liberties of the people is he who spreads among them bounties, donations and benefits.

— Plutarch, 1st century BC historian

When an elephant is in trouble even a frog will kick him.

— Hindu Proverb

Bury me on my feet; I have spent my entire life on my knees.

— Romani proverb

1

TEMPORARY REFUGE

Autumn 2011, Athens

Kolonaki was a scrap collector's paradise. Someone was always renovating an apartment in this Athens neighbourhood. Throwing away perfectly good things. Shameful, really. But their waste was Vijay's wealth. So who was he to complain? An asylum seeker didn't have the luxury of pride. He simply did what was necessary. If that meant being a garbage man for the Greeks who treated him no better than their trash, well, so be it. He provided an important service; he took their rubbish off their hands. Yes, he made a few euros, but how could anyone begrudge him that?

Vijay was so engrossed in trying to dislodge a large piece of pipe which would fetch a very good price he didn't notice the police cruiser pull up to the deserted construction site until it was too late. He had no time to escape, no time to hide.

One of the officers curtly demanded his identification, proof he was allowed to be in this country. Vijay kept his head down, didn't look the officer in the eye. Sweat stung Vijay's eyes, but he remained motionless. He'd thrown his papers into the sea during the crossing just as the smugglers had instructed. He couldn't tell the officers that. What could he say? Nothing. He turned his pockets inside out so they could see for themselves.

The next thing he knew, he was slammed into the side of their police car, his arms practically ripped out of their sockets. Metal bracelets cut into his wrists.

He didn't scream or complain. Why would he give them the satisfaction? They had the guns, the batons, and the handcuffs. What did he have? Nothing.

The policemen deposited him at the Amygdaleza Detention Centre. The Greeks said putting refugees in detention centres was more humane than letting them live on the street, but this depended on your point of view. Yes, Vijay and his wife Saphal and their son Sanjit were living in an abandoned shack he'd found in a suburb far from the centre of Athens, but they had a roof over their heads and no one threatening them with death. In Greece, they were beyond the clutches of Saphal's family and their petty grudges. And he was earning enough money to feed the family and put a little away for the day they would escape this country of so much sunshine and so little human warmth.

He was imprisoned for two weeks, but Vijay knew on the first day he had to find a way out of Amygdaleza. As long as he was trapped there, he couldn't support his family. During the day, he sat rotting with the rest of the detainees. At night they were packed into trailers as hot as ovens. Who could sleep with the wails, the snores, and the stench of so many?

Back in India, it had been hot and crowded too, but he'd always found ways to cope. Here, the fences were as high as towers. Sunshine hit the spiky ends of the razor wire and made them flicker. If he was ever tempted to take his chances with the fence and the razor wire, the armed guards at every corner of the compound reminded him he couldn't outrun a bullet. There had to be another way out.

Shiraz was at it again. A Pakistani who'd been thrown in detention like the rest of them because he didn't have documents, Shiraz was a troublemaker. Vijay knew this and kept his distance.

A small group of men had gathered in the yard to listen. "They can't treat us this way. We have rights," Shiraz proclaimed. "Even in this country of infidels."

Vijay sat on the steps of the trailer he usually slept in, trying to ignore Shiraz. He wanted to tell the Pakistani that only those with money and guns have rights, but instead he glared at the blazing sky as though challenging it to blink. He didn't want to get involved. If Shiraz wasn't careful, he'd get them all killed.

Vijay wasn't surprised when the guards came for Shiraz the next morning. Although the scuffle woke him, Vijay pretended to be asleep. It was none of his business. The Pakistani had brought this upon himself.

When he'd woken later in a heat-induced haze, the first thing he saw was Shiraz, standing by his own bunk. He fingered his split lip and squeezed his nose gently. Vijay wondered if the man's nose was broken. If so, why was he smiling like that? A smile that wide had to hurt.

He caught Vijay staring. "I leave tomorrow," he said and stretched, as though soothing achy muscles. He stood a little taller. "They finally see it my way."

"What did you say to these people?" Vijay whispered.

"You don't need to whisper," Shiraz said. "Everyone is entitled."

"You mean anyone who can pay."

"I claimed refugee status." Shiraz rubbed his face. "I didn't pay a thing. I am an asylum seeker." He shrugged. "I asked some simple questions. That's all." When he smiled this time, he winced. The scab on his lip split opened, seeped blood. He sucked at it as if he were a thirsty man. He ran his fingers through his hair. "I asked them if they wanted me to tell the caseworker what the guards did. Or perhaps I should speak to the doctor who comes here once a week? Should I show him some of my injuries?" He rubbed his shoulders and squirmed a little more, but the flicker of pain in his eyes was gone. "One guard hit me in the back of the head and again between my shoulders when I left the room. Maybe he was entitled."

"So how does it work?" Vijay asked him later that day. He'd kept to himself since he'd arrived at Amygdaleza because, really, what did he know about these people? Were they innocent like him? Or were they gangsters who'd fled their countries after some heinous crime? How could he assess another man's character? Still, he decided talking to the Pakistani was worth the risk. Sure, he was a troublemaker, but if he were to be believed, he'd be gone tomorrow. Shiraz had to know something that might help. Vijay had nothing to lose by listening to him.

They were squatting in the dirt in the courtyard, their sweaty backs against the fence that separated the yard from the air-conditioned offices where the guards reclined in their chairs watching their prisoners. Vijay saw them in there whenever he walked the perimeter. He pictured the guards now, laughing and joking as they juggled their batons or slammed them down in pantomime of striking some innocent man's back.

Vijay was closer to Shiraz than he would have liked, but he didn't want the guards or anyone else to hear their conversation. If the guards caught wind of what they were talking about, they might get the inclination to punish him. Vijay couldn't withstand a beating. He'd avoided them in India by escaping Saphal's family, never once succumbing to their invitations to return to Bihar where they promised to recognize Saphal's marriage and welcome him into their family. Other young men had succumbed to such guarantees only to be murdered in their sleep, their hands cut off and their bodies dumped into a wooded area or into the street for all to see. No, he'd kept his wits about him then and he would do so now. He hadn't come all this way to suffer at the hands of other oppressors.

And if one of the other detainees overheard their discussion, he might get a jump on Shiraz's advice before Vijay could take advantage of it himself.

"Ask to see the caseworker, tell them you want to claim refugee status," Shiraz told him. "You came to Greece to avoid a tribal war or some other type of conflict. You were afraid for your life. They have to offer you asylum if there is any threat to you or your family. They will start a file and you'll get maybe eighteen months or a couple of years out on the street to do whatever you like while you wait. It takes that long for them to figure out who you are, where you come from, the things you did to get into a place like this. Our embassies don't help the Greeks with identifying us either. They don't want us back any more than we want to go back. They're happy to offload us to someone else. You have no papers, so you can make up any story you like. This is your opportunity to be someone new. While they're figuring out whether you qualify for asylum or not, you disappear, find another country where you can get a job. In the meantime, you'll be free to do whatever you want."

Even though Vijay couldn't see his face, he could smell the sweat of too many days in the sun without a proper shower. I will wait, he thought. See if he gets out of here or if this is just another one of his stories. I have been a willing listener. But Shiraz cannot fool me. He is the kind of person who will say and do anything to get attention.

The next day, he watched Shiraz wave goodbye, a smile plastered on his battered face. If Shiraz could get out, Vijay decided, he could too.

He was excited to speak to Saphal when she came for their weekly Sunday visit. He knew it wasn't easy for her to make the trip to this place in the middle of nowhere. But she did it. She was a good wife. All honourable men deserved such a wife.

"Why did he choose you?" Saphal asked. "There are so many in this place, but he picked you to tell this story to."

"Why not me?" he retorted. Sometimes Saphal was so suspicious. These negative thoughts did not help. Not at all. Could she not see the opportunity?

"It could be a trap," she said. "I don't want anything to happen to you."

Even though a sheet of thick glass separated them, he could feel her doubts. She should take his word for things, but she always questioned him. She was his wife. She had her place. He had his. He would remind her of that once he got out of here. Subtly, of course. Saphal didn't like to be told how to act. She said she'd had enough of that with her own family and she did not need it from him either. What could he do? He had to keep the peace.

"Shiraz was a protester in this place," Vijay explained with as much patience as he could muster. "He wanted to spread the word to everyone, help all of us. I know he told others, because they were in the queue to see the caseworker the day after he left. I did not believe it myself, but Shiraz was good to his word."

Saphal's head tilted forward slightly.

He finally had her attention.

"It cannot be this simple," she said. "They must want money from you. Something. No freedom comes free of charge."

Vijay swallowed, fought the urge to fidget. He knew Saphal did not like to see him get too excited. She'd often called him a dreamer when they were in college, but, in fact, he was a survivor. He'd survived on the streets from an early age, something Saphal would never, could never, understand. She had come from a life of privilege, while he had had to beg on the streets. Vijay had long ago forgiven his mother. He knew her life had been shattered after being raped and giving birth to him. She had tried, but she had no way to provide for him. When he was four and old enough to fend for himself, she left him on the street. And somehow, against all the odds, he had found good fortune. When a group of wealthy Indian businessmen set up scholarships to raise street children out of poverty, Vijay seized the opportunity to get an education. He knew there would always be good fortune for those who sought it. If that made him a dreamer, so be it. Why should he hold himself back? He bent towards the glass, lowered his voice. "If I do this, it will give us time to make more money. Then as before, we will disappear. No one will be the wiser."

"How long are we going to run?" she asked. Again, her eyes pierced him.

It wasn't his fault they were running. He was happy in college. Then he met Saphal and her family refused to accept him. He'd left his future behind for her. "Until we find a home we deserve. That's all I want for us. For our family."

Saphal softened, as he knew she would. They had nothing to lose.

The next day, Vijay saw the caseworker. He filled in many forms, giving his real name and address. He didn't have to make up any story. Saphal's family would kill him if he went back to India. Yes, the politicians in his country enacted laws to protect his kind, but the caste system would never die for people like him. The Dalits. That was the truth.

The authorities took his fingerprints, and then they took his picture from every possible angle. The flashes of light blinded him. Still, he stared into the camera. He would not be intimidated.

The caseworkers were rushed and preoccupied, but he did not need these people to be nice to him. He simply needed them to do their job. He wanted out. Whatever they wanted, he provided. He would not see them again.

Within a few days his application was accepted and he was released from Amygdaleza. Free again. He had to report in every few weeks. This, he could do. As long as they left him alone, he could meet any of their silly demands.

Life was much easier with the temporary refugee card. When the authorities stopped Vijay, which was inevitable, given his chocolate colour in this milky-white country, all he had to do was show them the card and they'd leave him alone. He was making a good living collecting and selling scrap metal. Saphal and Sanjit helped with the business too. His son was small and hunched over like an old man, but he did what he was told. Vijay was tough on the boy because he had survived against all his hardships, and God willing, he would be a man one day. He had to learn how to take care of himself. Vijay would not be around forever, and there was no one coming to help the boy, no big lottery win for Sanjit or the family.

The Greeks played these games of instant fortune, as if this alone would help them out of their economic troubles. There were as many lottery offices and men on the street selling lottery tickets as there were bakeries and churches in this country. For Vijay and his family, there would never be anything more than work and struggle. It was the only way to get ahead. He'd known this his whole life. It would be easier for his son if he learned this lesson sooner rather than later.

Vijay's plan was working well. He saved every euro he could, hoping to leave Greece and perhaps one day open a restaurant somewhere, serving authentic Indian food, the same as they used to get back home. One day, he'd make use of the education he'd received before he was forced to leave college and India. This education and his skills would make his restaurant a success.

He'd found them a better place to live too, close to downtown Athens. Saphal liked the neighbourhood. It was called Ta Prósfygika, a Greek word meaning The Refugees. The place had once been an important complex of buildings housing some of the hundreds of thousands of Greeks chased out of Turkey between the two world wars. Some of those people still lived there. The buildings in the neighbourhood were now derelict and crowded, and the Greeks in the place worried that it would be torn down to make room for expensive homes. But this didn't worry him. He didn't intend to stay here forever. For now, they had a door to close and a lock to keep all those refugees in the other apartments out.

2

THE PRICE

Summer 2012

Ta Prósfygika, Athens

It was Wednesday and Vijay had to go to the asylum office yet again for an appointment to renew his refugee status. He'd been doing this for close to a year now. Sometimes he had to spend the entire day waiting for the meeting with his caseworker. It cut into the time he should have been on the street earning his living. Yes, he was free to come and go, but this bureaucracy was frustrating.

Bureaucracy or not, the authorities were letting him stay in Greece while they investigated his refugee claim. Who was he to complain? Initially he had had to report in every few weeks, now it was once a month. They trusted him. Buying time, even in one-month slots, was all he needed.

He wasn't planning on staying in Greece permanently. He hoped to get his refugee status here, and then move elsewhere in the European Union, a place where the economic situation wasn't so dismal. Saphal was happy here, though. She'd made friends in Ta Prósfygika. And now she was talking about Sanjit starting school. She'd settled in, and it would be hard to tear her away from here, but Greece was not where their future lay. Germany. Finland. England. These were the places full of hope and opportunities for him and his family.

Vijay reminded Saphal of this every other day. But he knew full well when she did not want to hear. She ignored what he said and instead told him again how good Sanjit's Greek and English were. How the nice old Greek lady in the building over to the right of theirs had brought Sanjit a few cookies. How would he get Saphal to listen?

Vijay couldn't believe his luck. He'd been waiting with the others outside the gate since six this morning, but his name was called right away once the doors opened, ahead of the two men in front of him in line. He'd be able to get back to work after he answered the caseworker's questions, told her what she wanted to hear. *We are doing well. Adjusting. No, we don't need anything. Thank you for your concern for us.*

Then he'd be able to leave and put in a full day of collecting.

He sat in front of the caseworker, his hat squeezed in his hands, his eyes respectfully downcast. This bureaucrat held the power over his future. And the hope for his family. Vijay had to stop feeling resentful. It was not as though there was no bureaucracy in his own country. He'd had to fill in one application after another, take part in several interviews just to get the scholarship money he needed to first get through the public school system, then to get to college. He was used to it, he reminded himself. This was nothing.

The caseworker didn't look up from her papers. She spoke quickly this morning, not making time for the simplest of pleasantries. He heard the words, but they did not make sense. He was reasonably fluent in the woman's Greek language and still he could not understand. "I beg your pardon?" he said.

"Your asylum claim has been denied," she repeated, enunciating every word, raising her voice as though she was speaking to a foreigner who didn't understand the language. Yes, certainly he was a foreigner, but he understood her language perfectly well. Why was she treating him like an imbecile?

Vijay's mouth was full of honey and charm when he was selling scrap metal, but now the stupid thing could not be bothered to find a single word.

This woman across the desk from him was young and usually she was friendly. But her smile had disappeared. She seemed kinder when she smiled. She should do it more often, he thought. It was the sort of smile that put someone at ease. But the way she looked at him now, he was sure he should be worried.

"There is no basis for your claim. I'm sorry." Her voice was quieter, ominous. She leaned forward, put her hands on the desk, and clutched them together as if pleading for him to understand. Her knuckles turned white, as she pressed her hands tighter still.

Vijay wanted to tell her not to be sorry. There was no use in apologizing. Just do what you have to do to help me stay. That's all. "But what about my wife's family? They threatened to kill us. This is all because I'm a Dalit and she is from the Kshatriya class, a higher caste. They do not accept anyone that is not like them. I know this seems silly, but my country is not as generous and open as yours." He did not believe a word of what he said, but what else was he going to do? At least his mouth was working again. Flattering and charming her. He was sure she did not want to hear the truth about how her country treated foreigners. The shame she should feel should be enough to grant him asylum, he thought. But what was the point of saying what should have been so obvious to this woman?

"But you can return to another part of India and be safe," she said. "This is the hardest part of my job. Believe me, I wish I could do more, but we are bound by rules."

"All sorts of other people are allowed to stay. Syrians. Afghanis. Why not us?"

"They come from war-torn countries. We can't in all good consciousness send them back to die. The Geneva Convention does not allow us to do such things."

"But we could be killed too. They are a powerful family with eyes everywhere."

The woman shook her head.

"Is there anything else I can do?" Maybe if she couldn't make things work out for them, he could do something himself. "Another process to give me more time? My wife likes this place so much, my son is going to start school soon." He smiled, shrugged. He hoped she'd see his predicament and show some mercy, check off whatever box on her forms she had to in order to allow him to stay.

She shook her head, leaned back in her chair, and took her hands with her, as though they too were done with him.

"Could I go to another country and make a claim?" Vijay bent towards her. He'd get on his hands and knees and beg if he had to, but he was sure it had been attempted by others before him, no doubt without much success. These caseworkers were probably trained to harden themselves against pleas and grovelling.

"Once you claim refugee status here," she said, "you can't claim status in another EU country. It would be a duplication of effort. Everyone's resources are already stretched."

He wanted to scream. Shiraz never mentioned this part when they were in Amygdaleza. Saphal was right. There was always a price for freedom. This was no one's fault but his own. He had let too much time pass, had became complacent because Saphal was content. They should have disappeared long before, but he hadn't wanted to be the one to ruin her happiness.

"All right, then," the caseworker said, as though the matter was closed, as though she had made him see what needed to be done and he had agreed to comply. But he had done no such thing.

She looked down at her papers. "We will arrange tickets for you and your family. You have a few weeks to get your affairs in order and then you'll have to report to the airport on September 15th. Good luck to you, sir. I hope everything works out for you and your family." She scribbled her signature on one of the papers, never once meeting Vijay's stunned gaze.

"Thank you," he said, but he wasn't sure for what. She nodded, but did not look at him. It took everything he had not to run out of her office. Someone would have chased him down if he showed his unwillingness to comply with the woman's demands. He was sure of this. Then, they would lock him away until his departure. He could not let anyone take him back to Amygdaleza.

All day, as he made his rounds of construction sites, shopping cart in front of him full of drainage pipes, aluminum window frames and stainless steel pans he'd scrounged up, his mind was whirling. But by evening, he had a plan. When he got home, Saphal was in the kitchen. He did not tell her about the plan right away. First he told her about the hours he waited in front of the asylum centre, how frustrating these monthly meetings were. None of it was true, but he wanted to make a show of it.

She wouldn't know the difference. She had worked alone with their son today. They had two shopping carts to their name. It made for more business. He had allowed himself to dream that one day he'd have a small truck like some of his Roma competitors drove around in. They were poorer than him, yet they could afford trucks, albeit ones without proper seats and doors. He'd have a brand new vehicle with a loudspeaker on top, urging those with junk to use his services. And of course they would because he'd be more professional-looking than the Roma, and his truck would be new and clean.

How could he fault Saphal for settling into life here? He'd done the same thing.

He would not tell her what the caseworker had said about his claim. He had decided this before he'd left the asylum centre's compound. Better for Saphal to think they were going toward something rather than running away.

"This is our home now," she said, as though she'd anticipated what he was going to ask. She said the same thing after each of his meetings with his caseworker. "I don't want to leave. We're making enough money. We have friends here. Greek volunteers come on Sunday and make food for us. It feels like home. In our building and in this complex, we take care of each other. We have a good life." Steam rose from the rice cooker she'd bought at one of the international stores in Omonia Square. She stirred the dal. The aluminum pot he'd retrieved from a dumpster and she'd cleaned up sat on the single-burner hot-plate. She could cook up an entire meal with the little they had.

The scent of ginger and turmeric made his mouth water.

"They are not all nice to us," he said. "You complain all the time about those people down the hall who have been asking when we're going to move out because they do not like the smell of our food. The others who stare at Sanjit and call him names."

"There will always be a few," she said. "Wash up, now. Dinner is almost ready."

"We could have a better future somewhere else," Vijay said later that evening. "Make a better life for Sanjit." The boy was finally in bed and settled for the night.

"Sanjit will be going to school in September. He has friends here." Saphal was at the kitchen table, darning a sock. Vijay stood at the counter.

He swallowed deeply. "You know we will never be accepted here," he said. "They will always look at the colour of our skin and treat us differently."

"Not everyone is like this," Saphal said. "And do you really think it would be any different elsewhere? We weren't accepted in our own country. This is the reality we chose when we married. Even when we went to Dharavi, no one accepted us. We were from Bihar? We were there to steal their jobs, take food from their mouths. Don't you remember?"

He took a mouthful of his tea, burnt the inside of his mouth and then his throat when he swallowed. His eyes streamed as he coughed and he choked on his words.

"Did something happen, Vijay? You haven't spoken about leaving for a long time." She stared at him now rather than the needle she was working through the sock. How could she darn without looking? he wondered, but said nothing. She knew he was up to something. One of his schemes. That was why she was looking at him that way. He turned to grab the glass behind him. Gulping water helped cool the rage in his mouth, the irritation in his throat.

He bit his lip. "I have never stopped talking about leaving. You have stopped listening."

"Why do we have to go anywhere?"

"That was always the plan."

"Come sit down and tell me what is going on." She placed the sock on her lap and moved one of the three kitchen chairs Vijay had found months ago, in a Kolonaki dumpster, closer so he could sit beside her. "Plans change. You are the one who says this."

Vijay remained standing. "I could go by myself." He expected her to come to him, somehow protest. Instead, she returned her gaze to her needle and said, "If you are keen to go, it would be easier and faster if you went alone. You could send for us later."

"You are my wife," he said and kneeled before her.

The needle fell out of her hand and onto her lap, but she would not look at him. "Saphal, I could not have come this far without you. And I will not leave you behind." He took her hands in his and tugged until she stood in front of him. He heard the faint sound of the needle hitting the tile floor. She bent to retrieve the needle. He stopped her and brought her in close. Kissed her forehead. "Leaving would be good for all of us. I only want what is best."

"You are a hardworking man," she said, looking straight into his eyes. "My family was wrong about you. They told me you weren't good enough to be my husband. They had other plans for a husband for me. But you were the one I chose." She pulled at her silver earrings. They had been a present from her parents. She never let them out of her sight. She'd told Vijay many times how they reminded her of her family. He supposed she missed them. But what was there to miss? he wondered. Her family never had any use for him. They only saw his caste, never what he'd been able to accomplish despite it. They made life impossible for them. Their views, their rules, their threats had forced them to run away before they were married.

"Wherever you go, we will go," she said. Pushing him away, she picked up the needle from the floor and turned to stick it in the sock. "I will begin packing what we will need to take. I will get Sanjit prepared. You find us the way out."

He had to tell her. "It would be quicker if we went on our own. You said so yourself."

She turned then. Her eyes filled with fire. "What are you talking about? I'm not going anywhere without my son."

"Sanjit is not well," he said. "You know that. He moves slowly. It would be better if we went on our own. Just you and me."

"But we are not young, and we have a family now. We have responsibilities." She pushed the chair into the table. The sound of scraping metal irritated him, but he was not going to let her see that.

"Yes, but if we go quickly, we can find a better home, a better life, and send for him faster. We could accomplish so much more on our own."

"You go by yourself," Saphal said. "On your own you would cover more ground. You wouldn't have us to hinder you. We will come when you are ready for us."

"No, you are my wife and I need you to be with me." He cleared his throat and reminded himself to remain calm. "And if we are together, it is more likely we will be accepted. Alone I look like a terrorist. Together we are a couple in love avoiding persecution. We will garner more sympathy and finally get what we wanted when we first left our country. It is still what we want. Nothing has changed." She had to understand he was not going to give her any options, but as with everything he had to be patient with Saphal, bring her around slowly.

"Sanjit is so small, so sickly. How could we possibly leave him?"

"How will he ever become a man? You baby him too much. He wants to become a man. You see how he carries large scrap pieces to help me. You refuse to let him. You want him tied to your sari forever. It cannot be this way."

"He is six years old."

"My mother abandoned me when I was younger than that. And I became a man without her," Vijay said with pride. Yes, he'd been a product of a rape. And his mother had thrown him to the streets as soon as she could. But somehow he'd survived. By the time he was five, he was sweeping streets. Later, he heaved out garbage for a restaurant owner. That owner taught him how to read and write, allowed him to go to school, and showed him how to apply for scholarships. That's where he fell in love with the bustle of a busy restaurant, dared to dream he'd have one of his own. He'd accomplished a lot, but there was still more to do.

"And is that what you want to do to your son too?" Saphal said. "Is that the only thing children are good for? To be abandoned like street dogs?"

They stood apart, but he felt himself backing away towards the counter, his arms behind him in the same way they'd been when the police first arrested him months ago.

"You know that is not how I feel," he said softly, but he was angry too. She should know better than to argue with him. He was the man of the house. Whatever he said must be respected, but there was no use saying this. Reasoning with her was his best chance of getting what he wanted. "You know it is expensive. We have some money. Okay. It will help. But it is not enough for all three of us." He hadn't spoken to the smugglers about this yet, but he knew it wouldn't be cheap. It had been expensive getting to Greece a few years ago. And had taken months. They could have gone through Russia, maybe secured a visa to go there as others had done, then entered Turkey undetected. But that was the most expensive option and they had needed the cheapest.

They'd taken a bus through India and Pakistan. A friend of Vijay's had an old school bus that he ran across borders, cramming as many people as he could into it. For the entire ride, Vijay had stood with one duffel bag between his feet and Saphal leaning against him. Sanjit sat on the other duffel, holding onto his mother's sari.

In Lahore, they'd found a smuggler to hide them in a semi-trailer truck through Iran. So many people squeezed together. The stench and the heat unbearable. Still, he'd withstood it. When they were finally released from the truck, his achy legs and sore back refused to allow him to stretch out or stand straight. Fresh air had been all he had prayed for when he was in the belly of the truck. It had taken days for his body to loosen. It took longer for the dizziness to leave him. Little sips of water was all he could handle. And still they had a long way to go.

It took nearly two months for them to walk across Turkey — Vijay and Saphal taking turns carrying Sanjit along with their bags — until they arrived in Izmir on the Turkish coast. They slept in parks where refugees gathered.

After that it was easy to connect to a local smuggler in one of the many coffee shops these people sat in waiting for customers like Vijay and Saphal. The smuggler was no more than a boy, Vijay had thought, a refugee himself from Syria, but it didn't matter who he was dealing with as long as the smuggler guaranteed their safe passage over the Aegean into Greece. The smuggler surprised Vijay by offering him a deal.

"We'll give you a lesson in steering," the smuggler had said. "They are not such big boats. There will only be twenty passengers to worry about. And you will save some money, three passages for the price of two."

Vijay nodded. What good was an opportunity if a person didn't take advantage of it when it came his way?

Vijay, Saphal and Sanjit were taken by van to Cesme, a small coastal town on the edge of a peninsula. Vijay was shown how to steer the nine-metre boat. The boat and the engine were not so big. How difficult could it be? he'd thought. But then forty-five people crammed onboard. Thankfully the journey to the Greek island of Lesbos was short and the coast guard was there to rescue them when the boat took on water. There were many families like Vijay's when they arrived in the town of Mytilene on Lesbos, and not many officials. Vijay, Saphal and Sanjit slipped away in the chaos. Vijay found a sympathetic tourist who was trying to help the many migrants by providing food out of his van. The man was a British student on vacation. After hearing their plight, the man stowed them away in his van and boarded a Greek ferry heading to Piraeus.

This time he would have to get false identification, find a way to guarantee their entrance into Germany. He had decided on Germany over Finland and England while he was coming up with his plan to persuade Saphal to leave Greece. Germany had accepted more refugees than any other European country. His best chance to secure refugee status was Germany. But, telling the truth as he had done with the Greek authorities hadn't helped. Concocting a story was the only way. This escape would be far more expensive than their first journey. It had to work. He didn't have the kind of money to make any further attempts at freedom.

"I will not leave my son behind," Saphal said.

"You know how Sanjit is. He needs help, more than this country can give him or than we can give him on our own. But in Germany, they have the finest of everything. We will have work, save money and get him the best care we can afford. This opportunity could make a big difference to him later. It could be the only chance he has to live a long, normal life. You know that is what is important to me."

Saphal shook her head. "So let us take him with us to this land of promise. If it is as good as you say it is, we can get him what he needs sooner."

"Crossing into Germany will be more difficult than it was getting into Greece. They will turn us away if they see something is wrong with one of us. You know how these border people are. Any excuse to deny us. Sanjit's cough will be our undoing. No. We will all be sent back to India and then what will happen to the boy? Our country boasts about its medical facilities, but none will be available to our son. You know that. Medical care is only for the rich in India. And let's not forget about your family. They have eyes and ears everywhere. Until you saw your cousin in the market, we were foolish enough to think we were safe in Mumbai. You know India isn't big enough to hide from your family. No, the best thing to do is to leave Sanjit behind, because he is settled now, and once everything is stable for us, we will send for him and give him everything he needs."

Her arms were crossed in front of her. She stared at him as though she was ready to hit something. Maybe him. And he looked right back at her. He wasn't going to turn away now. "I want what is best for Sanjit too. I promise you this."

She shifted her gaze to her feet.

Vijay reassured himself he was getting through to her and took a breath.

"Look, I have a friend. He and his wife lost their son when they moved here. They can't have any more children. They've tried. His wife is very depressed. They would be happy to look after Sanjit for a while until we can come back for him."

He'd already spoken to Kem, and he and his wife were keen. Kem was a good man, a family man without a family. He was poorer, less motivated and younger than Vijay, but Vijay had befriended him anyway. He saw his younger self in the Roma man, the person who desperately wanted more out of life. Kem hadn't had the same good fortune Vijay had enjoyed. In this matter, they could help each other.

"And how will we be able to get him back? If she is depressed and cannot have children, she may not want to give my son back to me."

"I have made it clear," he said. "They will be taking care of him only until we get settled. That is all. They are good people. Kem has had many opportunities to make more money selling drugs, just as I have. He has not done this. He is a family man." Vijay moved toward her, his arms open.

"What kind of name is Kem?" She stepped back away from him.

At least she was asking questions.

"We are from the same origins, closer than you might think."

"What kind of name?"

"Ukrainian. Something like that."

"And?"

She didn't believe him. Again.

"Roma. Ukrainian Roma."

"Roma? I am not leaving my son with people who steal! Who are illiterate. Poor. They cannot even use a simple telephone, let alone a cellphone. How will I contact Sanjit? Talk to him? Make sure he is doing well?"

"Just like your family, you think you're better than everyone else. We all do what we must to survive. There is no shame in that. And besides, how do you know they steal? They are not all thieves, just as we are not all women-haters and rapists. The Greeks say this about us all the time. It doesn't make it true, does it?"

She turned her back. "You always throw my family in my face."

Vijay put his hand on her shoulders. "I'm not trying to do that. I just want to give us an opportunity. Give our son every possible chance. We will come back for him." He turned her around to face him. "I promise." He raised her chin. He looked into her eyes. "I promise."

"If you've got the money, you can go in style. Fake passports, new names, flights, anything you want, we will provide," the man in the Armani suit said. "We're in the business of customizing to fit your needs and, of course, your pocketbook. But this is a business, not a charity. I'm sure you understand, we have to make a living too."

He didn't give Vijay his name. And what would he do with it anyway? He only needed a way out of Greece. Not on an old boat this time, but rather in a way that legitimized him and Saphal as true refugees. Fake identification, new lives.

"How much?"

"Five thousand euros a head. We're giving you a fresh start. It's a bargain."

Vijay had known it would be expensive. Even after the promise he'd made her, Saphal had argued further with him about leaving Sanjit. She had wanted to know how much passage for all of them would cost. Now that he knew the price, she couldn't argue with him any more. Either they would all be sent back to India, or he and Saphal would make a break for it while they still could. He would remind her this was what was best for Sanjit.

His own motives were genuine.

"How soon can we leave?" he asked the man.

3

One Step Ahead

Pefkakia, Athens

Even though I'm sitting right on the sidewalk, a lady wearing earrings like Ammi's almost trips over me. When she notices me, she says something I can't hear. She doesn't look at me or say she's sorry or anything. Some people don't want us to know they saw us, on our bums, hands out, begging. I try not to let that hurt my feelings because it happens a lot, people not wanting to look me in the eye. This didn't used to be my job, but because I'm not so big and my muscles are not so strong, I can't work with Abbu in the family business all the time. I thought this could be my way of helping. I used to find scrap metal for my abbu, but it is very heavy for someone like me, even when Ammi helps. I still do that job too, but not every day.

Besnik told me about this work. I met him wandering the streets with his sister Lala. Their clothes were torn and dirty. Their teeth were yellowy-brown like the pee of one of the street dogs. And they had sleep crud in their eyes. Disgusting.

They were nice to me, though, and helped me make a little bit of money for my family. I am a boy, so it is important to help my family. Abbu says that all the time.

The lady's earrings are gold, not like Ammi's at all. I can see that now, but I can't help watching her walk away. Gold Earrings is standing by her car now, her bags slipping down her arms as she tries to unlock the door. Her kid sits on her hip, screaming for his toy fire truck. Lucky him. He has toys. But you would not think so by the way he is crying. He pulls at his mother's hair, kicks his legs. If I did that, my abbu would slap me on the side of the head, or kick me in the bum. And if my abbu didn't do it, my ammi would. She loves me and everything, probably more than Abbu does, but there is no way she would let me get away with acting like a baby.

I want to ask Gold Earrings if I can help her with her bags. Ammi always says she wishes someone would help us when we have too many window frames or other metal pieces to carry away from those big garbage containers people use when they are building a new house or fixing an old one.

I am still thinking about this when the lady comes back and puts her bags down in front of me. I do not move. I am afraid she's going to hit me, so I bend my head down. I want to tell her that I did not do one thing, not one. I just looked at her earrings because they were like Ammi's. That's all. Maybe she caught me staring, but I didn't mean to. It just happens sometimes when I'm bored and waiting for people to pass by and put a coin in my hand.

I've heard stories from the other boys. I even saw it happen once. A man kicked one of my friends just because he was standing in front of the man's store, asking for money. The boy wanted to help his family. That's all. Rich people don't understand.

I hunch my shoulders up to my ears. I turn just a little because I don't want Gold Earrings to see I'm getting ready for a beating.

She doesn't hit me. She rummages through each bag, doesn't look at me, not for one second. Her kid stops wailing. He is curious too.

She takes out a bag of marbles and puts them in my hand. I stare at the bag, and I'm sure my mouth is open. In my surprise,

I forget and look right at her. "You need these more than he does," she says. "Do you understand?" I nod. "*Ne, sas efharistó.*" Of course I understand Greek. And I speak it too. My abbu says to speak and to understand a person is important. Gold Earrings meets my eyes and smiles. It is a sad smile, though, like she's thinking about something else, not me. She picks up her bags, puts the kid back on her hip, and walks back to her car.

The kid screeches louder than before, bats Gold Earrings's shoulder with his head, and pulls her hair again. If I ever did that, Ammi would yank my arm so hard I wouldn't be able to move it for days, and Abbu would bring out his belt. I know that for sure.

I rub the bag, feel the bag's mesh, and the cold balls slide under my fingers. Each marble feels smooth, like Ammi's earrings.

When I get home, it seems quiet for a change. This is strange because it is always noisy here. Abbu wants to leave this place where so many of us live together, but there is nowhere to go. That's what Ammi says, but I think she likes it here. I do too. At least we live in a small apartment. It is very old. I find chunks of the outside wall in the brown grass that we kids play on and sharp rods of metal stick out near the bottom of the buildings. I stay away from these because they could cut me. Some people have little pots of flowers outside their windows and those make me feel happy in my chest.

My abbu found this place for us. He had to fight others for it, but my abbu is strong and smart. All the time he tells me he brought us here for a better life.

Some of the Greek people who live in this neighbourhood don't want us here. My abbu says it is best for us to stick together with our own. It is safer this way. Ammi says there are good people here, people who care about us. On Sundays everyone from all the buildings meet to eat together and one Sunday, a nice old lady brought cookies especially for me. I don't know exactly where the old lady lives, but it is in one of these buildings.

It's late afternoon, so some are still out working. Ammi is here though, outside our building, at the picnic table.

I like it when I have her all to myself. No Abbu telling me what to do.

I show Ammi the bag of marbles. She just looks at them and shakes her head. "We can't eat those," she says. She's mad about something, but what it is, I don't know. It's good to stay out of her way when she's like this, but there are not many places for me to go. Ammi says I will start school soon. If it is true, I will have a place to go then.

I dump the bag of marbles down on the ground, and then sit down, my legs underneath me, one hand holding my mother's sari. My father says all I ever do is hold onto her, but Abbu is mean sometimes. A few days ago when I was trying to carry a heavy pipe to him, a nice lady with a big smile helped me. He thanked her, but as soon as she turned to walk away, he hit me across the head. It hurt too. "You do your job. You don't ask anything from anyone. Do you understand?" He hurt my feelings, but I didn't say anything because then I might start to cry and he doesn't like that either.

I use my free hand to flick one of the fat marbles. It is the colour of a rainbow I see sometimes far away in the mountains after a big storm. I try to hit some of the smaller marbles. I put those ones in a row, again and again. Straight as can be. I wish I could make my back go this straight, but it doesn't do what I want it to do. I bend a little into myself. Ammi says I'm just small. She says I will grow up to be strong like my abbu. But she looks sad every time I catch her staring at me. She tells me to straighten up. I try to remember to do that so she doesn't have to remind me.

The fire in the pit warms my back. I love the feeling because it makes me shake all over. I'm warm, I know, but I shiver like I'm still cold. Some of me is always cold. My feet are icy. Even in the summer, they stay cold. I rock back and forth to sit on my feet. That's better. I rub one of the marbles between my fingers. I like how smooth it feels.

Ammi stands over the picnic table Abbu built from scraps of wood. He's a collector. That's what he says, and when he's in a good mood, he laughs with himself like he is the only one who understands the joke. He collects mostly metal. But he will pick up anything. He says he goes all over the city, anywhere his legs will take him. He gets money for doing this because people always want to get rid of their own garbage and other people want to buy that garbage. The money he makes as a collector helps us more than anything my ammi and I do.

But it all helps, Ammi says, when I bring her coins. She never asks where I get them from, but I think she knows.

She has a garbage bag almost as big as me beside her that she's stuffing things into: toilet paper, some clothes, and the day-old bread the baker down the street gave us yesterday. She likes being outside in the sunshine. She always says our place is too small and dark and she can't see what she's doing in there. One day we'll have a bigger apartment in our building or one of the other buildings here.

When I look up at her, I catch her staring right back at me like I'm not even here. We used to play a hide-and-seek game when I was little. She'd pretend she couldn't see me, even though I was in front of her. The look on her face now is sadder than those other times when we played that game. But in a way, it's the same too. Ever since I can remember, which is a pretty long time, I always thought she was sad. She looks like I feel inside when someone on the street calls me a *zitiáno*, beggar. Or when they ignore me. Or, even worse, when they chase me with a stick. I don't know why they treat me like that, but it makes me feel bad. I want to tell them to stop being mean, but Abbu says boys are supposed to be strong. We are not supposed to complain or say how we feel. So I don't. Or, I try not to. It's not easy.

Ammi snorts and blows her nose, like she's crying or something. It looks like she's packing up our things. Maybe we're moving again and that's why Ammi is sad. She likes our apartment. We used to move all the time. Ammi said this is part of our life too. "We have to stay one step ahead. So bad people don't get us and throw us out of this country. Moving keeps us safe." But we've been in this place for so long, I thought we were safe already.

Where are we going this time? I wonder, but can't ask. Ammi's mouth is a tight, dark stripe. Her mouth reminds me of the heavy lines people print across buildings and fences close to where we live. I can read some of what the words say because Ammi taught me how. When I ask her about words I can't read, she looks at the letters, closes her eyes so tight I can see that blue vein poke out in her forehead. Then she says something like, "Never mind. It is nothing." I know by the way she shakes her head and hurries us back to our building she's afraid and doesn't want to scare me too. It makes me mad when she doesn't answer my questions. It's like she's hiding something from me and that's not fair. I mean, I'm almost seven and she calls me her man, but sometimes she treats me more like a baby than a man.

"Why aren't you with your friends," Ammi says now, "instead of being here under my feet? Can you not see I have work to do?" She covers her eyes with her arm.

"What's wrong?" I ask. "Did I do something?"

Her throat moves up and down. She swallows hard like she's trying to get something down that won't stay. I don't cry much now that I'm almost seven, but when I used to, I'd gulp the same way so the tears wouldn't come and embarrass me. Ammi's sleeve is wet when she puts her arm down, but her eyes are dry. "You will understand all this later. When you're older," she says. "This is the best we can do for you. We'll get the help we need for you if we do this. I know that now. Maybe you will forgive us one day and understand why we had to do this."

Her silver earrings shine in my eyes. I love those earrings. I used to tap them with my fingers when I was younger just to hear them tinkle. I still want to touch those earrings sometimes, but I'm a man now.

She grabs one earring and yanks at it. If she's not careful, she'll rip her ears wide open. Then what will we do? Abbu always says we have no money for doctors or things like that. Ammi asks him if she can take me to a doctor for my bent back and the cough. "What doctor would see him?" Abbu says. "These people don't care about us. They only want our money. Money we don't have. And you know as well as I do, they are not smart enough to know what to do. This isn't a disease they would understand." So we can't get sick and if any one of us did, well, we'd have to take care of it by ourselves.

She drops the earring on the table. It makes a noise like a little bell.

"Why not?" Ammi says, but she doesn't look at me, so I don't think she is talking to me. "Your father says she wants these too. A price for taking care of the one I should be taking care of myself."

Maybe she's talking to herself. She does that sometimes.

"She wants everything I have. Why not these too? They are no more important than my child, are they?"

I don't know what Ammi is talking about, so I stay quiet. That's always the best thing to do when you don't understand what the grownups are saying or doing.

She takes the other earring off, snatches the one on the table, puts both in her pocket.

She reaches down and hauls me up like I'm nothing more than one of those big sheets of plywood she carries for Abbu, so I have no choice but to let go of her sari. She tells me to go and play. I look away because I don't want to see her angry eyes. I do what I'm told. I know better than to argue with her.

I leave my marbles and run.

4

Candy Lady

Late Autumn 2012

Roma Camp, Néa Filothei, Athens

Candy Lady holds out another handful of candy. I mean to grab it and run away and hide like Mirela told me to do when Candy Lady comes to our camp. But then, her hand fills up with more and I can't help it.

When I get near her, Candy Lady clamps her hand on my shoulder and says, "We are going for a ride," I didn't think Candy Lady was this strong. Her hand is small, almost as small as mine. She's holding me so tightly it hurts, like Mirela does when she thinks I'm not listening.

I follow her to her car like the children who followed the man with the magic pipe in the story Ammi used to read to me so I could practise my English. Understanding and speaking and reading are just as important to my ammi as they are to my abbu.

I don't really want to go for a ride in her car. I only go with her for the candy, even though Mirela is giving me that look. I'm not doing anything wrong right now. I'm going with Candy Lady because Kem told me to. He calls Candy Lady Mrs. Shelby. I think Candy Lady is a better name for her, because that is what she brings me.

The others in the camp make a big circle around me and Candy Lady like they don't want us to leave, but Kem flings his arms like he does when he is pretending he is going to hit me and yells, "Mind your own business." They throw their hands at him and turn their backs. They don't like him anymore.

When I first came to the camp, Mirela wanted me to say she was my mother, but I only have one of those. Every day I sat by the fire for a long time and waited, trying to keep Ammi's face in my head. It scares me how I forget everything so fast. Were her eyes really brown? I see them sometimes in my dreams, but they disappear when I wake up.

When Kem tells me to go to work, I stop thinking. It is the same work I did before I came here. I didn't have to learn a new job, like I had to learn about the new food to eat. Abbu never allowed me any meat, but here I have to eat whatever Mirela gives me, because if I don't I'll starve. I don't like the smell sometimes and tiny bits get stuck in my teeth, but it's not so bad. Whatever fills my belly is okay until Ammi comes back for me. Then things will go back to normal.

Kem said I had to go to work to help support myself. That's what children are supposed to do. So that's why he took me out of school. I don't know why he let me go there and then wouldn't let me stay. It's not fair, but I'm a boy and I have to help. Kem said school doesn't help anyone.

I make more money these days. When I first came to live with Mirela and Kem, he told me I'd be good at it. "You'll bring in a pot of gold with your size and that bent back of yours," he said. "People will give you more money, more handouts. And don't forget to bring it home or you know what will happen. Right?" He lifted his hand like he was going to hit me and I ducked. But then he wiped away something on his cheek, laughed a big, long laugh that sounded like it came from somewhere down in his stomach.

In front of the grocery store where I work, waiting for people to come out and give me some coins or food, I sometimes hear Ammi's voice. Any time she felt we had enough food, like when the church people came on Sunday to make a big lunch for all of us who lived in those old buildings, she would sing.

Sometimes I think I hear her voice. But it's never her. The sound comes from the kids in a playground, the wind shaking the leaves on the orange trees. My chest hurts when I think she's there and then she's not, but I look every time, because one day it will be her.

My real name is Sanjit, but Kem and Mirela call me Bo now.

I answer when Kem yells "Bo, do this. Bo, where are you?" But I don't think it's as a good a name as Sanjit.

It's okay for me to have a new name, but I can't pretend Mirela is my mother like she wants me to. So I don't call Mirela anything.

When I say her name, it doesn't make her happy. "I am your mother now," she said one day, her hand on her hip, the other open and in the air close to my head like she was about to slap me. She didn't. But after that day, I didn't call her anything. That way I couldn't get into trouble. And I didn't call Kem by his name either. I answered when they said something to me and I did what they told me to do. That made life good for all of us.

When Candy Lady started coming to the camp, Kem and Mirela said I had to call them mother and father. There are words like this in their language and in the Greek language. But I wouldn't. I stopped eating and hid in the corner, changed into the shirt and pants I came to them in and wouldn't move from my spot. "Don't call us anything then," they finally said, "especially in front of Mrs. Shelby." I don't know why Candy Lady worries Mirela so much. Kem likes Candy Lady a lot. "It's like she's our grandmother," he says. "Bringing us food. Clothes for our little Bo."

"She wants what is ours," Mirela says, but never looks at Kem. It's funny how she never does. Look at him, I mean. Maybe she thinks he's ugly with his black-as-night hair, his cheeks that are not smooth but have lots of holes. His eyes are really black too, darker than any eyes I've ever seen before, so he looks angry all the time, even though I know he's not because he laughs and smiles a lot too and shows his gold tooth. Sometimes he draws pictures for me.

Whenever Mirela says anything bad about Candy Lady, Kem laughs at her and tells her she's just a jealous old woman.

Mirela and Kem have been pretty good to me. They even sent me to school, just like Ammi wanted. But I was only there for a couple of days. I wasn't allowed to stay. I liked school. The teacher was nice to me. She wasn't mean to me because of my dirty clothes or anything. There is no place here to take a bath like I used to do every day when I lived with Ammi and Abbu. Sometimes Mirela boils water and washes me all over while I stand in front of her. She likes to do this, but it's cold taking a bath outside and I don't like so many people being around looking at me. I don't ask Mirela why I can't do this inside our house because I know the answer. There is no bathroom in our house here like we had in our apartment.

We have a place to sleep and most of the time we have food. Sometimes it's cold, but it was cold when we were in our apartment too. Abbu wouldn't pay for heat in the winter. It cost too much money, he said. So we had to wear extra shirts and sweaters in the winter. This house is just for Mirela and Kem and me. It's especially cold when the wind blows, because the walls aren't really walls. They are made of some kind of heavy cloth, the colour of sand. And there are boards and other things keeping our house up so it doesn't fall down on top of our heads. It leans against a building, so our house has some help.

But the building has no roof and no walls, so it might not be too strong either.

For such a warm country, why is it so cold? I don't know.

Sometimes I let Mirela hug and hold me. Women like to do that. When she holds me, it makes her feel better. I can tell, because the next day she will buy me an ice cream and not tell Kem. We sit in the park in the shade. We don't look at those people who stare at us like they think we should not be in their park or eating ice cream. Do they think good things are only for rich people?

Mirela's dress smells of the smoke from the fire. I like that smell. I lean my head against her chest and hear her heartbeat.

When I first came to the camp, she found a pillow for me so I could keep my head off the ground. Mirela is good at finding things. I don't know how she does it, but she's the one who finds all of our food, not Kem. I'm sure Abbu would say she's more like a man than a woman, and maybe she is. She's very strong and knows how to get what she wants.

She likes to keep me close, she says, because I'm her lost boy. "God has given you back to me," she told me once, and then hugged me so hard I started to cough. This is the only time I saw her face shake like she might cry. Even her eyes got a little shiny.

"Let the boy go to work," Kem said one day when she didn't want me to go to work all by myself.

"I want him to go with me today," she said. "It's better this way."

"He'll make more by himself," he said. He pushed me towards the door. "He'll do what I tell him to do."

Mirela told me to leave then. She shooed me out the door, sneaking a few coins into my hand.

I didn't go far, though, not as far as I do when I have to go downtown on the train to work. I sat outside the flap to our house, listening. Slaps. Something falling to the hard ground. Kem breathing hard, but no sound came from Mirela.

I like Mirela and everything, but I really wish my ammi would come back. She said she would and I believe her. She wouldn't lie to me.

Abbu never hit Ammi. "You're not supposed to hit girls," he'd say if I had a fight with one in the park by our old house. "You must understand them first. What they like. Then you will know how to get around them."

I didn't really understand what he meant, but I could see when Ammi was mad sometimes, he would talk her right out of it. He was good at that.

I think Ammi left her earrings with Mirela to remind me of her. This makes me smile. She would not give them to Mirela for no reason. She loved those earrings and wore them all the time. Mirela does the same thing now. I don't like it that she wears what was Ammi's, but at least I can watch over them, keep them safe for Ammi.

Candy Lady drives with one hand and holds out more candy in her other hand. I try to resist, but it's hard. I love the squishy ones the most. They taste like the peaches, apples, and strawberries Mirela and I find in the alley behind the grocery store or near the bins after the open market finishes for the day. The candies are so much better than the real fruit, which is sometimes rotten right through to the inside and tastes and smells really bad. Mrs. Shelby looks at me as she drives and I know she wants something from me because no one gives you something for nothing. But I have nothing to give Candy Lady. I wonder if she knows that. She calls me her *little guy*, and looks at me with eyes that could eat me as quickly as I gobble the candies.

We drive for a long time. The belt she's put around me holds and squeezes me tighter every time she stops the car too fast.

I cough, but I don't think it's the belt. I cough all the time. If Mirela was here or if I was home with her, she would give me the medicine that helps me sometimes. Maybe Candy Lady doesn't know about medicines. She probably only knows about candy.

If I could get the belt off I could jump out of the car, I think, but Candy Lady will take me back soon so there is no point, except it would be an adventure to try to find my way back all by myself. I'm old enough and smart enough. After Candy Lady started coming to the camp, Mirela told me if anything happened I had to find my way back. I don't know what she means. What could happen? How would Ammi find me if I didn't stay where she left me?

Candy Lady talks and talks. She points to things and tells me their names. I look and nod, but don't say anything. It's a good thing Ammi and Abbu taught me English and Mirela and Kem know English because I wouldn't be able to understand Candy Lady. She talks very fast. And as nice as these buildings are — nicer than where I live in the camp — the grey haze in the sky still sits on top of them here too. The air feels heavy today, like it could squash those buildings and me in the same way I pound the cockroaches that climb up on my pillow at night. I guess it doesn't really matter where I live. The air that makes me feel like I'm choking is everywhere.

Candy Lady finally stops the car in front of one of the buildings. My stomach hurts now and I feel like I want to throw up. My teeth hurt too, like something very cold is sitting on top of them. The candy is stuck all over my teeth. My finger can't reach the stuck bits. There are too many and I give up. My hands are sticky.

"We're home," Candy Lady says. She gets out of the car and I don't know where she goes. I can't see her. Then all of a sudden, she's there again. Staring at me through the closed window on my side of the car.

She opens my door, leans over me and pushes a button. She smells of the camp, but nothing like Mirela. It is like she has some of the flowers from the park sitting inside her skin.

The belt around me lets me go. She holds her hand out. I'm afraid, but I take it.

I look around. There is nothing here I know. Where are we?

"This is your new home." She answers my question. I don't think I said it out loud or anything, but still she hears my thoughts, which is kind of scary. I wonder what other powers she has.

I would like to thank her for the candies and ask her to take me back to Mirela. As nice as it looks, I can't stay in this place. Ammi will never find me here. None of the words I know come out of my mouth.

5

<u>G</u>IFTS

Roma Camp, Néa Filothei, Athens

As he rushed home, Kem thought about how to please Mirela. The street was dusty from endless construction and reeked of the oranges dangling on the trees along the boulevard. He couldn't get Mirela off his mind. Maybe he would stack the gifts he bought her in the corner of their home in a pile taller than her. Or perhaps he would have her hunt for them one at a time as he gave her clues. She was still a child in many ways. Games made her happy.

The neighbourhood couldn't rid itself of the camp at the end of the block where he lived, despite all the new buildings being erected. There was supposed to be a recession in this country and still, they built new things.

The thugs who roamed the streets at night looking for people like him to beat up were not going to force them out. The camp was here to stay. And he wasn't going anywhere either. This stingy country was his home now. He had to make a life here. Somehow. And who knew? Maybe one day he'd get to live in one of those fancy apartments with a toilet inside, and drive a car like some of the rich drug dealers in the camp. Their children ran barefoot and were as snotty-nosed and dirty as his own son, but at least those kids rode in style when their fathers allowed them this privilege. He told himself to take it one step at a time, not to get cocky. Still, he didn't bother to pick any of the oranges from the boulevard trees today. You couldn't eat them anyway, but Mirela boiled the oranges with sugar she sometimes found in a dumpster. Then they were sweet enough for him to eat.

He walked into the camp, with its familiar smells of smoke and human waste, finally home with his own. Not quite his own, but close enough. At least these people in this camp accepted them, when others hadn't.

Mirela wasn't back yet. She was probably still out scavenging for food and anything to help make their lives a little easier. He would take a bit of her worry away today with the things he'd bought. He was sure of it. Wait until she sees all this, he told himself. Just wait. His face felt stiff from the smile he couldn't seem to wipe away. The wind was light and the sun hadn't set, but their home was already chilly. He shivered as he finished arranging her gifts. He'd get the fire going too. That would be a nice surprise.

When Mirela returned, she walked right by him and went into the lean-to. She didn't look at him, but then, she rarely did. Kem was sure her miserable mood would change when she saw the things he had stacked in the corner close to where they slept.

The wind kicked up, rushed the flames of the campfire towards him. Kem shuffled closer, patted at his arms and pulled at the lapel of his jacket. He stared into the blaze, letting the heat warm his face. He had even bought Mirela a heavy stainless steel pot and a brand new camp stove. A man wasn't expected to be this generous with his wife. But Kem prided himself on being a little above the other husbands in the camp. Different. His true nature.

It was cold tonight. Mirela's eyes followed him, demanded answers or something from him. Yes, he'd given the boy to

Mrs. Shelby. But why couldn't Mirela see what they'd received in return? She was never happy with what she had. She always wanted what she didn't have. She constantly needed something, that woman. Why couldn't she appreciate what he provided? That shirt with the tiny sequins that rippled and sparkled when she breathed he'd found in a bag of clothes dumped in the blue bin by the dumpster. Hadn't he picked through all those old sweaters and trousers and found this one beautiful thing for her? He didn't need to waste so much of his time. But he had.

He stamped his feet. They were like ice in the new shoes. And if he put his feet close to the fire, he'd burn a hole right through his shoes. It was this way with expensive things; they looked sturdy, but they couldn't withstand much when you put them to the test of his kind of life. Encased in the dust of the camp, his shoes had already faded. He rubbed his arms.

It was pointless to brood. He was here now, he told himself, in a Roma camp, even though he'd tried to avoid these people.

The Greek Romani, like the Greeks themselves, wouldn't allow him to enter their camps. No. He and Mirela were destitute, in need of a home, but those Romani would not offer them even a piece of bread. Did they think themselves a special breed of Romani? Better than the rest?

He'd tried the camps where the Romani were from Albania, Bulgaria and other places. Those people didn't want to accept them either, but when he and Mirela showed them how much they could help in the camp — sharing the food and firewood Mirela scrounged up — they let them put up their lean-to and stay.

He smiled, took a deep breath, as he did every single day before leaving the camp to eke out a living. He shook his head. He was only going to face his wife. A content one as well. Why so nervous? he asked himself and shrugged. Silly.

He crawled into the lean-to, keeping one hand on his fedora so it wouldn't tip off his head. The striped multi-coloured scarf around the rim of his hat brushed against his neck, left goosebumps on his skin.

The bags with Mirela's presents sat untouched where he'd left them in the corner. Mirela sat cross-legged on the ground beside them, sewing. She didn't look up when he came in. Ungrateful woman, Kem thought. He'd done everything for her, for the boy, none of this was for him. He fingered his new watch. Thank God the boy would now have more opportunities, a better life. The boy had been gone for one night and one day. He'd probably already had a hot shower and slept in a clean bed with a solid roof over his head last night. He would have a full stomach. That roof appeared magically, like one of the rabbits Kem's friend, Hanzi, pulled out of his hat to divert a tourist's attention while he slipped his hand over a wallet tucked inside a jacket or a bulging back pocket.

Mrs. Shelby had given them food and clothes and candy for Bo. It was far better than the money they'd received from the Greek government for enrolling the boy in school. That money had disappeared too quickly. Mrs. Shelby was much more reliable. She came nearly every day and gave them things all the time, without him having to do anything. Until yesterday.

Kem had pulled the boy out of school a week after receiving the government money. No one cared. No one asked questions. They didn't want the boy in their schools any more than he wanted to send him there. He just wanted the money the government types provided to make themselves feel better about what they were doing for those in the camp. Governments could be so stupid sometimes.

Mirela had wanted Bo to stay in school. Kem reminded her there was nothing to be gained from an education. "Better for him to learn how to support us." He stared at her. "Look at you. You know how to read and write. You knew how to before you came to my family. Where did that get you? What did school do for you?"

Glaring at her now, he thought Mirela had no idea what he had to endure to get these presents for her. Security cameras, security guards at the entrance of Carrefour, the chain store that carried the things he hoped they'd be lucky enough to have one day, God willing. The guards checked his bags, followed him through the store like the dogs he used to have in his parents' yard, always nipping at the back of his heels, his bare ankles.

One woman, another customer reading a toothpaste label, jumped when she saw him, then stared him down until he moved along without getting the soap he wanted. The clerk asked him whether he could afford to buy the camp stove when he tried to ask her a question about it. These insults he had withstood for Mirela. Couldn't his wife at least give him a smile, show a bit of happiness, just this once?

But she wasn't the generous type. Not like some of the Greeks who'd saved him and Mirela, given them money and a few things to start a new life after they'd arrived in Greece. The religious Greeks set up lines to hand out food and clothing from time to time at the neighbourhood church. Maybe this helped them purge their souls or maybe they were making up for the other Greeks, the ordinary, everyday bastards who beat the crap out of people like him. Because he wasn't a complete idiot, like his father used to call him, he understood the self-righteous glares of the people in this country who only wanted him and others like him to leave.

When they'd first arrived in Greece, the police had wanted to throw them into a detention centre. They'd almost succeeded too. "No documentation," the officer had said and stared at Kem's gold front tooth as though he'd wanted to steal it. Kem knew there were thieves even among those who said they upheld the law. Had he never seen a tooth like his before or would the officer just as soon kill Kem and pry it out of his head? Kem tried to keep his mouth shut, his head bowed.

"Go stand in that line over there. We'll get to you soon." Kem would never forget that officer's eyes. Gigantic, dark, penetrating, yet empty as though there was no compassion, nothing behind them. Kem knew that officer could easily kill him. Lucky for Kem, he and Mirela had managed to slip away right under his nose. They both knew how to use trees and other hiding places to move undetected. There were so many people waiting to be processed, no one would miss them anyway.

Vijay would understand. He was afraid of the authorities too, of being deported for no good reason except politicians wanting to win votes and make their citizens happy. But Vijay wasn't here, was he?

They'd become friends against all odds. Good friends. Why? Kem wasn't sure. Vijay's people and Kem's people fought against each other for the same territory, the same ways to make enough money to survive. But both had drawn a line when it came to dealing drugs. In Kem's camp and among Vijay's people there were some who sold this stuff to make a living. That business brought in money, but Kem saw what drugs did to some of his friends in the camp and he wanted no part of it. He had enough problems without adding a bad habit and senseless violence on top. Vijay felt the same way. Yes, they were meant to be enemies, but by God's grace that hadn't happened.

Vijay reminded Kem of his own old life. Before he'd come to Greece with Mirela. Maybe this was why they were friends. Or maybe it was because Vijay didn't live in the same camp or in the same neighbourhood as Kem did. He had his own people so there were fewer chances to get on each other's nerves. Kem didn't collect and sell scrap metal like some of the other Roma did. Kem didn't interfere in Vijay's work so he wasn't a threat. And Vijay wasn't an artist so he couldn't muscle his way into Kem's livelihood.

Vijay and his family weren't in a camp like this, but they all lived beside each other, in a place for refugees. As with pigeons, new people fresh off smuggler boats arrived and somehow found their way to the places where others like them flocked. Kem and Vijay had met while they combed the busy upscale neighbourhoods in and around downtown Athens. That was where the money was. Not in the suburbs.

We have the same history, Vijay had said. "Your people are the descendants of mine. Thousands of years ago, we came from the same part of the world."

But Kem didn't believe him. Vijay was darker skinned. Besides, Vijay was always working, focused and driven. The man didn't know how to relax. No, they were not the same at all.

He missed Vijay. He was really the only one he could talk to about his life, his strange wife.

Kem looked more closely and saw that Mirela was sewing a button on Bo's filthy shirt. Bo had been wearing that shirt with most of its missing buttons when Mrs. Shelby came yesterday. "It's my favourite," Bo said. It surprised Kem, because the boy rarely spoke to him. When he did say something, it was usually to Mirela. "He's a boy of few words," Mirela told Kem whenever he questioned her. "He holds many things inside."

"Maybe he hasn't accepted his new name," Kem had said. "We shouldn't have changed it so quickly."

"It has been months," Mirela said. "He has no trouble coming when I call him. I'm sure he's forgotten his old name and everything else about his other life."

He ordered Mirela to change the boy's shirt. He couldn't go with Mrs. Shelby looking like that. Like a good wife, she did as she was told. She knew full well what would happen to her if she didn't.

Why was she sewing the buttons on Bo's shirt now? The boy would be given clean clothes, brand new shirts along with his brand new life. There was something wrong with his wife's head. He knew that. He was the man, the one with the brains.

He kicked the bags closer to her. She didn't reach for them. He stood over her. She glanced in one bag, and then at him. "This is all you get in exchange for a son," she said. Her eyes were very dark in this light. They used to be such a beautiful green. The wrinkles on her forehead and around her mouth were etched into her tanned skin as though carved by too sharp a blade. Her face was bony and defined, skeletal. She was becoming an old woman already at seventeen. What would she look like at twenty?

He put his hands behind his back, knitted his fingers together into one clamped fist. "You've always wanted your own camp stove," he said. "It has a small propane tank so you won't have to always collect wood for the fire. It does everything. It will practically cook the meal for you." Held so tightly, his fingers were sore. This time he would be patient. She'd had to give up the boy too soon, Kem told himself, the son who would have provided for the family. He needed to be more compassionate.

But she had to give him some credit too. He'd done it, given her everything he'd promised her that night they'd met four years ago.

The first time he'd seen her, she was in his parents' barn, burrowed into the hay like a mouse looking for warmth, hoping to go unnoticed by the cats. He reached for her as he would to calm one of the many dogs in his parents' scrapyard. Her tangled hair felt wet and greasy in his hands. She whimpered and skulked deeper into the hay, away from his touch. Her eyes were squeezed shut. He patted her head, stroking her like one of the dogs.

She lay perfectly still.

Kem sat beside her and nudged her. She whimpered. It was then that he saw the padlock around her ankle, the chain's track ending with a locked bolt on the wall. "What did you do?" he asked. "Did you get caught stealing something from my father?" His voice, even to him, sounded as accusatory and critical as the foreign teacher's voice in the school he attended when he had nothing better to do. "You should know not to do such things."

She didn't move or answer his questions.

He pinched her to see if she was alive.

She put her hands over her head as if expecting to be struck. He shook the chain. Her leg moved involuntarily. The hay smelled of urine.

"I'll find out what you did. I'll talk to my mother."

He could only get his way with his mother when she was in a good mood. There was no talking to his father, who slapped or punched him whenever he felt like it. His father's anger seemed to come from nowhere. Still, Kem knew it would come. That knowledge made him cower whenever his father was in the room.

Kem found his mother by the campfire. She had a new floral print apron over her soiled black dress. She and his sisters were peeling potatoes and carrots they'd dug out of the weedy, dry patch of garden at the back of the shed they lived in.

"Where did the girl come from?"

"The same place my new apron came from," she said, smoothing her hands over the cloth. "Do you like it?"

"Who is she?" he asked. "The girl in the barn, what is she doing here?"

"She is our gift to you, our only son," his mother said. Her smile was a menace of crooked, dark teeth.

His father had probably bought her from a family in another valley far from where they lived.

His mother dropped a few potatoes, then a carrot into the pot. She examined another carrot closely and without warning tossed it directly at one of his sisters. It hit her in the head, but she didn't bother to look up. "Do a better job peeling these carrots," his mother shouted. "Or I will sell you to the first old goat who comes to our fence wanting a bride." His sister shrugged as if to say, what do I care?

"Why did God curse me with two useless girls?" his mother said.

Kem frequently roamed the alleys and streets looking for things to steal with his friends. They were the ones who told him about the things he could do with the girl in the barn. That was what wives were for.

"But I don't need a wife," he'd said.

"You might not, but that thing between your legs would like one," his friends had said. They all laughed at him. They were no better than a pack of hyenas, he thought. Why did he hang out with them? They were not his friends.

Kem would often bring Mirela a bowl of soup, sometimes an apple he stole from the neighbour's trees. At first, she wouldn't eat anything he brought her. But he was determined to take care of her. He had to. Otherwise, how would she survive long enough to be his wife? He began to leave bits of meat, fried potatoes and carrots behind. And in time, she ate. Like a horse, he thought. The plate was so clean he wondered if she'd licked it.

"Won't you look at me?" he said finally. He tapped her head lightly. She sat up. The way she stared at him with those watery

eyes made him ashamed of himself, his family, and his life. He
stroked her arm timidly to make her feel better, afraid to hurt her.
He would show her pictures he drew in a little notebook he stole
from one of those aid workers who came by from time to time.
But as the days wore on and she continued to turn away from
him, he slapped her shoulder, pinched her arm. "You are going
to be my wife," he said. "I can do anything I want. My friends
ask me all the time if I've done it. I will one day. Don't think I
won't. Don't think you're too good for me. You were probably
sold to my father, no better than the scraps we sell out of our yard.
And you were bought fair and square. Just for me. You might have
acted like this with your other family, but you gave up all your
spoiled ways when they sold you to us."

"Stolen," she said, the first word he'd heard her say since she'd
arrived. "Like my mother's apron. I was wearing it to school. It
was so pretty. I shouldn't have taken it, but I wanted to show
it to my friends. I was far behind them, though. Daydreaming
probably. One minute I was walking along singing to myself, the
next a bag was over my head, a hand over my mouth. I couldn't
scream. Or breathe."

He pulled at the chain around her leg. "You don't know what
you're saying. You were probably on the street, begging. My
father probably saved you by taking you away from that. And if
he did buy you, he was trying to save your miserable life," he said
and dropped the chain. "Grateful is what you should be."

She had begun to cry.

"I am strong. When I am your husband I will give you
sunshine every day. I am an artist. I will have money. You will see.
I will give you everything. You will no longer need your tears."

That was such a long time ago, Kem thought now. They had
been mere children. He fingered the new notebook, the two

ballpoint pens and the pencil kit he had bought himself today. This book would be so much better for collecting his drawings than the scraps of paper he had to use with whatever pencils or pens he could find. He would sell his drawings to tourists for money, real money. He'd write the tourist's name in the letters he knew and get something for his effort. As his mother used to say, "Good speaking is sugar for the soul," whenever he went looking for food or a handout. His father called him a *poponar* when he caught him drawing pictures in that long-ago stolen notebook. He'd rip out Kem's drawings and throw the scraps of paper in Kem's face, tell him he would not allow any son of his to be a *faggot*.

Mirela's life — their lives — hadn't been easy. She'd tried to run away on her own without him and when his father had found her, he'd whipped her with his belt until her backside and the tops of her thighs were a bloody mess. Mirela tried escaping again, but his father always found her. It wasn't until the baby came, a son they named Bo, that Kem and Mirela moved into a room of their own above the barn. Mirela began to talk to him about escaping together. She said it would be best for their son and for them to start a new life. Just them and their small family.

She smiled sweetly, didn't turn away from him. And each time, she made his knees weak. She finally loved him, he thought.

She came up with a plan for them to run away. She had the brains. He knew that, but he had the strength and muscle. And now he was the head of his own family. He would do the right thing by Mirela and Bo, better than his father had ever done for him.

They'd left in the early morning, heading towards the sea. She thought they should go overland to leave the Ukraine. But there were borders and border patrols. Every country had to have such things to protect themselves from what he and Mirela were about to do. But there couldn't be guards to protect every corner of the sea.

And the closest exit out of his country was by the Black Sea. If they went by land, his father would follow and find them. The man would go to hell to find Kem, beat the shit out of him just to recover the little money Kem had taken from him.

The sea would also give Kem and Mirela an advantage. Kem's father didn't like the sea. "It's too big. If you can't see to the other side, how do you know where you are going? It's a place for fish. Not men."

Kem liked the idea of going by boat. The aid workers used to read to him and the other children about these kinds of adventures. He fantasized about being on one of those large boats, sailing away. If they went by land, they'd have to cross into Romania. And once there, they'd certainly end up with the Romanian Roma, which wasn't far enough away. He was different. Better. Still a *tsyhany*, but better than a regular everyday Romani. He was from the Ukraine.

Besides, why do all that walking? For what? He had his father's money. Why not use it to make his life a little easier for a change? Mirela wasn't as smart as she liked to pretend. That's why his father had caught her those times she'd tried to escape by herself. His plan was definitely better.

They would cross the Black Sea into Turkey, then move on to Greece, crossing the Aegean. His friends had told him that both countries looked the other way when it came to refugees. For now, Greece would be a good starting point for a new life. Then, who knew?

He did worry about how quickly they'd be able to move with Mirela carrying the boy and how his family with the small child would go undetected. Kem wondered about leaving the child with his own mother and sisters, but said nothing to Mirela because he knew she would not go without the boy. When they boarded the small boat, there were other families just like his, all with the same idea of escape.

Kem paid for their passage with the money he'd stolen from his father. Mirela was the happiest he'd ever seen her. Not that she smiled or told him how happy she was. No, that was not her way. But he knew. She looked at him directly, without being pressed, her eyes clear and focused. Most of the time her gaze skirted him as though he didn't exist. Even at their most intimate, when he lay on top of her, she refused to look at him; her eyes squeezed shut, her face turned away, her lips drawn into themselves, denying him even a single kiss.

They were in Izmir, Turkey for only a few weeks, with all sorts of other people from countries he knew nothing about. Kem was anxious to get away from these strangers. They found passage on another boat, which was even smaller than their previous boat had been. When they arrived at the launch location, there were more than forty people jostling to get onto the rubber dinghy, double the number the boat should have been carrying. But no one was going to give up their pride and lose the money they'd paid for their passage. Kem and Mirela certainly weren't. They couldn't afford to throw their money away like that. And besides, it was the only way out of Turkey.

The seas were rough, soaking them through and through, even though they sat in the middle of the boat rather than its high sides. He threw up into a bag the smuggler had given him. Once, then again. Mirela stared straight ahead, looking for the sight of land in the distance. He too hoped it would come soon.

Their boat capsized near the coast of Greece. The smuggler had instructed them to sink the boat if they saw the Greek coast guard. "If you're in the water, they will rescue you. They won't let you drown. Believe me. They are soft. Get rid of your papers;

don't tell them who helped you. How will we assist others if they catch us? You'll be a refugee. The help will pour in and you'll live happily ever after, God willing."

Only a few families survived. God had spared them for a reason, he told her. Mirela had lost their child in the sinking — he had been torn out of her arms by the churning sea — and she was inconsolable. His parents would have said the child they lost was God's punishment.

Things happen you can't explain, Kem thought. Of course he was sad to lose the baby. But this was life. He understood. Why couldn't Mirela? No, all she did was weep, repeating that old proverb, "If there are no children, there is no luck." But what could he expect? She was a woman. She wasn't meant to be strong.

He finally had enough of her constant tears and her denial of him. He was a man and had his needs. So he forced himself on her. She gave him no choice. Maybe one day she'd like it too. Or maybe this was the way they played together, their own special game. Mirela, the woman to be taken by him, Kem, the man doing the taking.

As a man, he gave her what she wanted. A belly full of a new baby to replace Bo. That's all it took. Mirela had become tender with him again.

Now Kem wanted to rip the shirt out of her hands, slap some sense into her.

"Why are you sewing buttons on that rag?" Kem said. "We can throw it away."

"As you threw away my son," Mirela said.

Her eyes looked through him. She pricked her finger with the needle. She didn't wince or make a sound.

He saw the blood on her finger and on Bo's shirt.

He loosened his clenched fists and dropped them by his sides. Couldn't she see he'd reached a point where he could do more for her? All he had needed was someone like Mrs. Shelby to believe in him. He could be a better husband, have a little time to think about his own dreams. Maybe this was the beginning of some luck for him, and for Mirela.

He finally had some money to give Mirela a few things. And the boy had made this possible. Mirela had to understand. All a father wants is a better life for his son. That's what Vijay had wanted for the boy too. Kem was sure Vijay would approve of sending Bo to live with Mrs. Shelby.

He had only ever wanted to protect Mirela. Even when he was angry, he couldn't really hurt her, not the way some of the other men in the camp treated their wives. Still, he couldn't give her a child.

All those dead babies. Each time Kem packed her up with a child, she would love it, him, life. Then it would trickle down her legs, more blood than anything else. If it hadn't been for a little bit of luck and his friend, Vijay, they wouldn't even have had the boy.

Once she began using his gifts, he knew Mirela wouldn't miss having to take her turn at the campfire to cook the bits of chicken or eggs or vegetables she scrounged out of the restaurant dumpsters. He would miss the special smell and flavour only an open campfire could give. It reminded him of his home, his own country. Ukraine. He shook his head. Yes, the food would be different than how he liked it, but never mind. He'd made many compromises for her. What was one more? Besides, if it made her happy, the sacrifice for him was worth it.

"I have your favourites," he said. "Take a look."

He'd bought her a bag of pomegranates, so he could watch her suck the seeds out of their hard shells, lick her fingers. His chest felt heavy. He allowed himself a smile. She wouldn't have to share a single bite with anyone.

"I want my son back," she said, without another glance at the bags. Her eyes refused to leave his.

"He's in good hands," he said. Yes, it was true Bo wouldn't have Mirela to spoil him or Kem to look out for him, but he would have a chance for a better life. The boy, because of his looks or his size, or something Mrs. Shelby saw in him, had opportunities, opportunities no one had given Kem. He had done as much as he could for Bo. He had not let the boy or Vijay down. "Who needs family when you have an opportunity to get yourself out of this hole?" Hadn't he told Mirela this many times?

"He will be with a stranger, rather than us," she said when he first told Mirela about Mrs. Shelby's plans for the boy. "Who will teach him our ways? Who will protect him?"

"Do you mean the *tsyhany* ways? If they died tomorrow along with this entire camp full of Roma, no one would miss them," he said. And that was the truth, whether Mirela believed it or not.

"He won't be coming back at the end of each day as he did when he was in school for a little while," she said. "We fooled the government, took their money, then took him out of school, but we can't do that with this woman. She wants to keep him. Forever."

"Probably. But he might not like it. Then he'll come back."

"You killed my firstborn by bringing us to this country," she said, "and now, you've taken my other son away from me. You who promised me the sun." Then she laughed at him.

He struck her in the face with his fist, bloodying her lip and the pretty shirt he'd worked so hard to find for her. Mirela dropped to the ground, throwing her arms over her head. Kem forced himself to control the impulse to hit her again. He left their home and wandered, feeling the same kind of shame he'd felt as a boy when an aid worker teased him about his reading skills. That aid worker scolded him, and then laughed at him, said Kem was too thick-skulled to learn.

How could she blame him? It had been Mirela's idea to leave the Ukraine. He only went along. To make her happy.

He knew he could have killed her. She would have done nothing to stop him. She didn't care what happened to her. It wasn't the kind of submissiveness he saw in the other women in the camp. It was her own kind of defiance. Passive, yes, yet forever angry. He knew he would never beat it out of her. That was her greatest power over him.

The wind swirled outside, knocking at the canvas walls. Kem jumped, as frightened as if an intruder was about to slice through the flimsy material. He took a deep breath to calm himself, pushed his hat firmly down on his head.

She'd come around, he told himself. He had to be patient.

She sucked the blood from her finger. She picked at the bag for the first time, looked inside as if something else might appear.

"Do you like your presents?" he asked.

She didn't respond, but looked up at him with those eyes. Her face was as dirty as it was the first time he met her, and her lip swollen from yesterday, but still she was beautiful. Even now she could make him weak from wanting.

"What do you want from me?" he asked, exasperated. "I gave Bo a chance at a better life. And for this, I am to be blamed?" His words seemed unbelievable even to him.

Mirela continued to stare at him, not saying a word.

He smiled. "You know we can make another one," he said and reached for her. They were still young. He would be eighteen soon. There was still time.

She swatted his hands away. "Find my son," she said, as stubborn as those stupid dogs in the camp who persisted in chasing the rats that nipped at them, leaving them bloodied and whimpering. "And bring him back."

"I don't know where Mrs. Shelby lives."

"You'll think of something," she said. "You're always bragging about how resourceful you are."

"I will have to go to the police and ask for help. You know how they treat us."

Mirela said nothing, yet refused to take her eyes off him. This wasn't the same woman with a glance so lazy he usually had to turn her head towards him if he wanted her to look into his eyes.

"She will return," Kem said. "She comes almost every day. You know how these do-gooders are. They can't help themselves."

"It's been nearly two days," Mirela said. "She won't be back now that she's got what she came for."

Mirela turned away and began to cry. He went to her, rubbed her back. She didn't move away. Her sobs, hopeless and forlorn, broke something inside of him just as they had when he first met her. He swallowed hard. He'd have to find Bo. For her. For their small family.

Holding onto his hat, he ducked out the door and into the icy breeze.

6

Do No Harm

"**E**mpty your pockets," the young officer told Shelby, as if trying out his authority and voice for size. "Please."

An older officer said something to him in Greek. In the staccato mix of garbled words, Shelby thought she recognized a name, Christos. She was worn out after another brutal day and wanted to go home. Maybe it wasn't his name. Perhaps the older officer was swearing at the younger one.

The older officer looked at her in the same way the Greeks gawked at the beggars on the street, as if to say, "Why are you in my country? You don't belong here." She knew the smell of the camp permeated her clothes. She hadn't had time for a shower, or time to change. The officers had shown up not long after the ruckus. Still, the smell wasn't a good reason for his condescending stare. Didn't this man realize what she did to help those poor people? She pushed her shoulders back, tugged at her sweater. She'd show him, she wasn't a person he wanted to mess with.

The young officer repeated the request, his eyes pleading. He was just a scrawny boy. What was he doing in a place like this?

She pulled out her cracked Armani wallet, a few candy wrappers, and her apartment keys, plunked them on the counter. Then she turned out her pockets, making a show of it because she had nothing to hide. She wasn't a criminal. She was an aid worker, for Pete's sake, a volunteer who spent her own money to help others. But how could she expect them to understand? Social workers and the police were intrinsically at odds: one tried to help, the other incarcerated people.

The officer put what she'd given him in a plastic bag. The keys jangled.

She wanted to tell him he could throw out the candy wrappers. Her little guy had really enjoyed those gooey, fruity slices. She pictured his sticky fingers reaching out for her. She couldn't help it. She smiled before she realized the older officer with those dark saucers for eyes was looking right at her.

"You think this is funny?" he said.

He raised an eyebrow at the other officer standing beside Shelby in an unspoken command. He wasn't going to bother with the effort of words or common courtesy.

A hand fixed itself on her shoulder, directing her away from the two officers. The younger one's eyes didn't leave hers until she'd been shoved through a door. She was jostled down the corridor, and then pushed into a room the size of a large animal cage. He could be her son, that officer. But he wasn't. She knew that. She understood the difference. She'd said these words before to others, but couldn't at the moment remember to whom. She had a son, her own little guy, although he wasn't so little anymore. Ted. She needed to call him. It had been far too long. They'd be together soon. A holiday must be coming. She'd been working hard. And so had he. They could use some time together.

The door locked behind her. High above her head on one wall was a window she couldn't reach. She wanted some air. An airplane moved across the welted sky. Maybe it was time she thought about going home, giving up all this humanitarian work.

She could hear noise from the street below, voices arguing somewhere close. Her head felt heavy. She wanted to lie down.

Just for a minute. Clear her mind. A bed was against one wall. She'd lie down, rest for a little while. Then all this would make sense.

Néa Filothei was still an upscale area of Athens, even though some of the businesses in the neighbourhood had closed down. The camp grew in and around an abandoned warehouse and other derelict buildings left behind by the numerous Greek businesses that had gone bankrupt. Families of Roma had moved in, as they had in other deserted and unguarded buildings all over Athens, turning whatever they found into a home. Looming over the camp like a praying mantis was the giant metal façade of the Olympic Stadium. A busy freeway separated the camp from the stadium.

Shelby had walked around the isolated industrial part of the area when she first arrived in Greece. The cracked and sun-baked sidewalk sprouted dandelions, dog shit was everywhere, but that didn't deter her. She knew this place was as neglected as the Roma themselves. She had to do something. Do first. Think later.

She'd come to Greece for some time away from her work in Zimbabwe, but she was an aid worker. She couldn't look the other way when there was obvious need in Greece.

She began to regularly visit the shantytown. It wasn't easy to gain their trust, but the packages of food, the new clothes, the bags of candy she left behind after each visit eventually worked. Word got around that she was harmless, and soon she was accepted as a regular visitor. Not one of them. No. But welcome, nonetheless.

Again, today, as she was heading for the camp, one of the so-called law-abiding neighbours — the stubby, pale-skinned guy with a cross swinging back and forth from his thick neck — had yelled at her. His wife peeked from behind the trellis of bougainvillea. She must have caught her sweater on the spikey branches because she lurched back and forth as if to free herself. She stumbled forward into full view. That fat, prickly bush wasn't going to let her go without a fight.

The man spoke to Shelby in Greek. But after the puzzled look she gave him and the slight shrug, he'd figured out she was a *xénos* and switched to English. "You understand what I'm saying to you now, don't you?"

As impatient as the rest of his countrymen, he didn't wait for a reply.

"These shacks do not belong here among good people. These people are trespassers. They do not need your pity. They need to go back to where they came from. I do not want people like this in my country."

She tried to reason with him as his wife pulled on his arm. "I'm here to help."

He replied, "Why do you not help your own country? You people must mind your own business. We know how to take care of our own."

She let his words fall onto the street behind her as she would the dirty water that frequently spilled from balconies carelessly washed by people with no regard for those walking underneath. The man's anger was dangerous. She knew that, but there was nothing she could do about it.

Others had set fires to these slums, beaten occupants with chains and sawed-off pipes as they tried to run away. Who said Greeks were hospitable? Just last week, a migrant had been stabbed to death. No reason was given in the English-language papers. Was the fact that he was a migrant supposed to explain what had happened to him? If it came to violence against this camp, her camp, she'd stand guard all night and day if she had to, act as a shield between the Roma and those racist bullies.

Sometimes, you had to do what was right. Just last week, she'd stood up to a couple of teenage skinheads harassing a mite of a woman who'd been picking through a dumpster. They'd run off, sneering at her like two little boys who'd been scolded by their mother, but hadn't learned one damn thing. The Roma woman, from another camp, scurried off as well, without so much as a thank you. Next time, Shelby would call the police on boys like these. Someone had to do something. The organization she worked with, Volunteers International, wouldn't do anything about these daily problems. They were too busy worrying about their bureaucracy.

There was a dull thud, like a door being shut, then bolted. She realized she was trembling. This was silly. She used to be afraid when she was married to Robert, but that was so long ago. There was nothing to worry about now.

The breeze must have caught the metal blinds on the bedroom window. Maybe the bathroom door had blown shut, she thought.

Fresh air was good. She took a deep breath. Jasmine. The fragrance was overpowering. The sheets reeked of it, as though they'd been washed in one of those detergents that promised freshness, but only managed a bad imitation. She cupped a hand over her nose and breathed. She was sure she had washed her hands when she came in after her day at the camp, but all she could smell was the rot of the camp laced with phoney jasmine.

One of the old Roma women at the camp had grabbed at her today, just as Robert would when he was drinking, yanking at her arm as if to shake something free. The air above the camp clouded with the stench of human waste, decomposing garbage and smoke from the open fires. Sweat under each armpit stained the woman's black tattered dress yellow.

Shelby pulled her arm free and plastered a broad smile on her face, as she did whenever she was nervous. "Can I help you?" she asked as if she were an enthusiastic department store clerk, rather than an aid worker, neck deep and drowning.

Two shirtless and barefoot boys, no more than eight or nine, stood to one side. Mounds of small appliances, blankets, boxes, anything that could be dragged from the neighbourhood dumpsters, heaped the camp around them. A few red poppies — battered and thirsty — soldiered out from under ripped garbage bags. The old woman didn't reply and Shelby turned away from her accusatory glare. The noise and smells of human waste persisted.

The boys moved quickly. She caught them combing through the shopping bags in her trunk and yelled at them to stop. She wanted to hand out the things she'd brought in an orderly way so everyone got something, but they'd snatched a few cans of tomato sauce and stuffed them inside their shirts. Some of the teenage mothers, babies to bare breasts, yanked at the other bags. The old woman darted away, moving faster than her skinny legs and bent back could reasonably be expected to. A can of beans fell to the ground. A bare-bottomed toddler picked it up with both hands and stared at it as if it were a surprise gift. He looked at Shelby, his eyes hungry and frightened, and ran.

"Wait."

They scattered, the boys crawling through the holes of one of the derelict buildings. It was the same every day. The strongest won. She hoped they would share, but she knew they wouldn't. They were desperate. The whole lot of them. Gypsies. Beggars. That's what the Greeks called them. They were the Roma, the people she tried to help. In Athens, they were the unwanted.

She knew how it felt to be unwanted. Her son no longer needed her. He was a man, now. And independent. And he had been that way almost since the day he was born. She was proud of him, but still. And Robert. Well, he never really wanted her except when he was lightheaded and pleased with himself, in that brief phase before the next several drinks turned his silly grin ugly and mean.

Voices clashed against each other just outside her window, one raised in exasperation, another insistent. A third ran over the first. The conversation, if you could call it that, was strident and no doubt political. Everyone had an opinion in this country. It sounded like these men were in the next room. She couldn't understand what they were saying. They spoke too fast. Her command of the language wasn't great anyway, but she liked the shock of their angry, all-present rants. She caught the odd name of one of the political parties or a few words and filled in the rest. They steal from us. You can't trust them. Corrupt. Full of empty promises.

She could put simple sentences together, respond with the definitive *óxi* when someone shoved or yelled at her. Tonight, the voices made her feel like she belonged. Not so lonely. No, she wasn't lonely. Just off. These feelings, or whatever you wanted to call them, came at night, in that time between wide-awake worry and the oblivion of sleep.

The light breeze outside gathered the fragrances from the balcony gardens. She took a deep breath. Jasmine. This time, fresh. Almost. It should help her relax and eventually fall asleep except the scent always seemed to irritate her. She could never grow jasmine at home. Long ago, Ted had given her a jasmine plant for Mother's Day. She needed it to survive, but it wouldn't give her the satisfaction. She'd invested in a proper heat lamp, and plant food, nursed it with just the right amount of water. And the spray of buds kept their promise, bursting into delicate white.

Then she'd find one or two wilting on the floor, still clinging to their perfume. The plant continued to weep blossoms until only one remained, cleaved to a lower branch. Curling inward, the dark green leaves tinged brown at the edges. She'd hack the dead bits out, squirt more water, move the plant so it got more sunlight, then less, hoping her determination might make the poor thing recover. Eventually she gave up. She dumped the plant, pot and all, into the bin and replaced it, without her son being the wiser. She'd get it right with the next one.

Shelby was ashamed she couldn't make anything grow, not like her perfect-gardener-and-everything-else mother, who could make miracles spring from nothing.

She had taken canned food, bottles of water, jars of jam, bread, and cartons of juice to the camp today and some clothes she had bought at the discount stores. Unlike Canada, Greece did not have big-box stores where she could get five of anything for a buck. Still, she'd found a few places. They usually had a Chinese lantern at the front door or a sign scribbled in English. *Chinatown.* You could get a lot of stuff for twenty euros in these places. And now, One Euro stores were opening up all over the place. It took some work to find them, but she did. She'd become frugal, something Robert never would have imagined. If he could see her now, he'd know the money she used to spend had nothing to do with what she needed. His wallet had been the only thing he cared about. That and his bottle.

But Robert had given her this opportunity to rescue kids. He had had the decency to leave her a ton of money. He'd killed himself in his office. He'd left her long before that, but miraculously she was his only beneficiary. She'd been able to quit her dead-end job in Child and Family Services, where all her efforts came to nothing. How could anyone even call it child welfare when they took kids away from abusive homes and stuck them with foster parents, some of whom seized the opportunity to make a quick buck on the backs of these kids? Children never wanted to be away from their real parents anyway. They would stay, even when their own flesh and blood neglected them, used them as punching bags or ashtrays.

It was another sticky night. Her cropped hair felt wet against the pillow and her face felt flushed. The voices she'd heard earlier must have been coming from up the street, from the half dozen men who gathered at the kiosk in front of the brightly lit vending machine, hashing over the day's news of turmoil and economic disaster. They seemed to find their way there every night, just a few steps away from her apartment building.

She usually left the balcony doors open in the hope the air would circulate, but the whisper of the earlier breeze had hushed. Her neighbours never left their doors open. There had been a rash of break-ins recently all over the city. Since the economic crisis and the daily threat of Greece leaving the euro currency, Greeks had withdrawn their money from banks and insisted on keeping cash in their homes. Everyone knew this and some took advantage of this new opportunity.

But she wasn't afraid. She didn't have that kind of cash lying around. And Greece was one of the safest countries she'd ever volunteered in, even with the break-ins, the recent racial violence and the frequent street protests.

Beads of sweat accumulated on her forehead, but she didn't move. She was sure in a minute she'd be cold.

She'd get up soon; make sure the balcony doors were wide open. Or perhaps with some luck she'd fall asleep and not have to worry about it.

She had grown very fond of one of the Roma families and had kept something special for them today. She knew from her experience in Zimbabwe that she shouldn't make attachments, shouldn't get involved. More than once her supervisor had cautioned her, as if she were a child who needed everything repeated. "You're too close to all this. Maybe a break from it would help," he'd said.

But how could anyone with even the slightest shred of compassion not get close? She was doing something important in Greece, just like she had done or tried to do in Zimbabwe before she moved here four or so months ago. Had it been that long? She couldn't keep track of time anymore. Every day was busy.

Ted had always understood her need to help others. He knew the sacrifices they both made were worth it. "Whatever you need to do, Mother, I'll help."

She'd hidden a small box of fruit and vegetables, a couple of loaves of bread and a bag of fruit gummies she'd bought for Bo and his family under the front seat of her car and kept the car doors locked even as she opened the trunk. Once the crowd of Roma had disappeared with most of the things she had in her trunk, she drove toward her special family's lean-to, a lump of plastic sheeting and canvas that covered scraps of plywood perched against one of the only walls of the crumbling warehouse still standing.

"Hello, Bo," she called, as she got out of the car. The poor thing was wearing grimy, threadbare pants and a shirt with only one button left on it. He didn't even have shoes. No wonder his nose was always running. He'd been sitting on a log poking at the fire burning inside a blackened metal rim when she'd driven up. But as she came toward him, he dropped his stick and stood up, ready to flee.

"What's wrong, Bo?" she asked. "You know who I am. I'm here nearly every day. You're my little guy." She stepped toward him. "I'm sorry I scared you."

He moved back towards the lean-to, didn't take his scowling eyes off of her. He didn't greet her or say a word. This, even though she knew he spoke English perfectly for a Roma child of his age. Most didn't speak anything but Greek. In fact, she didn't know any Roma children who spoke English. When she'd mentioned this to Kem, he'd said, "We have no choice. We pick up a word here or there from tourists so they'll notice us and we can make enough to feed ourselves. Bo is bright. He has picked up more than most of the children here. And Mirela and I both speak English. It helps the boy."

"I brought this for you," she said, handing Bo a candy from her pocket. He came in close, didn't take his eyes from her, snatched the candy out of her hand and ran towards the lean-to before she could reach for him. If she could just hold him, she thought, they'd both feel better.

"Ah, Mrs. Shelby, you're here." Kem slipped out of the lean-to. He clamped his hands on his son's shoulders. The boy stood perfectly still.

He was a rough man, Bo's father. He was an artist who came across as harmless, but there was another side to him. She was sure of it. The shadows that sometimes came over his eyes reminded her of some of the men she used to encounter back when she did child welfare cases in her old job in Canada. Full of so much frustration, these men snapped and took it out on their kids. Not unlike Robert, in a way, although she doubted Kem drank the way Robert used to. But how could she really know? Everyone — her bosses, her friends, Robert — told her she was the type of person who saw what she wanted to see. True or not, she never gave it much thought.

Kem did appear to avoid those in the camp who were known to be dealing in drugs. So he was different in that respect. But he was also desperate, probably trying to do right by his family. He'd brought the family to Greece illegally, looking for a better life, a way to become the artist he dreamed of being. She'd seen some of his caricatures. He seemed to capture something about a person they couldn't see in themselves. She had to admit, he was a talented man, even if he hadn't gotten her exactly right in the drawing he had done of her.

His eyes lit up, his back straightened when he showed her his drawings. She saw the child in the man. He was young, late teens at the most, and his wife, Mirela, was about the same age. But like most of the Roma in the camp, they had a child. Children having children. This was the Roma reality.

Still, when she saw how excited he became about his caricatures, Shelby was proud of him. She wouldn't spoil his enthusiasm with pessimistic talk about the reality of his situation, life in this country for people like him. Kem should hold onto his dreams.

Kem sold some of his drawings along with black market or stolen packages of Kleenex, small breakable toys full of lead, and stolen bouquets of flowers. "My son needs a chance," Kem said every time she visited.

"Say hello to Mrs. Shelby." Kem pushed Bo forward. Bo's mother came out of the lean-to, adjusted her brightly patterned skirt and grabbed her son's hand, heaved him away, said she had to clean his face. She pushed him into their lean-to before Kem could say another word.

"You know, mothers." Kem's smile was clenched tight. "They are this way. Protective." The gold cap on his front tooth glinted. He was a man of some presence in his burgundy fedora and formal pinstriped jacket, even though the jacket was ill-fitting and shiny at the lapels. The breast pocket held a slightly frayed purple handkerchief that gave him a bit of flair. The hat had a long brightly coloured scarf around the rim. In any other setting he could be mistaken for an eccentric artist who would be revered rather than reviled. His pant cuffs hovered above his ankles, although the hems had already been let down.

"Yes. I'm a mother myself," she said. She moved to the other side of the car to fetch the things she'd brought for them today.

She handed the box to Kem. "There's some fruit and vegetables, a few other things. I hope it helps a little."

"This is very kind, Mrs. Shelby. The boy will like this. You see how small he is."

Will he get any? she wondered, but in the same thought scolded herself. These were honourable people who lived on the fringes of society. The migrants arriving from all over war-torn Africa made the Roma even more despised by the Greeks for some reason. They seemed to understand and pity war refugees, but couldn't do the same with the Roma, some of whom had been in Greece for centuries. She had to stop feeling like she couldn't trust Kem. That was what other people did.

Mirela emerged from the lean-to, Bo at her heels. She crouched by the fire and Bo followed suit. If he sat any closer to his mother, he'd be in her lap. As he chewed on the candy Shelby had given him, he kept his eyes on her, as though she might do something to him if he let his guard down. He stroked his mother's earrings. His nose was clean, his greasy hair combed. Smudged on his cheek was a bit of dirt, his mother's attempt to clean his face with a wet finger.

Seeing mother and son like that, Shelby thought about her own son, Ted, again. The night he was born, Robert had gone on a bender and hit her squarely in the face. The labour pains started shortly after he took off in search of another bottle. She drove herself to the hospital. The nurses wanted to mend her split lip, her crooked nose. "I fell," she said, pointing at her swollen belly. "Carrying this extra weight."

Her labour had been quick, the pain only slightly worse than her throbbing face. They placed the baby in her arms, but she felt too weak to hold him. Alone in her room later, Ted in his bassinet beside her bed, she couldn't look at him. She had no need to count his fingers and toes as she'd heard other mothers did. He began to whimper. His cries became breathless screams. She couldn't move. He was right there, but the gap seemed too far to cross.

She remembered thinking, as she did with all her child welfare cases: maybe she'd do better with the next one. How could a real mother have such thoughts?

The beating, the birth. It was too much. Perhaps she hadn't gone to Ted because she was simply tired.

A nurse had come in. "Are you all right?"

"Yes."

The nurse brought Ted to her. Shelby couldn't figure out how to place her arms so she could hold him properly. This situation was far beyond her capabilities. She was sure of it. She'd dealt with other people's children and had not been all that successful. How would she take care of her own? She didn't deserve this child. Or more correctly, this child deserved better.

"Do it like this," the nurse said. "See how I'm holding him?" The nurse again placed Ted in her arms. Shelby looked down at him and felt nothing but her sore lip, bruised face and her tender bottom. She told herself she should feel something for this child, but there was nothing. Emptiness.

As the baby calmed and nestled into her, she started to think about how she would protect him. Once a social worker, always a social worker.

It struck her that if Robert thought she cared too much about this child, he'd take him away or do something to him. Just to hurt her. He hated seeing her happy or enthusiastic about her work or her home or anything she loved or was excited about. As a successful surgeon, he had always craved all the air and attention in a room. And he'd do anything to get it.

Robert had eventually appeared, clutching a bunch of carnations, some wilting. He apologized for the flowers, said it was the only thing he could find at 7-11 this late at night. He set them down at the bottom of the bed.

The balled-up paper towel wrapped around the stems dampened the sheets covering her feet. She trembled and tried to kick the flowers away. Her feeble attempt at defiance.

"How is our boy?" he asked, all smiles, as though nothing had happened.

How could he look her in the eye? she wondered. "Here, why don't you take him," she said, feigning indifference, but holding Ted tightly, away from Robert.

"Aren't you afraid I'll drop him or something?"

"Maybe you can be better with him than me."

"Better than you, my little Miss Perfect? How is that possible?" His eyes were bloodshot and he had that puppy-dog forlorn look he put on when he was trying to be charming. Had this actually worked on her before?

She looked down at the baby, said nothing.

"You're always giving me that social work advice of yours. Trying to control my life." He threw his arms in the air. She turned away from him to protect the child.

"Even now," she said, "after all this, it's my fault."

He laughed and pried the baby from her. "You can't take a joke," he said. "You're too serious. I don't know how I ended up with someone like you when I'm a happy-go-lucky kind of guy."

"You were drunk that night too," she said, referring to the night they had met at the university pub crawl, but he ignored her.

She heard her name. And shook her head. These memories were from so long ago.

"Yes," she said and smiled.

"Mrs. Shelby, would you like to go for a walk with Bo?" Kem asked, getting her attention again. She thought she saw him nudge his wife. The woman didn't move or look up at her.

"Oh, that's okay. It's not necessary just this minute. Maybe in a little while."

Kem nodded. "As you like. You will have plenty of time together."

A motorcycle backfired in the distance. She bent tighter into herself, pulled the cover up under her chin, and clenched her fists close to her face. Bo was such a good boy and so close to his mother. Just like Ted had always been with Shelby. She needed to call her son. Find out how he was doing, although she knew he'd say he was great. It was his standard answer. He was growing his business and bringing in new customers. Like his father, he could only talk about his work. When she asked him about his personal life, if there was a new girlfriend in his life, he'd say something like, "There is nothing else right now."

He was an overachiever, yes, but unlike Robert, a caregiver too. She wanted him to have a good life, erase all the things he'd had to witness when he was a child and his father was alive. She wished she could have a conversation with Ted, really talk like they used to when he was a child. Sometimes he would come home from school sobbing because the other kids wouldn't let him play soccer with them. Through gulps and fits of heaving, he'd tell her they didn't like him because he couldn't run fast enough, didn't hit the ball with his head, was too clumsy, couldn't keep up. She'd listen and assure him if this was something he wanted to do, she could help him practise. But she knew he was too independent to ask for help.

No, they didn't talk like they used to anymore. Most of the time she had to think of a list of things to ask him before she got on the phone. Then when she heard his voice, the questions disappeared and the conversation was as stilted as ever.

She took care of others, listened to their problems, but Ted usually was the one who listened to her, gave her advice, particularly in those dark days after Robert left. Ted never wanted anything from her. Why had she given so much to others and so little to him?

In a way, she found it easier to work with strangers. She didn't expect perfection from them. Only to make their lives better. Well, maybe a little perfection. Just once, she would have liked to have things turn out for a family or a person she tried to help.

She would get up soon, make sure the balcony doors were wide open, take a look at all the lovely gardens across the way with the flowers blooming in fuchsia, yellow, white and pink overhanging their small concrete balconies. It was nice to be able to admire other people's handiwork.

Ever since that jasmine plant of Ted's and the subsequent ones she'd bought and killed, it was fresh-cut flowers for her. No more plants. That way, she knew right from the start what to expect. She knew they'd die and she would throw them away. No guilt involved. It made life easier, less complicated, when she knew the end-result right at the onset.

Her hip ached. The sheets felt like plastic. They squeaked as she moved. What had happened to the sheets she used to buy — made of the material and a thread count she insisted on — when she was married to Robert? She was a different person then.

At the camp today, Kem again had said, "You see how small he is."

Shelby had nodded. Yes, Bo was small for his age and hunched over like an old man. She knew as well as Kem did that her little guy needed a better life. Nothing more had to be said. If she could help, why wouldn't she? She'd already given them food, blankets and a little money. What was a little more? Money could solve any problem.

"Only for my son, you understand. To give him a future." Kem smoothed the rim of his hat as a too-confident salesman might.

His wife sat cross-legged and cross-armed, guarding the entrance to their lean-to.

The little guy would thrive, away from the brutality and poverty of this place. His mother had to understand. He could grow up in a good home.

Shelby could explain this to her agency too, but would they recognize what was best for the boy? It didn't matter. She had long ago stopped caring what the agency thought. Those agency types protected themselves behind desks in their plush offices. She had been on the front lines. Who knew better? The bureaucrats? Or her?

Something rattled. The noise must be the men up the street picking up their chairs, finally heading home. Pigeons cooed louder, as though beckoning their flock. The constant sound of traffic in the distance had deadened. It must be after midnight. She should check, but couldn't be bothered to turn over again to look at the clock. Her hip was stiff. Moving would be good. But she didn't have the energy. Her head churned with the sounds and images of the camp. The poverty and desperation had so consumed her. She couldn't let it go. If only it could be as simple as leaving all this desperation at the end of the day. It wasn't. Not for her anyway. She got involved. "Goes too deep, gets too close," her supervisor noted on her last appraisal. Yeah, Jerk, you're right. So what? She cared. Nail her to the cross. She was a volunteer. Beggars, like the agency she worked for, couldn't be choosers.

She shivered. First hot, now chilled. What was going on with her body?

Kem had taken Bo's hand and led him to Shelby today.

Shelby liked how Bo's hand felt in hers. He looked up at her and his eyes glistened. His lips were stained orange and traces of the candy she'd given him were stuck between his front teeth. "We're just going for a ride," she said. She took another candy out of her pocket and offered it to Bo.

He let go of her hand and tore the wrapper off. He shoved the candy in his mouth.

"You'll like my car. Wait and see."

Bo followed the candies she pulled out of her pocket.

Other women came out from their own tents and houses. They gathered around, would only let her pass when Bo's father yelled at them to back off. They covered their faces in their shawls and turned their backs. The frail old gypsy woman who had distracted her earlier to allow the others to steal food from Shelby's trunk threw a rock at her windshield as she left the camp. She'd helped them all in one way or another, and now they wanted to hurt her.

All she'd ever done was help these people. That's all she was doing.

She must stop all these silly thoughts. Maybe if she got up and had some water, her mind would calm down. She hadn't heard a peep out of Bo after she'd checked on him. Must be sleeping well. The poor little guy.

Yes, he'd cried and screamed when she'd brought him to her place, but he'd worn himself out and gone to sleep. The neighbours had banged on the walls and knocked at her door too, but she'd ignored them. They eventually went away.

It would take some getting used to for all of them. But it would work out. And Bo would flourish. She was sure. She'd get him into a school as soon as she could.

She pushed the sheets away. No point trying to sleep. She was still too worked up after the day she'd had. She heard something raked over metal. Someone pointed a flashlight at her. The light bounced off steel bars. She saw walls made of stone, the tiny window on the opposite wall above her head, the outline of a grimy metal toilet.

She wasn't in her apartment.

A guard stood outside her cell.

She sat up. "Where's Bo? Where's my little guy?" she screamed. "He needs me. I have to go to him." Shelby stood, lunged at the cell door, and wrapped her fingers around the cold metal.

The guard ran his baton across the bars in front of her, nicking two of her fingers before she could pull her hand away. The clanging hurt her ears. Her fingers smarted.

"You know what you did," the guard said.

He flung his chin forward as if dismissing her in that annoying way Greeks had of negating someone, making them feel insignificant. He tsked.

"This is how we say no, or disagree," someone told her once. "It's not meant as an insult."

"I was trying to help." She'd said the same words to her supervisor in Zimbabwe. Her bosses had wanted her to set up programs to help the locals deal with their own child welfare issues. Programming wasn't her cup of tea. She was and had always been hands-on. That was the work she did, whether her supervisor liked it or not.

The guard shook his head. "You Americans. You think you can do anything you want."

"I'm Canadian." She'd been saying it day in and day out since she arrived. It didn't matter. No one here seemed to understand the difference.

He walked away, leaving her in the dark again.

She sat back down on the bed. It was just a misunderstanding. Bo's father had agreed. Hadn't he? They hadn't made any concrete arrangements. But he'd hinted. In fact, it was his suggestion. Wasn't it? Why was her head in such a fog?

Kem said he'd discussed it with his wife. He said she wanted a better life for the boy. Both he and his wife did. But now as she thought about it, the woman's lip had been swollen, her cheek bruised. Mirela wouldn't look at her today.

She remembered asking Kem what Bo's name meant when she first met him.

"It means settler," he'd said. "And one day he will. With your help, of course."

7

SURRENDER

On a Street Close to the Amaroúsio Police Station

The police station was at the crossroads between factories and rows of high-end condominiums. The smell of the gardens around the condos, so different from the smoke and raw sewage of the camp, made Kem feel slightly dizzy. He took deep breaths as he stood in the shadows. He liked the scent, wondered what it would be like to lie down in the grass and sleep right there, out of sight and harm's way. But the angry graffiti slashed against the security walls of the condominiums — **Foreigners get Out, Greece for Greeks, Take back Greece** — urged him forward. He knew it was dangerous to be out alone, away from the camp at night, but it had been impossible to reason with Mirela. That woman's stubbornness would kill him one day. He was sure of it.

He hid behind a stand of shrubs, took another quiet breath and held it, listened for footsteps, raised voices, rattling, any sound that might mean he'd been spotted. He darted to a leafy orange tree. Crouched behind a car. Stood in the darkened space on the sidewalk out of range of the motion detector lights. He pulled his hat down on his head as a turtle lowers its shell.

He knew young Greeks with chains, steel pipes, and concealed knives roamed the streets at night looking for people like him. Just last week, a boy, someone who had been in this country legally, who had a real job and an apartment, his life ahead of him, was stabbed to death on his way to work because he wouldn't give up his bicycle. The thugs had chased him down with their motorcycles. That boy needed the bike for his livelihood. But you couldn't reason with thugs. Kem would have given up the bike. He knew that. Just as he knew it might not have mattered. They might have killed him anyway.

If they could kill someone who was legal, what would they do to him, an illegal *Tsyhany* from the Ukraine? Kem swallowed, told himself to stop thinking, it did no good. He shuffled as he gazed up the street, planning his move, the next hiding spot he needed to find. The police would understand when he told them his son was missing. Anyone would understand the anguish a father felt for his missing child. The police would help.

His shoes squeaked. He cursed himself for wearing them. He needed to move quickly and without being noticed. He knew how to do this. It's what he did to get his hands on the odd bunch of carrots or a handful of apples from the open market vendors busy with customers. If he could go unseen then, he could do it now. But how could he do that with these noisy, brilliant shoes? Though the camp's dust and grime had tarnished them, the shoes still stood out like a ridiculous beacon.

At this distance, the police station looked like any other factory, except for the looming fence of concrete and metal, and the hedge of razor wire. One guard, gun in holster, carried a machine gun across his chest and paced in front of the gate. There was a tower too, but it was dark. Kem doubted anyone was there tonight. Then he noticed a flare of light. A cigarette had been lit, igniting the tiniest of flames. It went out. Then it glowed bright again. Someone was in the tower, pacing. Likely with a gun. Kem told himself to be careful, make no sudden moves. These people would just as soon shoot you down as listen to anything.

Towels hung out the barred windows like a gesture of surrender. Maybe this was a sign. He should give up now before something really bad happened, before the police realized he was an illegal and threw him into a refugee camp, then deported him as they had tried to do with Vijay.

A man's thin arms drooped out of another window, hands clasped together, perhaps in prayer. Kem didn't want to think about those arms that looked so much like his own. He couldn't reason what he was doing. He had to go through with it, report the boy missing at the very least and get the police to help him find Bo. He couldn't go back to Mirela empty-handed. He couldn't go back to her anguished tears.

The men at the camp were right about him. Mirela had him under her thumb.

"Why?" they said one night when he said he had to get back to his family. "There's more wine." One man snickered and passed him the bottle. "And if you want something stronger, we have it too. Can give you a try for free, if you like. Won't cost you a thing."

He'd shrugged. "I just have to."

"He's as soft as those pencils he uses. His woman leads him by the nose." The men had laughed. "Or something. Poor bastard."

He should go back to the camp right now, forget about this foolishness. God had brought Bo to them and He had taken him away. That was all.

Kem had avoided the police station in the past, never walked on this block, even though it was a shortcut to the coffee shops and outdoor restaurants at the other end of the neighbourhood where he made a little money selling a drawing or liberating an unattended purse. He was afraid to get too close to this building. Someone would find out how he got to Greece and lock him away. But he had to go there now, for Bo. He had to get him back. For Mirela.

He closed his eyes and wiped his sweaty palms against his pants. He didn't know what to call what he felt for Mirela. It was like a craving that couldn't be satisfied. It made him feel happy and ashamed at the same time.

Kem stood a few metres away from the entrance, hidden behind a stand of trees. Should he make some kind of sound so he didn't alarm the guard? Or should he walk out into the light so the guard would see he had nothing to hide? He could wait until morning, right here in this spot. He wouldn't look so suspicious in the light of day and it would teach Mirela a lesson if he didn't come home tonight. She might worry about him. He wrapped his arms around his chest and crouched down to the ground.

His shoes squeaked.

And then he heard the sound of a gun being cocked.

"I will shoot if you don't come out," a voice shouted.

Kem scrambled to his feet, his arms stretched above his head. "Please," he said. As he fought his way out, the branches scratched his face and neck and knocked his hat off his head. He reached for his hat. Heard a gunshot. He quickly raised his hands and pushed himself out of the tangled arms of the trees, crushing his hat underfoot.

A cigarette tumbled slowly to the ground from the guard tower. He followed the ember until it was extinguished. He looked up at the tower. Kem couldn't see the person, but he knew there was a gun. There was always a gun. Pointing at him.

"On the ground. Now!"

"I'm here to ask a question. About my son. That is all."

"On the ground or I will shoot you."

Kem dropped to the ground. His brand new notebook and one pen fell out of his pocket. He reached for them.

The guard kicked Kem's arms further apart, did the same to his legs. He placed his foot at the back of Kem's neck and pressed down.

Kem coughed. Was the officer trying to choke him?

He heard the officer on the radio. "I need backup. I've got a live one."

"You don't understand," Kem pleaded. His eyes teemed, his cheek was wet.

"What are you doing with this notebook, this pen?" the officer said.

"I am an artist. That is all. I can draw a picture for you."

The foot came off his neck. "An artist, my ass." The officer picked up the notebook and pen. At this angle, Kem couldn't see what the officer did with his things. "You are thieves. Nothing more."

"I just came for help. My son is missing."

"No talking. There will be plenty of time for explaining once you're inside." As though he was stubbing out a cigarette butt, the officer ground his foot over Kem's hat, his once-prized possession.

Kem thought of fighting. He'd tried to struggle whenever his own father beat him or Mirela or one of his sisters. But he'd never been strong enough. He remembered the glint of a shiny belt buckle in the air. Images of Mirela taking one blow, then another as she lay crouched in the barn again, her leg chained to the post. His father's sweat sprinkling Kem's face like a morning drizzle, Kem's hands in his pockets, unable to move or flick away a drop.

There was no point in trying to fight back then and there was no point now. Would he always be on the losing end of men such as these? Was there no way to win?

8

FIRST STEPS

Vancouver, Canada

Y*ou cried the day you left, said you'd miss me.*
    "*Don't go," I said.*
    "*Mother will come back a better person," you said.*
    That's the year I went to boarding school. I was fourteen.
    "*It's perfect timing," you said. "You were going to have to go to a new school to go to high school, anyway. So why not boarding school? You won't have your mother nagging you about picking up after yourself. And you're practically a man anyway."*
    When we got together that first Christmas, you asked me a ton of questions. Who are your favourite teachers? Isn't school terrific? It must be hard to leave and spend time with your mother.
    We saw the Canucks beat the almighty Montreal Canadiens 5 to 2. It was crazy loud in the stadium, the crowd went nuts when Vancouver brought down the Canadiens. It gave you a headache and you had to lie down after. I didn't like it that you'd gone to the trouble of doing something for me and it caused you pain. I couldn't seem to do anything right, even when I tried.
    We visited your friends and we went to the movies. I wanted to see A Few Good Men, but you insisted I'd prefer Wayne's World. That was a kids' movie, not a movie for a teenager, but I went along because being together was more important to me than anything else. It just was.

Really, all I wanted to do was sit and drink hot chocolate and talk, really talk, to you. I wanted you to tell me what your life was like in Tanzania. That was the first African country you went to, I think.

I wanted you to tell me you'd had enough of that life and were coming home, that we were going to be a family again. I guess what I wanted was a real Christmas.

But ten days later we were back at the airport taking separate flights. You cried, clutched my arm.

I pulled away and bent down to get the present I'd bought you. A set of Canadian coins I'd bought at the post office. I thought it would cheer you up.

"Don't forget home," I said. That got a smile.

I still remember how stupidly happy I was to be able to make my mom smile. I always loved doing that. And once in a while I pulled out all the stops, mimicking one of your friends, retelling a funny story I'd heard on the radio, or repeating something one of my buddies said to a teacher. It didn't matter what it was, as long as I got you to give me a smile. I don't know why this was so important to me. Maybe it was because Dad never could do that for you. And maybe it was because you always seemed so preoccupied, like you weren't really listening. Sometimes it was like you weren't even in the same room.

Ted had to write about this stuff. No point thinking of where it would go. First get the shit down. That's what his sponsor said. And since he had to document this crap, it might as well be on the best money could buy. Notebooks, pens, clothes, booze, it was all the same — nothing was better than the best. His mother had taught him that. Nice things took the edge off bad times. Wasn't that what she used to say, whenever she'd bought him a new pair of Nikes or an expensive hockey jersey?

A letter. He should say what he had to say in a letter. At least then it wouldn't be just rambling nonsense. A letter might give him the purpose he needed to separate out the important stuff. He could decide what he did with it later. He could throw it away.

He spat out the stale gum, unwrapped a new stick and bent it into his mouth. Setting the journal to one side, he reached for a piece of paper from his desk. The paper was textured and weighty. He grinned when he saw his name embossed at the top of the page. *Theodore Holt.* Yeah. Some kind of big shot.

If people only knew.

October 15th

Dear Mother:

My letters are all returned Addressee Unknown. My emails to you bounce. Your phone number has changed. The operator insists it's unlisted. Reminds me of when I broke my collarbone in football practice in grade 10. The principal said they'd tried all your numbers. When he finally reached you, you told him you couldn't get away. "This is such a bad time. Drought is killing everything. I have to stay. I'm needed, you see. Please tell Ted I'm thinking about him. He's good at managing things. He's a good boy. Tell my son that, will you?"

In that first year you went away, we still had our house. But you sold that too. "We don't need it. We can stay in a nice hotel or rent an apartment. Someone else cleans for us and we play. We're on vacation, aren't we?"

Our visits always felt like a race to cram in as much as possible before a finish line I could see all too clearly, even if you couldn't. I wish I had said what I really wanted. I was too scared. I can write it down here because I doubt I'll ever send this. And even if I did, you'd probably never get it.

What I should have said: I don't want to run around sightseeing, Mother. I don't want to see the latest flick or even go to a hockey game. I just want to see you. Be with you. Maybe we would have found something to talk about, something of what other moms and sons discuss. You might have relaxed a little. But I didn't want to be the guy who disappointed you. You got enough of that from Dad. And besides, what were we going to talk about? Dad's bullshit? We were both good at avoiding that.

"Mother is doing what she needs to do," you said one night as I sat at the kitchen counter, shopping bags stacked at my feet. "Understand?" You were hunched over the stove, spicing a soup you'd learned to make in Africa. You were so proud of those spices. Browns and greens and yellows. And, really, I had to agree with you. The clear jars filled with those different colours were beautiful.

I remember seeing a tremor run through your shoulders, as if an icy hand had touched your neck. The kitchen was hot. Your blood had turned to water, you said, ever since you started working overseas. Vancouver made you feel cold all the time. I wondered if you meant empty. I wanted to scream, "This is where you belong. At home with me. Your son. I need you." But I said nothing. Why wasn't I enough?

You turned, but didn't look at me. And of course, with that distant gaze of yours, I couldn't say a word. "Be strong for Mother." You were good at drilling home a point. The program I'm in now is helping me understand some new things.

Step 1: We are powerless.

Ted pushed himself away from his desk, picked up his coffee cup and walked over to the window. He hated this shit. What was the point? What was going to change? He stared out at the vastness of the ocean. A few freighters hunkered in the distance. He watched their lights bob and imagined the waves slapping against their flanks. He sipped his coffee. Ice cold. He swallowed the bitterness, put the cup down on the table by the window. Wind bent the trees in front of his building. They were decades old, had withstood more than this, but still, an unexpected gust could split them into a million tiny pieces.

These trees wouldn't have survived if his mother had had anything to do with it. After his father left, she'd had the big pines surrounding the old house he'd grown up in cut down, then planted ornamental trees and flower beds instead. She said the garden needed the light. "And," she added. "those trees have always made me feel like I'm living in a prison. Or a grave. There will be plenty of time for that. I don't need this darkness in my life anymore."

One Saturday morning he'd found her in one of the flower beds, on her knees, hacking at the roots of a dandelion with a muddy garden spade.

"Weeds don't stand a chance," he said, hoping to make her laugh. Or at least smile, take away some of that too-serious concentration creasing her forehead.

She got up, inspected her work. Under her foot was a cluster of crushed phlox. When she saw what she'd done, she propped them up with the spade and a little soil. They fell over to one side despite her efforts. He pretended not to notice.

He rubbed his eyes now, until they stung. She was like that. In her need to make everything perfect, she would stomp on something else, even if that other thing was worth keeping. There was that jasmine plant he'd bought her for Mother's Day one year when he was a kid. He spent his whole allowance on it, then decorated the pot with a big red bow. The smell of jasmine was so sweet. He knew she'd like it. She loved sweet things. He later found the jasmine beside the garbage bin in the back alley. If she didn't like it, why hadn't she told him so?

Give her a break, he told himself now. He ground his gum between his teeth. She'd just wanted a happy family. Except how bloody realistic was that? He went along with it, too, pretending life was dandy. So who was the bigger idiot?

Down on the street, a lone jogger was struggling through the tempest of leaves and scraps of paper twisting and pitching in the air. He scrambled forward against the wind. Ted had always questioned the sanity of those guys who had to be out running, no matter what. But then again, he could understand discipline. It was really why he'd been able to succeed in his business, in his life.

He paced. Finally stopped and told himself to get on with it.

No one knows, not even Jack. He's been with me at Holt Communications for ages. A few weeks ago, right after I'd started the program, I went out for supper with him. I ordered a Perrier. And he was all over me. "What are our clients going to think, Teddy boy? The president of the company is a teetotaller. Perrier is for pretentious broads who want to show off and spend a lot of money on tap water injected with fizz. Real men need something stronger." Jack jabbed me in the ribs. I wanted to shove him up against the wall, say I don't give a rat's ass what anyone thinks. I'm the president of this company.

I gulped my Perrier, bubbles rushed up my nose and I choked on a fit of coughs. "Stay cool," Jack said. He thumped my back. "I was just pulling your chain."

Yeah, he was. But it was the first kick in the arse. Jack is my best friend and I was ready to beat the shit out of him because of a little bit of teasing. There was something wrong with this picture. Where had this need to hit something or someone come from all of a sudden?

I do it at home. Alone. Or, I used to. There was nobody around to notice the bottles piling up in the basement, the vomit on the kitchen floor, the shit on the jockeys. I would get rid of the mess before Janice came in to clean the place. I'm not trying to shock you, Mother, but I need to look at this straight on, stop hiding inside the person other people think they know.

Step 4: Make a searching and fearless moral inventory of ourselves.

Then write it all down.

Of course, I'm writing it down. I'm still the good boy. That's what you used to call me. And my science teacher would have agreed. He labelled me too. As if I was one of his stupid experiments. Give me an assignment and I do it better than anyone else. You can take the kid out of the school, but you can't get rid of his need to please. Really? Christ, I'm thirty-four.

Back in the day, I had everyone fooled. I was an honour student and the star quarterback. I also had the best supply of uppers and downers on campus. Didn't do the stuff myself. Made enough money to pay for university, start this PR firm and donate to some of those relief agencies of yours, Mother. I thought I had my life under control until the day I got the shakes so bad I had to leave a presentation I was supposed to deliver to the Starwood Group. They were a major customer and I was about to throw that deal away.

On stage, I was sweating buckets. That had never happened before. I left the conference room in mid-presentation, knowing all those faces were staring at me, went into the washroom, and threw up. Sat on the dirty floor until Jack found me. I told him I had the flu.

That's the reason I go to the damn meetings, have a sponsor to talk to now, have gotten involved in all this personal shit with complete strangers. I don't know what the hell I'm doing. I blab about all sorts of things at those meetings, like I'm cleaning out my guts or something. I can't even stop myself, for shit's sake. It's crazy. Or I'm crazy.

"What's wrong?" *Jack asked me later.*

"Like I said, flu."

He gave me that look. You can't bullshit a bullshitter.

I ignored him. But then I dumped the bottles I had in the apartment and made some calls until I found an AA group. It was time.

I don't want to lie to Jack anymore. I mean, shit, first I nearly punch his lights out over a bit of teasing, then I let us both down when my company, my goddamn company, is supposed to put its best foot forward. No more. It has to stop. I want to stop lying. Now that's a first.

I hired Jack away from my biggest competitor years ago. I really like Jack, and I'm lucky to have him in the company. But he doesn't know who I really am. Other people only see my public face, the successful businessman with everything under control. What a joke. I've got nothing to envy. All I know how to do is put on a decent act.

You know better than anyone, Mother, what an actor I can be, given the chance. Remember how you used to say, "I'm so glad I have such a smart son. Don't have to worry about you one bit." Guess I fooled you too. You were so proud of my grades, my accomplishments in school. But I suspect what you really liked was my independence. It gave you freedom. You no longer had to be Mother and saviour of the world all at once.

I promised myself I would never cause you grief. That's why I didn't say anything when life turned to shit at school.

Thoughts of his old school reignited memories: science lab formaldehyde, musty books. The reek of disinfectant and death he tried to mask with expensive colognes. Images surfaced: a tentative smile, hands on the back of his shoulders, stroking his neck. Black-rimmed glasses taken off and placed on a desk. A scuffed gold band.

Ted squeezed his eyes closed. "Focus," he told himself. "This isn't about that teacher. It's about you. It's time to face up to you."

He spat his gum into a Kleenex. His mouth was desert-dry. One side of his face throbbed, as if he had a mouthful of rotten teeth. As he took a sip of coffee, his stiff jaw loosened reluctantly. He massaged his jaw. Overworked and strained, the muscles at the side of his head ached at his touch.

I don't know how young I was the first time I saw you cry. I still remember my cowboy pyjamas though. You were on your knees, hands over your head. "Please. Stop. I'll go to the store right now. I'll go get your rye," you sobbed. Dad was standing over you, his fists clenched. I wished I had a gun then, like the cowboys. I tried to duck back into my room, like you told me to do if 'Daddy ever gets angry,' but my cuff got caught on something and ripped. You looked up and I saw the blood oozing from your lip. I rushed off. Left you with him.

The next day, I stuffed those pyjamas at the bottom of the garbage, made you a card. On the front of it, I drew a crude sunflower in a field of grass.

"It hurts when I smile," you said.

You bought me new pyjamas, one pair with stripes, the other checkered. My Superman pyjamas also disappeared. "Big boy pyjamas," you said, "for my big boy." Maybe you knew as well as I did, I didn't deserve to wear them. I wasn't big enough or brave enough to protect either one of us.

These bits of memory are stupid. This writing stuff down is supposed to be good for me, but all it does is dredge up this garbage from the past. I want to know how to fix things now.

When I was twelve, Dad left. You didn't get out of bed for days. I kept going to school like nothing had happened, making my peanut butter and jam sandwiches every morning, using the same sticky knife, the same red-smeared bag. For dinner, I'd make Kraft Dinner or Campbell's soup and we'd have a picnic on your bed. One day, after we'd finished our picnic, you patted the bed beside you. I got up and joined you in the heaps of pillows that surrounded you. "You're my Mr. Fix-it, aren't you?" you said. "I don't know what I'd do without you." You ruffled my hair, pulled me close. My ear squished close to your chest, I listened to your heart beating. I could have stayed there forever. But I knew I couldn't fix anything.

"I don't know if he'll come back this time," you said. "I really did try to help him. If he'd only listened to me, we could still be a family."

Ted dropped his head into his hands. Christ, when was he going to get over this stuff? His head hurt. His cheeks were wet.

After he left us, he'd show up from time to time, at night, drunk out of his skull. He'd want to take me for a ride to the lake or skating. "A son needs a father," he'd say. You never let me go with him when he was drunk. But you never called the cops on him either. Somehow you handled it by yourself. I don't know how. I guess you felt sorry for him or you still loved him. God knows why.

A few years later, Dad died. May 15, 1992.

I didn't know what I felt for him then. Even now, I don't know what I feel for him. He was my dad and everything and I knew he had problems, he should have gotten some help. He didn't have to hurt us.

I'm going to write this down because it's how I feel and I'm told I've got to be honest with myself. I know you won't like what I have to say, but I'm glad he's dead. Okay, I said it. He didn't do anything for either one of us. Maybe one day I'll see him for the sad, tragic guy he was, instead of the angry son of a bitch I knew. Maybe I'll even understand why he was so bloody mean and vicious, but right now, I have to take care of myself. I don't have any room left in me to think about why he did what he did. And I don't give a shit either.

Ted's Mont Blanc pen felt heavy. He rolled it around in both hands, felt the etching of his initials in his wet palms, and then dropped it on his desk beside the letter and the Moleskine notebook. He'd had the pen engraved with his initials and he'd written his name in his notebook, as he still did with most of his things. Leaving his mark, some record of himself on everything.

He traced his initials on the pen, recalled being teased at school for always putting his name on his things: books, shirts, equipment.

"It's not like anyone wants your junk," one of the guys on the football team said one day as he held up Ted's monogrammed gym bag.

"I know," Ted replied.

"It's weird," his friend said. "Kind of like you." He laughed and dropped the bag. Ted laughed along, but a rod of embarrassment jabbed at his stomach. How could others see so clearly what he didn't know he was doing himself?

He liked to know what was his, he thought now. What was wrong with that? Strange. He hadn't had any siblings to fight over stuff, just a mother who wasn't always around and a dad who didn't like anyone touching his things. He briefly thought about this latest revelation. Maybe he was a chip off the old block. Booze, weird habits.

He cracked his knuckles and stretched out his fingers. He barely knew how to use a pen anymore, except to sign contracts and deals. He had secretaries and assistants up the yin yang to type up those deals, clever guys who could make presentations sing, make his ideas look better than they probably were. He was the *ideas* guy, not the *do-it* guy. He hired others for that sort of thing. It was what he had worked so hard to achieve. He no longer had to get his hands dirty. Wasn't life grand?

His sponsor told him at some point he might be ready to show his mother the kinds of things he wrote about. It might help both of them. But Ted wasn't sure how.

He reached for another stick of gum, but then thought better of it. Instead he rubbed at his achy jaw; reread what he'd written.

One day, after Dad died, we were at the kitchen table and you suddenly said, "I want to make a difference with my life."

"How?" We were across from each other. I reached for your hand. You patted my hand. Looked at it, not at me.

"When I was in university, I wanted to work in a third world country. I thought that's where most of the need was. Your father agreed with me. We had the same goals then. Life happened and plans changed."

"And?"

"I've done a lot of reading and I think Africa might be the place for me. If nothing else, I can give it a try. I can do that now. You're almost a man and I've got the money to actually do what I haven't been able to do before. I know you understand. You know I haven't always been happy. This is my chance."

"How long will you be away? What happens next?"

You shook your head as if to say you didn't have all the answers.

"I know I can count on you."

"Of course, Mother." I said. Did I even know what those words meant?

As if nothing more needed to be said, you stood up and went to the sink. I drank some water.

Anyway, that was then and this is now. I want to come clean. But first, Step 5: Admit to God, to ourselves and to another human being the exact nature of our wrongs.

When I called your agency, they told me you were on extended leave. I know I shouldn't worry. You've moved around Africa a lot. You are a grownup, after all. But I can't help worrying when it comes to you.

Last time I heard from you, you were in Greece. Safer than Africa, I suppose. Will I get a scribbled note on the back of a photo like I did when I was seventeen — an out-of-focus snapshot of a kid with a tear-stained face and snotty nose, leaning against your chest? You were in Kenya then.

"This is one of my favourite pictures," you'd written. "Reminds me why I do it. Someone took the picture of us because I'd nursed my little guy back after his mother died. Nice to be needed."

I saw you — your satisfied smile, the kind I used to work so hard to get — as if you were standing right there in front of me. A strand of silver was out of its elastic twist and over your eye.

He'd thrown the photo away. He raised his eyes from the page in front of him now and looked over at the small trophy he kept on the windowsill. *Most Improved.* It was silly to keep such a thing all these years. But it was a reminder of what he could accomplish even without his father's blessing.

He remembered his father kicking the ball around with him when he was three or four. And buying him jerseys for his favourite team, Real Madrid. But Ted wasn't any good at the game. He knew it and his father did too. Only his mother remained completely oblivious.

Beside the trophy he saw the photograph he had kept of that trophy win. He was eight and in his soccer uniform, holding a ball. His mother was crouched beside him, her arm draped around his shoulders, their heads close, almost touching. She'd asked another parent to take the picture. "His father will be so proud of him," she said. Her smile was feeble, almost forced, her eyes partially hooded against the sunlight.

"Why do you keep this picture?" she had asked him once. "It's terrible. My eyes are barely open. It was such a bright day. Don't you remember?"

There was nothing he didn't remember. Sometimes he wished he could forget.

He stared at the photograph, willing other distracting thoughts out of his head. This picture was special to him. His mother was the one who helped him practise all those nights and weekends for the game he was so terrible at even his friends didn't want him to play. He'd told her he didn't need her help, but one day she'd suggested they go to the park anyway. She could be goalie if nothing else. And she kept asking to come along until it became their routine.

He shook his head. He had gotten better at the game because of her. Not perfect, mind you, but so much better. The other boys stopped teasing him.

It didn't matter to Ted that she wasn't her usual photogenic self in the picture. She was there, supporting him and being proud of him. They were together. Why wouldn't he keep that photograph?

I must have been about ten when I first took a sip of what was left in Dad's glass. He had passed out in his chair in front of the TV. Didn't even wake up when I started coughing. I hated the sour smell, but I choked down every last drop, licked the top of the glass. Sure, it burned my throat, but it made me feel cozy and warm, like how I felt those times we were close. I started sneaking his rye right out of the liquor cabinet. I have tried really hard not to face this, but I can't put it off any more. Not if I want to get on with this rehabilitation or whatever I'm doing.

I usually added some water to make up for the amount of rye I'd taken, but one time I drained the bottle. When he discovered the empty bottle he blamed you. And when you denied it, it set him off. You ended up with a broken arm that time. He did that to you because of me. I knew it was my fault then, but I never admitted it. I'm sorry, Mother. I betrayed you and hurt you as much as Dad did.

All I can say is that I never meant to.

Ted gnawed the callous on his thumb, ripped a piece of skin and crushed it between his teeth. He thought of Jack and the people who worked for him. They trusted him. He'd let them down if he didn't get his act together.

He'd ruin the business he'd built and hurt those who counted on him because he needed a lousy drink. How could that be? What he needed more than anything was a drink. As a child, he hadn't needed his mother. Or his father. Or anyone else. And now booze was controlling him. Stupid.

Sure, work and the day-to-day staffing and scheduling issues of running his business kept him busy. But as his workday wore on, he felt an agitation grow under his skin as if something had wriggled inside and persistently nipped at him. Although he wasn't sweating as sometimes happened when he hadn't had a drink, he knew what he needed.

He'd sneak off during the day for an hour or so, gym bag in hand. His office was surrounded by glass. He couldn't hide a bottle or take a swig in there as his father had done in his own office. Ted liked to get away anyway. When he'd come back, the smell of alcohol masked by mints or gum, he was right as rain, ready to take on the afternoon.

He had everything pretty much under control until he screwed up that presentation. It was then — on his way home, still jittery and sweaty, his knuckles colourless from holding the steering wheel so tight — he decided he had to do something about his problem.

"You should see someone professionally too," his sponsor had told him after he began AA meetings.

Ha. As if that would help.

His mother was a social worker. They were supposed to be good at seeing through the cracks of people like him covered with bravado and a quick smile. But she hadn't. Why would anyone else be any better? He'd take care of this himself.

He squeezed his eyes closed. An image of a man, the same man who startled him with cries in the middle of the night. Ted realized he was the one screaming and pushing hands, chest, and body away. Yelling, "Stop," and then pleading, "Please stop."

Ted opened his eyes, hunched over his letter and began to write again, his pen struggling to keep pace with his thoughts.

At boarding school, I couldn't figure out where I fit, what I was supposed to do with myself. Booze came to the rescue again. It was hard to make friends. Maybe if I had found even one friend, it wouldn't have happened.

I took to the science teacher. Thought he was a good guy who loved science and teaching. Maybe I thought he was the father I'd never had. Hell, I don't know what I thought.

At the front of the room, there was a quote of the day written on the blackboard every day. Sometimes it was something that would make you laugh when you got it, like, "Don't be afraid to make misteaks," but usually it was something like, "What have you done that's special today?" I liked that. It gave me something to think about.

After class I'd often stay and help the teacher unload a shipment of frogs or clean flasks or label things. He told me I was good at making labels, my printing was so neat and tidy.

In class, he'd pick me to demonstrate an experiment and he always said all sorts of good stuff about my homework. I liked being someone's favourite, even though the other kids bugged me. "Are you going to lick his boots clean, too?"

After it happened, I felt filthy. No amount of soap and water would ever make me feel clean — but the swigs of rye made it easier. In college I switched to gin, vodka, and sometimes wine. Rye reminded me of his breath against the back of my neck, the dead smell of the lab, that stupid wedding ring of his. He wore it most of the time. But other times, he'd take it off and tuck it in his shirt pocket as if screwing around on his wife was the worst of his sins.

The phone rang. Ted jumped, but didn't move. He had to finish this.

Shit. I don't think I can go any further right now. This personal inventory thing in AA is meant to help you face your past. It takes months, even years before a person can look clearly and honestly at his own shitty life. That's what my sponsor says.

And most of the guys in the meetings tell me to take it easy, one step at a time. But I'm already at Step 5. Want to get this done so I can move on from here. If I can get through this and out the other end in one piece.

The guys in the group say it doesn't work like that. But they don't know me.

I've been sober for ten days. It might be too soon to look at all my shit, sure, but what am I if not an overachiever? Couldn't change that even if I tried. No one knows what I'm capable of when I set my mind to it. Right, Mother?

Love, Your Good Son

The phone stopped and then almost immediately began to ring again. Ted hoisted himself out of his chair and walked over to the table by the window. The wind was howling. He could hear it whistling and churning. A small branch hit his window and startled him.

"Mother, I was just…"

"What?"

"Where? Athens?"

"Slow down. I don't understand."

9

EVIDENCE

Vancouver, Canada

"Look, Jack, I've got to go." Ted said into the phone. His voice caught in his throat. Why the hell did he have to explain every goddamn thing? He wanted to come across as calm and in control, as if leaving on short notice was no big deal. When was the last time he'd taken a vacation? Never. And that was why Jack was on his case. He knew something was up. Jack fancied himself an amateur psychologist. Ted humoured him most of the time when he started with the latest mumbo jumbo. Not today.

"I booked my flight last night," Ted said quietly. Jack knew him well enough to know when he lowered his voice it meant there was no room for negotiation.

"We need to close the Bales deal. You know they love you. 'Ted is the only one who gets our vision,' blah, blah, blah. They're always singing your praises."

"I'm not going forever." Ted fingered the miniature bottle of gin sitting on his desk. One gulp. That was all these bottles held. Nothing too serious. It was meant to be his insurance policy, his back-up plan if things got too crazy and he needed a little something to get him through.

"Maybe I should drop by," Jack said. "Go over a few things with you."

"I've got a ton to do," Ted said. The bottle tipped out of his reach. He lunged towards it, but it fell and banged about on his desk.

"What was that?"

"Packing stuff as we talk, Jack. Told you, I don't have much time."

Ted had drained every last one of his hidden bottles down the toilet when he started AA, then put the empties by the side of the dumpster for those poor folks who prowled the alleys making a living. He'd convinced himself that he'd found them all. He'd even made a show of it with his sponsor, going through the cupboards and drawers, the hiding spots under the bathroom sink, in his desk, in his underwear drawer, behind the dresser.

"Take a look for yourself," Ted had said to his sponsor, throwing down the challenge he knew the man would never take. Why would he?

"We aren't doing this for me," the sponsor said. "You know that."

Ted knew the sponsor wouldn't search his place. This was no different than business. You stood your ground and looked people straight in the eye, speaking with calm authority and no one called your bluff. No one, not even a fellow drunk would find this one; tucked inside the safe behind the layer of books on the built-in bookcase. He'd known it was there all along, even when he didn't admit it to himself. Out of sight and out of mind, he'd told himself. Just in case this detox thing got too tough. No one need be the wiser. What harm could it do? Just a quick swallow, enough to take the edge off. Only if he needed it. Except when he'd tried to quit before, one sip turned to two, one bottle turned to many. Then he was right back at square one.

"Come on, Ted," Jack said. "What's really going on?"

"You're in charge," Ted said. "The deal will go through. I trust you. We've been in this business together for a long time. You've got my cell number."

How could he explain that his mother was in a Greek jail accused of kidnapping some gypsy kid? No, Jack didn't need to know this. Ted would deal with it on his own.

"Is something wrong?" Jack asked. "We're buds, right? Let me help."

"Stop worrying," Ted said.

"Okay, so why do you have to visit your mom right now?" Jack said. "She needs you this very second. When was the last time you saw her? I mean, couldn't she wait a little longer?"

"It's been too long already, Jack."

He spit his gum into the wastepaper basket by his desk. It landed on the side of the plastic garbage bag and he was forced to take a piece of paper and push it down, out of sight. Why? Who knew? No one cared. He fisted the bottle, shrugged. Just one more thing to hide, for no goddamn reason except to keep up the stupid façade he'd created, the control he liked to think he had.

He stroked the bottle. The liquid swayed, teased. He took the cap off, whiffed.

Nothing like he expected. Strong. Sour. Similar to the smell that followed his dad.

His hand trembled and the bottle tipped over. It splattered his desk, blotting the few pieces of paper he had in front of him. He scrambled to right the bottle. When had he taken off the cap? Would it be enough?

Maybe he could lap up what was on the desk. He saw himself as a kid again, licking the last bit of icing left in the mixing bowl. His mother had finished decorating one of those fancy cakes she used to make during their visits. Her concentration and smile steady, proud. What was wrong with him? Was he really contemplating licking his desk clean? How could he think about drinking this shit?

He eyed the dregs at the bottom of the bottle. Holding the bottle as though it might explode in his face, he walked into the kitchen and stood by the sink. He took a swig before he allowed himself to think about it, swished it in his mouth. It burned his tongue. He spit the fire into the sink, splattering the backsplash. He washed out the sink and wiped the backsplash, then drained the remains of the bottle into the sink and threw the bottle into a plastic bag. His mother needed him to have his wits about him. Jack and the staff needed him to be honest. He needed to get off this shit. Everyone needed something. And a swig here and there wasn't going to help. Not now, anyway.

The buzzer downstairs rang.

He grabbed some paper towels and walked back into the living room. When he had wiped up the mess on the desk, he threw the wet paper towels into the plastic bag, put his notebook into his suitcase, stashed last night's rambling letter in his desk and locked it. He sprayed a bit of air freshener and then opened the balcony door slightly. Janice would be in to clean today. She'd scold him for leaving the door open. She worried about the grime and dust from the street below that landed on things in his condo. But who cared? The smell of booze would have evaporated by then and she'd be no wiser. That's all he wanted. Everything to be as it should be.

He wondered briefly how the hell his cleaner had become one more person he had to impress. Hide from. Christ.

He zipped up his leather bag. He'd received his mother's call last night and in the space of less than a day, she'd done it again, turned his life upside down. He would do what he could, because the one thing he'd always wanted to do was take care of her. He had to try.

He picked up his jacket, checked that he had enough gum to tide him over and headed downstairs, dropping the incriminating plastic bag in the dumpster before he climbed into the cab.

10

THERE BUT FOR THE GRACE OF GOD

Pangráti, Athens

Christos placed his gun and holster in the empty safe. He was thankful to be home after another difficult night shift. The sun had yet to come up over the hill and through the kitchen window. Buzzing above him, the fluorescent light shuddered off, then on. The light was faint, ghostly. He'd change it one of these days, when he had the extra money for bulbs and all the other things the family needed. For now, they'd need to make do.

He locked the safe, jiggled the door to make sure it was secure. He had children to worry about. Boys who liked to play cops and robbers. And a daughter who was a snoopy monkey always in search of new distractions, toys for her amusement. He would rather leave his gun at work. But that was not allowed. "Officer Pappas, a gun belongs with its owner," Commander Kefalas had reminded him.

The gun frightened him, the destruction it could cause. He hadn't told anyone, not even Tia, how afraid of it he was.

The safe used to hold the savings he and Tia had managed to tuck away, along with a few pieces of jewelry passed down through generations of her family. The money was long spent. The jewelry had gone to one of those new pawnshops popping up in his neighbourhood. They offered cash for gold or silver. He, like so many others, sold their jewellery to support their families during this economic nightmare. "Bloodsuckers" was what his mother-in-law called these stores. "They want to make money on top of our misfortune."

The safe had moved with them when they'd had to give up their home. Tia had wanted to sell the safe, get whatever they could for it. "We have nothing to guard anymore. We could use the money," she'd said.

"It won't always be like this," he'd reassured her. "And then you'll see, we'll need it."

"Always the optimist," Tia had said and kissed him. "It's good we have one in the family."

In the end, he'd been right to keep the safe. Who could trust banks anymore? No one. And who knew if the country would default on its loans and return to using the *drachma*. The newspapers warned of this every day. If Greece went back to its old currency, those euros socked away in a bank account would be worthless. Everyone wanted safes like his, sturdy, secure. It was hard to find them anymore. He never reminded Tia of what he had said. There was no point. She knew as well as he did how their lives had changed after the crisis.

He could hear water running. Tia in the shower. As usual, she'd put the pot on the stove to warm for him. His family's supper last night was his breakfast this morning. He came home after his night shift in time to see his wife off to work, the kids off to school. What a life they led. Hard to believe they were the lucky ones.

Feeding his family after he'd lost his project management job at OTE, the Hellenic telecommunications company, had been the biggest challenge he'd ever faced. During that dark period of unemployment, he'd have the same nightmare, night after night. His children were in a fenced playground. The boys kicked a ball, while his youngest, Alexandra, sat under the shade of a tree, staring at her brothers. It was so unlike her not to be in the middle of a game and he wondered why they'd excluded her. He called out to his sons, asked why they weren't letting Alexandra play. They gawked at him suspiciously, as though he were a stranger, someone they were not supposed to talk to. He tried again, his voice choked and not his own. Clearing his throat, he shook the metal fence. The thrashing sound and his own coughing woke him.

When he would wake from this recurring nightmare, he would stare at the ceiling. He asked God to help him find a job so he'd have the means to provide for his family. He didn't need very much, just enough to feed his children so they wouldn't be taken away and raised by others. He reminded himself he was not his mother. His situation was completely different than hers. She had dropped him off at a church when he was born. The nuns had been good to him. Strict, yes. But good too. They gave him his name, Christos Pappas. Christ and Priest. He wished this had given him some divine power. Perhaps then he could have done something to protect his family from the horrible economic crisis.

He never spoke to Tia about his nightmare. Instead, he'd assure her some kind of job was bound to come from all the applications he'd submitted, somehow they would make ends meet. And he'd take his children to the park, ignore their demands for an ice cream cone from the *períptero*, the kiosks set up to provide employment to disabled veterans after the war of independence. He thought it would be wonderful to have a small business like this, work for himself, make money for his family and have his friends gather there at night to talk, share a beer. But this was wishful thinking. Only disabled war veterans or widows or children of war veterans were allowed to own the kiosks. The authorization to set one up was strictly supervised by the

Ministry of Defence. Too bad the rest of the government wasn't as carefully watched.

Christos and his family continued to survive, despite the ongoing recession, thanks to God, his mother-in-law and Tia's cousin with government connections. When he'd worked at OTE, Christos used to say corruption and nepotism were Greece's biggest problems. If they could rid the country of the rot, they'd be better off. But that was before he found himself out of work.

His wife's cousin had told him the only places hiring these days were police departments and security companies. He had a few connections in the police department. "These days with the migrants and the Golden Dawn racists and the protests in the streets it's a booming industry. The only one. Go in there and show them you're tough enough for the job," Pétros said. "And keep your liberal ideas to yourself. These people don't care about such things."

As much as he hated the new order — daily riots in the streets, violence by and against foreigners — it had provided him with work.

Christos stuck the key for the safe into his pocket.

"You're home," Tia said as she walked into the kitchen. "How was the night? Has Kefalas's head shrunk any?" She smiled.

"It is always the same." He shrugged now. "People don't change."

She swung quickly towards the stove, turning down the element beneath the bubbling broth. "Too much on my mind and the day hasn't even begun."

"How was he last night?" Christos asked. He left a trace of a kiss on Tia's cheek. Standing at the stove, a ladle in her hand, she leaned into him.

"He ate a little. More than the first night," she said. "Yiayiá tells me he doesn't say much during the day, sits by himself, doesn't bother with any of the toys, even when Alexandra tries to interest him in her doll or pesters him."

"How is Alexandra getting along with him?"

"She thinks she has a new brother," Tia said, "who doesn't have to go to school with her other brothers." Tia stirred the soup. "The boys don't know why you brought him here. They wonder what their friends will say when they find out a child such as this is living with them. I've told the boys we have to help where we can. Where is their *filótimo*? They need to be reminded of what it means to be honourable."

"If they knew the way the Roma live," he said.

"The boy needs his mother," Tia said. "What kind of monster sells his own son?"

"We don't know he's done that. We only suspect it. Maybe it's a simple misunderstanding. We don't know."

"The child was found in the woman's apartment. Distraught. You told me so yourself." She turned and pointed the ladle at him. He watched as a few drops of soup dripped to the floor. She didn't seem to notice. "What was he doing there if his father didn't sell him? Thank God for the honest Greeks in the woman's building. It is nice to know there are still good people left in this country."

Yes, good Greeks, Christos thought. He saw again how the old woman had whispered and pointed to the Canadian woman's apartment door. Her husband stood behind her, his hands over his ears. Neither looked him in the eye. "What are we to do with these foreigners?" the old woman had said. "They are taking over our country. Ruining it. And our leaders let them in so they can walk all over us. When will it stop?"

"What will happen to that poor child?" Tia asked now. "What kind of life could he have with the person who calls himself his father?"

"We'll find his mother."

"And if you don't? Will he stay with us? I'm telling you now." She pointed at him. "We have to think of our own family first."

"Tia, I know this," Christos said.

Her jaw tightened; her eyes blazed through him as they did whenever she was trying to make a point. "What if the mother is worse than the father? At least the father went looking for him. We know nothing about the mother." Her voice rose; her shoulders hunched up, her posture stiffened.

"I don't have answers right now." Christos said. "I'm trying to understand what happened. I'm trying. That's all." He knew what she was thinking. *You are so methodical, so slow to come to a decision. So unwilling to push things. Sometimes you have to decide things without thinking. You have to take action.*

Pans banged against one another in the apartment next door. Water rushed. Would he ever get accustomed to others living so close? The apartment they used to own was in a newer building. They never heard their neighbours unless they were in each other's homes for lunch, a coffee. That kind of quiet, that kind of life, seemed so long gone.

Tia turned her back to him and faced the stove.

Christos ducked in to see the boy, who was asleep on a mat on the floor of his children's bedroom. He scanned the room, looking at each of his own sons and his daughter. They were so quiet, he wondered if he should nudge them to make sure they were alive, as he had done when they were babies. You're crazy, he told himself. Whenever he confided this to Tia, she would say, "Worry is the price of fatherhood."

The boy snuffled in his sleep. Christos stroked the boy's head as the nuns in the orphanage used to do with him.

What kind of woman would take a child who wasn't her own? Wasn't that the important question? Shouldn't the Canadian woman have known better? And what if the commander was right and the woman had bought the child from the father? The Canadian seemed disoriented, unsure of where she was, what she'd done. Maybe she was what the commander thought she was: another rich foreigner willing to buy anything, just because she could. He didn't see her this way, and he couldn't believe she'd kidnapped the child either, as the child's father had claimed. But what did he know about judging character? He was an engineer. Or at least he used to be.

He'd insisted on taking the child home with him rather than sending him to a church-run orphanage. Once the boy was placed in one of those homes, Christos knew there would be no urgency to find his mother. The child would disappear behind those doors. Christos couldn't allow this to happen. He couldn't. Every child needed a mother.

"Watch that kid carefully," Commander Kefalas had said. "Those people would steal your eyes before you knew they were gone."

The others, his colleagues, laughed at him. "You'll have some explaining to do at home. No way I could bring a kid like this to my wife. I'd be on the street myself, before I had time to take off my shoes. You have my sympathy." They looked at each other and shrugged, as though they expected something like this from him. They called him an *anthropistís*, teased him about his bleeding heart. It was going to get him into trouble.

He bent and kissed the boy's head as he would one of his own children. He closed the door and returned to the kitchen.

"I'll find his mother," Christos said to Tia. He lobbed his tie at the coat rack.

Tia turned to watch it float, then land, hitting its mark. "One day, you'll miss," she said, smiling.

They sat down at the kitchen table, across from one another. Christos tore a piece of bread and dipped it into his soup. Tia dunked her dry toast into her murky coffee.

"Foreigners have ruined this country," he said, without looking at Tia. He gulped his soup even as it burned his tongue. "Tourists, illegals, other governments, all of them. They've brought us nothing but trouble." He had only a few minutes of quiet with Tia before their kids woke up and started pestering him with questions about what kind of bad guys he'd caught last night. His sons had never taken any interest in his previous job. He knew they pictured him as some kind of hero now, like the ones they watched on the American programs flooding the Greek TV stations. But most days he didn't feel like he'd accomplished very much. What difference did he make? None. His sons would be disappointed if they knew the truth about the petty criminals he processed and parked in cells until someone could bail them out. Thankfully, his daughter, Alexandra, was too young to care about what he did. She just wanted to know why he had to go away at night. How could he explain that in these economic times, he was lucky to have a job?

"Are your colleagues trying to sway you to the right? Have you now joined Golden Dawn?" Tia asked. "I suppose you want to throw all the foreigners out of this country or into jail too." She crossed her arms, and her housecoat, belted tight at the waist, fluttered open near her breasts, exposing her tanned skin, a few freckles. Her face was not yet made up and she seemed pale this morning, as if she hadn't slept. He'd brought this worry onto her.

She pushed her bangs off her face. He thought about how she used to go to the hairdresser to have her hair done every couple of weeks when he had a job, when they both had their jobs. They were carefree then, even careless, if he allowed himself to think about it. They thought their jobs, the money, and their lifestyle would last forever. In this regard, they were no different than their government. Since the recession, Tia had let her hair grow long. Her mother trimmed her bangs.

"You're beginning to sound more and more like those ultra-nationalists. They are the ones who are an embarrassment to this country." Her voice rose and the vein at the side of her neck swelled. He loved that vein and every bit of her. She was opinionated and bossy, and still he loved her.

He'd met her at university, during a debate about the 1967 junta. Of course, she'd blamed the Americans. "Their meddling and obsessive fears about communism undermined our own government. And the mindless Greeks were no better," she'd argued. "They refused to see what was happening around them."

She'd spoken as if she'd lived through the junta, been jailed as so many others had been for their views and political leanings. In fact, she hadn't been born until long after democracy had been restored. How would she know anything about the struggles of those who'd lived through the junta?

He tried not to meet her gaze. He knew she was waiting for his response. Her hands clutched her coffee cup as she leaned towards him. Tia worried about him, as if he needed a strong hand to help him understand the difference between right and wrong.

She told her friends she had four children, not three. It irked him when he heard her say these things, but keeping the peace was more important, given their living arrangement and the tentative nature of the economy, their lives.

"You know the papers exaggerate," he said. "Not every police officer is a member of Golden Dawn, nor do we look the other way when someone is beating up a foreigner." He'd jailed three young Greek racists just a few days ago, kids who could easily be his own, for beating an elderly gypsy woman. Kids were committing such disgraceful acts these days — carving a swastika on a young

Pakistani boy's face, setting fires to Chinese-owned One Euro stores, kicking Roma children who begged on the street. Such senseless violence would once have brought so much shame on a family it would never have been thought of, let alone carried out. Where does such hate come from? He'd asked himself this question more than once since becoming a policeman.

"It's the economy," one of the other officers had said, "There is no hope for young people. No future, none at all."

He had watched his sons more carefully in the past year for any signs of this kind of anger and despair.

"Every day, one of our own does something that makes me ashamed to call myself Greek," Tia said now. She slammed her hand on the table. The coffee in her cup swayed and spilled on the white tablecloth.

Her ponytail was loose. She took out the elastic band and ran her fingers through her hair. The coffee soaked and stained the tablecloth. "We're going back to the days of the occupation."

"It's this horrible time," Christos said. "People need to blame someone." He picked up his worry beads, began to toss them over his fingers. The feel of the stones, the sound they made as they fell against each other, soothed him.

"It's easier to find fault in others," she said. "Those Golden Dawn criminals should be filling your cells, not sitting with immunity in our parliament. And the young people who follow those hooligans should be taught a lesson."

Tia was right. There had been too many incidents reported of migrants and other illegal foreigners being brutalized by the police who supported the antics of the Nazi party, Golden Dawn. A couple of Golden Dawn followers murdered a Greek rapper who wrote words against the racism growing in this country. Would they ever be convicted? Christos didn't know. "We picked up two Greek kids a few days ago for beating an Afghani. One of the mothers was already waiting for us when we got back with them. They had sent her a text. These people hire lawyers, pay someone under the table to let their sons go. I don't know. Maybe I'd do the same thing for one of ours."

"At least we have Yiayiá to watch over our children, teach them proper values."

"Yes." He held the worry beads still.

A toilet flushed somewhere above them.

Tia pushed away from the table and came to Christos. She kissed the top of his head. "I have to get ready for work." She was a secretary in Communications at the Attorney General's Department. She used to teach political science at the university. Her position had been cut, another in a long series of austerity measures.

Along with the other professors at the university, she had protested daily for months to get their jobs back. Then she finally found other work. But she continued to support those still unemployed, joining their protest in front of the Parliament once a week.

Christos didn't go to the rallies his colleagues at OTE had organized after their layoffs. What was done, was done. Nothing he did would change a thing.

Tia's mother had always bragged about her daughter and her lofty position at the university to the neighbours. Now, her mother sprinkled holy water and kept a large blue eye over the front door. She told neighbours there was nothing more they could do. At least they had each other and both Christos and Tia were working. "Too hard. But what can they do? If they complain, they will be out on the street again, with no work."

Sometimes Christos overheard his mother-in-law talking to the people next door. Their balconies were so close it was hard to believe they were two separate spaces.

"Why don't the politicians cut their own throats after the shame they have brought upon us? No, they take the bread from our mouths. How can they live with themselves while so many suffer?"

He held Tia close, his head against her stomach. Her silky housecoat felt cool against his skin. She ran her hands through his hair, then pulled away from him. "You need a haircut," she said. "Yiayiá can do it tonight, before you go in to work." Her mother lived with them. Or rather, they lived with her. She took care of the children, shopped and cooked the evening meal, and did all the things they would have done themselves if they weren't working such long, odd hours. They were squashed into an eighty-square-metre apartment, a kitchen, living room, three bedrooms and a bathroom for all of them to share. Still, Tia had found space for the boy, just like her mother had found room for all of them.

He thought about the boy's father. Christos could never give up one of his children. And yet, despite all his fear and worrying, his family had never missed a single meal during the crisis. How could he say what he would or wouldn't do if his family were at stake? His fingers began to work the worry beads again, the sound louder, more agitated.

Tia reached for his hand, stopping the beads in mid-swing. She kissed his knuckles. "I know I've asked you too many questions about the boy. You know how I am. I need answers. A plan." She kissed his hand again. "Bo can't stay. You know that. I don't need to tell you again why."

"I wonder what I would do in his father's situation?"

Tia raised her eyes to the sky, her chin forward. She crossed herself. "You would not do what he has done. You would not."

That night, Christos checked each of the cells as he did his rounds. The racist boys were no longer there. People with money knew how to make their problems go away. Of course, he didn't know for sure what had happened, but he'd been here for over a year and he had learned how money could make some look the other way.

At today's muster meeting, as the day shift exchanged information with the night shift, he'd heard the Canadian woman wasn't eating. Her trays remained untouched. "Our refugee camps are running out of money for all these migrants who wash up on our shores and this woman thinks she's too good for the food we provide her," Commander Kefalas said. A few officers shrugged. Others clucked.

When he looked in on her, Christos found the woman sitting on the bed in the cell, staring at the floor. Her hair was matted on one side. She seemed to have shrunk inside her sweater and appeared child-like even though she was probably old enough to be his mother. If he saw her in a café or on the street, looking so lost, he would have approached her, asked her if she needed directions, offered to help.

She gripped the metal frame of the bed. He saw the muscles in her hand tighten. She shook her head, leaned over and hugged herself as little Alexandra did whenever she was scolded. But unlike Alexandra, there were no tears from this woman.

"Mrs. Holt?" Christos said. He stood outside her cell, his hands limp at his sides. The corridor was dark. The damp air smelled of bleach tinged with sweat and urine. The floors were washed daily, but the bleach couldn't mask what had permeated everything in this place.

"Shelby," she said.

"Mrs. Holt."

"Just Shelby. Where is Bo? Is he all right?"

"He is in good hands, Shelby. We will find the boy's family. His father is not telling us much about how all this happened. I suppose he doesn't want to bring the police to the place where he lives. You could take us there. You could help us, Mrs. Holt."

"Take you there? Your officers have beaten these people, arrested them for no reason, and destroyed their homes."

So there was some life left in this tired woman, after all, Christos thought. Thank goodness. He was worried about her and wondered whether he should ask the commander if they could call a doctor to examine her.

He wanted to agree with what she said, tell her she was right. Nothing was fair. But this was how life was these days.

He thought about bringing a chair into the cell and sitting down beside the Canadian woman. She didn't seem like a bad person. Maybe she was even sincere. Anyone could be swayed to help the gypsies if they worked with them day in and day out. Hadn't he taken the boy in himself? Perhaps all she'd wanted to do was help. Maybe she'd wanted to give the child a hot bath, some food, a break from the camp. She intended to bring him back, maybe with some new clothes and supplies. But then she got attached to him, couldn't bring herself to leave him in that awful camp. Could she really be blamed? The Roma lived in such desperate squalor.

Someone flushed a toilet in a cell at the other end of the corridor. Christos jumped. This was his place of employment and yet he was afraid. Of what, he wasn't sure. The smell of urine was stronger now. Christos tried to breathe through his mouth.

"We have our work to do," Christos said, as though he felt he had to defend himself and his colleagues. If he could sit down with her away from this place and the bars dividing them, they might understand each other a bit better. But he was no longer at OTE, where people sat together to work out technical problems. "We don't go looking for trouble. We don't go into these camps. They are dangerous for us."

The woman stood up quickly and grabbed onto the bed frame as if to catch herself from falling. "Dangerous for you. How do you think they feel?"

"Are you okay?" he asked. He reached for his keys.

"No one is okay in a place like this." She looked directly at him and, for some reason he couldn't explain, he felt shame. "This was not my fault," he wanted to say, but didn't. He focused on the window just above her and cleared his throat.

"You must eat something," Christos said. "If you don't like the food here, I will share my sandwich with you, with pleasure. Would you like to try a little? My mother-in-law makes a very good ham and feta sandwich."

The woman smiled for the first time. "Your concern for me reminds me of my son."

There was a glimmer of light in those grey eyes.

"I'm sure he will be here soon."

"Yes, he's always coming to my rescue," she said, and sat on the bed again. "It should be the other way around."

"We take turns. Sometimes parents help their children. Sometimes children help their parents." He smiled, hoped this reassured her.

"I'm not sure I've ever taken my turn."

Christos didn't know how to respond.

She looked down at the floor.

He stood quietly outside her cell. He wanted to show her he really did care what happened to her and the boy. "Shelby," he said, but she closed her eyes at the sound of her name, his voice. He shook his head. He was weak, he told himself. Feeling sorry for this woman. He was not cut out for this type of work. He was too soft, just like they told him in training and just like the Commander said every time he looked at him. And when his wife would say, "My Christos has a good heart," he knew she was really saying that he was weak. He looked down the narrow, dark corridor, then at Mrs. Holt in her cell.

At the opposite end of the building, in a cell without windows, Christos found the gypsy, handcuffs bound around one wrist and shackled to the bedpost. He unlocked the door.

The key turning in the lock sounded loud to Christos, but the man inside the cell didn't move. Unlike Mrs. Holt, who was allowed to keep her street clothes, the gypsy had been showered and deloused and provided a prison uniform. He wore socks. His shoes had been confiscated. The man's face was bruised. Christos asked him what had happened.

"I fell," the man said, without looking at Christos.

Christos unlocked the handcuffs. "You do not need these." As he pulled the cuffs off, he noticed the bruises around the man's wrists.

The man flinched.

"You are safe here," Christos said.

The man nodded, but Christos knew he didn't believe him. He wasn't sure about the man's safety either, given the reports in the newspapers lately about police brutality against outsiders. He'd told Tia he hadn't witnessed anything like that at this station and he hadn't. Still, the reporting of such things persisted.

"Have you eaten?"

"Of course. They provided me with a four-course meal, complete with your famous Greek yogurt and honey for dessert just hours ago." The man put his freed hands behind his head.

"I wish for your sake this was true," Christos said. "But I know this place too well." He looked around to see if any of the other officers were in the hallway. He told himself he should be careful not to provoke more teasing, ridicule.

"They don't feed people like me," the man said.

"That is not true," Christos said. "I will find something for you and come back." Yes, but how would he manage that without getting noticed? he wondered.

Christos asked Dimitri at the front desk if the Roma man had been given food. He tried to sound casual.

"Oh, now we're calling him a Roma," Dimitri said, his feet up on a desk, a folded newspaper in one hand, a pencil in the other, working on a crossword puzzle.

"He's a gypsy," Lukas said. "Gypsies eat garbage and we don't have anything like this here." His grin reminded Christos of a painting of the crucifixion of Christ that hung in the church his family went to, the expression on one soldier's face as he stood at the foot of the cross, looking up at Christ. The soldier's grin was proud, as if he alone had hammered the nails into Christ's hands and feet, had spilled the blood of the King of the Jews.

"Just don't want us getting into trouble," Christos said. "You know what the media has been saying. And those human rights groups. Who knows if they'll send their spies in so they can complain about our treatment of the prisoners."

"Don't worry your engineer's brain about that," Dimitri said. "We cops know how to stick together and protect ourselves from trouble-making outsiders."

Lukas laughed. "You just take care of yourself, *mihaniké* and let us do the police work."

More laughter.

Christos turned away from them. So what if he'd been an engineer? He didn't flaunt his education. It didn't mean he couldn't be a good cop too. This job reminded him of when he was a child in the schoolyard being teased by the other kids because he didn't have real parents.

"Just going to check on a couple of people I missed," he said.

"You do that," Dimitri said. The others smirked.

"Good to see you being so fastidious," Lukas said.

Christos walked over to his locker, pulled out an apple and his sandwich, tucked one in his shirt pocket, the other inside his jacket. He headed back down to the cells.

"Here you go, Kem." Christos pulled the sandwich and apple out of his pockets. He placed both through the bars.

The man sat on the bed, one foot bouncing nervously. He stared at the sandwich. "The others call me gypsy. Gypsy do this, gypsy do that."

Kem stood up and walked over to the bars. Christos looked down the corridor one way, then the other, then passed him the sandwich and apple.

"Hey, Christos," someone called. "What are you doing?" It was Michelas, the commander's right-hand man.

Christos froze. With his eyes, he motioned to Kem, who tried to hide the sandwich and apple behind his back. Christos shivered as though his sweat had instantly dried and turned him into ice.

"What are you doing?" Michelas asked again as he stepped out of the shadows. "You know we're not supposed to get too close to these people."

"He hasn't eaten, Michelas," Christos said. "We can't let someone starve. I can't. It's not right. You know that."

Michelas nodded. "I know, but you also know better than anyone what the guys upstairs will say if they find out what you're doing."

"Who is going to tell them?"

Michelas paced, then looked around. "Okay, but if you get caught, do not bring me into this. I might agree with what you are doing, but I do not want to get involved. You know them. How they are. I do not want to be treated the way they treat you."

"Understood."

"You'd better," Michelas said as he walked away. "I have my own family. I need this job."

Christos took a deep breath, rubbed his hands together.

Kem fumbled with the apple, stepped back and placed it on the bed. He unwrapped the sandwich methodically, as if trying to control himself. He took small bites. "Very kind of you, sir," he said, his mouth partially full.

"I'm Christos."

He wondered about the Roma man. Was it just an accident of birth that this man was inside the cell and he, Christos, was on the outside? How different would Kem's life be if he had a job, a home and a family? But he did have a family. A son he'd possibly sold. So, maybe he wasn't any more than what he appeared to be.

"Have you found my son?" Kem asked.

"Yes," Christos said.

Kem jumped up, reached for the handle of the locked door with one hand, while still holding the sandwich in the other. His smile opened to bits of bread and cheese trapped between his teeth.

"He is safe," Christos said, putting his hand up, signalling Kem to stop.

"Thanks be to God. His mother will be happy. She hasn't given me a moment's rest since he was taken," Kem said and rattled the door. "So you'll be able to let us go now. My son and me. Yes?"

"We're still piecing things together. You say your son was kidnapped. Some believe you sold him."

Kem's eyes shifted slightly to the floor, then back at Christos. "No one thinks very good thoughts about us. They think we are all thieves, child traffickers and common criminals. This is not true."

He was probably right, Christos thought. But what could he do about it, except try to figure out what had happened and who was telling the truth? When he looked at this desperate man, more a boy than a man, his prison uniform too small for his lanky frame, he again wanted to return his son to him and just let the two of them go. "We want to get to the truth."

"You seem like a kind man," Kem said, dropping his hand from the door. "All I ever wanted to do was provide for my family. You are a father. Yes? You must understand this."

As he stood before him, Christos couldn't help but believe him. And yet, he also knew that what he thought wouldn't make any difference to Kem's outcome. The man had no legal documentation. Or at least, none was found on him. If he was an undocumented foreigner, there might not be anything Christos or anyone else could do for him. "If you tell me where his mother is, I may be able to return the boy to her. This might help."

"Help who?"

"At least the boy would be with his mother."

"And you'd tear down the camp and throw everyone out onto the street. This has happened to other camps."

Christos wanted to reassure Kem this wouldn't happen, but he wasn't sure.

"Look, I came here for help. My child was stolen. And now I'm the one in prison. Why don't you arrest the person who took him?"

"We have."

"You found Mrs. Shelby?" Kem turned and placed what remained of the sandwich on the bed. "But how?"

"Her neighbours complained about noise from her apartment. Screams. We were called. I went myself on that call."

"Did she hurt him?" Kem asked. "She better not have hurt him."

"He's fine. More homesick than anything else."

"So you see now who is to blame." Kem grinned. The look in his eyes, the way his lips didn't form a complete smile, reminded Christos of the neighbourhood cat who a few mornings ago presented him with a dead bird as he came home from work.

"You know those do-gooders. They say they want to help, but all they want is to help themselves. They take our things and push their beliefs on us, call it charity."

Again, Kem grinned. "You know the woman will say anything to save her own skin. The Americáni are like this. And she has money behind her. I'm sure she is a lonely rich woman. How will I defend myself against anything she says about me?"

"She hasn't said very much." Christos said. "But it seems as though she is trying to protect you from us. She worries we will do you harm."

Kem stared at Christos as if he didn't believe him. "I have nothing more to say. My coffin has already been nailed." He turned away and sat heavily on the bed. He bolted down the rest of the sandwich.

Christos heard a man's voice as he walked back to the front desk. He was speaking English.

"I understand my mother is being held here. What do I need to do to get your attention?" Dimitri and Lukas sat at their desks and glanced over at each other, nodded slightly in the man's direction. Christos knew they were waiting each other out, each hoping the other would bow under pressure first and actually get up and go over and talk to the man.

Christos walked to the counter. "It's crazy today," he said. "I apologize." He heard Dimitri say something about him being a *karfí.* I want to do my job and they call me an informer, a flunky, Christos thought. These people aren't worth my anger.

"Yes, I can see that," the man said. He stared beyond Christos. "I'm Ted Holt. My mother, Shelby Holt, is here. Is she okay?"

"Yes, of course." Christos saw hints of Mrs. Holt in the man's grey eyes and narrow cheekbones. The muscles in his balding head protruded and rippled, his jaw tight and inflexible, like computer wires. Mrs. Holt had described her son as a person who took care of her, but Christos was surprised by the harshness he saw in this man. Still, his mother was in a foreign prison and who knew how long the poor fellow had been travelling to get here from America. Maybe Christos shouldn't jump to any judgments.

"What will it take to get her out of here?" the man asked. He flipped open the wallet in his hand.

11

A WARM BED

Pangráti, Athens

The sound of the door opening wakes me up. It is very quiet, with only the sound of the other children sleeping, but I am sure there is someone else in the room. I pretend I am asleep too. I don't move even one toe.

I share this room with two other boys and a girl. The boys ignore me. I know they don't like me. That's okay. I don't like them either. The girl gives me her dolls to play with. Boys don't play with dolls. I want to tell her that, but I don't say anything. I don't know what I'm supposed to say to these strangers.

Suddenly there is a hand on my head. It is warm, and big, like a man's hand. No one but my ammi, Mirela and Candy Lady have done that. I want to lean into it. Maybe he will tell me everything will be okay, like my ammi used to say sometimes to make me feel better after I coughed so hard my chest hurt. I don't know, so I don't take a chance. I don't move a muscle. Instead, I slow down my breathing, pretend I'm sleeping.

The man kisses me on the head, says something softly. I can't hear it, but it sounds like a prayer. Then he goes away and I hear the door close behind him. I think he's a good man, this man, even though the boys say their father is a policeman and catches bad people and locks them up somewhere where no one can find them. He hasn't done that to me yet and when he talks to me his voice is always kind. I think he likes me. He doesn't seem angry with me like Abbu and Kem are all the time.

These people have given me a place to sleep where I'm warm for the first time in my whole life. Even my feet and hands are warm. They give me medicine. It tastes awful, but it helps my cough. They let me keep some of the nice clothes Candy Lady gave me too. My belly is full, every day. They even let me eat vegetables. That would make Abbu happy. I don't know how they know I'm not supposed to eat meat. Maybe they don't. Maybe they are just letting me eat what I want. I know one thing. I don't want candies any more. Ever.

It's nice here, but I cannot stay. Ammi will never find me here. I have to go back to Mirela and Kem because Ammi told me to wait for her with them. And I promised.

12

Past Transgressions

Amaroúsio Police Station

Ted rocked back and forth on a wooden chair in a room that was no bigger than his front hall closet at home. The officer had said they'd bring Mother to him, that he should make himself comfortable. Not bloody likely. He hadn't seen her in forever. And this, this hole of a place was where they'd have their reunion. Wouldn't you know it?

How would she explain this? How had the kid ended up in her apartment? Christ. Sure, she was great at her job helping others, but this was way over the line. Even for her.

He fanned himself with what remained of his boarding pass, but the hot, stifling air barely shifted.

A mound of black moving in the corner caught his eye. He looked closer. Ants toppled one over the other, scrambling for what looked like a crumb.

Down the hall, there was a loud bang as though a heavy door was being closed and permanently sealed. On his guard now, Ted listened to the sounds in the corridor. Heavy steps on concrete, the clanging of keys, and the barks of conversation in a sped-up, garbled, nasal-sounding language he had no hope of understanding. He thought about closing the door to this room, but he'd wait until they brought her to him. Then he'd see. His noise-cancelling headphones would have been nice, but they were in his bag at the front desk. He'd come straight from the airport in a taxi. The police had taken his suitcase from him, said something about security. Hopefully, it would be intact when they gave it back to him. Could he trust the police? He didn't know.

A tarnished cross hung at the juncture of two walls, a distraction from the institutional olive-green paint. Spider webs dangled from the ceiling, binding the cross. Wedged at the centre of the cross, a blue medallion in the shape of an accusatory eye glared at him. He averted his eyes and suddenly felt dizzy. Exhausted was what he was. Not enough sleep. Too much travel. Too little food. And detox on top of it all.

He probably should have checked into a hotel first, had a shower or washed his face after the long flight. But his mother had already been locked up in this place for days. His first priority was to get her out.

His jaw was sore and tight. He rubbed his cheek, let the gum lie on his tongue, still as a corpse. He thought of his father, a man he'd been trying bloody hard to forget his whole life. Why now? He didn't know, except Dad always blamed Mother when things went wrong. And now maybe Ted was blaming her too for having dragged him here to Greece and into this prison. Why? He was in over his head here. He didn't know how he'd be able to help her.

"It wasn't my fault, you know. Ask your mother," his father had said the last time Ted saw him. "She'll tell you." He'd tucked a bottle into the top drawer of his desk and brought his arm over his mouth to wipe his lips. He'd plopped himself down and stared at Ted. Looked right through him. "I'm sure she could tell you plenty, if she really wanted to," he'd said and choked on a laugh. "But that's not her style, is it?"

Ted gnawed at the gum again as though each chomp would take this picture — his father's slouched shoulders, red-rimmed eyes, and contrite gaze — out of his head.

He spun the chair around so he couldn't see the cross or the eye and now faced a fish-bowl glass window. Again he felt woozy and steadied his gaze. He looked at his reflection and wondered if someone was behind the glass in an identical room, watching him. If someone were there they'd get bloody bored watching him, he thought. He stared into the glass. He wouldn't be the first to flinch.

Ted knew he'd been lucky to have avoided places like this when he was dealing. That was a lifetime ago. Why think about this stuff now? No one knew or cared about his past misdemeanours, except maybe his AA sponsor. And this was hardly the time to be dwelling on it. Right now, his mother needed him to be the strong one. He pinched the bridge of his nose. Wasn't he always the strong one?

He milled his gum on his back teeth, shredding it. Yes, his problems could wait. And maybe they'd just go away. But he knew that was simply wishful thinking.

His brain had been fuzzy for days after he stopped drinking. But despite adding jet lag to the mix, his brain felt as though it had a bit of clarity now too. He had his mother to thank. Her emergencies snapped him back into focus.

The officer at the desk had told him to put his wallet away when he tried to… What? Was he really thinking he could bribe the guy? "I am an officer here. There is no need for such things," he'd said. "I will bring your mother."

The news at home was all about Greece's budget problems. The *crisis,* as they called it. Ted had read that the country was full of corrupt officials. You could get your way with these people if you had a bit of cash. Cash he had. So okay, he'd thought he'd try his luck. He'd try anything to help Mother. Wouldn't you know he'd get the one honest guy in the place?

"And you are?" Ted asked, tucking the wallet back into his pocket.

"Christos," he said. "Greek name for your English Christ. This will help you remember my name."

The other officers snorted. Although Christos's shirt was tucked into his pants, it puffed around him as if there was no one inside its neatly pressed folds. The collar hung loose despite what looked like a regulation-issued tie, cinched tightly. Laughter followed them as Christos led Ted away from the front desk. Ted hadn't looked back. Were they laughing at him?

He stood up, shook off the chill that had crept into his spine despite the heat. When were they going to bring Mother? He looked at his watch. He'd been waiting for twenty minutes.

The door was ajar. Men in uniform walked back and forth in the hallway, none of them paying him any mind. He stopped one of them. "Hey, do you know when they're bringing my mother down?" he said to one officer.

The officer raised his eyes to the ceiling, stuck out his chin as if he didn't see or hear Ted. He made a single, clear sound — tut — and moved on before Ted could respond.

Ted felt the anger well up from somewhere in his gut. The prick had a lot of gall. Ted made more in one day than this guy probably made in a month. He'll never have what I have, he thought: the Hugo Boss suit, the Tanino shoes and the goddamn Tag Heuer. The suit and shirt were wrinkled and he needed a shave, but what did they expect? He'd been travelling all night to get here. He told himself he wouldn't have to deal with these people for long. Still, the way that guy looked at him made him feel like he was not worthy of his attention.

He took a breath. There was no point in making things worse. And besides, Ted knew he was the kind of man who wasn't above breaking rules to get his way. Maybe the officer suspected that too.

Ted had felt guilty about something or other his whole life. And he knew, because he wasn't completely crazy, that he hadn't always had a reason to feel that way.

An image laced its way slowly before his eyes as though he was watching a movie about someone else's life. His father sat at the kitchen table. As he reached for a bottle his elbow knocked the platter.

Ted saw the platter fall and wasn't fast enough to catch it. His father was so close. Why hadn't he tried to reach for it?

His father watched the platter, as if this drama unnecessarily interfered with the rye top-up he drizzled into his morning coffee.

"Dad, that's Mom's favourite," Ted said. He gazed at the splinters on the floor, then glared at his father.

Ted picked up every last piece, cutting his finger and thumb on the sharp edges, and placed them in a box. He skipped school, bought some ceramic glue with allowance money he'd been saving and spent the entire day putting the fragments back together.

It was no use.

Ted called his dad at his office. "What are we going to do about Mom's platter? I can't fix it. I've tried, but I can't get the pieces to fit."

"You're calling me about a plate?" his dad asked. "Throw it out." His voice was distant and slurred. "She's got lots of those. Too many, if you ask me."

Why had he bothered?

He'd put the platter in the garbage. When she found it, she asked him what had happened. What was the point of telling her what his dad had done? It would lead to an argument between them. His father would get drunk. He would hit her if she didn't give in. Ted would make another ice pack, console her, tell her again, *Dad didn't mean it.*

No, it was better if she thought he was to blame.

She shook her head, refused to look at or talk to him.

That silence of hers. So many of his memories were of her quiet anger.

Other memories come into focus.

One day, he'd been playing with his train set in the kitchen, making whistle noises and beeping sounds, when he became aware of the surrounding silence. He was alone. It scared him. He was just a little boy.

He searched for her, found her sitting in a corner of the couch, staring out the window at the rust- and yellow-coloured leaves tumbling like snow in a burst of wind.

"Mommy?" he said from the door.

She didn't turn to look at him or acknowledge his voice.

"Mom?"

Nothing.

"Mother!" he screamed.

"What is it, Ted?" she said curtly. "Can't you see I'm trying to think?"

He'd slunk back into the kitchen and eventually she'd found him and wanted to play trains with him, long after he'd gotten bored with them. He played with her anyway — afraid to lose her back to that angry place. How old had he been then? Six? Seven?

It didn't seem to matter to her that he was just a kid and needed her. Silence was her weapon when she was angry with him. It was like torture. And it worked every time. Eventually he would apologize for anything. He didn't care what it was or why she was upset with him. He needed her to talk to him again.

His head was foggy again. The rush of adrenalin that had come with being in this jailhouse office trying to rescue his mother was waning. He needed sleep. Yet these past images were so clear.

He should be thinking about how he was going to find a lawyer for her. Would she need a lawyer? How was he going to figure this shit out in a country where he didn't speak the language and knew nothing about how to make things work in his favour?

He bit his tongue by accident and the pain shot through his face. The blood was bitter. He swallowed. He'd worked the same tasteless piece of gum since he'd arrived at the Athens airport a few hours ago. And this was the third time he'd bitten his tongue. Enough, he thought.

There was no garbage can in the room, just two chairs and a table against the wall opposite where he was standing. He swallowed the gum.

When he was a boy his mother had warned him about doing just that. He shook his head when he recalled the last argument they had over gum.

"It never disintegrates. Never," she'd said. "You won't be able to poop and I'll have to take you to the hospital. You don't want that, do you?"

"That's not true," he had said. He rarely defied her, but she was being silly.

"Okay, don't believe me," she had said. "You'll be singing a different tune when we're at the hospital." She walked out of the kitchen where they'd been standing.

"I swallowed it by accident," he had protested. "I didn't mean to." He followed.

"If you say so," she had said without turning to face him.

Ted rifled through his jacket pocket for another package of gum now, but found nothing. Another pocket. Empty. Since he started this bullshit detox, he never went without gum. Damn it all.

His tongue felt swollen in his mouth. It was no longer his to control. What would he say to her? What was there to say?

He paced the small room, but after a couple of steps crashed into the wooden chairs. Someone passed the room and tilted his head in as if to ask a question, said nothing and carried on down the corridor. Ted clasped the back of the chair and looked at the cross on the wall, remembered his AA sponsor giving him some focus exercises, but for the life of him he couldn't recall the words he was meant to repeat. He tried to concentrate. He closed his eyes. Maybe they'd come to him. Nothing. Sweat trickled down his face, crept down the space between his shoulder blades.

All this shit with Mother plus bloody detox, he thought. No wonder I'm sweating like a pig and these stupid memories won't leave me. I could use a drink.

"Ted." The voice was faint, unsure. He released the chair and turned. His arms dropped. His mother stood before him.

13

REUNION

Why had she been escorted out of her cell? No one had explained what was going on. Or perhaps they had. Who could hear above the ruckus of metal doors scraping against concrete, the endless cries in foreign languages?

The room in front of her was an oversized box. No exit except the door she was about to enter. On the floor, across the entrance to the room was a bump of heavy black tape she would have to step over. If she weren't careful, she'd trip on it. She teetered in the hallway as though she had a choice. She could barely catch her breath. Her brain was as gummy as the black licorice she devoured when she was stressed. Robert used to say her sweet tooth was far worse than the few drinks he liked at the end of a long day. The man never took responsibility for anything.

She saw Ted inside the room, his back to her. For a brief instant, she wondered how she might slip away before he noticed her. Could she go back to her cell and just let whatever was going to happen to her happen? But she knew it was too late for that. She called his name. Her voice came out as a whisper.

Ted turned and they stood staring at one another. She wanted to go to him, tell him how happy she was to see him, how she'd missed him, but her legs felt as heavy as if they were cemented to the grimy floor.

Her son was a handsome man, although right now he looked rumpled and weary. Bristles covered his prematurely bald head. Just like his father. Unlike his father, who resorted to potions to stave off the inevitable, Ted shaved his head. And kept it that way. "What's so important about hair?" Ted had said after that first shave.

She could see a vein throbbing on his right temple. Worry lines tracked between his eyebrows and she could tell he was gnawing at his right cheek from the inside. It was her fault he was standing here, nervous and uncomfortable, far away from his work, his life, anything he understood. She wished she could do better by him. She'd always wanted to, and somehow failed. She sucked in air, along with the fumes of bleach, urine and mould. She gagged, but nothing came up except the smell of her stale breath.

She must go to him, hold him. He had come all this way. Her cheeks burned. Why am I doing this to him? she asked herself. She tried to smile reassuringly, let him know everything was going to be okay. Somehow they would fix this.

"Ted," she called out his name again, gingerly. She hoped he understood she was embarrassed she'd brought him to this place. That's all. She wanted to go to him. She just couldn't seem to make her legs do what she wanted them to do.

He had yet to make a move toward her either. She guessed that, in this strange place, out of their usual context, he was no more sure than she was about what they were supposed to do or how they were supposed to be.

She took another deep breath. Her forehead felt warm, her hands wet. But her mouth was so dry. A sharp pain radiated through her back and her chest. Her breathing became shallow. The aching subsided.

"Mother."

His voice broke through all the noise, seemed to silence all other sound. His arms were open, he was moving toward her. Her Ted was here. He'd help her figure out what to do.

The young officer was beside her. He had brought her down from her cell, said her son had arrived from Canada. His hand now sat at her elbow like a prod. No, not like that. Christos had been kind to her since she'd been in this place. Perhaps he wanted to help her stay upright. Her wobbly legs felt as though they were pooling into the floor beneath her. Soon she'd disappear. Ted was just there. Close enough to touch.

She reached for him and stumbled over that bulging line. He caught her. She felt herself falling into his arms, Christos behind her. A commotion. A chair pulled out. She sat, but still her legs were boggy. "Are you all right, Mother? Mother? Please. What's wrong? What can I do?" Ted demanded answers. His voice boomed. It hurt her ears.

Ted crouched down in front of his mother and tried to peer into her eyes. "Look at me, Mother. Are you okay? What can I get you?" With one hand he held her shoulder back, afraid she'd fall forward if he didn't keep her in place.

"What have you done to my mother?" Ted barked at Christos. He stood, keeping a hand on his mother's shoulder. "I'll call the embassy. I'll tear this place wide open if I have to. You won't get away with treating her like this. No way. I'll get the papers involved. The news outlets. You might be able to get away with this bullshit with others, but I won't let it happen to my mother. We're Canadians." He pointed at Christos; his voice reverberated, out of control. He knew he needed to remain calm, but how in hell could he? This woman was his mother.

Two guards pushed through the door, batons in hand. They shoved Christos out of the way and stood in front of Ted. Eye to eye, so close he smelled the smoky remains of cigarettes on their breath. Firm and steadfast beside his mother, he didn't move. His hand clutched her shoulder. She remained seated in the chair. He'd pull her out of harm's way if any of the guards made a move towards her. He'd like them to try.

Christos jerked at the arms of the two guards. He was a matchstick in comparison to the thick-necked gym rats. They glared at Christos as if he were a piece of shit they'd stepped in. Weak men brawled to get their way, tried to stare you down to puff themselves up.

One guard raised his chin to Christos as if to say, suit yourself, we won't come to your rescue again. The other stared, wolf-like, in anticipation of something he might be able to seize and rip apart.

His hands up in surrender, Christos said to no one in particular, "Okay. Everything is under control. Let us start again. We are all reasonable people here."

As the guards walked out of the room, one pointed his baton at Ted.

"Asshole," Ted said. "Who would you be without that stupid stick?" Yeah, it was a ballsy thing to say, in a foreign country no less, but they might as well know what was what. They weren't going to intimidate him.

The guard turned, baton still in hand.

Christos stepped between them, shook his head. He said something in Greek. That's it. Put him in his place, Ted thought. Still, he reminded himself to keep his wits.

"We have to remain calm," Christos said. He crouched down beside Shelby, his hand on the back of the chair. "Are you okay, Mrs. Holt?"

She was slouched in the chair, her head down. "Water," she whispered.

"I will get some water," Christos said. "Are you okay here with her?"

Ted managed a nod. Humour the guy, he thought. He might be the only sensible one in this crazy place.

"He's getting you some water," Ted said. "Just sit still. Don't try to say anything. We'll figure this thing out and I'll get you released as soon as I can." He stood over her, his hand on her bony shoulder. His grip felt hard even to him. Staring out at the open door into the corridor, he loosened his hold and patted her shoulder.

With his other hand he searched his jacket pocket, then his breast pocket, looking for that goddamn cookie they'd given him on the plane. Where the hell was it? Finding it, he let her go. Ripped open the wrapper and handed it to her. "Take a bite," he said. "Please. Now. It'll help."

"Thank you, Ted," Shelby said. She put her free hand over his, looked up at him with those eyes that always seemed to ask for more than he had to give. He tried to free his hand from hers, but she held on. He was surprised at the strength of her grip.

"Save your energy," Ted said. "I'll work it out. Don't worry about anything right now." He extracted his hand, tucked both in his pockets and began to pace in front of the open door. How the hell was he going to help her this time?

"I'm sorry I brought you here," she said, meeting his eyes.

"Don't worry, Mother. Take a bite of that cookie. It will give you some energy."

"Where's Bo? Where have they taken him? Is he safe?" She tried to stand up.

He put his hand on her shoulder and guided her firmly back onto the chair. "Sit down, Mother. Please."

"He needs to be protected. And here I am, useless. I haven't made one bit of difference. Not for him or his family."

"Take a bite," he said. Where was goddamn Christos with that water? He kept his hand on her shoulder steady, even as his other hand trembled.

"Everything will be fine," she said and nodded.

Was that a sarcastic comment, he wondered, or was she telling him she didn't believe what she was saying?

He looked down at her. One hand was open in her lap like one of the street beggars he'd see in Vancouver. She nibbled at the cookie in her other hand. The way she's holding it, he thought, it'll drop to the floor and that will be that.

He wished he could take her away from this place. He wanted to do that for her. There was no question. Keeping her safe was all he'd ever wanted to do for her. But he couldn't do it before, so why the hell did he think he could do it now? All he could do was try. He was nothing if not her good boy.

Christos arrived with a paper cup of water. Ted took it from him and crouched in front of his mother, raising the cup to her lips. She tried to take it from him, but he continued to hold it. She gulped the water too quickly, coughed and dribbled a bit on her chin.

"Sip slowly, Mother, slowly."

"Has she seen a doctor since she's been here?" Ted turned towards Christos.

"No," Christos said. "But I don't believe she has eaten either. This could be the problem."

Christos didn't hold Ted's gaze. He wondered if Christos was ashamed of what they'd done to his mother. Well, he should be, Ted thought. She was their responsibility.

"You mean to tell me you don't feed your prisoners?" Ted asked. "What kind of place are you running here? Can we get her something?"

"I haven't been hungry, Ted," Shelby said. She placed her hand on his shoulder. "I didn't want any of it. Don't blame Christos. He's tried."

Ted turned to face her. "When did you last eat?"

"I don't remember." Shelby sipped her water, took a bigger bite of the cookie.

Finally, he thought. A little colour was coming back to her cheeks. "I can go out and get you something."

"I'm better now. This is what I needed." She squeezed his arm.

Ted pulled away. He didn't mean to. He got this way when he focused on problem solving. "Can you excuse us," he said, "so I can talk to my mother?"

"I will be right outside the door," Christos said. "If you need anything."

Christos left the door slightly ajar and paced in the hallway. He wasn't supposed to leave them alone, but where were they going to go? The woman, Mrs. Holt, didn't have the energy to walk, let alone run. And there were so many officers and guards inside and out, they wouldn't get far if they tried. Yes, there had been escapes in the past, but there hadn't been one since he started here, so he wasn't sure if the escapes were real or just what some of the officers liked to talk about to pass the time.

An officer ambled past him, on his way back to the front desk. Christos nodded in the direction of the room where Mrs. Holt and her son sat. "Her son is in there. Convincing her to tell us what she knows." Christos spoke precisely, tried to keep the eagerness and anxiety out of his voice. "Yes, I know I'm supposed to be in there with them. Tell me something I don't know. But what can I do? She refuses to tell us anything." The other officer gave him a strange look and kept walking.

Chris needed to remain calm. He told himself he didn't have to explain what he was doing. He didn't believe that.

If Kefalas saw him out in the corridor, Christos would say it was a good thing Mrs. Holt's son was here. The son was their best chance at figuring out what had happened. But when had logic played well in this place? Christos moved closer to the door, stood to one side, out of sight of Mrs. Holt and her son. He shook his head, then stood back.

Christos hoped Mrs. Holt's son could convince her to tell them what had happened and help them find the boy's mother, reunite the family. Then Mrs. Holt and Kem could be set free. That was how he'd like this case to be solved.

If the Roma was to blame for this, though, he would be detained for God only knew how long. Christos disapproved of the mass incarceration and subsequent deportations of illegal foreigners his country had started. It was shameful to treat people this way. All they wanted was a better life. Greeks, more than anyone, should understand this. They'd migrated and escaped to other countries since before the civil war.

He stared at the tape at the bottom of the doorway. When he realized what it was, he lunged towards the room. He needed to warn them they were being monitored.

Just as quickly, he stopped short of entering, nodded to Mrs. Holt, and backed away. There was no money to man the equipment. He'd thought these wires had all been pulled out. But they'd been left there because there was no money to remove them.

Christos leaned closer to the door. At the very least, he should be listening in. A good officer would. Their silence and whispers worried him. Hadn't he learned something about this in his training? Officers were supposed to be especially careful with the quiet ones.

It didn't seem right though. He moved away from the door.

He kneaded the knot at the back of his neck, but there was no releasing the cluster of muscles. As he listened to the whispered reunion of Mrs. Shelby and her son, he found himself thinking about his own parents. He didn't have a name or an image or even a sense of who his father was. He rarely thought about him or the mother who had left him at the orphanage. But for some reason, he wondered about them more now. Who were they? Where were they? What had happened to them? He remembered one of the nuns holding him when he was a boy. The scent of talcum powder on her habit and cornette made him feel close and comforted. Had his mother smelled the same way?

It had only been a few days since he'd met the Roma man, but he found himself thinking about him all the time. Had his father been like Kem? He would never know.

He wasn't sure why, but Christos felt a pang of guilt whenever he thought of Kem. The man was no more than a child, a child who found himself in a lie. He was in a hopeless situation. Where was his wife, his family? Stop feeling sorry for everyone you encounter here, Christos told himself. Some people are simply bad. It was true and he knew it. He'd met more than a few of those people in this place.

Commander Kefalas had said Kem would sell his own child for a few euros. "Where do you think he got those new shoes?" Kefalas had said. "That's the price you get for a child. You can't help but feel pity and rage. What's the point? They are all the same. They will never change. I've arrested these people for stealing, for selling drugs, for beating each other. And what makes me angry is not one damn thing I've done has made any of this better. In fact, it's only gotten worse." Kefalas slammed his hand on the desk. His penknife had jiggled and fallen to the floor.

Christos and most other Greek men had a *komboló̱i,* a string of worry beads, they flipped between their fingers to deal with stress. The commander had to be different. He didn't use worry beads. Instead, he liked to click his penknife open and then closed. The sound put Christos on edge, as did the commander's brooding stare. "I keep taking these people off the street. Nothing we do makes one bit of difference. I tell you this because what we do is a madman's job. We make an effort, try to help, but nothing changes. And nothing will change in our lifetime. Yours or mine. So get used to it."

Christos didn't feel any anger. Or at least he didn't think he did. He hadn't been around long enough in this job or dealt with refugees year in and year out. He was curious about these people, their lives. That was all. And he wanted to help too.

Whenever he asked questions about the background of some of the people they'd arrested, the other officers laughed at him. "What does it matter?"

"I'm interested, that's all."

He walked past the room. Mrs. Holt was taking a sip of water. Her son paced. "Everything okay?" he asked.

Mrs. Holt nodded. "Yes. Fine."

The son remained silent, his hands in his pockets. His jaw was set tight, that vein in his head pulsed.

"Take your time," Christos said. "I'm here if you need anything."

"Okay, do you want to tell me what happened?" Ted said. He stood over her again, then thought better of it and kneeled down beside her.

"I don't know what to tell you." She'd finished the cookie and drunk the water Christos had brought her. She stuffed the wrapper into the paper cup, pressed down on it over and over again. The crinkling sound annoyed him. Was that why she was doing it? She must have realized he was staring because she put the cup on the table and folded her hands into her lap. She appeared calm, as though she didn't remember what had happened or why anyone would make such a fuss.

He put his hands over hers and looked directly into her eyes. They seemed clearer, less confused. He was sure she knew where she was, why he was here.

"Well, how about you tell me how this boy ended up in your apartment?" Ted said. "Were you trying to provide shelter for him? Just for a little while? If I know you and your big heart, that's exactly what you were doing." He was trying not to get ahead of himself, but perhaps she needed some coaxing. "You were going to take him back to his parents, right? I mean, after you fed him and bought him some clothes and maybe took him to a doctor or something. That's how it was going to be. Right? Except he just wouldn't settle down. So someone called the police. And that's how you were arrested." She could be so naïve, he thought. She thought she could save the world one child at a time.

"He was frightened," Shelby said. She held his gaze, tears glistening in her eyes.

Ted focused on her face and waited. At least she was talking. The water and the cookie had helped.

Without meaning to, he gnawed at the inside of his cheek. The pain made him wince.

She put her hand against his cheek. "Your poor cheek," she said.

"This isn't about me, Mother." He didn't pull away, but her hand dropped to her lap on its own anyway.

"Bo missed his mother. I couldn't make him understand he was going to be okay. Everything would work out. He refused to eat. Refused everything I tried to give him. I thought he'd cry himself to sleep."

"So you didn't kidnap him or buy him or anything? You said on the phone they accused you of some such thing. But I knew it had to be a misunderstanding. We should be able to clear this up in no time. Explain to the cops what happened and they'll understand it was an honest mistake. In fact, they probably overreacted. We could make this point too. Put them in their place."

"But they have Kem," she said. "They'll blame him for all of this. They'll hold him without a trial. Just because they can. This is my fault."

"Who is Kem?" His raw tongue stung every time he spoke or swallowed. "I'm getting confused."

Shelby shook her head. With her eyes she pointed to the black tape on the floor, then the mirrored window.

"What?"

"It's not a good place to discuss this," she said. "I've probably already said too much. Who knows what these people will do?"

He threw up his arms. "This isn't the movies, Mother."

"They would jump on any bit of information if it meant getting rid of the Roma in this country. They are despised. Treated like vermin."

"You don't know that."

She leaned forward and whispered. "Kem is Bo's father. I know these officers would like nothing better than to have me implicate him. I won't give them anything. Kem deserves better. I'm not going to give him up just to save my own skin."

"How about we help you first? Then we'll help this guy and the kid after."

She rolled her eyes, as if he were nothing more than a naïve boy. "Who stands a better chance with the law here, Ted? A middle-aged white Canadian woman with an embassy behind her or a Roma man with no country willing to accept him? Answer me that."

"I want to get you out of here. You're my priority right now. That's it."

"He's not a Greek Roma either," Shelby whispered. "He's from the Ukraine, a non-European country, which is licence enough for these thugs to get rid of him. I won't let that happen." She looked at the cup and shook her head. "I've said far too much."

"Can we deal with one problem at a time? Please?"

"How is Bo? Do you know where he is? Where they're keeping him?"

Who the hell cares? Ted thought. He wanted her to concentrate on her predicament right now, not on the boy. Why couldn't she understand that? He stood up, his knees aching and creaking in protest. What was he? An old man? He palmed his forehead. Damp.

She reached out to him, laced her fingers through his. "I want to make sure the boy is okay. That nothing has happened to him. It's important."

"You mean nothing more has happened to him than being uprooted from his home." He walked away, propped himself against the blacked out glass.

Shelby shook her head. "These people live in such desperate circumstances, Ted. He's a small boy. Only six or seven. His future is ahead of him. He could do better."

"But you told me yourself kids want to be with their parents."

"Yes, but that isn't always the right thing for them," Shelby said. "Is it?" She looked at Ted as if to challenge him to argue with her. How would he know? It wasn't as though this was his line of work.

He squeezed his eyes shut. A bright pain ignited behind them.

"I have to fix this," she said. "Somehow I have to."

He moved towards her. "With you free, we can figure out our next move, find a way to help this kid or reunite him with his family. We can't do anything while you're in here. I don't know my way around this country. Only you do." If he could get her out of here, maybe he could talk her into going home, leaving this mess behind. The police would take matters from here. She'd done enough. "What do you think? Makes sense, doesn't it?"

Her shoulders trembled. "He's such a frail child, bent and weak. I wanted to help get him in a school, deal with that awful, awful cough he has. That's all."

"Well, unless you tell me what happened, I don't know what we can do."

She reached for his hand. "Help me free Kem. We'll reunite the family."

"What do we know about this guy? And how am I supposed to help him?" He turned his back to her, faced the blackened-out window again. "No, I think a better way to go is we help you first, then we figure out what to do about this character and his son. That's the deal." He slapped the window, but his mother didn't look up.

"Christos, are you there?" Shelby called.

Christos stepped into the room. "Yes, Mrs. Holt?"

"Take me back to my cell. I'm not going anywhere."

14

A Good Woman

"What?" Ted said.

Shelby stood. Might as well show them all she meant business. Steadying herself against the desk, she closed her eyes, shut out Ted and Christos. The walls disappeared. The mournful cries and decaying stink of this horrible place faded. For an instant, she was back in her own apartment, looking out her bedroom window. She watched the old men in the park across from her building, many with canes in hand. One in particular was impeccably dressed in a well-pressed suit, a starched white shirt and red bow tie. His white hair was thick and wavy and he was clean-shaven with delicate lines around his mouth. He walked more briskly than the others, though he had a slight limp. No cane. He stopped, looked up at her as though he knew she'd been watching him. He smiled.

Things always work out, he seemed to say. She knew that. The old man understood her better than her own son did.

Behind her closed lids, she could still see Ted's angry stare and Christos's forlorn expression. If they weren't prepared to help, she'd go it alone. They had no idea what she could do.

She opened her eyes. Bursts of light distorted her vision as though a camera flash had exploded too close to her eyes. The room seemed darker than when she first entered.

Although her brain was still a little fuzzy and confused, she hoped they couldn't tell. She was determined not to let them see any weakness.

Straighten up. She wasn't sure she'd pushed her shoulders back. Stop slouching. Not finding the energy to move, she took another breath. Then another. Her hands, the one on the desk, and the other one on the back of the chair, trembled ever so slightly. She felt it, but she hoped they couldn't see it. She had to be strong for Bo, Kem, their family.

Her son paced. Christos stood still, his hands behind his back.

The flickers stopped, the dizziness receded. The light in the room was dull, but she could see just fine now. She had needed to take a few breaths. That was all. Fixing her gaze on the blue eye and crucifix in the corner, she ignored the men.

"You want to stay here? I don't think I understand," Ted said, his voice not urgent and angry as before, but soft. He stopped pacing. She faced him. He jammed his hands into his pockets. His jaw tightened.

His eyes had become dark and withdrawn. His jaw stiffened and released, a mass of simmering waves rippled across his face. Another hint. He was containing something.

"I'm not going without Kem," Shelby said. "Period." She shrugged, and realized this simple movement only diminished her ultimatum. No matter. They couldn't make her leave if she didn't want to.

"But Mrs. Holt, we could solve this situation very quickly. There is no need for you to be here," Christos said. He stood fixed, but his hands were outstretched towards her. Almost like a little boy shyly asking for a favour. "This is not a place for a woman."

She turned to him. "This is no place for anyone." He wanted an easy solution, but she wasn't going to give it to him. "If I go free, so does Kem. We leave together. If he stays, I stay."

Christos rubbed his forehead. "If you tell us what happened, perhaps we can find a way."

She wanted to believe him. He had one of those faces, open for everyone to see what he was thinking. His oversized, baggy uniform hung from his shoulders and made him look as though he was in need of reassurance. But there was the gun on his hip, the nightstick and radio on the other hip, Shelby reminded herself. He was a jailer. "You want to persecute him like all the other illegals behind these walls. I am not going to help."

"This is not true, Mrs. Holt. We want to get to the truth and find Bo's family so everyone can go home."

At the mention of Bo, her grip on the chair loosened. Am I doing the right thing by the boy? she wondered as she stared at Christos. She had an urge to lunge at him, grab him by that oversized uniform of his and force him to tell her where Bo was. She remained still, breathed slowly to calm the quiver in her voice. "Where have you taken him? He needs to be looked after. He's just a boy. Don't you understand?"

"He is being well cared for," Christos said. "Please calm yourself, Mrs. Holt. Why don't we sit and discuss this reasonably? Find our way to a solution." Christos motioned toward the chair, but she didn't sit down.

Ted took the chair, positioned it between Christos and Shelby and sat down. "Mother, please sit. We can't get to the bottom of this without you." His hands pressed down on the edges of the chair as though he would jump out of it at any minute.

"Stop patronizing me, Ted."

"Mother, I'm trying to help here." Ted's voice was beseeching. "That's all."

"You keep saying that. And maybe I believe you, maybe I don't." She felt bad for being so harsh with him, but he didn't understand this situation one bit. "Ted, you don't know these people. Okay?' She pointed to Christos. "They persecute the *xénos,* as they call them. Strangers. That's what they call the Roma and others who are different from them. I can't let that happen. This is my fault and I have to fix it."

"How is it your fault? You tried to help this kid and his family. We tell that to a judge. You go free. Isn't that the case, officer?" Ted said to Christos. They glanced at each other. Ted smiled at Christos for the first time and nodded.

Her son had ganged up with the enemy, she thought.

"Yes, basically," Christos said to Ted, ignoring her. "We believe that the Roma man either gave or sold his child to you. But we want to understand what happened. How did this child end up in your custody? If we answer this question first, it might help us figure out our next steps. No one has been charged with a criminal offence yet. If we can resolve this the right way, no one will be charged and we all go our separate ways."

"She took him home to give him a good meal. That's all. This woman," he pointed at Shelby, "has worked her whole life to protect children."

"The Roma man says she stole him." Christos turned to look at her to see how she'd react to this piece of information.

"That's not true." She pointed at Christos. "If he said that, you must have coerced him into saying it. I don't believe you. Kem wouldn't." But desperate people did desperate things. She'd always said that. And it was true. Who could blame Kem if he blamed her? If she were in his position, she'd probably do the same thing to save herself.

Ted stood and put his arm around her. "She wouldn't do a thing to hurt a child, or a family, for that matter. She wouldn't."

Somewhere down the hall a door clanged open. Then slammed shut. Something heavy dropped. Shelby jumped. Ted's arm fell by his side. The sound of a smack, flesh being struck. A yelp. Heavy steps.

Two men dragged a third past the room. Shelby moved towards the doorway. Christos flipped out his nightstick, held it in front of her. She had known his true colours would eventually show.

Shackles around his ankles, handcuffs at his wrists, the man lunged forward towards the room. He stumbled and fell at Shelby's feet.

Ted pulled her out of the way, backed her into one corner of the room. She elbowed him, but he stood firm, like a wall she couldn't get around.

"I didn't do anything," the man shouted in English. "Please help me." His handcuffed hands came forward, resolute.

She ducked under Ted's arms, and sidestepped Christos's nightstick. "Kem."

Before she could kneel down, Ted grabbed her, put himself between Kem and Shelby. "What are you doing?" She pushed Ted away. She needed to confront these bullies now, get this thing settled. "He's done nothing wrong. It's my fault. Not his."

"Listen to Mrs. Shelby," Kem said. "She's telling the truth."

Christos held Ted and Shelby back with his nightstick. They stood to one side of the room. The two guards pulled Kem away, out of the room and down the hallway. Another door slammed at the end of the corridor.

"The way you people deal with your prisoners," she said. "You are no better than criminals." She rubbed her temples.

"I don't know what has happened, Mrs. Holt," Christos said. He holstered his nightstick. "I will find out about this."

She shook her head. "I want to talk to him." She refused to take her eyes from him.

"You could tell us what happened," Christos said. "That would help us all."

"Now." If she could talk to Kem, she felt sure they could come up with a story that would satisfy these guys.

She felt Ted's hand on her shoulder. "Look, officer, perhaps seeing the man, talking to him, might resolve this mess. What do you think? I'm sure you could make this happen, officer."

The two men gazed at each other.

Because of her, that family was separated. She knew this. Father beaten and in jail; son, God knows where. She'd set out to help, to do a bit extra for them, for Bo, the perpetually snotty-nosed, barefoot kid with a bad cough, and no hope for a future. A little money for Kem to buy the family some wood for their fire, some extra clothes for the cold nights. Some better food. That's all she wanted to do. Give Bo a chance.

"Then what?" Christos said. "If Mrs. Holt can't help us, we have no other choice but to keep the Roma man in custody until we get to the bottom of this." Christos said. He averted his eyes, put his hand on his holster.

She squeezed her eyes shut. She couldn't be angry with Christos. He'd been good to her. She caught herself. What made him any different than the rest of them? Nothing.

"I'm sorry. I can't help you." She wasn't going to admit that she was fuzzy about the details and who said what. And it was none of their business anyway. What she had done had nothing to do with the police.

Ted stood in front of her. "Can you just help them understand what happened?" He nudged her chin with his finger, forcing her to look at him. His eyes were as bewildered as they were those times when he was a child, kneeling in front of her. He didn't say a word then, but she knew he wanted to ask how his father could get so angry he'd bruise her face. She would glance at him through a swollen eye, unable to find a reasonable explanation, the words he might understand.

"Maybe the organization she works for can help, officer," Ted said. "I could contact them, see what they suggest."

"I'm in this alone, Ted," she said. "There's no one else." And before he could protest, she said, "Get my keys. Go to my apartment. Rest. My car is parked right in front of the building. The keys are on my keychain. Use it to come back. The officers have all my things. I'm sure Christos can get my keys for you. I will write down the address."

He ran his hand over his head. He turned to Christos. "How about I put up bail or something? I have cash with me. I'll sign whatever it is you need and will ensure she gets back here once she's rested."

"These things are not up to me," Christos said. "I'm sorry."

"Soon," she said to Ted to try to comfort him. "If we're lucky." Shelby knew it was not the answer he wanted, but it was the best she could do. He would have to go along. This thought made her realize how often she'd said this to herself. Every time they'd separated at an airport. Every time he'd gone to boarding school and she'd been off to some part of Africa where fragile peace had been restored or where a humanitarian crisis was brewing. She'd expected him to adjust to her schedule.

Christos led her back to her cell. "It doesn't have to be this way," Christos said. "You understand that, Mrs. Holt? Yes?"

She faced him. "There is never another way for people like Kem and his son. You know it and I know it."

He closed the cell door gently; still the clang gave her a start. She put her hand over her ears. The ringing continued to vibrate in her ears.

Christos wanted her to spill the beans so he could get Kem thrown out of his country. These guys played by their own rules. That was a fact. Bo and his family were her only priorities now.

She wouldn't fall for any of Christos's acts of kindness. That was all it was. An act.

A few minutes later Christos pushed a bag through the bars. "Please eat something, Mrs. Holt. You will need your strength."

"Thank you, Christos." She held the brown paper bag tentatively, as she would fruit or vegetables at the Saturday market, assessing whether the price was worth it.

"Mrs. Holt, you are a good woman who has helped these people. I understand this. But you have to see my position too." He shrugged and again his uniform puffed around him as though blowing on a clothesline. "I have to find a solution for the boy and his family."

"Where is he?" She moved closer to the cell door. The lines of metal bars severed Christos's face. Shelby couldn't take his face or its expressions in all at once.

"A safe place," Christos said. "He is only a small boy. I would not let anything happen to him. I give you my word."

"Thank you."

As he turned to leave, she asked, "And is my son all right?"

"I have given him your personal possessions, Mrs. Holt," Christos said. "He has gone to get some rest. But he will be back. He told me so."

"Of course he will," she said. "He's determined."

She sat down wearily on the cot in her cell. Her stomach growled and she looked down at the package on her lap. Christos was right. She would need her strength to fight for Bo and Kem. The cookie and water had helped, but it wasn't enough. Not for the fight she was about to take on.

She opened the bag and as she unwrapped the package, the aroma of spinach and cheese reached her. *Spanakópita*. She felt light-headed and unsure.

Looking around her cell as if someone might be watching, she took a tentative bite. The pastry melted in her mouth along with the spinach. She barely chewed. No need. She took another bite and another until all that was left was the oil on her fingers. She licked them.

Then she took the apple from the bag. Its crunchy sweetness made her mouth water. As she chewed, she pondered what Ted had said to Christos earlier. He was so adamant. *My mother would not do such a thing.* He believed in her, but she didn't deserve it.

She stopped mid-bite. Slowly, it came back to her.

"You see how small he is," Kem had said.

"Yes."

"The things you bring for him have helped so much," Kem said.

Shelby could hear the implication, the *but* in his voice. She could do more.

"He should be in school," she said. "He's a smart boy."

"Yes, but he must help the family."

In her hand a rolled-up fifty-euro note. That was the first time. Two months ago.

In so many conversations with Kem, in so many of the things she'd brought for Bo, in the money she'd given Kem, she had worked her way into that family. He'd said the boy needed a better life. "I can help him," she'd said, proud she could do something. Money could solve many problems. "I'll put him in school, make sure he gets an education." God, *had* she agreed to buy the boy? No, she just wanted to get the ball rolling. Get Bo healthy first. Then help with his education by providing the family with a little money to guarantee they kept him in school. Bo wouldn't have to go out every day and beg on the streets.

She'd take him for a few days to start with. Take care of that cough with medicine and a warm place to sleep. Some clean clothes.

Kem only wanted a good life for Bo. Wouldn't any father want the same thing?

She had known Bo was going to go with her that morning she went to the camp. And she knew the plan was for her to just give him a start, some opportunities Kem and Mirela could never hope to give him. It wasn't meant to be forever. And yet, how could it not be? How could he come live with her and then go back to that desperate place? She pictured his tiny shoeless feet, cold, dirty. That cough. The heaps of garbage, raw sewage, and smoke he lived among would never help rid him of that cough. Nor would the reality of the camp: no running water, no electricity, no heat.

She could help.

But what if she left Greece? Bo would be back to the same hopeless future. She had wanted more for him. He spoke English and Greek. He was such a bright boy, just like Ted in so many ways when he was a child.

It was a misunderstanding. That was all.

If she told the police everything that happened, she would probably get a slap on the wrist. Kem, however, would be convicted, and then deported. She pictured his bloodied face, the shackles at his ankles. How could she have thought she could give Bo a better life? Or that any kid, no matter how awful his situation, would want to leave his parents? She knew better. She was getting stupider with age.

She finished the apple and tossed the core into the garbage bin. She should rest. When Christos came back on shift, she would tell him everything. She imagined herself sitting in that room Christos had taken her to before. She would look right at that mirrored window and confess that she had kidnapped Bo from his parents. Lured him away with candy. Why? They probably wouldn't ask, but if they did, she'd tell them she was trying to help and got carried away. That was true.

She would insist either she or Ted see Kem released from custody. She visualized the police bringing Bo to Kem, the two of them walking away from this awful place, Bo's tiny hand in his father's.

She would make things right.

15

SURVEILLANCE

Amaroúsio Police Station

Christos knocked on the door to Commander Kefalas's office. He could see the commander inside sitting at his desk, but Kefalas made no attempt to acknowledge him. Christos took a deep breath and walked in. He had to know where and why they'd moved Kem. "Sir?"

Standing at attention in front of Kefalas's desk, Christos stared straight ahead. His hat was squashed tight under one arm, and his hands were gripped together behind his back. At least the commander hadn't thrown him out.

"So, Mr. Engineer." The commander looked up from his papers. "You didn't get any new information from our Canadian guest."

The commander had obviously come to his own conclusions about Christos's attempts to talk to Mrs. Holt. Christos wondered if he should say something or simply wait to hear what Kefalas had to say. Would the commander give him an opportunity to make his case, explain how he wanted to move slowly to get the information they needed? Kefalas had been a policeman his entire career. He probably made quick judgments, saw beyond lies.

Like the titan Cronus who consumed his children as they were born, the commander spread out in his chair, ready to devour anything put in front of him. His elbows grazed the top of the desk. He pushed the papers away, opened up a small space in front of him and dropped a napkin. His penknife in hand, he peeled an orange. Slivers of rind fell, one after another. The knife glistened with juice.

Michelas stood behind Kefalas, staring at something on the floor, his hands at his sides. Christos wondered if he was bored. Maybe if he could stand that still and disinterested, the commander would like him too.

"It is a slow process," Christos said, the words rushing out of his mouth.

"She had you in the palm of her hand," Kefalas said. "And squeezed. Women are this way. They shed a few tears and men fall, as weak buildings in an earthquake." He stared at Christos with those intimidating, empty dark eyes.

You do not know that, Christos thought. You're bluffing. I have seen you do this before to inmates and officers. It is not going to work on me. "We have to get her confidence," Christos said and moved closer to the desk. "Then you will see. She will tell us everything. We need to be patient." If Kefalas gave him the benefit of the doubt, trusted him this one time, Christos knew he would prove himself.

"She knows what she is doing. She is a sly one. No different than any of the other Americans we have dealt with in this place. They think they are smarter than us. They get themselves into trouble; pretend it was not their fault. Cry to their embassies to bail them out. I ask you, whose fault is it? Is it my fault they don't know how to behave, show any sort of self-restraint?" He put the orange on the desk, wiped his hands on the corner of the napkin. "They tell us we are too tough on them. We don't treat them well. We are backwards." He raised his hand toward Christos, as he himself might have done with a former colleague or client when he worked at OTE, to garner agreement, support. "They tell their embassies lies. As if their countries are any better. Those human rights groups should investigate American jails, like that place in Cuba where they hold those poor bastards year in and year out. No, others have no right to criticize."

"Excuse me, sir," Christos said, "but I do not think the woman is trying to deceive us. She is trying to protect the Roma man and his child. She didn't intend anything malicious. I'm sure of this. From what I can see and what she has told us so far, it seems to be a misunderstanding. I'm not sure the Roma is to blame either."

"Someone must be." Kefalas pointed his penknife at Christos.

Christos wanted to protest, but said nothing. Speak when there is a chance to be heard. He had told himself the same thing when he refused to join his colleagues at OTE in protest after they had all lost their jobs. Protest was useless then and it would be useless now with the commander.

"But she didn't tell you anything." Commander Kefalas wiped the knife against the napkin. He snapped the penknife closed. The sound startled Christos even though he should have been used to it. He blinked, his heartbeat quickened, but he remained still.

"She told me a little," he said quietly then cleared his throat. "A little is a start."

"Nothing at all from what I could see."

"You weren't there," Christos said, but his chest tightened. Could Kefalas have been watching him? Could Michelas have said something? Christos had seen Michelas in the corridor of the cellblock when he spoke with the Roma man the other day. As the commander's assistant and bodyguard, Michelas had a lot to lose by helping Christos. But he'd promised not to say anything and Christos knew Michelas would be good to his word. Who, then? The walls didn't have eyes.

"You would drown in a spoon of water if we did not take care of you. She had you wrapped around her finger. Am I right, Michelas? Or not?" Kefalas stared at Christos, grinned.

Michelas raised his eyes from whatever was preoccupying him on the carpet. "Yes," he said, as though he'd been caught doing something he was not supposed to be doing. "She didn't give us very much in the interview. And she did look as if she was controlling the situation." He glanced at Christos. Their eyes met briefly. Michelas turned away. Christos understood the man's predicament.

"How would you know?" Christos said. He took a step toward Kefalas. The commander stood, propped himself against the desk like a bulldog on his hind legs, eyes baggy and piercing. He slammed his penknife on the desk. Christos took a step backward.

"This is police work," the commander said. "It is my job to know. Are you so naïve?" He picked up the knife again and clicked it open and closed. Smiled. "Would you like to listen to the recording?"

Christos thought back to the black tape at the door of the room where Mrs. Holt and her son had spoken. The blackened window. Not possible, he thought to himself. They were always being told there was no money. They had to do their job with less.

"We have state-of-the-art monitoring equipment. I will not allow it to sit collecting dust. And I will not allow criminals to make fools of us. I find the money. There are many generous families who don't want to see criminals on our streets. They support the work we do. Simple. It's my job to keep things simple. And of course, there are the fines we collect from minor infractions or from foreigners who overstay their welcome."

"But we are obliged to tell her when we are recording her!" Christos said. It's only right, he thought. And what about me?

You should have told me. For the hundredth time since he started working here, he questioned his decision to take this job. How could he work in a place that made up its own rules? Why had he allowed himself to enter this hell?

His family. An image of Tia and his children, his mother-in-law last Sunday at the park crossed his mind. He was the breadwinner and couldn't let them down.

He straightened his shoulders, put his hands behind his back again, spread his legs and stared straight ahead. "And why was the Roma man brought in?"

Commander Kefalas closed his penknife, slid it into his pocket and walked to the front of the desk. "I will tell you this again because you are new to this work and your head is made for other things. People who end up with us are not to be trusted. Once in a while we make a mistake and arrest the wrong person. It happens. But this is not the case here. Believe me. Everyone is to blame for this mess with the boy." He gripped Christos's shoulder. The smell of the orange couldn't mask the persistent sourness of Kefalas's breath. As with other times the commander had been this close to him, Christos wanted to turn away, but he couldn't.

"You will see. There are no innocent people, innocent intentions, innocence, period, in our work." He slapped Christos's back. "And in answer to your question, the gypsy was due his time in the courtyard, some fresh air. We follow rules."

The commander's spittle flew from his mouth as he spoke.

Christos remained motionless.

"You can thank me for helping you with your case when this mess is resolved. That will be sooner rather than later if I have my way," Kefalas said. "Perhaps I will have a chat with him myself. That should get matters cleared up."

Bastard, Christos thought. There was no way the commander would trouble himself to question someone like Kem. He would leave that to others in much lower positions. And taking Kem out that way to the courtyard didn't make sense either. There was a direct door to the back courtyard. Did the commander think he was a fool? Kefalas had probably wanted to send some sort of message to Mrs. Holt or see how she would react when she saw the Roma man. Stupid games.

"They were recording the whole time," Christos said to Tia.

They were sitting at the kitchen table. The light overhead dimmed, and brightened, as if someone was toying with the wiring. Footsteps tramped back and forth in the apartment upstairs. Taps and toilets grunted as people in other apartments woke to the day.

The children, including the boy, were still in bed. Christos's coffee was cold. Tia had often scolded him for having coffee at the end of his shift, just before bed. But coffee didn't affect his sleep. Once the family was out of the house — Tia to work, the boys to school, Alexandra and the boy to the park with Yiayiá — he would get some sleep. His night shifts sapped him of energy. As if he didn't have enough with trying to solve the problem about the boy, Mrs. Holt and the Roma man, he also had to watch his every move. The walls did have eyes and ears, and there were many who would like to see him quit or be fired. That would provide an opening for an unemployed relative, a chance for someone else. Who could blame them? It was important to help your own if you could. He'd never felt he had to be on his guard in a job before. It exhausted him to the point that when he put his head down, he was asleep before he knew what had happened. Then the nightmares would jar him awake, so unsettling he was afraid to fall asleep again.

"They didn't even tell me." He rubbed his worry beads.

"We live in a police state," Tia said. "They are the only ones who have power now. The rest of us have nothing." Her hands were clenched around her cup. He put a hand on hers and her grip softened.

"He had guards bring the Roma man down the same hallway where I was with Mrs. Holt and her son. It was a show of some kind. But for what purpose, I don't know. It shook Mrs. Holt, made her quiet. I may have been able to convince her to tell us what had happened. Now, who knows? I doubt she trusts me anymore.

"Kefalas says they are all guilty. He speaks to me as though I am an imbecile." He closed his eyes, remembered again the commander's words. *You will see. There are no innocent people.* The nuns in the orphanage used to say the same thing whenever he gave one of the other boys his toy cars to play with and they were later lost or taken from him. "Those boys will answer to God, Christos, but you also have to learn not everyone is worthy of your trust," the nuns had said. "You will see."

"Who do you believe?" Tia asked. She brought her cup to her mouth.

"I want to believe both of them," Christos said. "It's so hard to know. Something happened. I understand this. But who is to blame? Why it happened, I don't know. There has to be something more than what is on the surface. But without Mrs. Holt's cooperation, I don't think we will ever know." His eyes were irritated and dry. He put his worry beads down, pressed the bridge of his nose with his thumb and index finger. Rubbed his eyes.

"Someone must be lying," Tia said. She put down her coffee cup, took his hand. "Don't you think?" She kissed the inside of his wrist. "Or perhaps they were in this together. Maybe they made some sort of deal and it backfired when the child began crying and making a fuss. It's only then the police got called. Otherwise how would you have discovered the boy?"

"We first got involved because the Roma man came to us with a story about his son being kidnapped. It was hard for anyone to believe, because who would steal a Roma child? The same night, my unit answered a complaint about a child in distress. For once we talked to each other and put two and two together. And that is how we arrived at where we are now."

"Why would the Roma man come to the police?" Tia asked. "If he was guilty, why would he come to a place he knows is dangerous for him?"

Christos picked up his worry beads again and began to run them over his fingers. "Maybe he felt guilty about something." Christos said. "Not watching him closely enough. They send their children to beg for money, sing or play the accordion on the street. Maybe Mrs. Holt stole the child and Kem knew it was his fault for not watching over him more carefully. And the boy's mother blamed him, told him he had to find the child. Kem said his wife hadn't given him any rest since the boy disappeared. Whatever we believe about the Roma, family is important to them. They are not so different from us."

Tia shrugged. "It's possible."

"But Mrs. Holt has worked with children and in camps like this for a very long time and according to her son, she is not someone who would do anything to harm a child. She has only worked to help them. That is what he said. And I believe him. If you saw her, Tia, you would not think this woman could do such a thing." He stopped the beads, choked them in his fist. "I don't know what to think about all of this."

"And her son?" She rolled her eyes.

"The son wants her released. He says we cannot keep her in custody if she hasn't been charged with a crime."

Tia nodded, as if affirming the obvious. She was forever the university professor.

"He seems like someone used to getting his own way. He's very demanding."

"You would be too if it was your mother."

Christos bowed his head.

"I'm sorry," Tia said. She reached for his hand.

He stood up, put his worry beads in his pocket, picked up his cup and walked to the sink. Even after it was rinsed out, the bottom of the cup remained discoloured. He left it on the counter upside down to dry.

"I didn't mean it that way," Tia said.

"I know," Christos said. He turned to face her. "There is something wrong with this whole mess. And I don't know what it is."

"The boy is settling," Tia said. "He slept through the night, the first time in four days. I didn't have to check on him once. He's getting used to us, I think. He likes Yiayiá. He sits with her while Alexandra plays around him or the boys get ready for school. Yiayiá is getting close to him too. I found her helping him practise his reading yesterday. He is a very clever boy. And she says God will smile on us because we are helping him, but I know the boy has already found a place in her heart."

"Thank God he has calmed down," Christos said. "At least he won't be badly damaged by this experience when he returns to his family."

"The damage has already been done."

Practical and blunt, that was Tia, Christos thought.

They would find the boy's mother. They would return him. He would go back to his life, to a father who was barely more than a child himself. And likely the mother wasn't much older either. And yes, the situation in the camp was not the best, but this was the Roma life. Who was he to question how other people lived?

Christos knew he couldn't fix the problems with the Roma or with Greece. But he wondered if he could help the boy. Just one little boy. What if the boy stayed with their family? Would that be so bad? He would always have food, a warm place to sleep at night. An education. This family could take care of him. He would have a future, better than the one he faced if and when he returned to the camp. The Roma didn't even send their children to school. What kind of life could the boy have without an education?

Christos shook his head. Since when had he become God? The boy needed to be with his own. There was no other viable solution. Still, these thoughts lingered like the commander's accusatory eyes, his bad breath. Overpowering and persistent.

Christos heard Yiayiá in the hallway. She opened the door to the room where his children and the boy slept and told them to get up. "I don't want to get up," Christos heard one of his boys say. The other mumbled, "It's too early." The boys were growing up, becoming stubborn. They always wanted more time in bed. He would have to talk to them again. They couldn't give Yiayiá a hard time every morning.

He heard nothing from Bo or Alexandra. That's good, Christos thought. The boy slept soundly. He needed his sleep. It would help him get over his cold and that terrible cough of his. Luckily none of the others had caught it.

Yiayiá continued down the hallway to the bathroom, her footsteps soft. Christos anticipated each step, heard every creak of the floorboards. She would soon get the boys ready for school. This routine of theirs kept them all from falling over each other. It made living together in such tight circumstances possible. When he was alone with his thoughts, he could admit how much he liked this arrangement. Yes, it was very tight, but they were together, close, the family he had never had.

The bathroom door closed behind Yiayiá. Christos heard the bathroom window being slammed shut. Who'd left the window open? he wondered.

Then Yiayiá was rushing down the hallway to the bedroom. Her footsteps were urgent, panicked. There was the click of a light switch followed by a scream. Yiayiá's voice. And then the voices of his boys. One falling over the other.

"What is it?" Christos said, as he rushed to his children's room. "What's happened?" He felt Tia close behind. "Are you all right, Yiayiá? What's going on?"

Yiayiá was bent against the wall, her hands covering her mouth. His boys sat up, rubbed their eyes. The mat on the floor, Bo's mat, was empty.

16

PAST, PRESENT, FUTURE

Germany

"When are we going to send for Sanjit?"

Vijay had just walked in the door, hadn't even wiped his feet yet and Saphal was on him, demanding. He had been working hard all day, washing dishes, scraping off the food people left on their plates. He could feed himself, Saphal and a few neighbours on the fare he had to throw out. Working as a dishwasher for a Greek restaurant in Berlin was in some ways cleaner than what he used to do, combing dumpsters for scrap metal, but in another way, it was dirtier because there was so much waste. He'd put away a few euros too. He could almost see his way to saving enough to buy his own restaurant in five, maybe six years. When that happened, his priority, aside from providing good vegetarian Indian food, would be to keep on top of useless waste.

Saphal's sari rustled as she paced back and forth in their small basement suite. Likely she'd been wearing out the carpet since she finished her cleaning job this morning. Vijay encouraged her to get out more, but she didn't want to. People stared at her, she said. Stare back, Vijay told her.

"They want to get rid of us in this country, too," she said whenever Vijay suggested she go to the park. "Have you not seen the marches by those who want to get rid of foreigners? Do you not see their signs? They complain about the Islamization of Europe and look at us as if we are all the same. Don't you see this?"

"There are jobs here," he'd replied. "This is what I see."

Can't I come home to some peace and quiet? he thought now. Just once?

He looked around and thought about all they had. They were luckier than most. The place where they lived was called a suite, but it was really one big room. It wasn't grand, but it was home. It had a foldout couch, a bathroom, a mini fridge and a two-burner hot plate. The small table in one corner with two chairs was their kitchen. What more did they need?

The place had come with the job. Kostas, the restaurant owner, took some money out of Vijay's pay each week to cover the rent. It was a good arrangement for all concerned. Vijay wasn't particularly happy about working for a Greek, though. He thought he'd left that country and those people far behind. But he'd come to realize the Greeks who owned businesses here were among the few who were willing to pay part of his wage under the table and not ask any questions. The owner knew Vijay was hoping to stay in Germany and he wanted to help in any way he could. Kostas had been an immigrant himself once.

"It's been over four months," Saphal said. "Almost five." She sat down at the table and he knew she was expecting him to sit down beside her and discuss this. He wanted to take a shower and have something to eat, but how likely was this to happen with her staring him down? What could he do? He had to hear it all over again.

"I haven't forgotten about Sanjit," he told her. "We just need this government to give us permission to stay. The process is in the works. I can't make it go faster. If I could, I would. You know this. And of course, we could use the time to save a little more."

"Maybe I should go back," she said. "Make sure Sanjit is okay. See how he's doing in school. Is he good with his studies? Does he need help? Has his cough improved? I want to know all of this. I miss him. There is no way to write or telephone those people."

Vijay sat down beside her. "You know we don't have enough money for that. And they might not let you back into this country. Now that we've started the refugee process, we shouldn't do anything to jeopardize it. We'll have all the rights and freedoms of this country and all the medical services for Sanjit too, once we get our papers." He placed his hand on hers. "When everything is settled, I will tell the authorities Sanjit is in Greece being looked after by a relative. They will fly him here for us with money out of their own pocket. It's what the government has to do."

He was confident he knew what he was talking about. He'd spoken to many others in the same situation and they had all said the same thing. Lie low, make some money, and get your refugee status. The long process bought him time and once he'd been here for a while, there was less of a chance the government would send Saphal and him back to their country, particularly since he had a job. They needed workers here. Kostas had said he couldn't run his business without people like Vijay. He had the best Greek restaurant outside of Greece. Or so he claimed. Even the politicians came to his place for their Greek food. With a legitimate job and a place to live, Vijay knew the authorities wouldn't turn them away.

"I don't know," Saphal said. "It's been months already."

"I think about how we will provide him with the best medical care once he comes here. That is my only goal. I think of him every day," he said. Maybe not every day, Vijay thought. He had work and savings and their future to occupy his brain too. And the boy was being looked after. He was a good boy. Sanjit knew, better than Saphal, that they each had to do their part to secure the family's future. Of course, Saphal had grown up with privileges Vijay never had. There was no mother and father to worry about him when he was a child. But never mind. A person couldn't go forward if they were always lamenting their past.

Saphal shook her head.

What else did he have to say to convince her he knew what he was doing and that everything would work out? "Are you missing those earrings of yours?" He tried to tickle her to show her he was teasing, but Saphal pulled away.

The earrings were simply a small payment to Kem's wife to care for Sanjit. The woman asked him not to tell Kem and Vijay hadn't. He didn't know why and he didn't care either. What was between Kem and his wife was none of his business. But Saphal had never let him forget it. "They were a gift from my family," she said whenever she wanted to remind him about the earrings. "The earrings were the only thing I had to remember them by. And you gave them away as though they were worthless." She was right. They didn't mean anything to him. They were just a bargain he'd made with Kem's wife, no different than any deal he would have made with others for his scrap metal.

Saphal got up, turned her back to him. "Sanjit will forget who we are."

"He won't forget. We are his parents. He knows that. He understands we all have to make sacrifices. We've taught him well. You've taught him well." Vijay went to her and squeezed her shoulder.

"Sanjit needs me. I can feel this. A mother knows."

"He's in good hands. Don't worry so much," Vijay said. "And you will see how well he will be when he gets the medical attention we've always wanted for him."

Saphal put her hands on her hips. "I hope you know what you're doing," she said. "He is our son. I can't wait much longer."

Was she threatening him? He shook his head. There was no point getting into a discussion now. He was tired and hungry and he needed a shower. Her family had never taught her how to behave. And the problem was made even worse because Saphal now lived in this Western country where women thought they were equals.

17

BELONGING

The Streets of Athens

At first I think I'll sneak out by the bathroom window, but it's very high and I can't quite reach it. I twist my ankle getting down, but I won't let that stop me. I wait for a few minutes to make sure no one has heard me and then I go down the hall and out the front door, quiet as a mouse so I don't wake anyone.

And now I'm running just as fast as I can. But my ankle hurts and my legs are so tired already. I can't get any air. Finally I have to stop.

I look behind to see if anyone is following me. My chest hurts. I swallow hard, hold my breath like Ammi used to tell me to do to stop the cough. It helps.

Ducking down behind a car, I think about how I will find my way back to the camp. It can't be far, but I will have to take the metro. I don't have any money, but I know how to sneak on without being noticed. I've done that so many times before. That's how I used to come to the rich places in the centre to beg for money. All those times I did that, I never saw anyone on the metro looking for people like me who had no money to pay for a ticket.

I close my eyes and picture the road I'm on and the park the grandmother took the girl, Alexandra, and me to every morning so the policeman could sleep. The other children had beds and

I had only a mat on the floor, but the floor was warmer than the ground I used to sleep on in the house at the camp. And the old lady was good to me. She gave me a nice warm jacket. Candy Lady gave me new pants and a shirt and socks and shoes, but the old lady gave me the warmest coat I've ever had. She hugged and kissed me all the time.

Ammi is like that. When she is in a good mood, she'll hug me for no reason. Not a lot, like the old lady. Just a little. Just enough so I know I make her happy.

I could have stayed with that family, if it wasn't for Ammi. She'd want me to go back to Mirela at the camp. Because if I didn't, she wouldn't be able to find me when she came back.

I can't help it. I think about the old lady again. She'd be waking me up right now, making sure I washed my face, asking me what I wanted for breakfast. She treated me like I was hers. And she took my side against those grandsons of hers, stood up to them when they teased me. They were her own flesh and blood, but she said, "When they are wrong, they are wrong. I don't care if they are my own, they have to understand the difference between right and wrong or they will never grow up to be good men."

I'd been sold to Candy Lady. That's what those boys said. The grandmother said it wasn't true, and Alexandra repeated everything the old lady said. She told me not to believe the boys. The old lady punished her grandsons for what they said. They had to scrub all the floors in the apartment. That's a lot of floors, more than the dirt one in the house I lived in at the camp. "What makes you her favourite, all of a sudden?" one of the boys said later when the old lady wasn't listening. "You're just a dirty gypsy whose own father wanted to get rid of you so bad, he sold you for a few euros and a pair of shoes."

I wondered if they were telling me the truth, but what could I do? Nothing.

Later, when the policeman came home from work, I heard him talking to his wife. Everyone else was asleep, so the house was quiet and I could hear everything. They were talking about Kem. "He should stay in prison where he belongs," the policeman's wife said.

Kem in prison. That was why Mirela was so mad that day. He was trying to get rid of me and she wanted to keep me safe. He's not my real father anyway, but I thought he liked me. I don't know how to tell if someone likes me or not. That's what Mirela says every time I try to play with another child in the park. The other kid and I swing on the swings or bounce each other up in the air on the teeter-totter until his angry mother finds us and yanks him away. Mirela scolds me then. "You know you have to stick to your own kind," she says. But what does that mean? I was just playing with another kid.

When I heard Kem was in prison, I knew what I had to do. I had to leave the policeman's house and find my way to the camp. It's the only way Ammi will find me.

But there is one stop to make first and from here it isn't far.

At the old apartment where I used to live with Ammi and Abbu, a woman answers the door when I knock. "What are you doing here?" she says. She has a broom in her hand and she holds it like a stick ready to hit one of the rats.

Even though she is very scary, I have to be brave. "Are my ammi and abbu back?"

"Back? Why would anyone come back to this country?"

"Ammi promised." I look her right in the eye, even though I know I'm not supposed to with grown-ups. But I know I'm right.

"Foolish child. You will learn soon about life and promises." She tries to close the door in my face, but I put my foot in to stop her. My ankle is sore, but still I have to be brave.

She opens the door wide now, lunges at me. "Go," she says and lifts the broom up like she's going to hit me.

The cough starts again and won't stop. I double over in fits.

"And take your diseases with you." She slams the door shut.

The cough this time brings tears. I sit in a corner outside the building out of sight. I gasp for air. After a long time, my breath comes back. I open my eyes. The sun is still hiding somewhere. What is wrong with me that no one wants me? Did Ammi and Abbu sell me too, like Kem did?

I know my ammi wouldn't. But Abbu, I'm not sure. No, Ammi wouldn't let him do that.

They had to get away because they wanted to make a better life for me. That's what Abbu said. I have to go back and wait for them with Mirela.

I stand up and look around. The sky is full of grey smoke, the same colour of the sky above the camp. It's far from here, but I know the way to the metro and I know how to get on it without being seen.

18

SECRETS

Maroúsi

Ted looked down at the keys in his hand, then at the door. There were so many keys and locks. Which one would work? He tried one key after another.

Finally locks tumbled and rattled. He heard several slide into place. The door snapped open on its own despite its obvious weight. He rolled his bag through the front door.

The fluorescent fixture inside the apartment hummed loudly and gave off a dull light. Ted found the switch and shut it off, thought better of it and turned it back on. He could hear voices, coming from above, below, and down the corridor.

Ted pushed the door closed, expecting the sound to disappear, but he was surrounded. Clipped and shrill, the voices persisted. He couldn't make out any words. Even if he could, they would be in Greek.

He stood in the narrow corridor, unsure whether he should go left or right. On the wall in front of him was an antique frame with a portrait of an old woman, someone he didn't know. The place probably came furnished, old hag pictures and all. The old woman was sitting on a wooden chair, her hands intertwined in her lap, her legs slightly apart. Her dark skirt reached the top of her buckled shoes. Her mouth was pressed so tight her lips disappeared. It felt as if she was looking at him, disapproving of him, letting him know he had no right to be here. He knew that. Had he ever had a place in his mother's home?

He'd always tried to be her good son. She called him that even when he couldn't do much to stand up to his father. But this time she expected too much. Ted chomped down on his gum. More cardboard than fruit, it was exactly what he needed. Something to gnaw away at.

He turned from the picture and went down the short hallway, which led to a bedroom. The balcony doors were wedged open and the blinds chattered in the breeze. Toeing the piece of wood out of the slider, he closed the doors. The blinds dropped. The voices from the other apartments dulled. He heard a siren in the distance, a door slamming somewhere above him.

By the time he'd gotten his mother's things and found her apartment, it was daylight. Now the sky was crisp blue, and the morning sun felt warm through the glass. This wasn't the low cloud cover that draped itself over Vancouver and made him feel cozy, safe. Here, this clarity, this bright light chilled him. He felt exposed and vulnerable.

In the park across the way, two boys were kicking a soccer ball, taking turns as goalie. Leaning into the blinds to get a closer look, Ted spotted an old man sitting by himself, watching the boys. Hard to miss his bright red bow tie. The man was smiling and his gaze seemed distant, as though he was reminiscing. You can't undo the past, Ted thought. Maybe that was what the old guy was thinking. He realized these were words he'd heard before. His sponsor had said something like that. "But you can face it," he had said.

The smile on the old man's face reminded Ted of his mother's vacant smile. She would disappear into herself sometimes when his father still lived with them and she was angry, then later after his dad died, she left him almost completely.

Ted rubbed his eyes. Why can't I just ignore all these memories until they don't bother me as much? He shook his head. Yeah, like that's worked well so far.

He tried to remember the last time he'd played soccer. He'd given up soccer long before he went to private school. It wasn't about his father. It had to do with him. No matter what anyone said, he never felt good enough to play the game. It would always be his father's game.

"Football," his father had corrected him every time he called it soccer. How often had he practised, how many times had he hoped his father had seen the last shot he made, the way he was able to balance and bounce the ball at the end of his foot? If he noticed the curtains in the kitchen move, he would always hope it was Dad watching. When Ted realized he couldn't please his father, he started calling the game *soccer* to spite him.

He shook his head. When he'd taken up real football, American football, at boarding school, he found a sport that gave him more control. That was fine by him. He became the quarterback running the show. He liked how others looked to him for direction. He'd been teased and ridiculed in soccer, made to feel the idiot. Football was different. He was in charge. The image of his father, absent-mindedly pouring himself yet another drink and raising it to his lips as he talked about Ted making a league team, finally disappeared.

Another balcony door slammed somewhere in the building. He turned away from the window and looked around the room.

The bed was unmade. On the dresser was a jar of moisturizer, a bottle of 30-plus sunscreen, and a tube of lip balm. He picked up the balm, twisted off the cap, smelled the lemony flavour. When he was a boy, his lips were always chapped and red because of his habit of sucking on them before a soccer game. His mother used to kneel in front of him and pucker her lips, miming what she wanted him to do, and dab his mouth with the same balm he later sucked away. He closed his eyes tight and opened them quickly again. The memory disappeared.

As he put the balm down, he noticed the outline of where it stood in the film of dust. He would tidy up, get the place ready for her return. As a boy he would help out this way, surprise her in the morning with a spotless bathroom he'd woken up early to clean. The smile in her sleepy eyes when he showed her what he'd done, the hug she gave him, the warmth of her body against his. Of course, that was all before she took off to save the world and left him to fend for himself against that creep of a teacher.

Stop, he told himself.

The top drawer was slightly ajar. He looked over his shoulder, and immediately felt ridiculous. Of course there was no one there. Who would know if he took a look?

He slid the drawer open another crack. You know better, he told himself. You wouldn't want someone looking through your stuff. He quickly put his hands behind his back as if his knuckles had been smacked. What the hell was he looking for, anyway? What could he possibly find in her underwear drawer? He pulled at the drawer before he had any further time to think. It slipped open too fast and began to fall. He caught it before it hit the floor, but not before he got a few good scratches on his wrist.

All this aggravation for a couple pairs of underwear and one fraying, grey bra. He put the drawer back in its place.

He pulled open another, then another. Empty. In the last drawer he found half a bag of jujubes. Mother and her stashes. That was one thing that hadn't changed. Under the candy, he noticed an envelope, then a drawing that lay flat at the bottom of the drawer. He could see the outline of hair on the drawing, but the envelope sat on top, covering the middle part of the sketch. The face.

Just as he reached for the envelope, his cellphone rang. Slamming the drawer shut, he swallowed a breath, held it until he felt the jitter in his hand still.

The cell continued to ring. Ted extricated the phone from his pocket.

"What's happening, Teddy boy?" Jack asked. "Enjoying yourself, are you? We're here sweating it out on the front lines."

"Yes, just fine. Long overdue," Ted cleared his throat. "Anything going on I should know about? The place going to pieces? Clients dropping off in droves, the doors about to close?" He had to keep it light. He looked up at the ceiling. What was in the envelope? The address label looked formal. He held his breath for another long second.

"It's your company, man," Jack said. "And you put us in charge. We're taking good care of it. Nothing to worry about."

"So you're just checking up on me." He rubbed his forehead. He'd been running for how long? Two days. It felt like more. He needed to lie down. Rest. The envelope was probably his mother's pay stub or something. He was making a big deal out of nothing. And the sketch? Who knew? Besides, it was hardly important.

"Do you need me to?" Jack laughed. "Getting yourself into trouble with your mommy, are you? Don't tell me you're doing double shots of Perrier. I warned you about that stuff, didn't I? Do I have to come over there and do an intervention or whatever they call it?"

Ted smiled. Jack could turn anything into a joke. He supposed that was why they'd become friends. Ted agonized and worried about everything. Jack kept things real and in perspective. Their relationship gave Ted balance.

"So, when are you back?" Jack said.

Ted shrugged. "Not sure yet." He took another deep breath, then held it, hoping Jack didn't hear the thick inhale. "Will keep you apprised as I figure it out."

"My, but aren't we formal," Jack said. "Must be Mom's influence."

Shit, Ted thought. Need to keep it lighter with Jack. "Talk to you soon."

Ted hung up and headed down the hallway to check out the rest of the apartment. Clean her place. That had to be his only thought right now. He needed to forget about going through her stuff. He chided himself for getting fussed about nothing. There was no point in looking for trouble. She would tell him what he needed to know when he needed to know it. That was the way she'd always been.

In the bathroom, he switched on the light. The space was only slightly bigger than an airplane lavatory. The living room was at the opposite end of the corridor; the kitchen to the right had one counter, some cupboards above it, and a table and two chairs. There was nothing on the counter, no coffee machine or toaster. A small European fridge, more like a bar fridge, sat underneath.

She certainly wasn't living a luxurious life. Maybe she'd spent all her money on the charities and work she did. If they paid her, it couldn't be much money. And she probably paid for her own travel and accommodation.

A blanket and pillow lay bunched up on the love seat. He assumed they had been for the boy. He'd have to get rid of them. Who knew how the boy lived, what kind of bugs he might have brought? Again, he thought about the envelope in her drawer.

Under the kitchen sink he found the boy's tattered clothes in a garbage bag. He tied it up, dropped it on the floor. He'd dispose of it at the same time as the blanket and pillow. He took out another garbage bag, and returned to the living room, where he scooped the blanket and pillow into it using a magazine. After throwing the magazine in as well, he twisted the top of the bag and double knotted it.

He opened all the kitchen cabinets. Two plates, two cups, two glasses, one pot. More dust here too. An unopened box of cereal lay on one shelf along with another bag of fruit-flavoured jujubes. The sink was tarnished. She used to like nice things: expensive pots and pans, Royal Doulton plates and bowls, crystal glasses. He hadn't expected to find her in a place like this.

Something cold pressed against his leg as he reached to the cupboard above the sink. The handle of the bar fridge felt like ice through his pants. Squatting down, he opened the door, faced a small bottle of wine. He remained still, staring.

Then he reached out, ran a finger down the side of the bottle, and licked his finger, as though the condensation alone might give him what he needed.

You're hopeless, he told himself. You haven't washed your hands.

The fridge held an unopened litre of milk and a container of Greek yogurt, also unopened. She must have bought some of these things for the boy, the wine for herself. There was also bread, sliced cheese, and a chocolate bar. Was this all she planned to feed the kid? For Christ's sake, she used to be such a good cook.

His stomach rumbled. When was the last time he'd eaten?

Sweat stung his eyes. He rubbed them. It wasn't hot. What the hell? He'd had this, plus the shakes when he first quit, but it had gotten better. Were the sweats back? Shit. Maybe a hit might help ease them.

His mouth watered involuntarily. There was no one around. He'd had one hell of a tough few days.

He took out the chocolate bar and shut the fridge door. Guilt. It was as though someone were watching him. Maybe it had been the call from Jack. Or thinking about Mother. Or maybe it was that creepy picture of the old woman in the hallway. He hadn't taken the drink. Give yourself a break, he thought. But the guilt didn't subside. He'd thought about taking a swig. It had taken everything he had not to do it.

His tired brain was all over the place. He thought about the envelope again. Sure, he had looked in some of Mother's dresser drawers. But he hadn't read what was in the envelope. And he could have. He had come all this way to help her, and then she wouldn't tell him anything. What did she expect? He should go to the bedroom right now and see if there was something there he should know. But then he pictured the letter he'd been writing to her the night she'd called him. He wouldn't want her to be rooting around in his desk and reading the hateful words he'd written. No, he couldn't do what he didn't want her to do to him.

Instead, he tried to ignore it as he'd tried to ignore the wine. Stay busy, he told himself, and you might have a chance.

He put a new garbage bag into the bin under the sink and spit out his gum. He scrubbed each finger under the tap. Foamy soap simmered in the sink and the hot water singed his skin.

Paper towelling his hands left them damp. He grabbed another piece of gum from his pocket, folded it into his mouth. His jaw and temples ached, but what the heck, the gum helped him stay focused, helped him stay away from that bottle in the fridge.

Back in his mother's room, he slid his finger over the dresser. Wait, he told himself. Wait. His mother used to say she'd wash the sheets a couple of times a week if she had time, just so she could have that fresh-laundry scent when she got into bed. He would wash the sheets for her. It was the least he could do. It would be a nice surprise.

She must have a washer and dryer in this place, but where?

He stripped the bed, located the washing machine in a closet in the hallway and threw in the sheets and the towels.

Okay, what if he read what was inside the envelope? Best-case scenario, he'd discover something that might help her. Worst-case scenario, he'd get nothing. No harm done. And if he was careful, Mother didn't need to know he was snooping around. But he'd know. Shouldn't that be enough to stop him?

He found a broom and swept the floor. Keep moving, he told himself. His body ached to lie down. But not yet. First, he'd finish cleaning the place for her. Then he'd get some rest before he went back to the jail. That officer, Christos, worked night shift. Ted wanted to deal with him. And only him.

The washing machine beeped anemically.

There was no dryer anywhere in the apartment. But there was a drying rack. He laid the sheets on top of it, then stuck the entire contraption on the balcony. Although the sky was hazy now, it was hot as hell out there. He began to sweat again.

The bottle of wine in the fridge beckoned. He imagined himself pouring a glass. Sitting down in the living room. Savouring it. His hand trembled. Another picture came to mind. He stood at the open fridge door, chugging the wine in gulps, the excess dripping down his face and onto his shirt. Stains on his shoes.

He unpacked his bag, put his notebook and pen on the table beside the couch. He'd sleep on the couch for now and when she was released, he'd move to a hotel for a night or two until they flew home. He would insist she return to Canada. When she was rested they'd figure out what she would do. She could live with him for a while or they could buy her a condo close by. She could retire or do some volunteer work in the community. In some sector completely different than what she'd always done. She'd been at this helping business for so long. Too long. A break, some rest, and a change in interests would give her perspective. And that couldn't hurt.

Standing in the living room, he could feel the pull from the fridge. The wine. Again. Still. He could replace the bottle. And Mother wouldn't think twice about it. So it was gone. She wouldn't think that was a big deal. If she asked, he could say he'd wanted a little sleep aid.

He forced himself down the hall, away from the temptation. A shower was what he needed.

By the time he finished, the sheets on the balcony were dry. That hot Mediterranean sun. This would never happen in Vancouver's cool dampness. His stomach growled, but he ignored it. It would only take a minute to make his mother's bed. Then he'd lie down, grab something to eat later.

He'd almost forgotten about the envelope. He slid the drawer open. Just enough to get the envelope out. He moved the candy and came face to face with the sketch.

Mother stared back at him. He swallowed. Took a breath.

The sketch was more a caricature than an exact likeness, but he recognized her eyes, soft and caring. And there it was: the barely there smile, reluctant and aloof. The drawing showed exactly what he'd always known about her. There was an absence there. The artist had captured it completely. She had always held a piece of herself back from others. He was certain she wouldn't have liked the sketch.

Who knew her this intimately to have captured her so well? Did she have a love interest here? What else didn't he know about her? And her life?

He picked up the envelope, closed the drawer on her eyes.

The envelope had been opened already. He wouldn't have to fiddle with that. It was just lying there. If anyone asked, he'd say he was cleaning up and found it.

He read through it quickly, and then read it again, focusing on one paragraph. "I am sorry to inform you we have terminated your volunteer position. You are a caring person, but you continue to engage in personal relationships with our clients. Your role is in fact to set up programs and allow locals to deliver them. This has been pointed out to you on numerous occasions, but we have not seen your behaviour change and you have not availed yourself of any of the courses or counselling your supervisor has suggested. We have no options left. We hope you will take time to reflect and find volunteer work that is more suitable for your many skills and abilities."

Fired. Mother. Who fires a volunteer? And particularly after all she'd given. Christ, who were these people? Why the hell had they done this to her?

He replaced the letter in the envelope and returned it to its spot. He shook his head when he saw her eyes again. He couldn't think straight anymore. His brain was woolly, and he was bone tired.

He closed the blinds. He thought about the letter, dated months ago from her bosses in Zimbabwe. This must have devastated her. If they didn't appreciate her, her hard work, why hadn't she come home?

The sounds from the other apartments quieted. His hands stilled too.

He stepped out into the hallway, heading for the kitchen.

One sip. That was all he needed.

This was the last clear thought he had before all thought vanished.

19

CONFESSIONS

Amaroúsio Police Station

"Listen, Bo came with me," she said to Commander-whatever-his-name-was. Her own words startled her, but she'd made up her mind to do this and there was no turning back.

Strikingly large, the commander's eyes burrowed into her. There should be warmth in eyes like that, so perfectly round and dark chocolate brown, but she couldn't see or feel it. She saw a void.

She didn't believe the smile either. He lounged in his chair, large, resolute and confident. She wondered if the chair could withstand such weight.

"His situation was desperate in the camp. No running water, no electricity, living in filth. The only food was what they could scrounge up from the dumpsters." Don't avoid his eyes, she thought. Like social workers, police officers know how to read a person's expression. The absent glance away. The obsessive rub of a forearm. Rocking a chair back and forth, fidgeting. These were clues. He would see right through her. "I knew I could help. At the very least, I thought I might get him to a warm place so he could get rid of that awful cough." She leaned back in her chair, crossed her legs. Her hands sat open on her lap. She had nothing to hide.

The commander's chin was covered in greying peach fuzz. Tufts of hair, curly and wild, protruded from his ears. His uniform bulged in the middle, where a button was missing on his wrinkled shirt. She could see right through to his undershirt. A cross rested against his chest, the gold chain barely visible in the folds of his short neck. His shoulders were gentle-giant broad, but she wouldn't trust them.

You don't scare me, buster, she thought. Still, she realized it would have been better to wait until Christos came in. She had intended to, but then couldn't sleep, her head spinning with schemes to get Kem out of jail and Bo back to his family. And besides, she'd seen this commander-whatever the night she'd been brought into this place. He was always around. And she thought he was someone with clout who might rectify this situation. If she could only get him to see it her way.

They were sitting in his office, the door open. A policeman stood in one corner close to his boss. Just outside the office it was chaos — men in handcuffs, men with name tags, others with uniforms — scuttling back and forth in the hallway. The shrill voices, the ringing phones were unrelenting. The noise irritated her. It didn't seem to faze the commander or his henchman.

"I am having some difficulty understanding, Madam," the commander said, "why a woman like you would want to take a gypsy child home. Is this the way you Americans like to help?"

"It's very noisy here," Shelby said. "Perhaps if we close the door?"

The officer behind the commander had a face like one of those ancient statues in the Acropolis museum. The least he could do was close the door. What other purpose did he serve? What was he standing guard over? She thought: this commander fellow hardly needs protection from anyone, least of all me.

She shifted in the chair and caught herself. The commander watched her. She settled, crossed her legs again and stared right back at him.

"I do not think this situation has anything to do with the noise. I can hear you perfectly, Madam, but I do have some difficulty understanding your actions."

"I know. It was a foolish thing for me to do," Shelby said. "I got carried away. I didn't know what I was doing. I'd like to correct that." She leaned forward toward him. He was not going to frighten her. If he didn't agree to help her, she'd cry bloody murder, accuse him and his officers of abusing Kem, a defenceless man. She would tell him what she saw when she was in the interview room. She'd threaten to bring in the embassy, report his men. He'd be held accountable. This type of guy ran like a coward when his job was on the line. She was sure he didn't want any more negative publicity. The police treatment of foreign detainees made the English papers weekly.

"And how, Madam, do you propose to do this?" The chair scraped as he rocked himself forward, closer to her. He fingered his penknife, and then noticed she was staring at him and shoved it in his pocket.

"I've explained what happened," she said slowly, as though speaking to one of her former child welfare clients, who simply couldn't understand why his children had been apprehended and placed in foster care. "You can let Kem and his son go. Then deal with me how you will. I'm the one in the wrong here. No one else needs to pay for my mistakes. I see it as plainly as that."

"How much did you pay for the child?" he asked as he heaved himself up and out of the chair. He lumbered in front of her, stuck his hands in his pocket, and tried to appear harmless, with that wide-eyed grin and seemingly naïve question of his. He towered over her. He's no fool, she told herself.

"I've already told you," she said. "I kidnapped him." She leaned against the back of the chair, recrossed her legs, and folded her hands into her lap, star-pupil style. A shower, her own bed, a good hot meal, a visit with Ted. That was what she really needed. Ted had told her not to talk to anyone until he got back. He wouldn't be happy with her, but once she'd explained her thinking, she was sure he'd understand.

"It is very interesting that we found the gypsy with no more than a few euros on him. Where would the money have gone, I wonder. Drink? Drugs? Women?"

While he asked these questions, the commander paced in front of her.

"Kem is a family man. If he had any money, I'm sure he would have spent it on his family. He's a good person."

The commander rubbed his face. Fluff floated innocently from his bristles. She knew he didn't believe her. And he was probably ridiculing her too. But it didn't matter. The only thing she cared about was Kem and his family. The way to beat this commander was with patience. She wasn't going anywhere. "I didn't give him any money. Okay?"

Again, the commander said nothing.

"I'm sure he told you the same thing," she said, sitting still again so as not to show the nervousness tightening in her stomach, the subtle twitch she felt in her eye.

"Oh, yes, he told my officers the same story. It makes our job easier when the stories coincide. Still..." He walked behind her, slammed the door shut. She jumped at the bang.

"Oh, forgive me," he said. "I do not know my own strength. I did not mean to frighten you."

The office was slightly quieter. The voices were down to a murmur. A ringing phone persisted.

Stay calm, she told herself. Don't play into his hands. Don't say too much. She didn't like having him behind her, not seeing his face. It was too tempting to look around. She wouldn't give him the satisfaction. She gazed straight ahead at the other officer. She smiled. Like one of the mannequins in a store window on Ermoú Street, he remained unmoved.

"Fine, Madam." The commander stood beside her. His cologne was overpowering. She gulped and began to cough.

"Water?"

She shook her head, swallowed again, trying to calm the cough. Her nose dripped. She swallowed, swiped at her nose with the back of her hand.

"I have your statement. We will take it under consideration as we proceed with our investigation."

"What investigation?" she asked. She looked over at him. He was trying to manipulate her. "I've told you the truth. What more do you want?"

"I have to assess all the facts, not simply what you've told me," he said. "I have been doing this work for a very long time. We Greeks have a saying: we must look below the surface for the truth. That is what I intend to do. And your statement has been very helpful, Madam." With a nod he signalled the officer, who finally moved toward her.

"But wait." She leaned forward. "You are not going to let Kem go?"

"I only have your word."

"And his."

He looked at Shelby with the same kind of knowing sneer Robert had always used whenever he thought he had something over on her. She felt her face becoming red with exasperation. He was not going to release Kem. Not now and maybe not ever. Time to play her last card. You asked for it, she thought. This could have been so much easier. You jerk.

There was a sudden knock and the door opened. She turned. Christos's eyes slid over her, then away.

Yes, she knew she should have waited until he came on shift before she spoke to anyone. She understood that. But maybe it wasn't too late. Christos could still help convince his boss she was telling the truth. Maybe there was still a chance.

"Can you not see we are in the middle of something?" the commander said in English. He pulled at his pants, tucked in his shirt.

"Commander Kefalas, can I speak to you in the hallway?" Christos replied in English too. Then he said something in Greek.

"If this is about this case, we can speak here. Whatever you need to tell me, you can tell me in front of our guest," Kefalas said, pointing to Shelby. "In English. So we all understand each other."

"I am not so sure it is a good idea," Christos said, his eyes again dodging hers.

The commander watched him in that sort of way that said *I make the rules here.*

Christos seemed undeterred.

She turned around in her chair and sat perfectly still, staring at the other officer. She had to let Christos do his job. It was better not to interfere. He knew what to do. He could take it from here.

They spoke in Greek. She could pick out a few words here and there, and understood they were talking about Bo. *Agóri*, the Greek word for boy.

The conversation was brisk, Christos doing most of the talking. He was trying to convince his boss. Good, Shelby thought. This was good for all of them. Bo. Kem. Me. Maybe Christos would have a little more luck with the commander than she'd had. They spoke the same language. They were supposedly on the same side.

Their conversation ended and Christos and the commander turned to her. She looked for some hint of what they might be thinking. Nothing. Grave stares. Christos stood at attention, hands clasped behind his back. His pant leg quivered.

"What is it?" Shelby asked.

"It seems as though Officer Pappas has lost our young charge."

"Kem is gone?"

"The boy."

"But where? He's a child. How could he disappear? Who was responsible for him?" She stood up, agitated, got very close to Christos and his boss. Neither moved. The officer behind the desk stepped forward. Kefalas put out his hand as though to stop traffic. The officer stepped back.

"We'll find him," the commander said. He glanced at Christos.

They escorted her back to her cell without a further word about Bo or Kem. Again, her efforts were for nothing. Bo was missing and Kem was still in jail. And with all this going on, Ted hadn't been to see her either. He was supposed to be here to help. Why did he disappear when she needed him the most?

She told herself to calm down. He would come. He'd probably taken a nap and overslept after the long flight. She held on to the bars and watched the officers walk past. She asked another officer if he would get Christos for her, but he shook his head. "No English," he said in Greek. They all spoke English. That was why it was so difficult for her to learn Greek in the time she'd been in the country. Still, they only spoke English when it suited them.

She sat on the bed, her head in her hands. She didn't know how much time went by. Maybe an hour. Maybe two. She lost track and there was no way to tell anyway.

"Mrs. Holt."

"Christos." She moved quickly toward the bars. "Oh, thank God."

"One of the officers told me you wanted to see me."

"What happened to Bo?"

Christos eyed the corridor in one direction, then the other. She wanted to tell him to pay attention to her, but he seemed overwrought.

"My family was taking care of him. He disappeared during the night. Walked right out the front door. We don't know where he is."

"Why was he with you?" she asked. "Shouldn't he have been in foster care or something like that where he could be watched?"

"Our systems are overloaded," Christos said. "I volunteered. I hoped to find a quick solution."

"So you did what I did. You took Bo home. You see how easy it is to do."

He glanced away.

"I'm sorry. I know you were trying to help."

"I understand you told my commander you took the child."

Was he trying to trick her? Christos wasn't like his boss. Right from the first night, he had tried to help her. She knew that. "Yes, I did. This mess wasn't Kem's fault. He should be set free. Maybe Kem could find his son. He could probably help."

Christos shook his head. "The situation is not so simple."

"Why not? I've admitted guilt. Let Kem go. He'll find his son. Charge me. They can get back to their lives. You solve your case. And you get on with prosecuting me."

"The Roma. Politics. Illegal immigration. Things like this."

She heard someone else enter the corridor. Christos stood back. And there was her son.

"Ted, where have you been?" She reached for him through the bars.

"Mother, this is our lawyer."

The man accompanying Ted was pudgy and appeared out of breath. He wiped his forehead with his handkerchief, nodded and smiled, but didn't bother to introduce himself.

She could always count on her son knowing what to do, she thought.

"We've been working on this nonstop," Ted said. "He's negotiated your release. We can go home," Ted said, beaming like he used to when he was a boy and brought home a present for her, a little necklace or a plant he got at the farmer's market.

"I'm not going without Kem, Ted. And now the boy is missing." She sat down on the cot. It sagged. The iron bedframe pressed against the back of her legs.

"Mother," Ted said. His tone was sharp. He gripped the cell door as though he intended to bend it open with his bare hands. "Mother, you know as well as I do, we need to get you out. You can't do anything while you're here."

"Ted, they won't let him go if I don't push this." Her eyes focused on him. She wanted him to understand she knew what she was talking about.

"And how much can you do while you're inside this place?" Ted said. "I can tell you. Absolutely nothing."

The lawyer nodded. Christos didn't look at Ted or the lawyer, but gazed at her.

She sat quietly, stared at the floor, thinking. Ted was right; she would have a better chance of finding Bo if she got out. Once she found him, she'd get the lawyer Ted hired to help Kem.

She stood, went to the cell door. She stared at Ted. "You promise to help me."

"Yes." Ted shifted his eyes away.

He couldn't fool her. She'd hold him to it.

"Please look at me. Do you promise to help me?"

"I've come all this way," he said. "What else would I be doing here?"

20

Opportunity

Amaroúsio Police Station

Kem trudged the strip of cracked concrete, then turned, retraced his steps. Over the muffled din of traffic and construction, the stubborn clanging followed. His face hurt. He rubbed his cheek. He'd already tripped once with these damn leg irons around his ankles and hit the ground hard. It happened quickly. More bruises.

Those officers who'd thrown him out here could have removed the leg irons. The cuffs dug into his ankles and the chain holding the two ends meant he could only take small strides. Otherwise he would fall flat on his face again. It was probably what they wanted to see him do.

The guards could have made the short sixty minutes of fresh air he was supposed to get, according to his jailer's rules of decency or human rights or whatever they called it, a little better.

Dandelions pushed through the concrete. The walls looming around him opened at the top to a slip of Mediterranean-blue sky. Bone-warming sunshine, clear skies: no clouds in the way. Thorny hoops of razor wire sat on top of the walls. The bands of bright silver reminded him of the earrings Mirela wore. Dangly. Layers of smooth silver triangles. Spikey at the bottom. Jabbing him, and in the way when he was trying to get close to her for the little something he was sure she liked too. Yes, her tiny fists hammered his chest, and she kicked at his shins like a donkey when he got too close. It was true she turned her face away from him when he tried to kiss her, but this was their private game. She liked it. He had seen how she tilted her head into the purse-size mirror he stole for her. After he was done with her, she admired the whisker burns on her neck or the odd bruise he had left on her shoulder or her small breasts from his enthusiastic bites. It had always been the same.

"Why are you wearing those earrings again?" he'd asked for the thousandth time.

"I found them after the boy came to us," she said. "They are for good luck."

They looked familiar, but he couldn't remember where he'd seen them. He was a man. He didn't pay attention to such things. But he was sure he'd seen them before.

She'd probably stolen them. Not that she'd ever admit it. She thought she was better than him. Or at least that was what she told him every single day. "I survive honestly," she said anytime she brought home a bag of overripe fruit, a fully cooked, half-eaten roast or a barely used blanket. "I keep our family fed. With my hard work. And honesty," she'd said when he'd asked her where she got the blanket. She'd slipped it over one corner of the dirt floor of their lean-to to keep a layer of warmth between them and the pebbly ground. The blanket wasn't for everyone, of course. She'd placed it in Bo's corner rather than her own husband's.

"Diving into a dumpster is honest?" He poked at her ribs, teasing her. Her eyes burrowed into him. Again, he'd stepped over an invisible line she'd drawn, one he usually didn't see. She had a hair trigger, his woman. Sometimes this was good in a woman, but he knew, better than anyone, that wasn't always the case.

"The Greeks leave food for us, hanging on the handles of the dumpsters," she'd said. "It takes some work to find the places where the people are generous like this, something you and your friends know nothing about."

"Work or generosity?" he'd asked. "Which one is it that I know nothing about?"

She'd stared right through him.

Ungrateful woman, he thought now. He rubbed his wrists where the handcuffs had been. When he first came to the police, that bastard who put the handcuffs on him had dragged Kem's arms behind his back, cinched the cuffs on tightly. The angry slashes of red were turning into gloomy shades of blue, the tender skin bruised anew when the guards put him in handcuffs to escort him to the courtyard.

They were supposed to remove all their chains and shackles when they placed him out here for fresh air, but they didn't like to do it. One of the guards had told him as much. "Easier for us to watch over you people. Anything that can make my life better is good for me," the guard had said, and chuckled. "You understand. It is not a personal thing. I have nothing against you."

Kem nodded.

"But we have a dilemma," the guard had said, light and friendly, as if they were sitting together around the open fire at the camp enjoying each other's company, rather than separated by bars and locked doors. "If we don't take the cuffs off as we're supposed to, someone will report us and they'll close places like this. You will all be thrown out of the country. Which wouldn't necessarily be a bad thing." His laugh, reckless and natural, came from somewhere deep in his belly. His holster shuddered, but the gun on his hip, clipped in place, didn't move.

"I keep you in a job," Kem said. He could look at this guard straight in the eye. Others wouldn't allow it. They'd stare him down or raise their chin in that dismissive, insistent way. He'd avert his eyes.

"You have a point."

Okay, so not all the guards were bad. One had even given him back his notebook and pen. "These are yours, aren't they?" the officer had said. Kem wasn't sure if he should admit to anything, but he nodded. The officer smiled. Kem had drawn boxes and lines shaded in black. Dark lines. Over and over again. He wasn't sure why he'd started these abstracts. They helped pass the time, kept his hands busy, his mind focused on the bars he was drawing rather than the ones he was behind. He was fresh out of ideas for the caricatures he typically drew and besides, it would be suicide if he did such things in a place like this. You never knew who would take offence. No, it was easier to do the abstracts. He'd fill a page with black shapes, then start on another one, the heavy lines and shading of the previous page leaving a dent on the subsequent pages.

So the guards had a job to do. Sure, some of them shoved him harder than they had to, taunted him, threatened him or ignored him, but some could be reasonable too. The guard who'd taken him out to this courtyard, as the Greeks liked to call this enclosed space of weeds and cigarette butts, had given him a couple of cigarettes and had even lit one for him. Kem smoked both, one after the other.

He was light-headed and queasy. The guards chose the exact time Mrs. Shelby was in one of those offices to take him through the corridor, put him on display for her. What the hell were they trying to do? Give her a reason to put another nail in his coffin? These do-gooders helped you on their own terms. If things didn't go their way, you became disposable. He would be the one to be thrown away like garbage. He nodded as though he were talking to someone else, agreeing to the point made.

Yes, at first Mrs. Shelby brought them food, then clothes and candy for the boy. She came every day, as a member of the family might. Mirela didn't like her from the start.

"She is a good woman who wants to help us," Kem had said. They were sitting on opposite sides of the spitting campfire. Bo was somewhere roaming the camp with the other children, no doubt finding trouble, as Kem had when he was the boy's age.

Mirela poked at the fire. Smoke and ash kicked up in the breeze. Kem rubbed his eyes. Mirela stabbed at the fire again. His woman rarely smiled, and when she did, it was usually because of the boy. Still, he was sure he saw her grin as he took out his handkerchief to wipe away the soot and tears from his eyes.

"I don't trust her," she said, staring into the fire.

"You're jealous," Kem said. "Bo is always happy to see her when she comes."

Her eyes pierced him as decisively as if she had stabbed him with her knife, the special one she used to pry open the dented cans of beans or soup she sometimes found in the dumpster.

"Any child is happy to see the person who is offering him candy," Mirela said, pointing the poker at him. "This is not new. Look at how you act around her."

"Bo loves you, like any boy loves his mother." Kem stood and walked over to her. He squeezed her shoulder. "Like his real mother."

The comment was off-hand, a small thing to say, something to put her in her place. He had to do it once in a while. Otherwise, she might guess at the power she had over him. And that was never good for a man. Vijay used to say the same thing when they spoke about their wives. "My wife has ideas about being treated as an equal. I have to humour her. It's the only way to survive."

The blow had come out of nowhere. Mirela hit him with such force he toppled over close to the fire, singeing his hair and burning his hand. "He is my son," she said, pointing the hot poker at his eyes. "He has no other mother." She threw the poker down and went inside the lean-to.

She didn't talk to him for days, not until he stole a flowerpot full of white daisies from a neighbourhood florist and left it by her side of the cardboard they slept on. "It's a good thing we understand each other," Mirela said. That night she lifted her skirt to him without force or suggestion on his part. He pulled at her underwear, rubbed his face against her long neck and again was gouged by one of those earrings of hers. After a few pumps at her, her face still turned away, he'd forgotten about the earrings and everything else that bothered him.

He crouched down against one of the walls of the courtyard. The sun-warmed concrete against his back made him shiver. He should never have told Mirela he would look for Bo. It was too dangerous to go to the police. They were illegals in this country. They'd been lucky enough to escape being documented and tracked once before. But he'd given in. Her tears, his weakness. That woman had an evil spell on him, something that made him do reckless things.

He should have said, "Look Mirela, life is this way. The things that come easily can be taken away easily. Bo is gone, but we'll find another son." Their world was full of strays. She knew this just as well as he did.

Hadn't he produced a son for her? It wasn't his fault. She was the weak one. Not him. His father had said as much to him, once. "Useless in every way," he'd told Kem. "She barely carries her weight around here." Kem's father had come from the barn where they kept Mirela.

"Doesn't want to help your mother or sisters."

He'd cinched his belt, doing up his fly as if he'd had his pants down, but how could that be? The outhouse wasn't close to the barn. "And don't expect her to be pleasing you. She's all fight and nothing more."

She was as small as a child. That was what Kem liked about her. She wasn't like the other women in the camp, with swaying hips and asses that easily carried water, children, couches and junk they found discarded.

Mirela never paid much attention to him. She spoiled the boy, though. Kem should have been angry. As the man of the house, he was the one to teach the boy right from wrong, what he could get away with. But Kem wasn't that kind of possessive, angry man. That was his father, not him. Kem had wanted to see Mirela happy, if for no other reason than to soften her mulishness and make his life a little easier.

He thought of her stubbornness, her better-than-him attitude, her rebuffs, and felt his skin shudder, his *pulă* stiffen. She hadn't even come to ask about him and still he wanted her. It would be dangerous for her to come to this place. There was nothing she could do to help him. Still, he wondered if Mirela missed him.

Foolish thoughts. He stood up. His legs creaked and wobbled. He needed to go home. As the man of the house, he had responsibilities. He couldn't be sitting around in a place like this wasting time. He didn't have the kind of money a woman like Mrs. Shelby had. He looked up at the wall again. No towers, no guards watching.

If he got out of here, the only place he could go was the camp. He could hide there until the police lost interest in him. It wouldn't take long. People like him only got noticed when they troubled the Greeks or the tourists. It was true. The Roma were the scapegoats for the problems the Greeks had with their economy, but he didn't think someone as insignificant as he was would be the object of much attention, given all the other problems in the country. One day he would draw pictures about these things and people would see his work and understand how he'd been treated.

If he went home without Bo, though, Mirela would force him to go back out until he found the boy. The police had him somewhere, but Kem was sure they wouldn't tell him where. They wouldn't let Bo go easily.

He hadn't thought about where the boy might be until now. Mirela was right. He wasn't much of a father. She said this all the time. He'd show her.

"Your time is up," the officer said. Kem startled at the sound of the man's voice. Preoccupied, he hadn't heard the door unlock, the guard step out into the courtyard. Now they stood face to face, the guard in the doorway that would lead Kem back to his cell. "You can't stay out here all day," the officer said. "We're not running a country club. Others need their turn."

Kem shuffled toward the door, his head down. Another prisoner entered the courtyard. As he passed, the man slipped something into Kem's hand. The edges of the paper were sharp, but Kem closed his hand around it tightly, jabbing his palm. He thought again of Mirela's silver earrings.

Kem was ready, had been for more than an hour. He'd followed the instructions in the note, stuck his scrap of a towel between the bars of his cell. He was part of the group, part of the plan. He tucked his notebook down the front of his pants, his pen in his back pocket and his jailhouse blanket under his shirt. It would protect him from the strike of a baton if it came, and if he didn't need it for that, he could use it to get over the razor wire. If it got out intact, the blanket would be a present for Mirela.

Why they picked him, he wasn't sure. And it didn't matter. Vijay had always said, "When opportunity knocks, you don't slam the door." Was Vijay talking about his own escape from a prison, or his refugee claim, or something else? Kem wasn't sure, but now that chance had smiled on him, he knew he had to act.

The more of them that escaped and fanned out, the harder it would be for the police to track them all down. This would give him time to hide for as long as it took for the police to lose interest in him.

Footsteps, urgent and decisive, were coming down the corridor. He heard keys in locks; doors opening. Whispers.

Someone at his cell door. A key rattled in the lock, but it didn't budge. Something was stuck. The man wiggled the key. Other voices behind him urged him to hurry up.

"Leave him behind. They'll catch us if we don't hurry," someone hissed.

"Don't leave me," Kem said. He tried to keep the panic out of his voice. Weakness was never a good thing.

The sound of grating metal on metal. Nothing.

Then, as if by magic, the door clicked open.

Following close behind the man in front of him, Kem's breath was caught in his chest. He was unsure how many men there were. How were they going to get out of this place? Follow, he told himself. Just follow. His breathing calmed. Images of Mirela came to mind. For her, he told himself. This was for her.

The blanket fell and tangled in his legs. He nearly tripped. "Leave it," someone muttered. Kem kicked it aside.

A door at the end of the corridor opened. Fresh air, shimmering black sky, the sound of traffic nearby. Kem gulped air. No wire, no fencing, just out the door. How could it be this easy? He didn't know and didn't care. He wouldn't question good fortune.

The others scurried in all directions. He ducked down low into a bush, waited for the searchlight to swipe over the trees, streets, and buildings in front of the prison. He stood up, stole away.

21

BONDS

Maroúsi

*I*n a few hours, she'll be dragging me to God knows where to find the kid. I don't know why I let her talk me into this. We were supposed to go home. That's why I spoke to the commander today. He found me a lawyer, or at least someone with a suit and tie, to help with the paperwork. I could have gone to the Canadian Embassy, but figured the fastest way to get things moving was to go to the source. I didn't have time for diplomatic mumbo-jumbo and government officials wrangling to save face with their counterparts.

The commander was at the front desk. He's a self-righteous prick who hides behind a supercilious smile. But I knew if anyone could make something happen, it had to be this guy.

The commander played hardball at first, told me Mother had admitted to taking the kid. He didn't believe her any more than I did.

But then he told me there was a problem with her extended stay. He said something about the EU Schengen Agreement, whatever that is. They're the ones who saw her stamped passport. Not me. I had to take his word for it.

What can I do for her? I asked. Happy to do whatever was necessary.

People enjoy our country, he said. It is a problem for us.

I let him ramble on.

They like our food, our fine wine.

He stared at me like he knew something about me I didn't know myself. But how the hell would he know anything?

Okay, so I screwed up yesterday. It was too fucking much. That bottle of wine just sitting there, this shit with Mother, all these fucking memories. I drank it. Every last fucking drop. Didn't stop to think about it either.

An hour later it came out. Didn't know which end to stick where. Sat on the floor in the shit and puke, bawling my eyes out, like I was a kid again. I don't want to ever forget that smell. Or what that drink cost me.

People who come here never want to leave, the commander said. We have to levy fines and put people in jail and deport them. And still they come.

I can't wait to leave, I thought, but I humoured the guy and listened to him rattle on. I acted like I had all the time in the world to listen. Guys like him just want an audience. Meet a lot of them in my world.

The commander shook his head, said something about how Americans think they can solve all their problems with money. He tucked his hands in his pockets. As if that would hide what he was doing. Reminded me of Mr. Weston.

Ted put his pen down. His hands were clammy. He stared at his former teacher's name. He could feel the man's hand on his shoulder, again. Ted had stood still as his teacher brought him in close, held him. Ted wished his father could have hugged him like that. But that feeling had lasted only long enough to take a few breaths, the brief moments before he realized what Mr. Weston had really wanted.

He felt surprisingly calm, considering the images skittering through his brain. Having written the man's name made him feel as though he'd released something he'd held too tightly in his hand. It hurt, but a little relief had also come from letting go. He would need to deal with Mr. Weston. Remember again what had happened. Every bit of it. Ted knew that, understood it.

He put his journal and pen down on the table.

Ted sprawled lengthwise across the couch in his mother's living room, head drooped over one end, his legs, at the other, touching the floor. So many thoughts. Booze. Mother. Mr. Weston.

His jaw throbbed. His neck ached too. He licked his lips. Sandpaper ridges. His mouth dry from the Greek salad they'd shared when they got back to her apartment. Not enough olive oil, too much salt. Exactly what you'd expect from street vendor food. She wasn't up for a nice restaurant. She wanted to go home, take a shower, and hang out with him. He'd accommodated.

How old was he when she asked him to do this one thing for her? She'd asked him for this or that favour many times. Small things. "Pick up the groceries after school, will you? I'm going to be late." "Can you take the garbage out? It's a bit heavy for me." "Ted, if Alice calls, please tell her I'm not home. I've listened to her problems three nights in a row. I don't mind helping her. Just exhausted tonight."

There was no way to say no to Mother.

But that one time was different; it was more than she should have asked of him.

He was almost fourteen. He'd come home after school that day just like every other day. He was surprised to find her at home already. She was back from the office early for a change, said she'd put in a lot of overtime. It was time they paid her back. That was it. She was always particularly quiet when she was worrying over a problem or a client or mad at him. He didn't think he had done anything to piss her off, so he figured she was worried about a client. No need to push it or keep asking her what was wrong.

He did his homework and came downstairs when she called him for dinner.

She didn't look at him, forked the clump of onions on her plate, but didn't put anything to her mouth.

Laying the fork down, she stared out into space, oblivious to him. She didn't even smile. Man, he thought then, she must be worrying a tough case this time.

He was never sure when she'd come out of herself, so he just concentrated on finishing his dinner.

"Your dad is dead," she said bluntly, as they were putting their dishes in the dishwasher. No warning, no gentle setup, nothing.

"Dead? When? How?" He stood still, blood rushing to his head. He'd eaten too much, too fast. He controlled a burp, afraid he might throw up. Stuck in his throat, the vinegary taste and smell of the onions he'd wolfed down at dinner with his overdone steak. The onions burned angrily in his chest.

"They need next of kin to identify him." Her eyes trained on him.

"Dead? How could he be dead?" Ted shivered, even though it was an unusually hot spring night. The kitchen window was open, a fiery breeze badgering the curtains. He registered these things, but none of it made sense. He rubbed his arms. Nothing. Inside, his bones were turning to ice.

How could his father be dead? He'd seen him in his office a few days, a week ago, no more. He said something about it not being his fault. What wasn't his fault? What other things had they talked about?

He should have stuck around. Talked to his father. What the hell was he trying to tell him? Why hadn't he listened more carefully?

"They want me to identify the body," his mother said. "I can't do it." Her hands gripped the countertop behind her. Her back was to the sink, her chest open as if cornered. And still she wouldn't take her eyes from him.

Each time he recalled that night, he couldn't remember exactly what he'd been thinking. How and when had he agreed to identify his father? The picture of where they were standing. Yes, he saw that clearly, right down to the old sunflower-patterned curtain. The early spring heat. And how cold he was. Yes. After several swigs of whatever was kicking around in the liquor cabinet, he got into bed with his clothes on and an extra blanket. It didn't matter. He was sweating, but he wasn't sure he'd ever feel warm again.

He remembered the man who'd asked him a few questions the next day in that sterile room. He'd answered every question. The man read the authorization his mother had signed to allow him to identify his father, and nodded.

The bright lights made the room feel barren. The smell was stale and antiseptic. Do what they want you to do, he said to himself. Get it over with. There is no making sense of this. Don't try.

He stared at his father. He looked like he was just asleep. A little pale, that's all. His complexion was not unlike the colour of the ashes in the fireplace. But he often looked like that after a bender. Why was this time any different?

The man put his hand on Ted's shoulder, frightening him. "Are you okay, son?"

Dead. He'd wished it so many times. His father dead. "Yes. Fine."

"I need you to sign some paperwork."

Despite the man's morbid work, there was hopefulness behind his eyes, like a smile. How could that be?

"Whatever you need," Ted said. "My mother. She couldn't do this."

"Understood," the man said, but his eyes shuttered closed.

How could this stranger understand, when Ted couldn't? She was this way. She couldn't handle the really bad things. Not by herself, anyway.

Ted had planned to skip school and go home. But as he walked to the bus stop, he began to chuckle. His father was gone. What the hell was he laughing for? The man would never hurt her again. He'd fantasized about killing him, but hid when he knew his father was hitting Mother. He only came out afterwards. To get her an ice pack, make her a sandwich, hold her hand and try to make her smile.

And now that his wish had come true, he didn't know how to act or how to feel. Why couldn't he stop laughing? He ducked into an alleyway, crouched behind a dumpster, gulped down the contents of the mickey in his pocket. He'd only brought it in case he thought he might need it. He laughed, choked. He coughed up phlegm. Spit. Slipped down in a heap on the cold pavement, his back against a grimy brick wall.

His father was gone.

His sides ached. Face wet. He couldn't stop. He'd laughed himself into tears. Arms across his knees, he put his head down, his forehead sunk into the cradle of his arms. His eyes startled open at the sound of the silence. Where had the cars gone, the traffic? He watched the pool of blood grow, one drip at a time. Another drip. One after another. He watched. That's all. Did nothing to stanch the blood coming from his nose. Everything else — sound, thought, his laughter — had stopped.

Ted sat up in Mother's apartment, planted his feet on the floor. The living room was hot and humid. Odours of grease and cooking seeped through the walls. How do these things infiltrate concrete and steel? he wondered.

The noxious stench of the morgue where he had identified his father was exactly the same as the one that permeated the walls of his science class at boarding school a few years later. Mr. Weston again. His grin. The stupid wedding ring he'd tuck into his breast pocket. Hiding it. To make what he did to Ted legit. Images drowned so long ago floated to the top. One overlaid on the other. The hand of the person at the morgue on Ted's shoulder is kind, fatherly. The other hand rubbing Ted's neck is his teacher's. Rougher, urgent in its longing.

He closed his eyes, squeezed every muscle in his body tight. And held on.

A locked classroom door. Mr. Weston's breath in his ear. The man's hands squeezing Ted's nipples, finding their way down his pants. He'd trusted Mr. Weston. Disgust. What had he done to make it happen?

One by one, the images faded, although he knew they'd return. He took a deep breath, then another.

He heard something down the hall. His heart quickened. His mother must be up. He had no idea what time it was. He heard the bathroom door shut.

The curtains allowed morning light to filter through and the room was already bright. He reached for a piece of gum. His dry mouth moistened slightly with lemony bitterness.

He saw his open notebook and pen on the coffee table, where he'd left them. Get your shit together, he told himself, and tucked both away into his carry-on bag.

"Knock, knock," she said, as she walked in.

He jumped.

"Planning on making a quick getaway?"

His hand was still pushed into his bag. "Just tidying up," he said, and zipped the bag shut. "You look good," he said.

She was in her housecoat and her hair looked fluffy, as though it was freshly washed and dried. Her eyes were engaged and bright. Rest and food went a long way, he thought.

"I'm finally going to do something tangible to help Bo and his family," she said. "And I'm so happy you're here, too. You're going to come see where I've been working. We're in this together." She plopped down beside him, leaned her head against him. The flowery scent of her hair annoyed him.

What work? he thought. You were fired. He hadn't realized volunteers could be fired. But she had been. He patted her hand, as she used to do to his when he was a boy. He stood up, walked over to the window and pulled the drapes open. Facing her, he kept the gum in his mouth still under his tongue. "Shouldn't you be talking to your bosses?"

"Oh, they're not involved in the day-to-day stuff." Leaning closer to his bag, she ran her fingers over the initials engraved on the side of the bag. "You're still putting your name on everything." As though she was recalling a fond memory, she grinned wistfully.

He shrugged. "You taught me that. Remember?"

"Yes." She sat up straighter, moved away from the bag, pressed her hands over her housecoat as if brushing a crumb of toast or a piece of fluff away. "Your father was always worried about the money we spent on toys, books, games, anything and everything. Don't lose your toys, your books. They're expensive to replace. Remember how he used to say that? He went on and on about every single purchase. It made me crazy. He liked to put his initials on everything too. Remember?"

He nodded, as though he could see his father just there in front of him, yanking at a toy, shaking it in the air, demanding what it cost and why Ted needed it.

"He still has his influence over us," she said quietly, as if talking to herself, "so many years later."

He wanted to disagree. That man had no power over him, or her, for that matter. Instead, he asked her about her job again.

"But shouldn't you report what happened?" He leaned towards her. "Your organization might be able to help."

"We're on our own, Ted," she said and smiled. "Like always. It's just you and me. That's the best way to be." She nodded. "Don't those words sound like they come from an old nursery rhythm?"

"I'm hoping when we arrive at this camp of yours today, the kid will be there. We can tell the police, take a picture for proof, and they'll let his father go. We book our flight home and we're done with this country."

"You're forgetting one small detail in your happily ever after. The police will want to deal with me too, and who knows what will happen."

He turned toward the window. No, I've already taken care of that, he thought.

The day was hazy and colourless, the heat suffocating already. The sun wore a leash of smog.

"Don't worry so much," she said. "You got us a smart lawyer, the embassy is involved. It'll work out."

He lowered his chin, but didn't turn to face her. He'd have to tell her about the arrangement he'd made with the police commander. They'd find the kid first. That would make her happy. It would be easier to tell her once they'd solved the problem with the kid and his father. Then maybe she'd come clean too.

"How about breakfast?" she said.

He hid the gum against the inside of his cheek, turned away from the window to tell her he'd love to take her out for breakfast. She was already out the door.

Ted swallowed hard, held his breath as he followed her. Why hadn't he bought a mask or a handkerchief to put over his nose?

The stench — urine, human waste, rotting garbage, smoke and greasy sweat — were overpowering. Constant. And somewhere, there was the smell of alcohol. A still. It all made him queasy, like the other night after the wine.

Coffee and bits of the fruit he'd had at breakfast came up his throat. He swallowed to keep it down.

Shacks, tents, and lean-tos sat one beside the other in and amongst heaps of garbage, old furniture, and open fires.

Everywhere eyes stared at them. He knew they would just as soon kill him as see him here. Trespassing. He quickened his step, ensuring he stayed close to his mother. An old woman spat onto the broken cobblestone. Another man threw trash at his feet, spraying his pants and leather shoes. He'd buy a new pair as soon as he could, then chuck these out. Mother had told him to wear jeans, a shirt he didn't mind getting dirty or smelly. He didn't have any such thing. It wasn't as if he'd packed for a trip to the dump.

In front of a lean-to erected against a gutted concrete building sat a woman with a garbage bag between her spindly legs. Her elbows were on her knees, and her hands picked through a garbage bag. She wore a headscarf, cracked, plastic sandals, a black skirt, and a T-shirt with an imprinted image of Snow White. The air was swirling with ash. The fire seethed.

Ted stifled a cough.

"Look who is back," the woman said barely glancing at them. She picked up a poker, jabbed at the bits of burning wood. A spark flared briefly, and then subsided.

"Is Bo here, Mirela?" Shelby asked, moving closer to the woman. The woman glared at her. Shelby took the hint, and squatted down across from the woman, eye to eye.

"What business is it of yours?" the woman said. Her earrings were bright against her dark skin. The beads on her headscarf jingled and made a faint tinkling sound as she stabbed the fire. "He is my son."

"We're trying to find him and make sure we get him home to you. Then we can help get Kem back. He's in jail. But he shouldn't be."

The woman stood up, the poker still in hand. Her earrings vibrated furiously. "Go away and leave my family alone." She tightened her grip on the poker.

"If we can prove Bo is home safe with you," Shelby said, "they will let Kem go. You can be a family again and I will not bother you anymore." She remained crouched down, even as the woman stood over her. How could his mother be so calm in the face of all this? Ted wondered.

"My husband can take care of himself."

"But we can help him." Shelby extended her arm toward the woman. "I can do this small thing for you."

Muffled cries came from the lean-to, along with the noise that sounded like a chain clanking. Ted wondered if some kind of dog was going to lunge out at them.

"Bah! Like you helped us before?" the woman said. She turned, signalled to a young girl to stand guard outside the lean-to. The woman disappeared inside.

The girl stared at them.

Shelby stood, rubbed her hands. She called out after the woman. "Look, I'm just trying to help. Is Bo with you? I won't take him away again. It'll be okay."

There was a commotion inside the lean-to. A boy staggered out of the flap, dragging a chain. His ragged shirt hung open. The woman, close behind him, yanked at the chain. The boy stumbled. She tried to drag him back along the ground closer to her.

"Bo!" Shelby rushed to him, pulled at his outstretched arms. Ted took a step forward, unsure what to do. He'd stood back so many times when his mother took his father's fists. Not anymore.

The woman dropped the chain, grabbed the poker she'd left by the door. She jabbed the air, just in front of Shelby's face. The girl lobbed a rock that caught Ted in the elbow. He grabbed his arm. The rock fell at his feet.

"She is not my mother," the boy yelled. He crawled to Ted and held onto his legs. Despite his throbbing arm, Ted helped the boy up, shielding him from the woman.

The woman stood in front of Ted, her jaw clenched, the smell of rotten meat on her breath.

"I will not let you take my son." She edged closer to Ted, poker in hand.

"I am not your son," the boy insisted. Ted felt the boy shiver against him.

"I thought Mirela would help me find my ammi," the boy said.

"What did you do to him?" the woman hissed. "He never spoke these insults before."

The woman and Ted continued to stare at each other. Ted was at least four inches taller and he pulled himself to his full height. He'd show her who was in charge.

"Bo, what are you saying, honey?" Shelby said. She crouched down beside him. "You came back here. This is your family."

The boy shook his head. "I thought she would help me. Ammi told me to wait for her here, but I've waited and waited and she has not come back."

"Help you how?"

"Quiet now, Bo," the woman said. "You know these people are dangerous. They took you away. You know that. You were told to listen to us. Ammi and Abbu. Remember what they said."

She pointed at Mother. "He does not know what he is talking about. You people did something to him when you took him away. He does not recognize his own family. This is your fault."

Now what? The kid was behind his legs. His mother was kneeling down beside the boy and the woman in front of him wouldn't get out of his face. She was not a big woman. She had the body of a teenager in a lined, sunbaked face. Probably a kid herself. Why hadn't he seen this before? It didn't matter. He knew she was dangerous. Her face was set like stone. And that poker in her hand wasn't helping either. He had to find a way to get them out of here.

"They gave me to her because they went to find a better life for me. Ammi told me they would come back. I had to stay here or my ammi would never find me again."

"These are lies," the woman shouted and pushed at Ted to get to the boy.

He stood firm, stared at her.

"The earrings. They are Ammi's. She left them with Mirela. I knew she would be back. She would never leave them. Ever."

"She sold those earrings to us like she sold you to us," the woman spat. "She didn't want you. You ungrateful boy. I'm the one who loved you, took care of you, gave you everything. She never wanted you."

The boy tried to kick her. "That's not true."

The woman lunged at the boy. He cowered again behind Ted. Ted pushed her back.

"She is a liar," the boy said now. "She's lied to me to keep me here."

Shelby stood up, eyed the woman. "You want to tell us what's going on?"

The woman shifted her eyes away from Ted. He followed her gaze. They were being circled. Men, women, children surrounded them.

"You people think you have all the answers. You know nothing about us."

"I came back here so she could help me. That is all," the boy said. "She does not care what I want. I know that. She wasn't keeping me safe until Ammi came back. She was keeping me." The chain around his bare ankle rattled. "She won't let me go."

"We're taking him with us." Mother said. She put her arm on the boy's shoulder.

"Mother," Ted said, quietly.

"We have to, Ted." The look she gave him made it clear there was going to be no argument.

"Take a look around you."

Grumbling whispers. Men, women, children — dark, menacing and desperate faces — were closing in, some with metal pans in hand, others with rocks.

Ted stood firm. How the hell were they going to get out of here? Sweat dripped into his eyes, burned. Still, he wouldn't give the woman in front of him the satisfaction of a blink. If he had to take her down with him, he would.

"Look." Shelby turned to the woman. "I am taking Bo with us. Period. And you are not stopping us."

"Back off," he told the woman in front of him. She kicked him in the shin. Someone else threw a rock. He absorbed the blow between his shoulder blades. He would have liked to throw it right back at whoever threw it. But there was no time. He had to protect Mother. And the kid.

Sirens split the air. A loudspeaker crackled with words he didn't understand. Thunderous footsteps. The mob that had been circling them a minute ago scattered. It was as though they'd disappeared through invisible doors and openings he hadn't realized were there.

The woman remained. She stared at Ted, her eyes daring him to look away.

22

FREE

Roma Camp, Néa Filothei, Athens

After separating from the others he'd escaped with, Kem hadn't come straight back to the camp. He'd kept to alleyways, hiding behind parked cars and dumpsters. Eventually, he'd ended up in the park behind the camp. For hours he waited there in the dark, deserted park with large oaks and no trails, listening to the sirens in the distance, wondering if they were tracking him. But no one came looking for him. The police didn't know where he lived or which camp he'd come from. He'd given them nothing and he doubted Mrs. Shelby had told the police where he lived. The officer, Christos, had said Mrs. Shelby would not say anything about the boy or what had happened. He hadn't been wrong about her. She was a good woman, just like he had told Mirela.

From the littered hillside, he watched the camp. It was quiet. He could easily avoid the few late-night stragglers who were still wandering the dirt laneways. He was back in territory he knew and he always knew how to make himself invisible here. He'd have to get rid of the prison clothes and get into his own. And his hat? As easy as things come, they go. He'd find a way to replace it. At least he still had his notebook and pen. Now that he was home, he also had the other pen and pencils he'd hidden the night he'd gone searching for Bo and disaster had fallen on him. These things might be the source of his livelihood when his escape became yesterday's news. He had to protect them, as he had protected his family.

Sneaking into the camp, he'd made his way to the lean-to, then crawled right in while Mirela was asleep. The light was dim. The streetlights above were still on. They always shone over them, into their tiny home, as though they were on display. When he wanted to sleep, he covered his eyes with his arm or his jacket to block the light.

The boy was curled up on his piece of cardboard. Seeing Bo startled him at first, and then confused him. Had he dreamt all the misfortunes the boy had brought down on their heads? How had he returned? The boy was smart, Kem had to give him that. But smart enough to escape an orphanage after Mrs. Shelby was locked up? He didn't think so.

Mirela had found him somehow and stolen him back. She had her ways. She could have saved him a lot of trouble in the first place, but never mind, Bo was home now, and they were all together again. This was what was important. He had avoided the catastrophe of being sent to the big detention centre outside of Athens. He would have rotted in there for months and then like his friend, Vijay, he would have been told to leave the country. He would lose his family forever if that happened.

He told himself to relax. He'd escaped again. It was lucky for him he was like a cat. He had nine lives. He wondered if he could escape to a better country, as Vijay had done. Maybe it was time to think about another move. But he didn't know where he would go. He would have to talk it over with Mirela. She was the one with the ideas.

He noticed something around the boy's leg. It caught the soft light and glimmered. Perhaps it was an ankle bracelet Bo had found. Shiny things struck the boy. He loved touching Mirela's earrings when he sat close to her. Kem thought this wasn't right for a boy of his age, but Mirela told him to leave Bo alone whenever he complained about the boy's fascination with her earrings.

Kem tucked in beside Mirela, slipped his hand over her breast. He squeezed.

She turned quickly, punching at him. He held her arms down and climbed on top of her. "I see you're happy to see me," he said and smiled.

One hand holding both of hers above her head, he unzipped his pants, pushed her skirt out of the way, pulled at her underwear and forced himself inside of her. He tried to kiss her, but she turned her face away.

"I've been in that awful prison for days, but I see nothing has changed," he whispered. "That's okay with me."

She lay still, as though she were still asleep.

Once satisfied, he remained on top of her to catch his breath, his weight teetering on his elbows. She was a tiny thing. He had to be careful, forever careful, not to squash her. After all, she was his wife, from now to eternity.

He rolled off. "You sent me to look for your son and they threw me in jail. It was your fault. You owe me this." He didn't have to provide an explanation for what he wanted. Still, it was the right thing to do.

Sitting up, she dragged her underwear up, shoved her skirt down.

"They will come for you. They'll look here first," she said. "You can't stay."

He was on his back, arms behind his head. He could feel her glare. "They don't know which camp I come from," he said, his pants still down against his thighs. A dribble of sticky wetness warmed his leg. He was relaxed and content and Mirela was trying to spoil the moment with details. Her worries. She never stopped.

"This is the closest camp to that station. They will come here first." He was sure she expected him to jump to her bidding. He'd done that one too many times. Not again, he told himself. "And besides, they probably know you're not Greek Roma. This camp is for foreign Roma. The police must know that too."

"They wouldn't think I was stupid enough to return here. They know I'd just try to disappear like everyone else who escaped. And besides, they want some of the others more than me. I'm sure of that. Word travels fast. I'm not a big fish. They'll go after others, like those student anarchists, first." He released his arms, tugged his pants up, and tried to pull her down close to him. "And you know as well as I do, they don't like coming into our camps. They're afraid of us."

"But you did come back," she said, and remained sitting up, staring at him. "You made it very easy for them to find you. The boy."

She rarely looked at him directly, but now her gaze was fixed and unrelenting. What was she saying? Was she saying he was stupid? He'd obviously been gone too long. "You got the boy back, I see," he said. "And he's back wearing the awful shirt. I thought Mrs. Shelby would give him lots of nice clothes. I thought he'd do better by her."

"I sewed the buttons back on the day he left. I knew he'd be back," she said. Her mouth twisted and sneered at him. "You didn't want him back. But I knew he would come back to me. I'm his mother."

"So why the chain? Didn't you have enough of those things in your own life?" It had come to him as she talked. That was what he saw around Bo's ankle. "And if you knew so much, why did you send me out there to find him?"

She'd turned her back. "You have to leave," she said. "I don't want you bringing your troubles on to us."

"The trouble I'm in is because of you." He sat up, jabbed a finger into her back. He was a man, not a boy. Why did he do such childish things? Like his own sisters who used to tease and torment him, Mirela egged him on this way, brought out the child in him. And sometimes, she pushed so hard he became angry and violent with her. These were the things he'd seen in his father and promised himself he'd never do to his wife.

She shrugged.

"Where are my other pants?" he asked. "I've got to get out of these clothes."

Without looking at him or moving to get his pants as a good wife would, she pointed with her chin to a bundle in the opposite corner.

She lay back down on her side of cardboard, away from him.

Kem wasn't sure how long he'd slept, but the sun was already high when he woke. He changed into an old pair of pants, a tattered shirt, and the jacket he usually wore when he had to scrounge around for firewood. He put on the old shoes he'd wanted to discard when he bought his new shoes. Mirela had told him he might need them again one day. And besides, she said, they did not have enough of anything to begin throwing things away. He'd wanted to get rid of the shoes if only to spite her, but in the end, he couldn't do it.

Now he was glad to have them, even though the laces were long gone, the tongues disfigured, the heels chipped down to nothing, and the leather scuffed. They were better than no shoes at all. The police had taken his new ones. One of the officers had probably taken them home for himself or his children.

He left the lean-to, found his way through the alleyways of the camp and scrambled up the hill for a piss. Just as he finished relieving himself, the sirens began. The noise was deafening.

Now his feet refused to move. He stood stock still, his zipper down, his hand trapped in his pants. He had wanted to take a piss. That's all. He stared at his lean-to, just there.

Standing on a scrap of dirt, he watched the uniforms swarm in.

Finally, the sirens stopped. He removed his hand from his pants, zipped slowly. The noise of the zipper seemed amplified. He gritted his teeth, and squeezed his eyes shut as if these actions alone would ensure he didn't give himself away.

Opening his eyes, he squatted down warily. He could see Mrs. Shelby clearly. Had she escaped too? Why would she come back here? No, that couldn't be. Escape wasn't for white foreigners. They could afford better means. The bald guy standing beside her was probably her lawyer, here to help her get the boy back. They'd have a fight on their hands. Mirela wouldn't let the boy go so easily again.

He heard murmurs, but couldn't make out what was being said. The police escorted Mrs. Shelby, the man, and Bo away. Mirela stood her ground.

They weren't here for me, Kem thought. He watched the last of the police cars leave the camp. He turned. Mirela's eyes speared him where he stood. The police hadn't found him, but of course, she would. In her stare, he knew, she was commanding him to her.

He scuttled down the hill as quickly as he could without falling.

"Did they ask if you'd seen me?"

"The boy has told them," Mirela said, the poker still gripped in her hand.

"About me?" He put his hand on her shoulder. She was always this way, giving him bits and pieces of information. Torturing him. The police were using Bo as a way to get to him. They would hold him until Kem turned himself in. Was that it? What the hell was he going to do now? Mirela would want Bo back. Even if it meant he had to go to prison. His hold on her shoulder tightened. His legs trembled.

"About our arrangement." She knocked his hand off her shoulder. His legs gave out and he fell to the ground. He got up unsteadily.

"You mean with Mrs. Shelby? Did she come back to take him without giving us anything more for him? These rich do-gooders." Kem shoved his hand in his jacket pocket and fiddled with a hole he found there.

"Bo told them he wasn't our son."

"So what?" Kem said. "His family left him with us. That is not a crime. We are taking care of him. And good care, too. Did the police not see the toy truck I bought the boy just days ago?"

"They're not going to bring him back," she said and dropped the poker. Her eyes glistened; she nibbled her bottom lip.

He tried to hold her, but she pulled away, punched him in the stomach. "This is your fault."

Kem was stunned. He was not the enemy. "Look, they didn't arrest you," he said, and rubbed the spot where she'd hit him. "So it can't be that bad."

"They are investigating the boy's claims. They told me I have to go to the police station tomorrow."

"I can't go with you," Kem said and realized he'd spoken too quickly. He could no longer hold her gaze. He saw her lip curl.

"You'd just be more trouble. We already have enough of that." She slipped back into the lean-to before he had a chance to tell her he would go with her if he could, he'd go anywhere with her. She'd never believe him, but it was true.

He stood over the dying fire. The sun had broken over the parched hills and concrete buildings in the distance long ago. It would turn the camp into an oven soon. He was thirsty, but too exhausted to find the water jug now. The old pot sat on a rock close to the fire. As he lifted it, the lid slipped and fell against the rock and into the ashes. Someone yelled at him to be quiet. People were trying to get some rest after the excitement. He shrugged, dug into the oily remains of the meat and eggplant he found at the bottom of the pot.

After he'd had his fill, Kem found a heel of a cigarette in his pocket, matches by the entrance to his lean-to, and lit up. He sucked in the smoke. It burned his chest and warmed him.

He was a free man. Thank God. Everything hadn't gone to shit.

He stared at the ashes in the pit; flicked his match into it before he burned his fingers. She'd like it if he started the fire for her. She liked the fire to burn all day, just to heat up some water when she wanted it or anytime she wanted to wash her face. A good husband would. Later, he told himself. Then maybe he'd be able to convince her to let the boy go. He'd done all he could by the boy and his friend, Vijay. That was all that could be expected of him.

23

THE RAID

Athens

When Christos came out from behind the short concrete wall where he and the other officers had been hiding, the boy staggered to him. He held onto Christos. The other officers placed Mrs. Holt and her son in one of the police cars, but the boy would not release his leg or go with another officer. Christos picked him up as he would little Alexandra and held him to his chest. The boy's shoulders were bare and dusty. His shirt was torn open. Tears stained his dirty face and his nose was runny. He coughed into Christos's shoulder. The chain rattled as his chest and his body heaved. Christos held him closer.

"My ammi said she was coming back for me. I have to stay here. I didn't want to leave your house. You were nice to me and I miss Yiayiá. But Ammi would never have found me there." His words were muffled in Christos's shoulder.

Christos smiled. The boy called Christos's mother-in-law the name all his children called her. Yiayiá. Grandmother. He set Bo down. He unravelled the chain from his foot while the boy held onto Christos's shoulder. It came off easily, more a symbolic shackle than a real restraint. He flung it into a heap of garbage behind him. He straightened the boy's shirt, and took Bo's hands in his.

"I will find your mother," Christos promised. "But you will have to stay in the place I'm taking you to. It will be warm and clean. They will take good care of you and bring a doctor to check your cough. And I will see you every day and tell you how we are doing with finding your mother. Okay?"

The boy nodded, but didn't meet Christos's eye.

Putting a finger under Bo's chin, Christos smiled when their eyes met. "Can you promise me you won't run away, Bo? I will find her. I promise I'll do my best."

"My name is Sanjit. She will only know me by that name. Please tell her I've been good. I've been waiting for her, just like she told me to."

Christos nodded. "I will."

The boy smiled.

Christos wheeled the squad car away from the well-lit building where he'd left the boy. In the rearview mirror, the façade and the grounds looked cheerful, the floodlights nudging back the shadows of the large trees in the yard, and the doubts that wouldn't let him be. He headed towards the station, his thoughts on Sanjit.

He would have liked to have taken him home. But he knew that wasn't the right thing for his family. He couldn't put them through more. Yiayiá and Alexandra asked when the boy would be coming back, his sons asked if Bo had been thrown in jail or kicked out of the country along with his lazy parents. "Is that what happened, Babá? You can tell us the truth. We're not babies like Alexandra." He knew Alexandra was listening. "We don't throw children into prisons in this country. You know that," he'd replied, angrier than he could ever remember being with his boys. "He is an innocent boy, no different than the two of you. Do you understand? He is no different than the two of you."

It hadn't been the right thing to take the child home, as he had done before. He realized it only after the boy had run away, after his sons' questions, his mother-in-law's tears. Work and home had to be kept separate.

Antonis sat beside him, nattering about going into the Roma *kataskínosi*. "That was something," his partner said. "Never thought we'd do it. Those camps are dangerous. And those gypsies are so loyal to each other. They never report all the things that go on, drugs, violence, beatings. But still we went. Because of your plan. Only an engineer could figure out how to get into a place like that without being noticed."

He punched Christos in the arm, as though they were old buddies. The man had barely spoken two words to him when Christos had first been assigned to be his partner. "You drive," was all he'd said back then.

The Office of the Ombudsman for the Roma had a list of all the Roma camps. Christos had suspected Kem was living in the one close to the police station. He wouldn't be in the neighbourhood otherwise. Christos downloaded the plans of the derelict buildings. The camp was situated in a natural basin, so they could watch the camp's main entry from various viewpoints without being detected. He knew the Roma had other ways to enter their camp, but surveillance of the main entry would have to do. If nothing else, it was a start. He didn't know whether they would enter the camp when he initially spoke to the commander, but when he saw Mrs. Holt and her son, he radioed the rest to be prepared to storm the camp if the need arose.

"We got lucky," Christos wanted to say. And fortunately, most of the Roma in the camp had been too concerned with Mrs. Holt and her son to notice them.

Antonis couldn't stop talking. "Those people are something else, the way they live. How could she chain him up like that? The boy isn't a circus monkey. Luckily, he stood out like a fly in a cup of milk. So we could rescue the imp. He's not even hers. I always knew they were thieves, hiding cans of food under their shirts or slashing purses to steal the wallets inside, but I didn't know they took other people's children. I don't want people like these in my country. Call me a racist, but I don't want them around my children. We have values that are important to us. If we allow them to keep having children, soon they will outnumber us. Then what will happen to this society? They have no idea what it means to be civilized. It's good we sent them all a message today. If we could get rid of them all, well, so much the better."

"It's a good thing he was already outside that shed or whatever it was where they were keeping him. It wouldn't have been easy for us to storm through all those tents and lean-tos," Christos said. "The narrow passageways they've built are impossible to manoeuvre. There are too many concealed spots, hidden traps. We don't know enough about their ways."

"No, you're right, but their rocks couldn't stop our tear gas and batons if we had wanted to use them." Antonis laughed, a snort of bravado. He sounded nervous, even now that they were in the safety of their vehicle and away from the camp. "And your engineer's brain."

"We didn't find the Roma man or the other escapees. The commander won't be happy." Christos was thinking ahead.

"You know why he's tough on you, don't you?" Antonis said. He turned toward Christos as though he wanted to share a secret. His seat belt held him in place, stopped him from getting any closer.

Putting his arm against the back of Christos's headrest, Antonis tugged at the belt.

Christos tightened his grip on the steering wheel. Yes, I know what Kefalas thinks. I'm not cut out for police work. I'm made for desks and computers and not the mean streets and people Kefalas has worked with his entire career.

"He thinks you have potential," Antonis said, raising his eyes and chin slightly as if affirming what he said. At the same time, he seemed to say he didn't understand why the commander bothered with the likes of Christos. "He only pays attention to the ones he sees as worthy of his effort. He ignores everyone else. Haven't you noticed?"

Christos glanced again at Antonis. The man was not beneath practical jokes. He'd been the one who jammed Christos's locker so he couldn't open it, put drops of glue on the steering wheel of the squad car, then told Christos to drive, hid Christos's files and notepad. Then, he'd laughed his head off and encouraged the others to laugh. All those incidents had happened when Christos was first partnered with Antonis.

Christos stared at the cars in front of his vehicle. There was always traffic in this city of cars and pollution and people and chaos. It didn't matter what Antonis said. The commander would be angry they hadn't found the Roma man.

Christos had been the one who had convinced Kefalas that they should watch the camp.

"At this point, I don't care about the boy," Kefalas had said. "I want that gypsy back in custody, along with the others who escaped. The only way to make this right and avoid shame is to find them all and make an example of them."

He showed the commander his drawings, where they could set up their surveillance posts. "He'll probably go back to his family, the camp he came from. These camps are great places to hide. They don't bother us and we don't bother them. That's the unspoken rule. Right? So he may let his guard down and simply head home to his family."

"You still don't understand." Kefalas picked at his teeth with the plastic toothpick he'd dug out of his penknife. "These people have no attachments to anything or anyone. Why do you think we have so many in this country we haven't been able to catch? I will tell you. They are like cockroaches. They find holes to dig themselves into, out of our reach. Undisturbed and hidden, they just keep multiplying."

"But sir, the man came to us, looking for his son in the first place," Christos said. He sat across from the commander and leaned an elbow on the desk. "Why would he do that, take such a risk, if he didn't care about the boy?"

Kefalas threw up his hands. The toothpick remained stuck in his mouth, giving him the look of having an extra tooth. The penknife dropped to the desk. Christos flinched.

"Do you think I understand these people and their motivations? Who knows why he came here? Maybe he was trying to get more money from the American woman. Blackmail. Said he'd go to the police if she didn't give him more money. Or perhaps his wife threw him out because he sold her son to the first stranger willing to take him off his hands for a shiny euro or a pair of new shoes. I don't know why these gypsies do what they do. I'm here to make things right, not to figure out all their twisted motivations. I leave that to the psychologists and engineers like you."

Christos sat back in his chair. "We have no other leads, sir. It may be our best chance of finding him," Christos said, then added, "and the others who escaped with him." Kefalas wouldn't be concerned about the escape of one detainee, especially a guy like Kem, who was a gypsy and would find his way back into a place like this many more times in his life. It was the others, or rather the number of escapees, that was likely the commander's major concern.

Kefalas would be called on the carpet for lax security. News like this would hit the papers and the law-and-order guys and the other mean-spirited Golden Dawn-type politicians would make a big deal of the escape, use it as a platform to target foreigners again.

"The police are too incompetent to keep us safe. We will do it for you by cleaning up the country of this human garbage. We're the only ones who can." Christos could already imagine the headlines, the interviews, and the sound bites in the press and on television, every politician vying to be the person the public trusted to keep them safe. With the escapes, the politicians would have been handed an issue they could run on besides the abysmal economy. As for guys like him or the commander who tried to maintain order, no one would care what they did to prevent the escape or find the escapees. The commander couldn't be fired. He'd been around too long, but if someone wanted to get rid of him, they'd find a way. He'd be reassigned or demoted or forced into early retirement.

"Two days, that's all I'm giving you," Kefalas said, and tilted his eyes toward the door. "Bring me back something." He approved the overtime so Christos could work the day shift too. It would be easier to watch over the camp during the day, Christos had argued, and less dangerous than during the night shift.

Yes, I have something for you, Commander, but it's not what you are looking for, Christos now thought as he drove toward the station.

The boy was safe. That was important. Christos focused on his destination. What would happen next to the boy he'd promised he'd help?

He shut out Antonis, who was humming a popular song about unrequited love and revolution. How these two things could be combined in verse, Christos didn't know.

At the station, Christos was ushered into a large boardroom. There were a few pats on the back and smiles from some of the other officers as he passed by. He'd gotten them into a Roma camp and back out without incident. So he was suddenly some kind of hero.

This attention embarrassed him. He wanted to do his job well. That was all.

Mrs. Holt and her son were already in the room behind the main desk. He saw them through the wall of glass. As she watched her son pace, her posture was relaxed, face as calm as someone waiting for an inconsequential appointment. Her son had his hands shoved into the pockets of his pants. His shoulders rode high around his ears as though in a permanent, strained shrug.

When she saw him, Mrs. Holt stood up. "Christos, finally. How is he? Where is he? Is he safe? That cough of Bo's has gotten much worse. He needs to see a doctor. Is that possible?" She fired her questions at him one after the other.

"He's fine, Mrs. Holt. Let's sit down." He offered the chair again to her.

"Yes, Mother, let's stay calm," her son said. "I'm sure the officer has made arrangements for the child."

Mrs. Holt sat down. Her son remained standing.

"The boy is in a safe place. He has assured me he won't run away again and I gave him my word I would find his real parents."

"Well, well," Kefalas said as he walked into the room. "Everyone is back." His eyes penetrated Christos. "Almost everyone." His grin looked like a badly disguised sneer. "Madam," he said and slipped his penknife into his pocket. "You're still here."

Christos did not meet his eyes.

"And you are back," Kefalas said to Mrs. Holt's son.

The son nodded.

Christos wondered what was going on between the two of them. Kefalas ran his hand over his whiskers. The son's eyes seemed to drift, focusing on everything and nothing at all.

"Officer Pappas, did you see any of the escapees?" Kefalas spread out in a chair across from Mrs. Holt. He gave her a glance and her son moved to the spot behind his mother, put a hand on her shoulder.

"What escapees?" the son asked. "We went to find the boy. That is all we were doing in that camp."

"And you didn't see his father?"

"What is this about?" the son asked, this time considering Christos.

"A group of prisoners escaped a few nights ago. The boy's father was with them."

"Kem?" Mrs. Holt said. "He shouldn't have been in here in the first place."

"We thought he might end up back at the camp."

"We didn't see him," the son said, his lips pursed, his shoulders still uncomfortably high. "Only the boy, and his mother. Well, not his mother. The woman. Whoever she is. Where is she now?"

"My officers have left her there at the camp until we figure out what is going on. Maybe her husband will come back there, maybe she'll cooperate with us to get the child back," Kefalas said. "We never know with these people."

"But Bo isn't her child." Mrs. Holt leaned her elbow on the table separating her from Kefalas. "We have to find out where his real mother is and why Bo was with Mirela."

"Did you check her shack?" Kefalas asked, eyeing Christos.

Christos nodded. "No one else there."

Kefalas rocked so far back in the chair, it creaked as though it might shatter into pieces. It held. He snapped forward onto his feet.

"So you went for one case," Kefalas said, "and you came back with two. Now we may have a kidnapping as well as an escape on our hands."

Christos nodded.

"What are we going to do about finding Bo's family?" Mrs. Holt asked. She leaned forward in the chair as though she didn't want to be forgotten.

"You have done quite enough, madam," Kefalas said. "This case no longer concerns you. This is police work and we know how to do our job. You are free to go." He turned to leave the room.

"But I need to help find the family." Mrs. Holt stood up, placed her hand on Kefalas's forearm.

"There is no role for you here," Kefalas said. "You have only a few days. I hope you have made your arrangements."

"But I told you I kidnapped that child in the first place. There must be charges pending against me. I can't just leave the country. My son has hired a lawyer. We'll be ready when the time comes, but for now, I can help you find Bo's real family."

"The situation is under control. The Roma woman is coming in to give us her statement. I'm sure she will also tell us about the arrangement she made with the boy's family. We will locate them and solve this problem. You don't have to worry. You are not speaking to just anyone here. You are talking to the Greek police."

"And what about the charges against me?" Mrs. Holt asked.

"Your son has taken care of this," Kefalas said. "I'm sure he will explain things. In the meantime, Officer Pappas will see you out."

Christos remembered the first night he'd met Mrs. Holt's son, how eager he was to pull his wallet out. Mrs. Holt glanced at her son, questioning.

Kefalas was out the door quickly, and then turned to smile at the son. "We understand each other. Yes?"

"I will explain, Mother."

Christos pointed the two of them towards the door.

24

BLOOD TIES

I promised the nice policeman I would stay here. And I will for a little while just to see if he finds Ammi for me. He looked right at me like he wanted to see me. Even though he looked scared, his eyes were like the tiny lights I see in stores at Christmas, bright and warm and, I think, filled with love. People who are not the same as us stare at us as if we are someplace we shouldn't be, that we don't deserve to be here on the same street, in the same world they live in. Both Ammi and Mirela told me these people think they are better than us. I don't think this man is like all the others. I believe he's going to find my ammi.

When I came back to the camp, Mirela gave me back my favourite shirt, the one Ammi got especially for me from a real store. I know it's old and only has one button left on it, but Mirela had put some buttons back on. The buttons were different — plain black, not like the shiny silver ones I used to have on it, but they worked. It was the first thing I put on when I came back. That shirt and Ammi's earrings were the only things I had left of her, so I had to guard them good.

The night I got back, Mirela was happy when she saw me, but then she got really mad the next day if I wasn't by her side every minute. And if I left the camp or our little house and didn't tell her where I was going she'd pinch my ear when I got back, tell me

I had better listen to her or else. I don't know what she meant by *or else*. She never said.

I was only back for two days and she was mad at me all the time. I guess she was afraid another person would want to take me away. I told her I wouldn't let that happen again and even kissed her cheek and hugged her tight because I know that makes her happy. She smiled big and wide then, in the same way she did when I first came to stay with her. Her teeth looked sharp, though, like those of some of the dogs running around the camp. And they were kind of black too, like she'd chewed on dirt every day of her life.

I forgot this was what her teeth looked like because she didn't show them all the time, and maybe that was a good thing.

She put a chain around my ankle and attached it to a heavy can whenever I was inside where we slept. When I was outside, she would pull at the chain if I got too far. I would fall and my knee would bleed. She'd wipe the blood away so gently that I wondered why she wanted to hurt me in the first place.

"It's for your own good," she told me. "That woman who stole you from us may have given you some ideas to run away by yourself. And besides there are other bad people out there you have to watch for." We were sitting by the fire then. I wanted to tell her Candy Lady didn't steal me, Kem gave me to her. But I didn't.

She wrapped the chain around my ankle again, making some kind of knot. I watched her, not really knowing what else I could do.

"And that policeman and his family who you said took you to his house? Maybe he will come and take you away again," she said. "When you're out running around, away from me, not paying any attention to anything, but playing and goofing around, they'll sneak up on you and take you. You don't know these people. Believe me."

"I don't want to go out to play. I have to go to work," I said. "I have to help the family and I can't do it in the camp. And the other kids laugh at me too because I'm not working. It's not fair."

"They will find you and take you," Mirela said. "They are like the devil himself." She made a face that was supposed to scare me, and then used her fingers to make it look like she had horns growing out of her head. She didn't have to go to so much trouble. She was scary all by herself.

"Then I will run away from them again," I said. "You wait and see. I'm almost a man. No one can make me do what I don't want to."

She smiled and I thought she was crying too. She wiped her face with the bottom of her shirt.

I got tired of the chain and worked at taking it off. When she caught me, she slapped my face so hard it felt like everything in my head shook. I felt a little dizzy and started coughing like I do sometimes, but this time a lot harder. I threw up right in front of her, spraying her face and her feet and I bet her dress too.

She cried then for real and hugged me hard, smearing my snot and the stuff I threw up. I knew she was sorry for what she did, but there was no way I would hug her back. I thought, just wait until I tell Ammi.

That was when I told her I wanted to know where Ammi was and how I could find her. Mirela was in front of me hugging me, but she stood up, then, wiped my mouth with her dress and said she was my ammi and I'd better get used to it because no one else was coming for me. She said these words so quietly, it was like she was holding something tight, boiling inside of her. It scared me more than if she'd just hit me again.

But I got even with her. I tore my shirt open, the buttons she'd sewn on, popping off one by one. I didn't want her new buttons. I didn't want anything from her.

"Suit yourself," she said. "It will be cold at night, your chest will be exposed and your cough will never get better. But if that's what you want, that's fine with me." She turned her back to me and sat down close to the fire.

"You are not my ammi and you'll never be," I told her. But she ignored me. "Do you hear me?" I hit her on the back with my fists, but she didn't move. "My real ammi is coming back for me. You wait and see, *Scroafă*." I punched her again, even though I surprised myself calling her that name I heard other boys use in the camp when they talked to a girl they really liked, who wouldn't pay them any attention. *Bitch*.

She didn't turn around. "You can wish all you want, but she isn't coming back. They never come back. They find better lives and forget the past." Her voice was quiet and soft like those times she told me stories at night before we went to sleep.

That was the night Kem came back. Maybe they let him out of prison so he could go home. If only someone could do that for me too.

I heard him sneak in, but I didn't move. I pretended I was asleep. I wasn't. I was awake, trying to plan how to get the chain off my leg and leave this place so I could look for Ammi myself. I would have to find a way to steal Ammi's earrings back for her before I left and that wasn't going to be easy. I needed to be nice to Mirela. Then maybe I could talk her into letting me hold them. I would disappear and she'd never find me.

When Kem came in he lay down beside Mirela. I moved to my side so I could see them and hear what they were talking about. I wondered if she would tell him what I called her. Then I'd be in for it. But Kem didn't do any talking. He climbed on top of her. He grunted kind of like one of the pigs in the pen at the other end of the camp, and then rolled beside her. Mirela never made a sound, even though I was sure he was trying to kill her. I wondered why she let Kem hurt her whenever he felt like it.

Kem laughed out loud like he was suddenly surprised. No one here laughs very much so it made me feel warm inside. Maybe he wasn't trying to hurt her at all.

I didn't move again and I guess I fell asleep. I woke up to voices outside. Kem and Mirela weren't in the corner where they slept.

It sounded like Candy Lady was back. It was her voice. I was sure of it. And she was arguing with Mirela. I listened some more, but I wasn't sure what they were saying. That's when I knew I had a chance. If I told the truth, maybe Candy Lady would help me. I don't know why I thought this, but I had to do something.

The chain was around my ankle, but it wasn't hooked to anything, so I could wriggle around with it still attached to me. But then I started thinking again. Candy Lady liked me too much too, kind of like Mirela. She liked me enough to want to keep me. She might not help me find Ammi either.

As I thought about what I should do, I heard more angry voices. It sounded like everyone in the camp was right outside our house. I had to decide now. At least with Candy Lady, I might have a chance of escape. If I stayed here with Mirela, there might never be another chance. I had to get away to find Ammi myself.

Mirela walked into our house and when I saw her, I knew what I had to do. I ran outside. She held onto the chain and tried to drag me back. But I got away and shouted everything to Candy Lady and the man standing beside her. I didn't even know him, but he looked strong, so I held onto him.

Then before anything else could happen there were lights and loud sirens. And the policeman who took care of me came and talked to me and held me and told me he'd find Ammi. He promised and I believed him. I could see it in his eyes. Even though he was different from me, he seemed to understand everything I was thinking.

So I'll stay for now.

A boy in one of the other beds down from me just told me to be quiet. I haven't said a thing, but I guess it's my coughing. My chest hurts. I try to cover my mouth. But still it comes. I turn over and try to bury my head in my pillow away from the little light on the wall beside my bed.

My eyes adjust. That's when I see it. I watch as it soaks the pillow red. I scream. I don't know how I can with all this blood, but I do. The lights come on and worried faces surround me. Their wide eyes all looking at me. No one turns away like other people have done before. That is the last thing I see.

25

Mirela's Dilemma

Amaroúsio Police Station

Christos watched the woman walk past the front desk and into the interview room. The other officers moved away and averted their eyes, allowing her the kind of space they might give to one of those government senior officials who have started visiting this place looking for human rights violations and any opportunity to cut jobs and save money. But it was not respect they were showing. It was closer to revulsion.

Christos had seen her yesterday. Frighteningly aggressive, she had stood, poker gripped in her hand. In the morning shadows of the Olympic Stadium and the freeway just above the camp, the flames in the fire pit had played across the woman's cheeks, making them look as hardened and misshapen as the gargoyles adorning the corners of the ancient buildings in central Athens. Her eyes were barely visible, yet he knew in her stony glare she was telling them all she'd just as soon kill them as let the boy go. At the sight of the police uniforms storming into the camp, most of the Roma vanished. This woman hadn't moved or flinched. He suspected she wouldn't today either.

She gave her name as Mirela yesterday and again when she checked in at the front desk just now. No last name. "This is my name. That is all I know," she told Pétros, at the front desk. He shrugged when he caught Christos's eye.

Her back was as straight as that of the famous ballerina his little Alexandra liked to mimic. Her eyes flared with a hint of emerald. Her sunbaked face was chiselled and emotionless. Cut into the corners of her mouth and eyes were tiny white lines, cracks in the skin missed by the unrelenting sun. Still, she seemed smaller today, a girl rather than a woman.

Pétros led her in the direction of the offices and Christos followed. Her black skirt and blouse looked clean, or at least cleaner than the dust-covered skirt and stained T-shirt she had been wearing yesterday morning. Her shawl was a rainbow of colour, her headscarf black as night. Yesterday, she'd been in sandals, but today she wore a pair of polished children's loafers that looked too small for her. She squashed the backs of the shoes with every step now as if to mould them to her will.

He noticed her silver earrings and wondered if she'd stolen them. He caught himself. He was being unfair. He was starting to think like his colleagues. Nonetheless, he wondered how she could afford such an extravagance. Silver wasn't cheap. Tia didn't have earrings like that.

He stopped himself. This wasn't about her jewellery. There was the boy to consider and the promise he'd made to him.

"Thank you for coming," he said as he walked into the office behind her and closed the door. He glanced at the camera, wondered if Kefalas was watching. And decided he didn't care. The boy was more important than this job or his commander's pettiness.

She stood waiting, her eyes fixed on him.

"Please sit down, Mrs. Mirela."

She gazed at the chair he pointed to, and then she looked at him with an expression of disgust, as though he'd asked her to sit in a pile of dirt.

"Do I have a choice?" she said and walked behind the desk to the chair meant for him. "You have my son. You have Bo and I want him back."

Christos stood, leaning against the back of the opposite chair, the desk between them. "His name is Sanjit, Mrs. Mirela. He isn't your biological son."

"That woman who stole him from me put thoughts in Bo's head with her poisoned candy." She stabbed the desk with her finger. Her eyes didn't leave him. They flickered. Loathing. Anger. Frustration. Emerald again. "She's the one to be blamed."

Christos sat down. "I understand your fear for the boy."

"Where were the police when we needed you?" Mirela shook her head. "You harass us on the street. You think we are here to steal your things. You are suspicious of us even when we keep to ourselves. You look at us as if we are insects to be stepped on. You don't protect us. And now you are accusing me of what? I don't know." She crossed her arms, leaned back in the chair and for the first time did not stare at him with those raging eyes. "She did something to him. I know she did."

"Mrs. Holt had him for less than one night," Christos said as calmly as he could. Did she think he was born yesterday? Who did she think she was? The boy would not lie about such a thing. But this wasn't the time to be heavy-handed and logical. She'd only become more entrenched in her position and he wouldn't get anything useful out of her. Remember why you're doing this, he told himself.

"She's been visiting the camp almost every day for months. Bringing him candy. He's a child. He is led by his sweet tooth and nothing more. He doesn't know any better. Did you when you were his age?" She stood up, leaned towards him, pointed at him as though he was the one being interrogated. "Bo is lucky enough to have a mother who wants to protect him from strangers. I'm sure your mother did the same for you."

Christos wanted to say, "You don't know anything about me," but instead said, "Sanjit is a child. Yes?" He felt his Adam's apple move up and down, as he tried to swallow, but whatever was irritating his throat remained.

"You have no reason to hold my son. I take good care of him. He wants for nothing. He should be with me." She sat again, crossed her arms over her emaciated chest.

"And your husband." Christos leaned forward.

"So this is what it's all about." Her arms released. She brushed her hands over her skirt. She crossed her legs, turned away from him in the chair. "I don't know where he is. If you think I do, you don't know my husband. I can't help you. I can't exchange information about him in return for my child. I don't have this to give. And I doubt he will come back to the camp with the police watching. God knows he's not a completely stupid man."

"I haven't asked you about him." He stared at her, willing her to turn around.

She shrugged, shuffled in her chair and observed him, as she had yesterday, full of rage and condescension. The green spot in her glance was back.

"I have no doubt that your husband can take care of himself. He is not my concern," he said.

"You say this and you expect me to believe you. But why don't you people see? My son has been taken, and the woman who started this is free to come back and take him again. Why was she at the camp? Why is she not in prison? Is it because she is a tourist with money to spend? This is all you people care about." She moved forward in her chair, closer to him. "For the rest of us, you have not even an ounce of pity."

"I'm only worried about the child at the moment. He is ill."

Mirela stood up, wrapped the shawl around herself. "If my son is ill, then I must go to him. Why am I here? I should be with him. He needs his mother."

Christos stood too. "He is asking for his real mother."

"I am his real mother," Mirela said. "You can't trick me into saying I'm not. Bo needs to come home, so he can forget about all this nonsense." She leaned toward him, put her hands on the desk. "He needs to forget all of you. And he needs the love I can give him."

"He may not be able to return to you."

"What do you mean? He's mine."

"We know that is not true."

"But I'm telling you the truth," she said. "What more do you want? I will swear on my life, if I have to."

Even though he knew it wasn't true, he could see she believed it. He had to make Mirela understand the gravity of the situation. Maybe then she would help him find the boy's real mother.

He pushed his chair closer to the desk and stood behind it. "Mrs Mirela, his health is deteriorating," Christos said.

"He has a cough," she said. "There is a pharmacist who gives me medicine for Bo. When he takes it every day, his cough is better. I know it was helping. But Bo hasn't been home for days, ever since that woman stole him from us. He hasn't had his medicine. If I can take him home I will make sure he gets it. And I know the pharmacist will help me because he, unlike so many…" She looked at Christos, and then averted her eyes. "I mean to say, he is a kind man."

Christos knew what she meant. Greeks had changed since the recession, in ways he didn't like. Even he could see that. Just the other day, some farmers had charges dropped against them after they shot and wounded protesting migrants who hadn't been paid in over six months. If migrant workers were treated like this, he could only imagine how the Roma were dealt with. In fact, he didn't have to imagine. He knew.

"Mrs. Mirela, I'm afraid it is much more serious than a simple cough. He is very ill," he said, his voice held in check.

Like Tia, he was sometimes ashamed to be Greek. Yes, some would say they didn't have enough money to help their own, let alone the foreigners who kept coming daily by the hundreds to Greek shores, and that was probably true. Wages, pensions had been cut. New taxes introduced. He never had more than a euro to give to the many begging in the streets. But a lot were also afraid of the foreigners because they'd heard someone somewhere had stolen something. Urban myths. That was all it was. The Roma were feared because they were different. Hadn't he himself suffered at the hands of bullies at school because he was an orphan, because he was different?

He was afraid for the boy. He had to get this situation resolved before the boy... No, he wouldn't think of what could happen. Not now. He had a job to do.

"I don't want to frighten you, Mrs. Mirela," he said. He looked at her directly. "But the boy is in the hospital. He needs to be treated. It's already been left too long."

"But the medicine was helping." She wiped her eyes with the tip of her shawl. "They can cure him. Yes?"

"I don't know. The doctors are doing everything they can, but the medicine they are giving him now may not help him either. We have to find his mother. This is his wish and it might help him get better."

"Your laws are the problem," she muttered as if to herself. "You won't let us live in peace. All we want is what everyone wants. A good life."

Christos said nothing. He wondered if his own mother had felt this way. Perhaps she had given him up because she couldn't provide the kind of life she thought he deserved. His mother. Always present. He was a man. She shouldn't matter any more, yet she did.

Mirela rubbed her eyes. Her shoulders hunched further still. She didn't look at him. "Bo's parents were forced out of the country. They thought their son would be better off here until they found a place. His parents, especially his mother, wanted him to go to school, but that is not always possible for us. Everyone must be put to work from an early age. They said they would come back for him."

"Who are his parents, Mrs. Mirela?"

She sat down heavily in the chair. "I had my own son once," Mirela said quietly, as though she was alone in the room and thinking out loud. "I lost him in the sea. The others would not stay in my body. I don't know why.

"When Bo's parents came to us, I thought God was giving me a gift. The mother thought she would come back for him once they had made a better life. She insisted she was leaving him behind only for a short while. But who ever comes back?" Mirela wiped her eyes again with her shawl. "And then the Canadian woman came with her clothes and food and candy and convinced my husband the boy could do better with her." She looked at Christos now and shook her head. "I'm not meant to have children. But I love them. I only wanted one of my own. I got Bo and was grateful. I worked hard to take care of him. Maybe this was my punishment for being careless and ending up with my husband's family. I don't know. It feels like a long time ago that I was with my own family, in school with my friends."

Christos realized that Mirela was probably no more than sixteen or seventeen years old, although she looked much older. She should be in school, she should be thinking of books, other things young girls think about at this age. And yet, she'd already lived through so much tragedy and loss.

Mirela shook her head as if throwing off a trance and looked up at Christos. She said, "I only know their first names. Bo's real name is Sanjit, as you said. His father was my husband's friend. His name is Vijay. And the mother's name is Saphal. They were from India. I don't know anything more about them. In our lives, the less you know about people, the better. We keep our secrets to ourselves."

"They haven't been in touch with you? To see how the boy was doing?"

She shook her head. "How would they reach us? We have no phone. Most in the camp can't read. I can. But I have no address, nowhere a letter could be sent to."

"You can't help us find them." He sat down across from her, leaned his elbows on the desk. You were my one hope, he thought.

"I don't know how," she said. "I would do anything for him, but I don't know where his parents are. I'm sorry. I'm very, very sorry." Her eyes disappeared into her shrunken face.

"We will put his picture in the paper here and in other EU countries. We will put out a bulletin to other police authorities. Maybe someone will come forward."

"Can I see him?" She slipped off one of the earrings. "This is silver. It will bring you some money. Or maybe you would like to give them to your wife. Whatever you want to do with them, it doesn't matter. They are yours. I want to see my son." She took off the other one. Put them both on the desk and pushed them in his direction.

He stood up, picked up the earrings and put them back in her hand. "I will do what I can for the boy and for you. This is not necessary."

Her hand balled up around the earrings. Her eyes glistened with tears.

He guided her out of the office as he might assist an elderly woman cross the street. "I will do what I can," he said again and handed her his card. "Come and ask for me anytime if you think of anything, any clue about how we might find his mother."

His throat constricted again, and he realized it was his frustration, and hopelessness for the boy that was stuck there like a sob.

"You want to do what?" Kefalas said. The commander was behind his desk, shelling pistachios, putting the shells to one side, the nuts to the other. He didn't look at Christos.

"I want to put out a bulletin to locate the child's real parents," Christos said. "I want the media involved, the other police forces in Europe and maybe around the world. We have to find the child's parents before it's too late."

"Does he know where the man who called himself his father is? Does the boy know? And if not the boy, does the woman know anything that might help us?"

"I haven't asked," Christos said. "The boy only asks for his mother."

"People get sick all the time," Kefalas said. "He won't be the first. Our doctors will cure him and he'll be back to his life in no time."

"I am going to reunite him with his mother. And I'm going to do whatever it takes to make that happen. I am not asking for permission. I'm only advising." Christos put his hat on his head and closed the door as he left the commander's office.

Christos stared at the tabletop, at a smear of last night's tomato sauce from the pasta his family had eaten for dinner.

"Why reunite the boy with the mother who left him with the Roma?" Tia asked.

"They were deported. They probably thought leaving him in Greece would be safer for him than to take him to their country."

"Do you know this for sure?"

Tia was hinting at his naïveté, but Christos knew he had to trust his heart. "I believe what both the boy and the Roma woman told me."

She stroked his hand. "You're doing the right thing, then."

He hoped so. "I don't know if it will be enough."

"The bulletins are out. It's all over the news. The parents will be found. I have no doubt about it." Tia said. She held his hand. They sat across from each other at the kitchen table, the sun beginning to rise above the night-time gloom.

"It's going to work out. You'll see."

Christos looked up. "He's such a small boy. It's not right he has to be without his mother. He has Mirela and Mrs. Holt. They ask about him all the time. They want to see him. What right do I have to stop them? None. He has so much love. Why the hell can't he get better?"

"You don't know that he won't."

"The cough is getting worse. His muscles are weak and he's bent over. The doctors say he is suffering from something called congenital myasthenia syndrome. It is a rare, inherited disease. It is difficult to diagnose, but one of the doctors spotted it quickly in the boy. He had worked in India and Pakistan for some years and had seen other children there with this same disease. The doctor told me there are ways to treat it, but the boy is so weak he cannot tolerate the standard dosage of drugs. He has a severe respiratory condition that they must treat first. He didn't sound hopeful."

"The boy is young," Tia said. "And resilient. He will get better and stronger."

"Why can't we find his mother, the one person he wants?" Once Sanjit's story hit the news, donations of money, food and clothing began arriving at the hospital where the boy was being treated. The outpouring of support for the lost boy found among the Roma felt to Christos like too little, too late. Where was their compassion before the newspaper headline?

Christos sighed. He smiled weakly, realizing he and Tia had switched roles. Usually she was the pessimist and he was the optimist. He told her this.

She smiled. "Well, someone in the family has to be." She pushed herself away from the kitchen table and deposited a kiss on his head as she collected their breakfast dishes.

His cellphone buzzed in his pocket. He scrambled and got it after several rings.

Tia stood at the kitchen sink, watching him. "Who is it? She mouthed.

He shook his head. It wasn't the hospital or the doctor. "Just Yannis," he whispered. Her cousin.

"Yes, okay," Christos said into the phone. "I'll go. But I'm not sure it's what I want to do anymore."

Tia turned. She shook her head, questioning him.

"I'll see," Christos said. "I can't make any promises right now. I'm in the middle of a case. Then we'll see."

26

Memories

Maroúsi

Shelby couldn't stop the whirlpool of thoughts in her brain. If Bo was not Kem and Mirela's biological son, whose child was he? Christos had assured her the boy was safe and that he was looking for Bo's parents. Kem had escaped and was still at large. According to the police commander, she was free to go. Just like that. No charges. No need to appear in court. Nothing. But how could that be? She'd confessed to taking Bo. The lawyer Ted had hired hadn't said two words, so he couldn't have been much of a factor in her release. And beyond all this, there seemed to be some kind of catch to her freedom. "Your son has taken care of this," the commander had said.

He'd looked at Ted and then at her with a knowing smile. "I'm sure your son can explain." Shelby caught how the muscles in Ted's face tightened and flexed.

Ted was walking so quickly she couldn't keep up. Achy and stiff, her legs threatened to give out. Even though she'd started eating properly again since being released and she'd slept better in her own bed, she wasn't a hundred per cent.

She should let Ted go, she told herself. Give him a few minutes to himself. Still, her steps quickened. He was trying to run away from this. Who could blame him? She'd like to run away too. Wasn't that what she'd done herself in the past? After Robert died. And after Zimbabwe. Oh, Zimbabwe. She'd been so busy worrying about Bo and his family, she'd completely forgotten about the mess she'd left behind there with that other family.

All she ever wanted to do was help. But lately it seemed everything she touched turned rotten. She was always hired to set up programs that locals would eventually run: child welfare programs, sex education programs, counselling programs. But she liked working with families. And at first, the families appreciated her efforts, happy that someone cared. She had a clear picture in her head about how everything would be. They'd become friends. She would make a difference one on one. She was happiest in those early days, all her efforts filled with promise. She gave it her all. That was what you were supposed to do in this business. She understood she had a tendency to get too close. But with Bo and his family, she knew she'd crossed a line.

This time, she wasn't going to run away though. She was going to fix her mistakes.

"Ted, wait," she called, as she stopped in front of a café to catch her breath. A few tables and chairs were arranged outside. Inside, the lights were out. Stores and restaurants often did this to save money. Electricity was expensive. Since the crisis, people did what they needed to do. Except who was going to walk into a dark tomb of a café?

The glass doors that faced the sidewalk were open. "Why don't we get something to drink?" she said. "This place is open."

Ted stopped, but remained turned away from her.

They sat at a round table barely large enough to hold their two coffees and a slab of pound cake. The cake had arrived on an oil-ringed napkin.

As Shelby leaned forward to tear off a piece of the cake, their knees touched. Ted swiftly moved his legs to one side, giving her his shoulder and profile. His jaw rippled. His mouth was clenched shut. Yet somehow, he was working the gum in his mouth. The sun clipped the expensive watch on his wrist and glinted in her eyes.

Looking at her greasy fingers, her stomach felt queasy. She left the cake, wiped her hands on the napkin straddling her lap.

Ted took a sip of coffee, cradled his cup in his hands. The sun coming through the tree above them left parts of him in the light and the rest in shadows. It was hard for her to see his expression, anything, except the glimmer of his watch. She couldn't guess at what he might be thinking. The light breeze stirred the leaves, a few of which dropped onto the table. Ted took no notice. She found it maddening when he cocooned into himself like this.

"Please talk to me, Ted. I know you're angry at me about all this, but you promised you would help."

He turned and looked into her eyes. "It's you that needs to start talking, Mother. I can't help you if you're not going to be honest with me."

She wanted to explain things so he could see it from her perspective, see what she was trying to do for Bo and his family. But before she could even begin, a pair of buskers, an old man and a young girl, were at their table, standing in front of them, playing the harmonica and violin.

Roma.

She wondered which camp they lived in. She wanted to ask, but she saw Ted's expression of distaste. This wasn't the time to get chummy.

The buskers were not particularly loud, but they were close. The music sounded like a good rendition of "Never on Sunday." Many of the buskers played the same tune over and over again; she imagined they knew which ones roused the tourists to open their wallets.

She'd wait to say what she needed to say. The buskers would soon finish.

She wondered if she had any change. Normally she carried lots of it, just for this kind of situation. She didn't know why she was thinking about change when she had so many other things to worry about. It was ridiculous how her brain worked. Planning. Churning.

As he watched the buskers, Ted muttered something, but she couldn't make it out.

She took out her wallet, which still had a couple of euros in it. The man was by her side, practically on top of her before she had a chance to look up. She gave him the coins. He eyed them, then looked at her with his sorrowful brown eyes, his head slightly tilted as if to say, *is this all you have?*

She wanted to tell him she wished she had more to give, but she smiled and hoped he understood.

He looked at Ted, who gave him a dismissive nod. Bowing his hat to her, the man returned to stand by the young girl, his hands on his hips. He no longer played his harmonica. Eyes squeezed shut, the girl continued to play her violin as though she was in the country's best concert hall rather than a grubby street.

The café owner lunged out the door with his broom, and told the buskers to stop bothering his customers. The old man grabbed the girl's arm and she abruptly stopped playing. They hurried down the sidewalk, and out of sight.

The café owner apologized for the disruption.

"They weren't bothering us," Shelby said. "We don't mind."

The owner shrugged. "These people are not good for my business," he said, and walked back inside, muttering in Greek. He was probably cursing them too. Even though they were white foreigners spending money here, Shelby knew the Greeks thought they were too sympathetic towards the other foreigners, the unwanted immigrants.

There were no other customers in the restaurant, so Shelby didn't know why the owner was making such a fuss, but what was the point of saying anything? The poor man was trying to make a living.

She put her wallet back in her purse, and said, "I wish we could do more for these poor people."

"You've always wanted to save the world, haven't you?" Ted said. He licked the foam from the rim of his glass of iced Greek coffee, avoiding her gaze. "Dad used to say that."

Whenever Robert accused her of this, she knew some petty, hurtful comment would come next. "Don't you know you're just pissing into the wind?" Robert had said more than once about her child welfare work.

It was easier to help others. That was true. "Your father never understood why I did the work I did." She slouched in the chair. Now it was her turn to avoid his gaze. "Because he was a doctor, I'd thought he would. When we met in university, I thought we had the same goals, that we were motivated by the same things."

"Money?" Ted said.

"What?" Shelby asked. "You know I never cared about the money."

"Who had to have the best sheets, the best garden, the best this and that?"

Ted sounded just like his father, accusatory and belittling. She knew she should simply let the comment go. But she couldn't help herself. "Who are you talking about, Ted? Me or you? Who has to put his name on everything he owns? Who has to have the very best money can buy? I only have to look at your watch to answer that question. You see how I live. I'm not here for myself. I find it hard to believe that your father has been gone for so many years and I'm still defending myself. I thought you were here to help me, not to make things worse. I was hoping you would understand."

She pushed her cup away, turned to face the street. A plastic water bottle floated in a puddle around the grate in the gutter, knocking at it again and again, trying to find a way through.

"When I was a kid and you sent me off to boarding school so you could go make a difference halfway across the world, you asked me to understand. Do you remember?" His voice was slightly raised and he was pointing at her. "I didn't understand what you were doing back then, and frankly, I don't get it now. I know you wanted to help people, but if I'm honest with you, Mother, and this is difficult for me to say, I wish you had given your family as much attention as you did your work."

Here it comes, she thought. So he's not talking about my work at all. Just bad mom crap. All the ways I screwed him up. Why can't he ever remember the good times? They happened. Every time we got together. I'd get all the stuff I had to do done: paying his tuition and getting his books and supplies, buying traveller's cheques, finding tickets to a Canucks game, figuring out what was going on in the city he might like to do just so I could make every minute of our time together count. But even as she thought this, a picture of the two of them in the Vancouver airport drifted into her mind. She knew he was barely holding back tears, but he smiled and reassured her by letting go of her hand first. He went to one gate and she went to another.

She remembered how his lip trembled when she'd tell him to leave her alone so she could think. He was just a toddler then. Robert hadn't wanted her to go back to work after her maternity leave finished and she complied. Adding work onto taking care of Ted was more than she could face at the time. She'd been working so hard battling the depression that constantly threatened to engulf her, she'd had nothing left for him. She'd been a drowning woman who could not reach out to save anyone else. Little Ted just took whatever came his way. But if he was quiet when he was angry he'd learned it from her.

She finally went back to work when he was four and started in pre-school. Work was her escape from Robert's drinking and the exhausting weight of trying to be a good mother to Ted, when her energy was forever spent.

"I know my work has come between us, Ted. And it might have seemed like I cared more about it than I did about you. But that was never true. I always made sure you were okay, looked after. I got you into the best school."

"Believe me, bad stuff can happen to a kid, even a kid in an expensive school. I needed you then and you weren't there."

"What do you mean, Ted? Did something happen? Were you bullied? You never said anything. I thought you were happy there. And you were such an independent kid, I thought you'd like the kind of freedom you'd get from being away at school."

"They call that outsourcing these days, Mother. If you've got the money, but no time or inclination to do a certain task, you get others to do it. You outsourced your parenting responsibilities."

"Now, really, Ted."

"It was fine to have me around if you needed a bandage or an ice pack for a swollen lip Dad gave you. To feed you when he left us. But as soon as he died, you didn't need me anymore. I could maybe see you sending me off to boarding school before he died to protect me from his drunken rages, but no, it was after. I was shipped off, like I had served my purpose. You only kept me around as long as you needed someone to share your misery."

He was just being hurtful and she was not going to rise to it. When he calmed down, he'd apologize and they'd go back to being how they had always been.

"Maybe you're right. I'm too close to my work. It's probably time to take a break. And there are some things we need to deal with in our relationship too. I get that. But I need to resolve things here before I go anywhere."

They sat apart, each now facing the street. The only sound came from the din of distant traffic, the coffee machine gurgling in the café, and the thrashing of the water bottle. The occasional person wandered by, but this wasn't a busy street. There were no other distractions, even as she searched for one.

She held her breath for several seconds, and then let it go. Why were they arguing? There was no reason. It didn't make sense. Somebody had to give in a little.

"Ted, your dad and I," she turned toward him, buying some time, unsure what she was going to say. "That happened a long time ago. It's not important now."

"Maybe it is. You keep getting into messes. Why do you do it? Do you know?" Putting his coffee down on the table, he turned to face her. Finally. He bumped one of the legs of the table and spilled some coffee. He didn't move to wipe it. And she didn't either. The cake remained stuck to the napkin, the ring of grease growing. "You need to figure it out."

"What do you mean, messes?" she asked. She straightened in her chair. "This is the first time I've asked for your help. It's the first time something like this has happened."

Ted squeezed his eyes shut, rubbed his temples. "I'm trying to understand, okay? That's all. But right now it doesn't look good from my vantage point," he said. "For God's sake, Mother, how could kidnapping that boy be a solution for his family?"

"I didn't kidnap him." She looked down at her coffee cup, but she could feel his critical eyes on her. She wanted to get up and walk away from him.

"That's what you told Commander Kefalas," Ted said. "He told me himself."

Again, she leaned forward. She had to make him understand. "I would have said anything to get Kem out of that place. It was the only thing I could think of."

"So you never kidnapped that kid?"

"Ted, you know better."

"I actually don't."

She looked beyond him and saw Bo. Then saw Ted as a child. "He was such a smart boy," she said. "He spoke English and Greek and his eyes always watched over what was going on. He reminded me of you when you were his age."

"So you took him to relive some old memory or something?"

She stared at Ted. He would never understand. He wanted a quick and simple explanation for her behaviour. She couldn't wrap it up in a bow for herself, or for him.

"Okay, I gave the family things to help them. But it all happened so fast. Kem talking about a better life for his son. Me thinking I could provide it to him. I don't know how it all came to this. It was a misunderstanding. My fault. I didn't mean to buy him, but I know maybe that's what happened. I got carried away with trying to help. I knew he was going to come with me that day. I didn't think ahead about what would happen after that. Then I didn't know how to take him back.

"You have to believe me. I thought Kem and his family needed my help. I was happy to do what I could. That's all. I may have screwed up, but that was never my intention. Things just got out of hand," she said and turned away from him.

"Don't they always?" Ted said. "Why did you have to leave Zimbabwe, Mother?" he asked calmly. He looked directly into her eyes.

She stared right back at him. How could he possibly know?

His eyes quickly shifted. He glanced down at his own coffee, then toward the street. She followed his gaze to a cyclist moving along the road, jacket and bow tie, back straight. She recognized him as the man she often saw, sitting in the park across the way. "You were in my bedroom. You saw that letter," she said. "You tell me."

He shrugged. "It was there. I read it."

"It wasn't just there," she said. "I know exactly where it was, Ted. You had no right to go through my private things."

"What did you expect me to do?" He raised his voice, looked her in the eye. "You were in trouble and you weren't giving me any information so I could help. I needed to find some clues. That's all."

"In my drawers?"

He shook his head. "I had to do what I had to do, just like I had to do what I had to do to help you after your fights with Dad, what I had to do when you made me identify Dad's body after he died because you couldn't, and what I had to do to survive that boarding school, what I had to do at the police station, what I've always had to do. I'm nothing if not your *good son.* That's what you've always called me and like an idiot I've complied."

"What do you mean?" She reached for his hand. He shifted in his chair and turned away.

"Nothing."

This time she put her hand over his. "What did that police commander mean when he said the situation was taken care of? What did he mean, I'm free to go, Ted? How is that possible?"

Ted moved his hand away. "Fine, I'll tell you. I fixed things with the cops."

"What exactly do you mean, you fixed things?" She gripped his forearm, forced him to look at her again. "Tell me."

"You know these people better than I do," Ted said. "What's the one thing that talks in this country?"

"You didn't pay them off." Her voice rose. "Tell me you didn't."

"Let's move forward, Mother. We need to be out of the country within a few days, and we've wasted too much time already. Now we can go home. Or you can go anywhere you like and help yourself to another bloody poor kid."

She stood up. "You can go, Ted, but I'm not leaving until I've made things right." She snatched up her bag and strode away. She didn't know why she'd called him in the first place. She could solve this on her own. If money was all it took, fine. She had it to burn. She didn't need anyone's help.

27

Maroúsi

Ted watched his mother walk away. He hadn't intended to say all that he'd said. He wanted to understand what had happened and get on with his plans to get her home. Suddenly, he was spewing all sorts of stuff from the past. Sure, she'd made an attempt to understand. Wondered if he'd been bullied at school. If only it had been that simple.

He should go after her, apologize, and do whatever he needed to do to get them out of the country. She didn't deserve the comment about outsourcing. He was mad at her, but really, for what? She'd done what she'd always done. Why had he expected anything different from her?

He put his head in his hands. He had to deal with his shit on his own. And it wasn't all bad, either. It allowed him to find solutions to every problem he'd been handed. That was his strength. His parents, both selfish in their own ways, gave him his independence. This strength.

He wished Mother could give a shit about him, instead of her work, for a change. She had in some ways. He knew that. But he had to stop wanting more from her.

His father had probably felt like Ted did now. Ignored. He remembered his father trying to get off the booze. He'd go for weeks without a drink. Mother watched him carefully, told Ted to be on his best behaviour. "Daddy's going through a rough time," she'd say. "We have to be extra specially good so we can help him."

But she'd watched him with the same look captured in the caricature of her: reserved and questioning, as though anticipating Dad's fall. And somehow Dad always complied. He'd eventually start drinking again.

She never seemed upset about it. She was used to his father's tumbles and she seemed prepared to deal with it. "Well, we'll just have to wait and see when he's ready again. We'll be ready, won't we, Teddy?" she'd say singsong-like.

He wondered if she enjoyed the rescuing part better than the times his father was actually sober. Maybe it gave her a purpose, something to fix. Maybe Ted was the same way.

He sipped his coffee. Even though he'd lost his temper and Mother had taken off in a huff, he felt better. He was seeing his parents as if for the first time. He didn't want to repeat their bullshit. He had to quit blaming them for what they did. He had to stop feeling helpless, that his only lot in life was to help her. If he did that, maybe there was a chance he would stop blaming himself for not preventing his father's angry outbursts and for not helping his mother more.

His cellphone vibrated on the table. He saw Jack's number flash up on the screen and picked up before it went to voicemail.

"Do you want to tell me what the hell is going on?" Jack said. His voice was clipped.

Christ, now what? "What do you mean?"

"Your mother, the little gypsy boy, the family that isn't his real family," he said. "It's all over the news. You said you were visiting her because you hadn't seen her in quite some time. You were catching up. Things were going well. What the hell happened?"

The tremble in Ted's hand was back. He was suddenly hot. He hadn't noticed the absence of the tremors and sweats until just now when these things came back all at once.

"If you're worried about the business," Ted said, "no one is going to make the connection between my mother and what she's doing and Holt Communications. So don't worry." Jack was always worried about the firm. How to build it. Where to get new clients. New projects. Slicker campaigns. Communications and public relations was a competitive business. And Jack was a family man. He needed to put his kids in swimming classes and ballet and God knows what else. University one day.

"I don't give a shit about the company," Jack said.

"Well, thanks for that."

"You know what I mean, Ted. I want to know what's going on with you."

"It's a long story," Ted said. He would have liked to tell Jack, get the entire mess off his chest, but where would he start? He was still piecing it together himself. And hanging by his fingernails while he was doing it.

He'd lied to his business partner, conveniently left out some key details. It was no wonder Jack was pissed. Ted had been hoping not to have to tell Jack or anyone outside his AA circle about the booze, or his mother's problems or any of those other things that haunted him. He'd hoped to clean himself up, put a shiny new coat on his old life. Shit.

"We've been friends for a long time," Jack said. "You could have told me why you had to go."

"I didn't know what was going on," Ted said. "Not in any kind of detail, anyway. I'm still not completely sure. New stuff keeps coming up."

"You didn't think I'd understand. You could have given me some credit."

"Sorry." The word scared him.

"Okay." Jack chuckled. "I guess it could be a lot worse. Right?"

"I had a drink the other night," Ted said.

"Maybe you needed it, with all of this stuff you're dealing with," Jack said, but the tone of his voice had changed. It was quieter, as if he was waiting for something.

"I'm an alcoholic, Jack," Ted said calmly, as though he said these words out loud all the time. The knot in his stomach unravelled. The quiver in his hand was gone. There was silence on the other end of the line. Had he gone too far?

"I know," Jack said.

"What? How?" His grip tightened around the cellphone, he brought it closer.

"You can hide a lot of shit," Jack said. "But you can't hide this. Christ, I can read you like a book. I saw the sweats, the nervousness when a dinner meeting went on too long. I saw how you poured glass after glass for others, usually filling the glass to the brim. I could see you staring at the booze other people drank, watching as it went down. And I knew something was up when you couldn't finish that damn presentation with the Starwood Group. I knew you were going to do something about it, then. You'd hit your bottom. Finally."

Ted stood up, hit his knee against the table. "But you never said a thing."

"What was I going to say? I couldn't force you to get help. That wouldn't have worked. All I could do was wait, keep an eye on you, and make sure you didn't kill yourself. And besides, I knew you'd pull through, even if you didn't know it."

He'd been hiding out for so long. He pictured the furrow on Jack's brow, the way he'd lean in to make a point about a presentation they were putting together.

He began pacing in front of the café.

"And don't think I bought what you were telling me about going for a workout at lunch," Jack said. "I may look stupid, but I'm not that stupid." He laughed. "You know what I mean?"

"There's more I have to tell you," Ted said. "And I will. Spilling my guts is new for me, but I seem to be getting the hang of it." His own laugh was almost giddy. "But right now I've got to get this situation resolved for my mother."

"What can I do?"

"Nothing I can think of," Ted said.

"What's next?"

"I'm going to do whatever she needs me to do," he said. "I've got to start accepting her for who she is. I've always wanted her to be different. Better. As much as I want her to admit that she made some mistakes with me, I'm not going to hold my breath. I'm the one who has to change."

"So you're good."

He smiled. "Yup."

"So, I don't have to come over there and fix things for you, like I do every day of my life with your damn company?" He laughed.

"I'm good."

Ted spit out his gum in the ashtray, pulled out a euro ten-note from his pocket and left it on the table.

28

THE PAYOFF

Maroúsi

Shelby had heard Ted come in. He called out to her, said he was sorry. "Let's talk this out, Mother. Figure out what to do. I'll help. I promised I would, and I will."

She didn't get out of bed. What was the point? He had said these words before. He'd made up his mind about all this and hadn't listened to a word she'd said. He blamed her, for what, she didn't know. Said she hadn't been around for him or his father. If it wasn't her, who was it who cleaned up after Robert's messes, took Ted to his practices, helped him with his homework? Got him into that great private school when she went overseas? Where would he be today if it wasn't for her? Didn't she deserve to have a life too? Couldn't a person be both a mother and a professional person who had her own interests?

And he'd been in her things too. That was unconscionable. No, she would let him stew for a bit. Maybe he'd come to his senses. Besides, she could use a bit of rest to think about what to do next.

She closed her eyes, but couldn't shut Ted out completely. He must have been no more than eight months old. They were upstairs in the nursery. He was lying on the change table and she was babbling away about the new shirt she'd bought him just for this day. They were going to the in-laws' for dinner. She wanted

Ted to look extra special. He was such a gorgeous baby, but the in-laws weren't the warm and fuzzy types. They weren't much different from her own parents. Still, she hoped for more.

As a young girl, she had watched her homemaker mother on her endless quest to create a magazine-perfect domestic scene — cooking extravagant meals that included all her husband's favourites, putting together stunning floral arrangements from her own gardens, setting the table just so. And then she would wait for him to get home. Often he would call to say he wouldn't make it home for supper. He was a criminal lawyer, a partner in his firm, and his work came first. She watched as her mother paced, looked out the front window, reheated already crusted-over soup.

Shelby vowed she would not live her life like her mother. She would have her own career. In university, studying for her degree in social work, she volunteered to read to the blind, visited the elderly in old folks' homes and finally found her calling when she worked as a camp counsellor at a summer camp for disadvantaged kids. She loved everything about university, from studying to the discussions to her practicums. And university brought Robert into her life. He was going to be a doctor. They had the same goals of helping others. They planned to go to third world countries, provide services many of these places had no access to. With Robert in those early days, before they each finished their degrees, before Ted, their dreams seemed possible. Then Robert's drinking started to get out of hand. Ted was born. And Shelby felt herself gradually slide into the same hole her mother had never escaped.

She looked at little Ted. Her in-laws would not be able to resist him in his new royal blue and light purple striped polo shirt.

Robert was at the bottom of the stairs, bellowing at her to hurry up. She could picture the drink in his hand. She ripped off the packaging on the new shirt quickly. Just once she wanted them to have a Sunday dinner like other families. She didn't want any upsets or tension. Just warm, polite conversation. Maybe a little gushing over her son. Their only grandchild, Teddy. Was that too much to ask?

"Why do we always have to be late?" Robert complained again. She heard the tinkle of another handful of ice thrown into a fresh glass. "You know what sticklers for time they are and you insist on being late."

She tickled Ted, who laughed a laugh that could only come from a place of innocence. "Look at the shirt Mommy bought you." She held it up. "You will look so handsome. I can hardly wait to show you off. They won't be able to resist you."

She put the shirt over his head and started to work his arms through the sleeves.

Ted screamed out suddenly. It scared her to death.

"What?"

Ted's cries were so loud, she could barely think. She hadn't done a thing. "What's wrong?" she said. "What is wrong with you?"

"What are you doing to that child?" Robert's voice demanded.

She tried tucking Ted's arm through the shirt again. He screamed even louder. She felt as useless as she had just after he was born. Whenever he'd cry out then, she couldn't find the strength to go to him. She was so exhausted, his whimpers didn't move her to do a single thing.

But on that Sunday, it was rage that rose in her. She wanted to stop the screams, stop him. She put her hand over his mouth. He gulped for air.

"Stop it," she said, her voice quiet in fury. She didn't want Robert to hear her frustration. Not today, after she'd gone to so much trouble.

Ted's face turned even redder, as though he were choking.

What the hell is wrong with you? she thought. Don't you like the new shirt? What would you know about new or old? It's just a shirt. Stop it. We're already late and you know your father hates being late. Stop it now. Don't make my life harder than it already is. You're supposed to be what's good about my life.

She was shaking and still she held her hand over his mouth.

Ted gasped for air. Okay, have it your way, but we have to get going. She took her hand away. He shrieked into her face. She went about getting him dressed, shoving his arms through the sleeves of the shirt. Enough of this. She yanked at the buttons. The action jostled his tiny body in one direction, then in another. God help her, it took everything she had not to shake him when she picked him up. Why was he doing this to her?

When she put him back down, she saw them. Just under his armpits, the heads of the pins hung limp from the shirt. Tiny and almost invisible. She'd missed them, two of them, one under each arm. The heads were harmless. The sharp ends had poked and scratched his tender skin every time she'd tried to straighten the shirt. Why hadn't she noticed them when she took the shirt out of its stupid packaging?

She pulled the pins out of the shirt, tucked them in her pocket. She held Ted close, trying to calm her breath. Her shoulder absorbed his cries.

Lying him back down, she rubbed a cool cloth over his face, and then kissed his cheeks. He reached for her and smiled as though he had forgiven her.

Putting her head down against his shoulder, she wept.

She heard Robert's footsteps on the stairs. She raked her fingers through her hair and a sleeve over her eyes, as quiet and in control as she could be.

"What's the holdup?" Robert said. He must have suspected something or seen the blotches that always dotted her cheeks when she cried.

"What is it?" He didn't walk towards her. Or reach for her. But, there was softness in his voice, something in the way he looked at her, like the old days when they'd first started seeing each other.

"I'm sorry," she said.

"If we're late, we're late," Robert said. He kissed the top of Teddy's head.

During dinner, her in-laws were amiable and kind. Robert's mother bounced Ted on her lap and tickled him. He laughed and smiled. It was exactly the kind of dinner she had imagined. Still, she reached into her pocket from time to time, as though forgetting the pins were there and jabbed her fingers and the palm of her hand. It felt like relief.

Long after the angry pinpricks under Ted's arms healed, she'd wake up in the middle of the night in a sweat, unable to get the bloody spots out of her head.

She turned onto her back, focused on the ceiling now. Enough of feeling sorry for herself. This wasn't getting them anywhere. She'd try to make it up to Ted. They'd have time together afterward to talk things out, maybe go on a vacation together. Some place luxurious where they might both relax enough to find their way back to those good times they used to share when she'd come home from one of her overseas assignments. She couldn't undo the past. All she could do right now was fix what she'd done to Bo. His family.

She heard Ted pacing in the other room, then after what seemed like forever, nothing. She sat up in the dark. No light under her bedroom door, no sound.

She waited a few more minutes.

Feeling pretty safe, Shelby snuck out of her room and walked down the hallway to the door. Thankfully, Ted had plugged the night-light in. It helped her, except she saw the old woman's eyes in that awful picture on the wall.

The key wasn't in the door. Hopefully, that meant he hadn't locked it. She tried it and the door swung open easily, without a sound. She closed it behind her. She needed to tell Christos about the bribe. He'd be surprised what his boss was up to and maybe he'd do something about it. Then she'd ask to see Bo. It was too much for the boy to handle all this by himself, in an orphanage somewhere, with strangers. At least he knew her. She'd be the familiar face. The one he could trust. And besides, he needed someone in his corner to make everything right.

Shelby's back was as straight as a board when she entered the police station. "I'd like to speak to Christos."

The man behind the desk clucked in that way Greeks did when they wanted to say no. He raised his chin. Be as condescending as you like, she thought, I'm not going away. She stared at him and he finally went off to find Christos.

"Mrs. Holt."

She heard his voice behind her.

She turned to face him. "Are you just coming on shift?"

"I was at the hospital," Christos said. "I'm a little late."

He seemed preoccupied.

"I'm sorry, Christos. Is everything okay with you? Should you be here?"

"I was with the boy," Christos said.

"At least he's getting the treatment he needs now," she said. "Was he moved to a hospital to help deal with his cough? It will have a chance of getting better now. He's a resilient kid. Thanks for taking care of him, Christos."

"He's very ill, Mrs. Holt. The doctors are doing everything they can."

"What do you mean? He's young. He'll be fine. It's probably nothing more than bronchitis. It'll clear right up with some antibiotics. Can you tell me where he is? I'd really like to visit him."

"I think that would be good. I took Mrs. Mirela to him a little while ago because I think the woman really cares about him. And I know you do too. He needs that more than anything. At least until we find his real mother."

"Who are you taking where?" the commander asked as he walked in. Other officers circled around behind him like a pack of dogs waiting for a kill.

"Christos, I need to talk to you alone," she whispered to Christos. "There's something I want to tell you."

"Madam," the commander said. "Whatever you have to say, you can say to me. I am the commander here. Officer Pappas is one of my men. I am the ultimate authority."

"You took a bribe from my son," she said. "That is why I was released and you kept poor Kem behind these walls until he escaped. My son had money and you took advantage of that. Kem had nothing." This oaf of a man wasn't going to scare her. They might as well all hear it too. She was not going to allow this to happen and not say a bloody word about it.

"That is a very serious allegation, madam." He grinned, but his eyes turned a darker shade, as though he knew as well as she did that he had been caught. He turned out his pockets, catching his penknife before it hit the floor. "If your claims are true, I have surprisingly little to show for it."

A few of the other men laughed. He gave them a stern look. They stood at attention.

"This is not possible, Mrs. Holt," Christos said. "We are officers of the law here."

She stared at him, but he looked away. He knew full well his commander was capable of anything. But what options did Christos have? He had to go along with the goon and his henchman or he wouldn't be able to survive.

"Mother. What are you doing?"

"Ted." Her face was warm. She'd been hoping to tell him about it later, once she got what she wanted. "I'm glad you're here. Now you can tell them what you told me. You paid to get me out of here. Go ahead, tell them." She moved towards him.

She could hear his intake of breath. He shook his head.

"Yes, please enlighten us," the commander said. "I believe Mrs. Holt is a bit confused about the conditions under which she was released."

"Apparently you've been in the country over three months, Mother," Ted said. His hands were on her shoulders, as if he were trying to explain a difficult math problem.

"So? I can stay as long as I want. There can't possibly be a law against that. I'm spending money here. Doesn't that help the country?"

The commander said, "Am I correct in assuming you are not a citizen of another Schengen Agreement European country?" A smile covered his face and his dark eyes lit up as though some switch had been thrown behind them. Shelby looked around. The officers didn't meet her gaze. They stood at attention.

"You know as well as I do that I'm a Canadian. So what?"

"The Schengen Agreement allows foreigners such as yourself to stay in a EU-member country for only three months. Then you must apply for a special visa, which I understand you do not have. Correct?" the commander said.

"What does that have to do with anything?" She felt like slapping that smile right off his face. She clenched her fists instead, steadied them at her sides.

"You have to pay a fine when you overstay your welcome in the EU. We are not as corrupt as you Americans like to think we are."

"Okay, how much is it? I can pay the fine right now. But that isn't going to let you off the hook, Commander. My son paid you to set me free. And that can't be legal."

"Your son paid your fine, Madam. We appointed a lawyer so we could make the process as smooth as possible. But part of the arrangement was to have you leave the country or more fines would be levied. These are not my rules, Madam. They are EU rules, and Greece, as a member country, follows the rules to the letter."

She turned to look at Ted again. He nodded. "It's true, Mother. This is how it works. Once I paid your fine, you were free to go. You didn't give me time to explain."

"But I told you I took that child."

"In fact, you helped us uncover an even bigger crime, Madam," the commander said. "That's the one that concerns us now. We have to find the boy's real parents, reunite them. The Roma man probably abducted that child to use as a street beggar. It is our job to put the boy back where he belongs." He rubbed his face. The smile returned. "And we have you to thank for alerting us to all that was going on in that camp."

29

DENIED

Germany

Customers were always leaving newspapers behind in the restaurant where Vijay worked as a dishwasher. Kofi, the cook, liked to take his break on the back stoop of the restaurant, and he'd take the newspapers out to read and then just leave them there. Whenever he'd go out for some fresh air, Vijay would collect the scattered papers and put them in the dumpster. Somebody had to show some propriety. He didn't bother to read the papers. The world was a mess. He already knew this. What could he do about it? But today, one of the pictures stared right at him. It was his son.

He looked at the headline and suddenly felt as if all the air had been sucked out of him.

Boy Found Among the Roma.
Police Search for Biological Parents

If something had happened to Sanjit, Saphal would never forgive him. Never.

Vijay read the article. The child was being treated in an Athens hospital, but wanted desperately to see his mother. The police believed a Roma man who was allegedly a fugitive from justice had kidnapped the boy.

Kidnapped? These newspaper people could never get anything right. They wanted to sensationalize everything, even the most mundane. It was good that Sanjit was finally getting the medical care he needed and Saphal and Vijay could never afford.

Their son was fine. Nothing had happened to him. He shook his head. Hadn't he told Sanjit to behave, not to bring any attention to Kem and his wife? The boy never listened. Instead, he had to call for his mother and suddenly everyone got involved.

As for Kem, there was nothing he could do. He hoped his friend had managed to stay out of the clutches of the police. I brought this trouble on him, he thought. Me. And my son.

He put the newspaper in the garbage and went back to work. He had an appointment today with his caseworker at the office of Migration and Refugees. He had a job, and his boss had vouched for him. That would make the authorities happy. If his refugee status was approved today, he'd call the hospital where they had Sanjit. He would give them whatever proof they needed and make arrangements for the boy to come to Germany as soon as he was discharged from the hospital. They'd start all over and finally settle into their new life. Saphal would be happy. Maybe she'd stop nagging him once and for all.

"I don't understand," Vijay said to the woman, who spoke English with a throaty accent. Her words were clipped and to the point. Her navy pinstriped suit was severe. Her shirt was buttoned tightly to her neck. Her eyes were hard. "I have a job in your country. I have filled out all the paperwork. I've done everything that you required. Why can I not stay?"

"You originally claimed refugee status in Greece," she said curtly. "Under a different name."

"There must be a mistake," Vijay said and raised his head a little higher, looked at her as though he was indignant. "I came here directly from India. Did what I was told. My employer says he can't get by without me. His restaurant is very busy.

He's written these words in a letter to you. Please look at your papers. This information will all be there." One country never knew what the other was doing, so Vijay knew there was no way she could know he'd claimed refugee status in Greece. She was bluffing. And he wasn't going to play her games. She wanted him to jump to her command, but he didn't live in India anymore. He didn't have to do this for anyone. So sign the stupid paper work, Miss, and let me go on with my life. "All your politicians go to that restaurant. Even some of your bosses. It's a very, very busy place."

"Yes, I know."

"I'm contributing to your society. I'm needed here."

"Our computer files don't lie," she said in that same no-nonsense, severe voice. Yet she was supposed to be on his side. She was supposed to be helping him. "We know you and your family claimed refugee status in Greece. You were denied there, changed your name and found your way to us."

"I don't know who you are talking about. But that person is not me." Again, Vijay didn't flinch. She looked at her computer, and then turned it so he could see the screen.

"This is you," she said. "Pictures don't lie. And if we must, we can also take your fingerprints again and compare them to the ones we have on file."

"Send me back to Greece," he said. "I will go."

"Correct. Under the Schengen Agreement we could send you back to the country where you entered Europe. But as you must know, Greece is suffering under a great economic crisis. They haven't been able to deal with the influx of migrants either, so we've stopped this practice. Your country poses no threat to you, sir."

"But you do not understand what my wife's family is capable of. Please."

Her eyes left her screen and she nodded to someone behind him. "I'm afraid that until you are repatriated you will be kept in custody, as you are considered a flight risk."

He heard footsteps and he knew there was more than one person behind him. "It's not fair," he said. "All I wanted was a place where we could build a life. Have a little freedom."

30

SEEING AMMI

Eginitio National Hospital, Athens

I don't know where I am or what happened, but the room is very, very bright. I remember I was in a place where the nice policeman left me, but then I started coughing a lot and now I'm someplace else. This cough is always getting me into trouble. Everyone notices coughs like this and my bent back and small muscles. Sometimes people are nice to me because of how I am and give me money or cookies or marbles like that lady did once a long, long time ago. I wonder where those marbles are now. Sometimes, people give me food too. But most of the time people tell me to move along. They don't want a person like me around. I thought my back would grow straighter and my cough would stop as I got older, but I'm seven now and nothing has changed. My birthday was a little while ago. I kept the day in my head so I wouldn't forget. No one said anything because I didn't tell anyone, except the grandmother I lived with at the policeman's house. She said she was going to make me a cake, but I didn't stay there to see if she really would or not. I hope she's not mad at me like Mirela and Candy Lady are.

I would like to turn the light off, but I don't think I can reach it. My body hurts the same way it does when I've been lying on one side on the ground for too long. I open my eyes just a little, but it's too bright. They don't want to stay open, but I keep trying because I want to know if the nice policeman found my ammi yet. If not, I'm going to have to find her myself. When I get better. Pretty soon.

I try really, really hard and open my eyes as wide as I can. There's a window. I can see the sky. It's dark blue. Rain taps at the glass. My eyes shut all by themselves.

I force them open again. There are flowers, pots and pots of them. And toy trucks and other toys. There's even a big teddy bear. He looks soft. It feels like I'm in a park or one of those big toy stores I see sometimes, but can never go into. I have a blanket around me too and my feet feel warm like they did at the nice policeman's house. It must be special, this place.

There's a funny smell in here, like the medicine Mirela used to give me, and there are lots of beeping sounds.

Voices. I think. Too. Quiet and calm. It feels nice.

I turn my head. There she is! My ammi! I knew the nice policeman would find her. I knew it. And he's here too.

I try to keep my eyes open, but they close all by themselves. Sometimes I think I see Ammi and other times I think I see Mirela. Who is here? I'm not sure.

It must be her. The policeman promised. Ammi's here and she won't go away again. My eyes fall shut. But I can feel a smile as big as the sky on my face. I'm sure Ammi can see it too.

I feel Ammi's hand in mine. Her hands are rough. She's been working too hard trying to make a better life for us, just like Abbu says we'll have one day. She's holding me. I think I hear her crying. Her earrings are shiny. I'm glad she has them back.

"I'm sorry," she says. "I'm sorry for what I did. I just didn't want to let you go. I love you so much. I wanted to protect you."

I want to tell Ammi that it's okay; I knew she would come back for me. But I hope she understands I'm too tired to talk.

"Please don't leave us again," she says. "Please."

I want to tell her that she left me, but I don't. She already feels bad and as a son, I should make her happy, not mad.

"When you get better," she says, "We'll go for ice cream again."

I don't remember having ice cream with Ammi. She always said we couldn't spend our money on foolish things. I thought it was Mirela who took me for ice cream. But it's hard right now to keep everything straight in my head. I just want to sleep.

"Okay, Sanjit? You get better and we'll go get an ice cream and sit in the park. Just the two of us. You remember how much fun we had, just you and me. Don't you?"

I haven't heard my real name in so long except when I said it to myself in my head. That's the name Ammi gave me.

"Maybe we should let him rest right now," a man's voice says. It's the nice policeman again. I know because he touches my head the way he did when I stayed at his house with the nice old lady and the little girl.

"I can't leave him," she says. "I know you said I could only stay for a little while, but please, I can't leave him now. Please don't make me."

Why would the policeman want to make Ammi go now that we've found her?

"All right," the policeman says. When I get better, I'm going to ask him to come with us for ice cream.

31

THE RIGHT THING

Eginitio National Hospital, Athens

Seeing how the boy responded to Mrs. Mirela made Christos feel as though he'd done something good for Sanjit. But was the boy aware of who was in the room? Christos wasn't sure. The doctors said the boy was weak. There was so much damage to his lungs, they weren't sure if anything would help him. And on top of this, Christos hadn't found the boy's mother, either. The only thing the international exposure had accomplished was to have Greeks and others come forward to offer their homes for the boy. They had ignored Sanjit when he was on the street, but now that it was in the news, people wanted to adopt the boy. People were strange. Maybe it was easier to be a good Samaritan when you had an audience.

The boy had opened his eyes only briefly when Christos brought Mrs. Holt to the hospital the day before. Then he turned his head away. But he had responded to the Roma woman. Christos hadn't been sure about allowing her to visit the boy, but when he saw how tender she was with him, so completely committed to him, Christos knew he'd done the right thing. It was hard to imagine she was the same woman who had once chained him.

This brought a surge of emotion in Christos he found difficult to gulp down. Still, he'd swallowed it, because more tears would accomplish nothing.

He wasn't sure where the emotions came from. He was frustrated he couldn't find the boy's mother. He was angry with the commander, who seemed so totally absorbed in finding Kem he didn't care about anything else.

He could give up this work tomorrow. And he should. It was more than he could reasonably handle. What had he accomplished here, anyway? Nothing. He couldn't even keep his promise to a sick child.

He squeezed his eyes shut.

He had another job prospect as a systems engineer for a shipping company. He could leave this police work behind. That would be the easiest and smartest thing to do. But he hadn't jumped on the opportunity Yannis had called him about the other day.

Christos's thoughts were interrupted by the realization that the beeping from the monitor had changed, sped up. His eyes flew open as he peered at the monitor screen. The wavering line went flat and an alarm went off.

A doctor was by the boy's side in an instant. He checked the boy's chest, then his eyes. He put his hand on the boy's chest, muttered what sounded like a prayer. "Such a pity," he muttered.

He gazed at Christos, shook his head.

"No," Mirela cried. "No." She caressed the boy's face, shook him urgently, as though he had overslept. "Please," she said. She held the boy to her, rocked him, and chanted something Christos didn't understand.

Christos couldn't speak. He made the sign of the cross, and left the room. Quickening his pace, he walked out of the hospital doors.

Someone bumped into him. It didn't stop him. He heard the apology, then "the commander wants to see you." The words fell behind him. He didn't know what to do with them, what was expected of him. He realized he didn't care, either.

Outside, Christos ran. He didn't know where he was going. Was there someplace he was meant to be? He couldn't catch his breath and still he ran faster.

Sitting at the kitchen table, his forehead down against his crossed arms, Christos couldn't control the tears. He'd tried, but they came by themselves. Tia rubbed his back. She waited for him to explain, but how could he put into words what he couldn't understand himself? He'd failed Sanjit. He couldn't give that little boy the one thing he wanted more than anything, his mother. His chest ached, and still the tears came. He thought of the Roma woman and saw her with the boy again. Her tenderness. She was the one who made Christos long for a mother he'd never known, a mother who might have loved him as much as the Roma woman loved Sanjit.

"You did everything you could," Tia said. "You brought him to our home, found him when he ran away, got him to the hospital. You tried to find his mother. You made a difference in that little boy's life."

"I know," he mumbled. "I know."

He felt her hand on his back. He was thankful. But right now, nothing soothed him.

"Yes," the commander was saying as Christos entered the station to a horde of reporters and cameras. "We have found her. We will reunite the boy with his mother. She's on her way as I speak. This is what we do. Reunite families, make lives better. It's what we're known for. Our *filoxenía*." He obviously hadn't heard about the boy. The commander's smile was open and generous. His eyes, less piercing and intimidating, seemed to soften for the cameras and all those microphones thrust in his face.

"It is our dedication and our resources that helped track her down. We did it for the boy and the family. You know how important family is to us Greeks."

"So how did you find her?" one reporter asked.

"Our ads and coverage in the media helped." The cameras clicked non-stop. The commander grinned.

"Did the woman see one of those ads?"

"Yes. And came forward to our embassy."

"Where was she?"

"Our embassy put her on the first plane back," the Commander said. "She'll be here soon. We have sent officers to meet the plane. I'm not giving you that information because she doesn't need to face all your cameras. She will need some privacy right now. Maybe later you will get a chance to speak to her. Understood?"

Well, maybe the man wasn't completely without compassion, Christos thought. He would have to tell him that the woman had arrived too late. He swallowed. Even after all the tears, this thought still touched a spot in him he knew would always ache.

"And what about the escapees?" a reporter from *To Vima* asked. "Any further leads? Can you tell us more about the escape? How did it happen?"

The commander held up a hand. "Are there any other questions about the boy? About our Herculean efforts to find his mother?"

"What about the escapees?" another reporter asked.

Christos knew two guards had been suspended for helping the men escape. Apparently, the November 17 anarchists had bribed the guards. It was said that the group had disbanded in the early 2000s, but there were always followers, young people rising to the cause, particularly since the start of the economic crisis.

The guards weren't charged. The whole thing had been hushed up to save embarrassment. And the guards hadn't even lost their jobs. They would be sent off for some remedial training course or another and be back on the job in a few months. Christos knew they probably had connections to someone high up in the government.

"A manhunt is underway," the commander said. "We think the Ukrainian gypsy who had the boy masterminded the escape plan. And we believe he kidnapped the boy because he saw the boy as a good source of income for him. A sick child on the street begging for money. The gypsy knows how to play on our Greek compassion. He's a terrorist. No doubt he came here to cause the same kind of trouble he did in his home country. These people are the ones we have to watch. The ones who don't value the kind of life we have."

Christos's hands were fists by his sides. He knew the Roma man was too passive to plan an escape. In these jails, like in society itself, the Roma were never the leaders. A terrorist. God, he hated that overused word.

"The man had entered the country illegally a few years ago and escaped before he could be documented and sent to one of our refugee camps. Because there are so many trying to cross our borders, and we have so few resources, we never caught up with him then. It looks like he's back to his old tricks."

"Where did that happen?"

"Who was in charge then?"

"Was it public knowledge?"

The questions came one after the other from various reporters.

The commander held up his hands. "That's enough questions," he said. "We'll talk again after we reunite the woman with her son. We have done good work today. My men should be proud." He made his way through the crowd of reporters, Michelas in front of him breaking his path.

That's why the commander had his sights set on Kem, Christos thought. The commander had been in charge of the camp where a few dozen refugees walked away some time ago and were never found. It was hushed up then. It never made the newspapers, but he'd heard about the incident in basic training. No names were mentioned. It was just an example of how mistakes could happen if officers weren't constantly vigilant.

Kefalas never forgot a thing. That's why all the attention on recapturing Kem. It was a bloody sick system when people like this were in charge. Christos would like to tell all these reporters the truth about the Roma, the life he and others like him lived on the country's doorstep.

He thought about the other escapees. Why had they taken Kem along? What use would he be? Christos then realized they knew. One of the guards who helped them probably told them the commander would set his sights on finding Kem. So if they took him along, all effort would be put into finding the Roma man and this would give the rest of them time to disappear.

He heard Tia say again, "You made a difference in that boy's life."

Maybe he did and maybe he didn't. But how could he live with himself if he walked away from this job and didn't bother trying?

32

REGRETS

Maroúsi

"Look, Mother," Ted said. He was sitting beside her on the couch, completely focused on her. "Bo was ill. There was nothing you or anyone else could have done for him. He had that syndrome, whatever Christos called it. The way he lived in the camp, he didn't have much of a chance. You did everything you could."

She leaned forward, her head buried in her hands. He instinctively put his arm around her. When was the last time he'd done that? It didn't matter. He felt just as useless as he did when he was a kid holding a bag of peas over her swollen eye, whispering, "Things are going to be okay. You wait and see. Dad just gets really mad sometimes."

"I know," she would say, cupping his cheek and smiling, even though he could see her wincing at the pain in her face. Then she'd hug him to her tightly. She'd comforted him during those times too.

"That's all I wanted to do," she said now. "I wanted Bo to live in a better place, give him some opportunities. Hopefully, help clear up his cough. That awful runny nose. But, I made things worse. If he'd stayed with Kem and Mirela he may have had more time. They took care of him. She truly loved him. I'm such a fool."

"I know you were doing your best, Mother. I know that."

"But?" She sat up, scanned his face without meeting his eyes. "I keep screwing up. You said it before and it's true. I know that's what I do." She wiped her eyes. Her face was puffy.

"You've always tried to make things better for everyone. And I don't just mean the people you've worked with." He squeezed her shoulder.

"When I went to see him in the hospital, Bo wouldn't even look at me," she said. "He opened his eyes and when he saw it was me, he turned away. As sick as he was, he knew he didn't want anything to do with me. I started this mess."

"I saw that camp," Ted said. "Anyone who saw those conditions would want to try to make things better for the people who lived there."

"I took that child. He didn't want to go with me. I could never have provided him with what Mirela did naturally. I don't think I'm capable of loving anything properly."

"Anyone can see that you wanted to help the child and his family. You can't blame yourself for caring. So many people can't or won't. You do. That's special."

"I've made some incredibly stupid decisions lately. Somehow my boundaries have disappeared. Maybe I never had any. I'm so bloody driven and sometimes" — she looked at him — "I don't do enough." She stood, blew her nose.

"Come on. You're not being fair to yourself." He wanted to reach for her, find a way to console her. Instead, he leaned back, rested his head on the back of the couch. Let her get it off her chest, he thought. Right now, he needed to listen.

She turned her back to him. "I could see the bond between Bo and Mirela and I tried to break it. This time it was Bo, before it was…" She hesitated.

"Who?"

She faced him, her eyes now clear, the tears gone.

"Your father loved it when the two of you kicked the soccer ball around. Remember how it was his game? He would brag about every kick or trick you did. Especially when you were a toddler."

"I sucked at the game. And Dad knew that too. That's why he gave up on me." Ted was stating a fact. As long as he faced it, this truth couldn't hurt him anymore.

"You practised so hard." She sat back down on the couch. Their arms touched. He'd missed this closeness. All that anger he'd directed at her for everything that had happened to him had made him blind to the good in their relationship.

"I used to take you out to practice," she said. "Remember?"

He nodded. "Yes, but I never got any better. The nicest part of that was we were together. I had you all to myself. But it didn't improve my game one bit. It wasn't your fault. I just didn't have enough talent for the game."

"It was my fault."

He shook his head. "Look, Mother, you weren't the one playing the game. That was me. And no one had to tell me how bad I was. I knew it. Dad didn't even bother after a while because he was so ashamed of me. You tried to help. You practised with me, took me to practices, and listened when I was frustrated and angry. That was you. Let's not rewrite history. I was there. I know what happened." Ted didn't want to get angry with her, especially now, but there was no point to not seeing things as they were. He remembered perfectly well what had happened.

She shook her head and leaned into him, took his hands in hers.

"I was the one who rushed to put you into an organized league," she said. "Your father was so proud of you. I thought it would please him if you got better. Faster. He told me it was too soon, but I didn't listen. I thought I knew better. But you were so young and so small in comparison to the others. You couldn't keep up and then pretty soon you hated the game. It was my fault. You were a natural and I ruined it for you because I was selfish. I wanted your father to love me, us more." Her eyes were clear. Sad. Yes. But absolutely clear and focused, as though a curtain had been lifted.

Ted sat still, not sure what to do with this confession. He shrugged and his hands fell away from hers. "We can't undo the past," he said. "You try too hard. That's all. You want everything to be perfect. Life isn't that way. You know that better than anyone. Look at the work you do, the people you deal with."

"Maybe," she said, "but I've screwed up many times. They fired me in Zimbabwe because I didn't want to do the job I was assigned. I was supposed to only set up programs, mentor locals. That's it. But no. I wanted to do more. One of the teams I was training finally complained that I was spending more time with the families. I wasn't allowing them to do the job, instead I was rushing in to do it for them. And they thought I was talking about adopting one of the children and taking him away. I wasn't. I don't think I was. It was another boy. But, like you said, maybe I'm trying to recreate something here. I don't know. And look at what I did to you. I sent you off to private school after your father died. You needed me and I left to go save the world, as you put it. Right?" She shook her head. "And your father…"

"Enough, Mother. Enough." He didn't really want to hear any more. He needed to continue to love her and he wasn't sure he could if she told him anything else. He stood up and went to the window, staring out at the now empty park.

"I was the one who reported your father's drinking," she said. "He lost his licence because of me."

"And you probably saved some lives. Right?" Ted said without turning around. "He shouldn't have been practising medicine in his state." That day in his dad's office so many years ago came back to him. His father had been cleaning out his desk when Ted walked in. He saw that now. Quickly tucking something back in his desk, his dad had slammed the drawer shut. Files maybe. When he remembered the incident, before, he always imagined it was a bottle. Now he wasn't so sure. He remembered fragments of their conversation though. He told Ted it wasn't his fault. Ted should ask his mother about what had happened. What wasn't Dad's fault? He hadn't asked and he'd never dug into it deeper with Mother. Funny how he called his father the informal Dad and his mother the more formal Mother. When did that happen? He couldn't remember.

Although he'd stopped chewing gum a few days ago, his jaw was suddenly sore, as though he'd been grinding down on something that wouldn't give. "Dad was a drunk. That was his problem. You didn't cause it."

And that's what I am too, he thought. There's no one to blame but me. I've been deadening myself with booze and keeping everyone at a distance. It's gotten me nowhere. My parents weren't always there for me. And I wasn't always around for them either, except to pick up the pieces. A teacher I trusted molested me. I've hidden and manipulated and been a jerk. So what? Shit happens, but I'm not going to let it dictate my life.

"I could have done more to help your father. All I did was belittle him. As if that approach was going to work. I don't do that with my clients. I felt sorry for myself and escaped into work. I didn't want to deal with it. I left him long before he left us and still I fell apart when he took off, as if it was some sort of surprise. I've never been honest with myself. Never. Somewhere along the line I made a decision I didn't care about him anymore and would do better the next time around with someone else if the opportunity came. Who makes that kind of decision about their marriage, about their child?" She stopped talking suddenly, as though a puzzle had finally come together. "I hate myself for saying it, but I wanted another chance to do better than I'd done with you." She buried her head in her hands.

He sighed quietly. Okay, she'd screwed up. In her, he saw himself. He was his mother's son. And his father's. If he couldn't show compassion towards them, how could he be compassionate with himself?

He came back to the couch and sat down beside her, putting his arms around her and drawing her close. "I don't know anyone who hasn't done something they're not proud of. We do our best. Let's go home and figure out what happens next. Okay?"

33

WAITING

Hidden behind a tree overlooking the camp, Kem had been waiting for Mirela for hours. She'd gone to the police station against his wishes. Not once, but several times. She wanted to get the boy back and she wasn't going to stop until she got him. She may have come back when he was wandering the parks, trying to stay out of the camp and any police detection. She'd told him the last time he saw her that the police were looking for him.

They'd probably arrested her. How was he going to help her now? That woman would never learn. For someone who had always told him she was smarter than he was, she sure didn't show it. One day she would ruin him.

He had done a drawing of her shortly after he'd met her in his father's barn. It was his way of trying to coax a smile out of her. He made her eyes large in that drawing because that's the way she had stared at him back then, as though she was looking right through him to something bigger than him, something more. But those cold eyes had never flickered with even the slightest acknowledgement of his drawing. And he'd done such a good job of capturing her. Not just her eyes, but every detail, right down to the single line of her mouth, the proud cheekbones in her sallow face.

Enough, he told himself. Maybe he needed to find someone who would share the same things he wanted from his life. He was not so old, only eighteen years now. He could start again, find another way to get out of this country. She wanted to destroy her life? Okay. That was up to her. But he was not going to let her take him down. No, he wouldn't. If he had to leave her behind, he would have to do it to save himself. He had important things to do: draw the pictures he wanted to draw for people who would appreciate his work.

He'd wait another few minutes, though, in case she came back. He wanted to make sure she was safe. A good husband did these things. He'd been nothing but a good husband to Mirela.

34

ANOTHER CHANCE

India

Three days after his meeting at the Migration and Refugee office, Vijay was flown back to India on an airplane, as if he were an important businessman rather than the rejected migrant he knew he was. He was sent to Delhi, where the authorities thought he could hide from his father-in-law and Saphal's brothers. But they were a powerful family. He knew they could find him if they wanted to.

Saphal's name had been kept out of the papers, but he had no doubt it was her when he read about what had happened to the boy. She never came to ask for Vijay after his detention that day, and if the authorities tried to track her down after they arrested him, she'd probably eluded them, no doubt using all the money they had to fly back to Greece and Sanjit. At least she'd avoided his fate. He couldn't begrudge her that.

Their son died anyway. They knew it would happen. The doctors had told them about his disease long before they left India, but Saphal would not listen to reason. "What do doctors know?" she'd said. "They don't know the power of a mother's love." She'd looked at him and seemed to realize she'd crossed a line. "I mean a family's love."

He had loved his son. He had intended to keep his promise of bringing him to Germany. But when he was honest with himself, he knew he had given up on Sanjit when he was first told about the boy's disease. Something inside Vijay had closed. He'd seen other beggars on the street with the same swayed back and underdeveloped muscles. He'd heard the same cough in the Mumbai slum they used to live in years ago. He knew his son would only get worse. At least he'd brought him into the family business and didn't leave him on the streets to beg. He'd done better than others would have with a sick child. They would have abandoned the boy, left him to fend for himself. If Vijay had done that, his son would have died long ago. His love and care for the boy had given Sanjit a few more years.

Even when he'd had to escape to Germany with Saphal, he had made sure Sanjit had a home to go to. He hadn't just left him on the street as Vijay's mother had done with him. He was sure Kem and his family had taken good care of Sanjit too, until that meddling aid worker got involved. These people who wanted to help were all the same. Why didn't they send money instead? No, they wanted to get involved, change people.

He read that there were two migrant women at the boy's funeral along with so many Greeks, including top-ranking government officials. He knew the women had to be Kem's wife and Saphal. They'd buried him with a set of earrings in his hands, Saphal's earrings. The boy had always liked them. Maybe they would remind him of her in the next life.

There was nothing in the papers about Kem. Wherever Kem was, Vijay hoped his friend was safe from the police.

Anyway, he liked to think he'd done his best for Sanjit, trying to toughen him up, make the most of the little life he had coming to him.

Vijay had been planning to go back to get the boy. He had. But time moved too quickly.

He had to stop thinking about all these other things and figure a way out of his country. There was only one way for people like him to leave. Money. Vijay was meeting a man today, near the train station. That man would name his price and Vijay would find a way to get it. Since returning to India two years ago he had been working hard and saving what he could.

He would have to ask how the smuggler planned to get him to Turkey for a boat to Greece. Would he be concealed in a truck, or a compartment of a train, or go on foot? He didn't know, but it was getting tougher to migrate anywhere these days, because border guards more closely monitored trains and intercity buses in border regions.

Whatever way he went, it wouldn't be easy. If he got to Turkey, he wouldn't have much money left. He could tell the man that he could operate a smaller vessel as he'd done before in exchange for free passage. But more likely, he'd have to take one of the larger, more dangerous vessels. He would be squeezed on one of the lower decks of a tanker with women, old men, crying babies and others who didn't have enough money to be on the higher decks. He'd heard some people were locked up on those lower decks. There would be no escape if the boat sank. This is what you could expect in the lowest class. How many times could he cross the sea and not be taken by it?

He knew more about getting around the refugee system now. With any luck, he'd get his happy ending this time. He had to take the chance.

Saphal was probably in the old neighbourhood in Athens. The papers never said what had happened to her, but he knew she could never come back to India. Her family would have killed her. The day she had married him, she had practically signed her own death warrant. She was too headstrong for her family's backward traditions.

He had to find her. There was no life without her. He should have told her this. Perhaps, it wasn't too late.

35

New Beginnings

Late 2014

Kem had never met the pharmacist who used to give Mirela medicine for Bo's cough, but he and his wife seemed to treat Mirela well. They'd given her a room to live in and a place to work. She wore a nice, clean uniform. Her face had lightened and the lines had disappeared. She no longer wore her earrings. She must have finally sold them. She looked like the girl he had met in his parents' barn forever ago, no longer the sunbaked and dried-up old woman she was when they lived in the camp. He saw her sometimes in the park, sitting on a bench, licking an ice cream cone. She sat by herself, reading a book. People wandered by and said hello and she looked up and smiled. During these times, Kem was sure he saw the emerald in her eyes again.

She went to a school at night too. She was always so smart. Mirela had crawled out of the hole of a life his family had tried to sink her into. He was happy for her. She deserved this better life.

Their old lean-to had been torn down not long after Bo died. The whole camp had been bulldozed to the ground. The police were probably looking for him, got frustrated and ripped up the whole place to get even. Somehow the others in the camp didn't blame him though. They understood he was only doing what his friend had asked him to do: protect the boy. Any one of them would have done the same thing. And he was one of them. That was the good thing about living in a camp like this and being Roma. Loyalty.

Everyone watched out for one another. Yes, some bullied and beat up on their own or others, and some sold drugs, but no one went running to the police with their problems. They settled things among themselves without the help of outsiders. Strangers brought problems, and with their lives being what they were, no one needed more of that.

Besides, they'd found another abandoned piece of property and set up another camp. No one bothered them there. No police. No do-gooders. It was too far and too isolated from any neighbourhood in Athens.

He moved into the camp along with the rest. He lived in a lean-to just like he did before. The police had given up on him long ago, but still he avoided them when he saw them on the street in riot gear, getting ready for another one of the many protests they had in this city. People protested here because they thought they could change things. The Greeks weren't smart in the same way the Roma were. The Roma knew nothing would ever change. They accepted what was. This was the way the world worked.

Kem's new wife didn't know anything about his old life and that was the way he liked it. She knew her place. She didn't argue with him and didn't ask questions when he came home late and hadn't been able to make much money from his drawings. After all, she was only fourteen. She'd given him a child. A son. Maybe he'd grow up and make enough money to buy his father a car.

When he watched Mirela, he made sure she never saw him. The best thing for her was for him to leave her alone. But he had been her husband once. He couldn't ignore that responsibility. He would have it for as long as he breathed. He owed her that much.

At night, in the park, hidden away from view in a clump of bushes, no one to bother him, he drew in his notebook. It wasn't new anymore, but it had some blank pages left, room enough for his new drawings of churches and parks. One day maybe someone would see his work and think they were good enough to sell in a gallery.

The commander continued to ride him, but Christos ignored him. "You're an anarchist," the commander said, as they sat in his office. "Like those foreigners you like so much."

"People don't pick up after their dogs," he said to Kefalas. "Others double-park as though they own the road, they yell at each other in the streets. They make up their own rules because they think they know what's best. The foreigners do not do these things. We Greeks do these things. People like you and me. And as long as that continues, there will always be anarchy in this country."

Kefalas shrugged, snapped his penknife shut. "The only thing I know, Mr. Engineer, is you'll always have a bleeding heart. Maybe when you have as many years in this job as I do, you'll see things differently."

The man could use some worry beads, Christos thought, and wondered if the commander had been a different person before he took on this job. It didn't really matter. Christos had found a way to do what he needed to do despite Kefalas's interference.

Greece was heading into another election. More promises had been made. *Dignity will be restored to Greeks. We will end austerity. The shackles will be lifted.* That's what they said. But the crisis continued. At least some things had improved. Many of Golden Dawn's senior officials were now in jail, awaiting trial for murder, running a criminal organization and more. Because of this, Christos was hopeful for the future of his country.

Christos had begun to like this work. He felt like he was making a difference. Tia understood this need in him. She only complained when he worked late or didn't hear her when she tried to tell him something. He was always somewhere else, thinking about something else. Every second weekend, he volunteered at Ta Prósfygika, that once stately complex in downtown Athens. He helped cook meals there.

He'd started going there after Saphal moved back into the place. When she came back to Greece for Sanjit, the government gave her refugee status. The public insisted the government help her, because the boy died before her return.

She worked in a café down the street from where she lived. Every Sunday, he caught up on what she'd been doing all week.

On his other days off he worked with an organization that helped Roma children integrate into the school system. Christos provided what was once given freely to him by the nuns in the orphanage — love.

This quitting hadn't been easy on Ted. Each day was better, but sometimes, when he was stressed and unsure of himself, it took everything he had not to crawl back into the bottle and hide. He reminded himself he had dealt with a lot of shit on his own and he could do whatever it took to stay sober. "That's your strength," Jack had said. "You're a survivor. You should be proud of that."

Ted promised himself he'd take one day at a time, just like his sponsor reminded him he should. He knew this was the only way forward.

He was on his way to Bishop's tonight to celebrate his mom's latest news.

"Mom doesn't know about my problem," he'd told Jack. He'd kept the letter he'd written to her in the early days after he started the twelve-step program. And he'd added much more to it. He looked at it from time to time to remind himself of how far he'd come. He wasn't sure if there would ever be a time when he'd give the letter to her. "You'll find a way to tell her when you're ready," Jack had said.

Ted hugged Shelby, and then sat down at her table. "That's my mom, the author," Ted said and smiled.

"I still have to write the thing," Shelby said. "Lots of interest now, with this upcoming Greek election, the ongoing economic crisis and austerity and the talk of the large number of migrants on Greek shores. There's renewed interest in all things Greek. But who knows how long that interest will last? What am I going to say about Kem and Bo and Greece and the whole mess that seemed to capture the world's attention for about five minutes? And who is going to care? What difference will it make?"

"Mom, when has that ever stopped you?" Ted said.

She smiled. "You might have a point."

"Can I get you something to drink?" the waiter interrupted.

"I'll have a glass of white wine," his mother said.

The waiter gazed at Ted and smiled. "And for you sir? Can I interest you a glass of wine or perhaps a cocktail?

"You don't have enough back there to get me started," Ted said.

"I know what you mean," the waiter said. "I'm one of those too."

Ted smiled.

"Some Perrier then?"

"Perfect," said Ted.

Shelby gave Ted a quizzical look as the waiter walked away. "What does that mean, one of those?"

Author's Note

The United Nations refugee agency (UNHCR) says at least 124,000 people reached Greece's shores by sea in the first seven months of 2015 — more than seven times as many as during the same period in 2014. This influx of refugees has stretched the resources of an already cash-strapped nation. And yet, Greeks who have had to deal with unemployment, rising taxes and diminishing resources venture out daily to provide whatever they can to new arrivals. The combination of the economic crisis and the increase in migration has spawned racist rhetoric and political parties like Golden Dawn, but the majority of Greeks still come forward to welcome new arrivals and help in anyway they can. This comes from the nation's sense of *filótimo* (honour) and *filoxenía* (hospitality).

For more information, here is an excellent article and video on the migrant route from Izmir to Lesbos:
http://www.ekathimerini.com/199285/interactive/ekathimerini/special-report/migrant-traffickers

ACKNOWLEDGEMENTS

This novel came to me while I was in Greece finishing my first novel. I lived in the neighbourhood I described in this book, close to a Roma camp, which has since been torn down. When I returned to Canada the novel lay dormant, but the sights, sounds and people I met never left me. I made a phone call to the Greek Consulate General's office in Vancouver. My thought was to talk to someone about my novel's themes and to get some advice about how I might proceed to meet officials in Greece who could confirm some of my early impressions. Ilias Kremmydas, the Consulate General, listened to what I was trying to do, spent a great deal of time giving me advice and helped me focus my research plan.

He forwarded my proposal to the Greek Embassy in Ottawa. The contacts I made in Greece and the research I completed could never have taken place without his support. It was his initiative and desire to see my project succeed that made everything else possible.

Shortly after Ilias forwarded my proposal, I received a call from Athanasia (Sia) Papatriantafyllou, the Press Office Director for the Greek Embassy.

Sia connected me with Elena Soupiana of the Public Relations Directorate for the Secretariat General of Information and Communications in Athens. Elena set up the meetings I had requested, including those with Maria Stavropoulou and Eleni Petraki of the Asylum Service for the Ministry of Public Order and Citizen Protection, Commander Evangelos Triantis and Sergeant Anthoola Siouti of the Amygdaleza Detention Centre, Daniel Esdras, head of the International Organization for Migration (Greece), as well as an interview with author Nikos

Hasapopoulos, who has written extensively about the Nazi party Golden Dawn, a group that plays a minor role (as well it should) in my novel.

The access and openness I was given was more than any foreign author could have hoped for, particularly given the difficult nature of my subject matter.

Elena also sent me information about the Roma community, answered all my questions and my many, many emails and phone calls. She was my go-to person during my time in Greece and she never wavered.

It is through some of the documents she sent me that I found Kostas Dimanatis Balaskas, Anastasia Belesca, and Maria Panayiotopoulos of Action Synergy, who collectively deliver various programs to the Roma community in Athens.

I met lots of people of all cultures in cafés and on the street and at protests. I pestered them with my questions and had wonderful discussions in my bad Greek and their excellent English. Their views and impressions, challenges and struggles infused my work.

My cousins kept me sharp with questions and discussions about my project as well as so many other topics. While we don't agree on a number of different issues, I've enjoyed the discussions we've had and the teasing. It has kept me grounded, and that's a good thing.

And special mention and thanks has to go to my cousin Elias Vranopoulos, who made inquiries through his friend Professor Asteris Huliaras at the University of the Peloponnese (Corinth) on my behalf. This led to a meeting with Maria Kratz-Larsen of Children's Ark and a tour of a Roma camp.

No matter what anyone else tells you: *filoxenía* (hospitality) thrives in Greece. Many things may have changed here following the economic crisis of 2008, but this has not. The people I met were incredibly generous with their time and information and eager to help me. And furthermore, as migrants come to Greek shores in record numbers daily, the coast guard and everyday private citizens come out to help, providing food and shelter and hospitality even as their resources are diminished.

I'd also like to thank my friend Paula Dauns, who is a lawyer and has worked with refugees here and abroad. She answered many of my questions. If I've made any errors, they are mine alone.

Thank you to the women who always have my back, fellow authors and awesome critiquers: Sue Oakey Baker, Rebecca Wood Barrett, Katherine Fawcett, Sara Leach, Mary MacDonald, Libby McKeever, Nancy Routley in Whistler, and to my friends in Vancouver, authors Eric Brown, Veronique Darwin, Jennifer Honeyburn, Linda Quennec, and El Jean Wilson, who saw various chapters and provided their insight.

Access Copyright and the BC Arts Council provided me with support so I'd have the time and resources to work on this novel. And my publisher, Karen Haughian of Signature Editions, provided sage advice and pushed me to complete this work. She has an incredible eye for detail. I also want to thank Terry Gallagher at Doowah Design for her brilliant design of the novel's cover. She captured the essence of *The Brink*.

I'd like to thank Sophia Balanou, Alexandra Courcoula, and Marilena Tzartzanou for providing homes to call my own while I was in Athens at various times working on this project. And finally many thanks and love to my husband, Dave, who accompanied me on this and so many other adventures.

I've questioned my sanity more than once along this journey. I mean, how much reality does one need to inject into a work of fiction? But I've never questioned my belief that no one succeeds by him- or herself.

ABOUT THE AUTHOR

Stella Leventoyannis Harvey was born in Cairo, Egypt and moved to Calgary as a child with her family. In 2001, Stella founded the Whistler Writers Group, which each year produces the Whistler Writers Festival under her direction. Stella's first novel, *Nicolai's Daughters*, also set in Greece and Canada, was released by Signature Editions in 2012 and released in Greece in 2014 by Psichogios Press. Stella's short stories have appeared in the *Literary Leanings* anthology, *The New Orphic Review, Emerge Magazine* and *The Dalhousie Review*. Her non-fiction has appeared in *Pique Newsmagazine, The Question* and the *Globe and Mail*. She currently lives with her husband in Whistler, but visits her many relatives in Greece often, indulging her love of Greek food and culture.